LIGHTS OUT IN
WONDERLAND

LIGHTS OUT IN WONDERLAND

DBC PIERRE

W. W. NORTON & COMPANY   NEW YORK · LONDON

Copyright © 2010 by DBC Pierre
First American Edition 2011

For information about permission to reproduce
selections from this book, write to Permissions,
W. W. Norton & Company, Inc.,
500 Fifth Avenue, New York, NY 10110

For information about special discounts for bulk
purchases, please contact W. W. Norton Special Sales
at specialsales@wwnorton.com or 800-233-4830

Manufacturing by Courier Westford
Book design by Ellen Cipriano
Production manager: Anna Oler

Library of Congress Cataloging-in-Publication Data

Pierre, D. B. C.
Lights out in wonderland / D.B.C. Pierre. — 1st American ed.
    p. cm.
ISBN 978-0-393-08123-7 (hardcover)
1. Men—Fiction. 2. Self-realization—Fiction.
3. Relationships—Fiction. 4. Quests (Expeditions)—Fiction.
I. Title.
PR9619.4.P54L54 2011
823'.92—dc22

                              2011020688

W. W. Norton & Company, Inc.
500 Fifth Avenue, New York, N.Y. 10110
www.wwnorton.com

W. W. Norton & Company Ltd.
Castle House, 75/76 Wells Street, London W1T 3QT

1 2 3 4 5 6 7 8 9 0

LIGHTS OUT IN WONDERLAND

Per els somnis d'una nit

If your ethical model defeats you,
change the model.

LONDON

When sewers burst, their waste to spew,

Our street to brown foam will succumb;

Flying kids will follow in grungy shoe,

To scurry and splash through the scum;

Now society cracks under similar laws,

Gushing truth, wit, and wisdom like pee;

But as the mess edges across our floors,

No more scampers or splashes you see;

This lack of chutzpah dishonors our day,

Forcing history to implore me and you:

Come attend! Let's do this reckless decay,

And dance through an empire's last spew.

There's no name for my situation. Firstly because I decided to kill myself. And then because of this idea:

I don't have to do it immediately.

Whoosh—through a little door. It's a limbo.

I never have to answer the phone again or pay a bill. My credit rating no longer matters. Fears and compulsions don't matter. Socks don't matter. Because I'll be dead. And who am I to die? A microwave chef. A writer of flyers. A product of our time. A failed student. A defective man. A bad poet. An activist on the fence. A drinker of chocolate milk, and when there's no chocolate, of strawberry and sometimes banana.

In times set up for the survival of the fittest—not the fittest.

Ah, well. I always avoided mirrors, but here, naked in a room with a basin and a mirror, I steal a glance. Whoosh—the weasel is gone. Suddenly I'm a sphinx with choir-boy eyes, as luminous and rude as a decadent portrait in oils.

Because nothing matters anymore.

Rehab isn't the place for this kind of inspiration.

By way of celebration I pee in the basin—after all, a porcelain appliance plumbed into a drain—then I flush it with the faucet, which I feel shows refinement. Reason and refinement are shown in my last living hours. Proof that I'm not deranged, that I came from good people. Or, at least, from stories of good people. Dressing quickly, I don't bother to wash, it doesn't matter. I only pause to stretch at the window and marvel. My depression's gone. Whoosh—down a rabbit hole it went. Everything's whoosh. That's the rush of this limbo.* Of course, it only works when the decision to die is final. Which mine is.

The reason is simple: that of the many things I was supposed to be and have and do in life, I am, and have, and have done exactly none of them. I flounder in the wake of modern times, watching them speed away. This may sound pathetic except for one thing: I don't lack inner forces. I have inner forces, more than enough. But they never found expression.

Unexpressed force, more pointless than no force at all.

In the course of this writing it might seem to you that I recommend this fatal path. Well, I do recommend it. Make up your own mind according to what you see, but in the meantime I count you my partner. And I say this to you: everyone regrets leaving a party early, hearing laughter from a room behind them. Death must feel that way. But I don't feel it at all; because this party's over. Bottles are empty. Kegs are spitting foam. Our empire of

---

*What is this limbo? A kind of detachment from the object world, a club-mix of what we fleetingly taste in moments of shock. Already I sense that it has an envelope, a zone we must stay in to keep it afloat, pushed by fear, pulled by comforting oblivion. Science would call it *dissociation*; but in life we have a choice between the clinical and the romantic—and *limbo* is the romantic choice. In case you need arguments for choosing romance over science, remember this: science still doesn't know why we sleep.

shopping is in its last dying twitch. Bye-bye free markets, farewell terms and conditions, ciao bogus laughter, ha ha, whoop, wa-hey. The last revelers are the dregs we see at any free event, now vomiting wine. It's not regret but pride I feel at detecting the state of things, and bailing out in good time.

So adieu, Modern Day, adieu. Another chance to prove ourselves capable of self-control, and therefore worthy of freedom, is gone. Deep down we know it too; for over a decade we've only reheated the past, glorifying our hundred best moments over and over like old-timers with snaps of their frisky days, unconsciously saying goodbye.

Now watch the lights dim in Wonderland.

Whoosh. What a decadence.

A ball smacks between rackets somewhere outside, and to me it's a ticking clock, uneven like the real time of nature. I have to vanish from here—quick, before anyone goes to work on my mind. I'm going to live it up for an hour or two. Because I'm worth it, ha ha. As far as the behavior my limbo suggests, just look around. If we're supposed to follow our peers, we don't need any greater morals than them.

It means carte blanche for Gabriel Brockwell.

First things first—I'll call on the most accomplished profligate I know: my friend Nelson Smuts, a man always close to wine and debauch. With him riding shotgun we'll turn my last hours into a perfect miniature of the age I leave behind, nothing less than a last wanton dive to oblivion.

Ah, decadence. I smile out through the window. The rehabilitation facility sits festering like a family secret in the countryside north of London, England. It has nooks, shrubberies, and empty ponds coated in slime. Inmates—so-called clients—drift around sucking leaf mold—so-called fresh air—and wearing trousers that don't touch their legs but hover empty over the wrong kinds of shoes.

My room isn't locked. The hallway outside is ripe with that mechano-pubic smell of vacuum cleaning. I plunge through it as late sun whacks the building, a golden blast that lights galaxies of dust against the lobby's dark. Whoosh. The Ancients would call this a good sign. It seems big decisions call for signs from the divine Enthusiasms, those ironic and whimsical energies which a limbo must attract. Who knows if they favor life over death, if they give signs along the path of an adventure, or save their lessons for the end?

Come, though—we'll see.

A long-faced girl slumps behind reception. She watches me, hoping I won't approach. Whoosh—I swirl through the light toward her. My shyness is gone. The secret that I will die makes it irrelevant, so I go up till her face is in shadow, and ask for a pen and paper. We'll take notes—yes!—while everything's so clear. As the girl fumbles around, I see checkout forms behind the bench, and reach for one. She recoils, as if my arm has some stunning force field. But then I see she's a person who flinches at everything. All movement is a slight surprise to her. She puts down a notepad, arranges a pen beside it, and stands back while I square the checkout form on the bench, frowning with intent. With a flourish I take up the pen:

"All happiness not derived from intoxicants," I write, "—is false."

Her mouth opens slowly: "O-kay. I might just get David, or Rosemary—who have you been seeing—David, or Rosemary?"

Her face seems to grow longer, melting toward the bench with every word. This is a Salvador Dalí girl, someone to fold over the branch of a tree.

"Neither one," I say, and continue to write:

"All self-knowledge, courage, and resolve not attributed to intoxicants—are false."

"I'll call David." She reaches for a handset.

I settle into my stride, spilling out of the *Reason(s) for Discharge* box, into *Mentor Comments*. "The notion does not stand up," I write, "that those few dropouts susceptible to the wealth of sensitivities that make them human, traits and passions even celebrated by their peers—"

"David West, David to reception."

"—should, for their failure to harmonize with mediocrity and automatism, be shut away with passive-aggressive profiteers who spend their hostilities passing off manipulation and dogma as some kind of curative therapy."

"David to reception, please."

"The need of this assortment of new-age ano-extremists to patronize, wield authority, and lord false compassion over others is a more breathtaking and sinister disturbance of character than anything I could aspire to. If one thing convinces me to stay out of rehab it is this shocking realization: not that such a hoax could find allies—but that the allies it finds should be so menacingly installed in one place."

Dalí Girl twitches. She straightens flyers. "Who knows where David is? Shall we find you a seat in the Quiet Room? While we—figure things out?"

"No," I say.

She blinks, nodding slowly. "The thing is—this isn't your form that you wrote on. Your form is in our files. So we'd have to write this out again."

I stand watching her for a moment. "Then why don't we copy my registration details from the form you have, onto this one?"

"Well, no, but—this isn't the form we have on file for you. You see? Really you're not meant to write on the form anyway."

I level my gaze.

"Also your form will have comments and—"

"No, it won't. I haven't attended anything."

"Well, yes, but it still will, because—well, *that's your form.*"

"Then why don't you get that form?"

"I'm afraid it's confidential."

"Hm." I shift my weight.

"I'm sorry—it's just that, for example, clinical notes will be there, and of course your payment details—"

"Would you even charge for a half-night stay?"

The girl stiffens. "Well, the course is prepaid. You see? The terms and conditions—"

"No, no—the term and condition in the existential world is that I arrived during the night, and now I'm leaving." I don't say it unkindly. I even leave my mouth open, smiling. The tuft of my chin beard bobs up like a squirrel.

Dalí Girl squirms.

Ah, well, well. Even here we find profit picking over the bones of the fallen. I take a step back. Dalí Girl shuffles papers while I try to accept the facts.* "I don't know where David could be." She frowns down the hallway.

---

* Ah, Customer Service. It falls to Dalí Girl to work the gulf between a photograph of a glamour model in a telephone headset and a collections department not based at this address. She squirms because despite efforts to erase her common sense, culture has left a nodule of reason intact. That fragment of tumor makes her uncomfortable enforcing outrageous terms. Her employer should have picked up on this.

"Well, it's an outrage." I calmly pocket the notepad and pen.

"David West, urgently to reception, please."

My stare passes over a potted palm beside the desk, then over some letters at the back that spell "Hope." I muse how much better a word like "Smashing" would look. Or even a sign from a Chinese supermarket, "Excellent Soiling" or "Hymen News."

"The thing is"—Dalí inflates with a new idea—"you'll be wanting your personal effects? Your wallet, phone, and what have you? I'll need a senior staff member to sign them out, I can't just do it. That's the thing."

"Look—in the space of three minutes your reasons for not helping have been: that I'll have to write on a different form; that I'm not allowed to write on any form; that I'm not allowed to see the form; and that you need professionals to open a locker."

"That's the thing," she says, happy to just leave the topic. "I can get you some mineral water? While we wait for David?"

That's the Thing. I see in her face the power to call people who come quicker than David, and with medications. Whoosh. I just take the water, frankly, whose fizz crackles noisily around a slice of lemon, and mope down the passage to the Quiet Room. This is a vacuum of passion overlooking the yard. Just where you'd expect to Wait for David. It smells of paint and damp. I find it empty, and sit on a pus-colored sofa facing a window through which trees thrash their bristles in the wind, a pummeling wind choked with dead leaves.

I should've just walked out. Reception was a mistake.

A chessboard sits on a side table with some magazines on relaxation and breathing. Light from a table lamp glares off their covers. The organism who needs tips on breathing, I muse, should probably be allowed to die. And I wonder if light would bounce as well off a copy of *Bacon Busters* or *Fisting Wives*. We'll never find out; that's why these out-of-town rehabs cause discomfort. Because a once-voluptuous mansion where waltzes were danced, where the air churned with fragrance and with the barks of beloved children and dogs, now a monument to shame, condescension, and bean sprouts—will have either a copy of *Fisting Wives* or a row of corpses under the kitchen garden.

It won't have both.

I switch off the lamp and soak in a violet glow. The chessboard sits waiting for a game; I inspect the rows of pieces. Pawns line up to die, knights ponder doglegs, rooks measure straits. With one imperious swipe I take the white queen and plow through both camps, batting the black king to the floor. This is the kind of attitude we'll need this evening. Whichever odyssey we've embarked on, you and I—and I feel it is an odyssey, if only a brief one—should show the same disregard for life and nature which they have shown for us. We'll chase pleasure without restraint.

Go out like animals. Like capitalists!

Ah, this moment before death is a virgin arena. Not to say I'm the first to discover suicide, even you've surely cradled the idea, lifted its flap in a certain dark moment, sniffed it, sized it up. Not that you've planned it like me; but still you must sense, in the combinations of chance already in play around you, at least one outcome where the price is your death.* I wonder if that's

---

*About suicide: imagine the spirit as a mansion. You'll guess we don't use many rooms. Apart from a few moments in childhood we don't dance around it in sunlight. But there's a traffic of things in and out, and what happens is that unwanted bulks can gather inside. Gather and gather, menacing us. Unable to shift them, we hide in ever smaller spaces. And in our last hole,

where we get a sense of being lucky, watching destiny's fingers whirr past our triggers, watching other people's triggers being hit. Surely this is what makes news so profitable.

Anyway—mine were hit.

My mind drifts to Nelson Smuts. What a party we'll have. What a bacchanal. Last I knew he was just back from Brussels, in a private kitchen down south. A while ago, this was. A year ago, maybe. Ah, Smuts.

In the middle of this reflection, the Quiet Room door opens. A thin young man looks in. He wears a skinny sweater and has a pale, unformed kind of face, like the fetus of a horse. He just stands looking at me.

Then after a while he points at my shoes:

"That's leather," he says.

Not sure where he's going with this, I look back for a moment and, after he offers no more clues, raise a finger at his top and say, "That's wool."

"Yes, but the lamb survived," he says.

I turn away, blinking.

After more silence he says: "Aren't you coming?"

"No," I say.

Another few seconds pass. Then he goes out and shuts the door behind him. Other murmurs pass in the hallway, and as they fade, a set of footsteps approaches.

"Gabriel Brockwell?" a man says at the door. He says it with

---

life offers a choice: to play out our demise in parallel theaters—psychosis, zealotry, religion, cancer, addiction—or to bow quietly out. But beware: life doesn't ask these high questions when we're confident and fresh—it waits for hopelessness.

out effort, in a tone that won't leave him looking stupid if there's no answer.

I ignore him. I'll wait here till all's quiet, then run. I sense him looking stupid behind the door, but feel no stress in ignoring him, or any care at all. Those tensions are gone now, because I could kill myself at any moment.

"Gabriel?"

As he says my name, I write it on the notepad.

A title appears: *The Book of Gabriel.*

Then a subtitle: *Anything—for Monkeys, Dogs, & Poets.*

I put *Anything* rather than *Everything* because it seems all things arise in the same way.* In order to support a mass of pseudo-industries, markets have led us to believe that every fragment of life is highly specialized, and therefore in need of goods and services to control it; whereas in fact all nature has a predictable and pretty boring character, whether you're a bug or a radiographer, escaping a bird or scanning a breast. As for the creatures in the subtitle, I feel they're ambassadors of human spirit, motifs from where charm and self-loathing are born. They might even have their own heaven—why not?—if Swedenborg says there's a special paradise for Turks and the Dutch.

With the notepad officially open, a spirit of research prevails in limbo. Our notes should therefore be clear, and you'll forgive me if the language seems formal—surely to throw light on a decadence we have to step away from its lingo, twisted as this has been to sanction outrage. Because isn't language the buttress of civilization? Honed to explain quirks and crimes in all subtlety,

---

*Remember Hobart Loots said: *Lots of things are included in everything; but there's only one anything.*

without margin for error or escape?* With this decisive stroke I get up off the sofa. My belongings can stay at reception, Smuts will have money, Smuts will have food and wine.

But as I reach the door, new shuffling sounds approach.

A man's head pokes into the Quiet Room:

"Ah—there you are," he says

---

*To take hold, a decadence relies on communal thoughtlessness, and this is first brought about by language. Through language the acts and notions which a few years ago would have caused outrage come to be accepted. Ever more careless words introduce attitudes into the culture which make reason unfashionable. Vocabulary shrinks, forcing more concepts to live behind fewer expressions; and in this process the acceptable and unacceptable come to mix, and are passed off one for the other.

2

David West is a sallow man who would bruise easily. His eyes are like boiled eggs, without sheen, and a shadowy yolk even looms under their whites. Sockets like egg cups hold them in place. I don't warm to him.

"You're not an easy man to find," he says. "The session's started, won't you join us?"

"No," I say.

He leads me from the Quiet Room, frowning and smiling at the same time. "You look rough. I wondered if you'd even wake up."

"It's nothing. I just need some cakes."

"Ah, David." Dalí Girl cranes from reception, cheered by his appearance. "Mr. Brockwell needs some assistance." And mouthing silently: "He seems *agitated*."

This is an alarm code. They look at each other, and pause. Dalí Girl uses blinking to lure David to my form on the bench, angling it for his convenience. In a gesture of fake brotherhood, some cynical technique of human touch, he grips my shoulder as he passes to read it. But when he reads he begins to droop like a hiker finding the distance way farther than he thought.

Finally he turns to the girl—"Would you get Gabriel's file?"—before saying to me: "Gabriel, Gabriel—so baroque! I don't know whether to treat you or publish you!"

Now he's a funny man. This doesn't sit well with me. "Hm." I look around. "If I could just have my things."

He hovers closer, chewing his lip. "You should know I'm disappointed. We're here for you, but you have to take the first step. Let us in, Gabriel. It's a contract—and it has to work both ways. I can't let you hide from that."

I vaguely scratch my curls. "Mr. West—two weeks' charges for a one-night stay doesn't much suggest that things will work more than one way."

"Listen," he says, "you might not be the model shopper. And that's fine. But you're from the same planet, you know how things work. This isn't a hotel. For us to be serious about helping you, your room has to be held for the full course. I feel the same way as you about terms and conditions, but—"

"Then why don't you do what you know is fair?"

"Gabriel, this is also our trade. It's how we live. No person, under any system, can be expected to forfeit their livelihood. Survival isn't a capitalist concept."

"Excuse me—a thousand percent penalty in small print is a capitalist concept. And a little above survival."

"But it's not a penalty; you booked a product of two weeks' duration. It's specified on the contract for you to accept or reject—the terms are clear."

"And that's fine and good except for one fact—I personally booked no product, of any duration, under any contract."

David pauses, checking his watch. Then he sighs: "Whether it was your father or you doesn't change the facts. And actually, as it was your father who guaranteed the booking, should we discuss the contract of trust you stand to break with him? On top of everything? Couldn't your forfeiture be construed as a kind of theft? From your father?"

"I was asleep when he brought me."

"Asleep." This brings a gleam. "Or unconscious?"

My face reminds him that both states are plainly sleep. But he goes on: "You see, Gabriel, the course lasts two weeks because it takes at least that long to get to the bottom of things. It's complex. *You're* complex. You can't spend less than a day here and complain of poor value for money. Forty-two sessions—one individual, one group, and one ad hoc session per day—try getting that in London for what we charge."

Dalí Girl returns with a lilac folder and hands it to David. I turn on her: "*Can you just get my things!*" and she jumps.

"Now, now." David raises a hand. "Susanna has a right to a civil working environment."

As he speaks I notice his skin: it's dry and thin like paper. This, along with his pinched features, makes me realize a sign is being sent by the Enthusiasms:

David West is an origami person.* Spread, creased, and

---

*How self-righteous are those conditioned by fear. Holding back is their main drive in life, and hence all they preach. Origamis take no risks, wear mediocre clothing, and say mediocre things. They have a smug air, or an air of overly reasonable bonhomie, which is a high form of smugness. Look at how solely they're responsible for most counteractions to endeavor, and for marginalizing people with traits outside their own rigid norm. Origami people are the identifiers of the problems of others, the foretellers of downfall owing to all but themselves. These ignorant, dogmatic lurkers are secret enemies; and even as you read this, they're out there busily hoarding evidence of your failings.

folded by culture into a clever likeness of a man, a napkin adorn-
ment without ideas outside his own folds, unfolding others to
crease them back in his own image. As he looks up from the
folder he must see a horror in my gaze, because his face gets even
sharper.

"You'll make me quite mad," he says. "I'm being very patient
with you, even though you've made me late for the other clients.
Aren't their issues as important as yours? Should everyone forfeit
their right to treatment because of your behavior?"

I wait as these next turds slither out of his psyche. Now we
find out he also favors the anal ploys of a police officer. Only
police officers and eight-year-old girls open their dealings with
such stupid questions: "Do you always leave your vehicle in the
middle of the street, sir? I suppose you call that a correct way
to behave, sir? How would you feel, sir, if somebody did that
to you?" and et cetera. These, while expressing native smugness,
are also ploys meant to force your submission; because an honest
answer would make you an idiot—and a sensible response would
leave you a prisoner.

I have overestimated David West.

I take a cigarette from my pocket.

"Not in here, come on." He lowers his voice: "Don't let's get
off on the wrong foot. You're living through hard times, and I'm
sorry. You've lost a partner, lost your job. You've lost all that goes
with that. You've lost—"

"All this is in the file, is it?"

"Don't forget, I signed you in from your father. My point
is, Gabriel: things have been a struggle, and I empathize—but
you don't have to struggle alone. It doesn't have to be this hard.
Just pay me one courtesy: sit with me for a moment and open

a dialogue. We can start anywhere—for instance, these bipolar issues I see in your notes."

"I was depressed." I fumble for my lighter. "Now I'm fine."

He shuts the folder. "Well, here's my concern—manic depression doesn't swing between depression and fine. Or it'd be called fine depression. Don't you think?"

I light the cigarette.

"You're going to make me very mad."

Hoisting my gaze, I take a wholesome drag and look along the room's high cornices, elegant braidings of vines, cornet-shaped flowers and leaves, some cuddling droplets of water. All are now painted a dull cream. I picture them gilded, bordering an aquamarine fresco of treetops and sky, as might be seen looking up from inside a grave.

"Gabriel: you are breaking the law."

Dalí gives a cough. It's unconvincing. She means to evoke cancer, but comes across like a housewife signaling boogers on someone's lip. I quietly continue my restoration of this demoralized structure, throwing Italian marble on the floors, erecting in the lobby a Frascati villa fountain overgrown with sacred lotuses and water poppies.

"Gabriel: you are violating our rights and breaking the law."

What a psychological sewer the place is. How rotten and insane. I turn to David, after a thoughtful drag on the smoke:

"How dare you violate this place?" I say. "You cunt."

3

Mistake. I should've just walked out. Fading daylight gives the Quiet Room sofa the tone of an infected wound. The nurse steps out, leaving me alone.

The door latches shut behind him.

Women were right: cunt used to be a harsh word. I wore Winnie-the-Pooh pajamas the first time I heard it. That was the night things started going downhill. I say night—it was a late afternoon passed off as night by adults manipulating time for their own gain. One minute I was skipping up the hall, fluffy after my bath, singing like a fool. I was seized by this sudden flamboyance, one of those little deliriums that can erupt in the young like bubbles from insanity's worm: "Wo-wo," I sang, "take the money and run!" I didn't know what it meant, I just liked the tune. And I never guessed what significance it had at that time.

Next thing I knew, my father smacked me through a glass door:

"*Cunt*," he hissed. "*You little cunt!*"

I didn't know what that meant either, but its sound was cutting. It blended well with the boosh and clank of my body through glass. Afterward I lay on the hallway rug, coated like a sauce ladle in blood from all the jags quietly in me. And I remember thinking cunt was just the right sound for that action.

I thought this while trying to get back on my feet.

But in a certain way, I never got back on my feet.

That little dude has lain there bleeding ever since.

My friend Nelson Smuts was over to stay. He ran alongside me in cowboy-gun pajamas, with his tan fresh from Cape Town. After the crash he stepped through the door, gathered up shards of glass, and solemnly laid them on my chest. Where they belonged, I guess, with all the other fragments. That's Smuts.

The glass door was a turning point for me. To seal the lesson, my father, hearing his then-girlfriend's footsteps, stood over me to yell: "How many times have I told you don't run indoors!" When she arrived he added: *"Nicht hier drinnen!"* He was playing the Euro-man with her. Guy Brockwell was one of those beardie guys who went to East Berlin after the wall came down. He put a shoe through a deserted factory window and started a club with a car stereo and a bottle of ginger wine. When the glass door happened we'd only recently returned from that last lanky phase of his youth. All he had to show for it were some weird pants and a few German phrases he could use around women. As for me, I still think some things in German today, even after all these years. The infant brain is as soft as oatmeal, those raisins sink in.

Plus I came back with a book called *Frederick*. Frederick was a mouse who saved up colors in summer; then, in winter, when fellow mice only had gray things to think about, he recited back all the colors he'd saved. At the end the mice rejoiced, saying: *"Frederick, Du bist ja ein Dichter!* You're a poet!"

I knew Frederick was me. I even looked like him. I used to

pull up a chair in front of our bullet-holed building in Prenzlauer Berg, climb on top, and tell poems. I never looked at anyone, I hid behind the rhymes. But I always began my readings as Frederick did: "*Ihr lieben Mäusegesichter*—my lovely mouse-faces."

East Berlin after the collapse of communism was like a kindergarten sandbox. Nobody knew who owned anything, nobody needed money or permission for their projects, all they needed was a beanbag chair, some wistful music, or a watering can with an eyeball painted on it. Westerners flocked to wear bad clothes and lurk around like little gray Workers from the East. Eastalgia became a new human condition.

Not that I recalled this as I lay bleeding that night in England. My father treated me on the kitchen table with iodine and tape, trying to sound calm through gritted teeth. The kitchen smelled like a clinic. Highlights flashed off Smuts's eyes in the dark of the doorway. We were all afraid, as animals are after violence.

My father was worried about money, that's why he was aggressive. To be fair, he didn't even look for the worries—like most people he just got lighthearted one day and signed something to boost who he thought he should be. Some carefree music, vivid colors, pictures of young women, and he signed something. Catheters slid into his accounts and his money trickled, flowed, or flooded out depending how the faucets of the economy were turned. He grew troubled, I watched him change. His sense of himself came to rely wholly on the flow of goods and credit.

Profit smashed me through that glass, not him.

And the infection soon laid him waste. I confirmed it years later when he saw the book of Frederick and sneered. The pointless mouse found a niche in the market, designed a product to fill it—then gave it away for free.

A loser's guidebook, Dad called it.

My father had embraced capitalism. It was the system that said he didn't have to grow up. That said he could just be his child's best friend. The same system that's now asking what have things come to.* What things came to is that for thirty years there were no parents.

Only casual friends you couldn't trust.

Anyway. I won't burden the notes with history, it doesn't matter now. Beyond the Quiet Room door I hear David West's voice approaching. From his pauses and inflections I sense my father is on the line. The next obstacle.

"Technically he could be," says David. "Into your care. But I'd advise against it until we assess him at law."

My brow falls. He means Mental Health Law. I drift back to the window, watching autumn whip the dark outside. At some point all summers are over, the view seems to yell. And did I enjoy the summer just past? Did I squeeze every drop of its juice? No. Because I didn't know it was the moment before this moment here. Had I known I may have scampered through sunlit fields, tossed my shoes up at the sky. But who can know which moment is the one before? And even if you knew, how could the moment be preserved? These are the riddles behind living.

So badly packed for life am I with my baggage of riddles.

---

* Despite this being a grubby decadence, we've responded correctly as a culture. It's been emphatically promised that a hamburger delivers happiness, togetherness, and security. That a sofa and credit card deliver them. But all that truly delivers them is a drink. Since we worked this out, the government has actually stifled drink advertising. But not sofa advertising. To quote from our day: you do the math. The key to consumer markets is unhappiness, individualism, and insecurity—where promises shine brightest.

Limbo has faded. It makes me thirst for death. Which brings the idea: I don't have to do it immediately. Which lands me back in limbo. It's a circuit.

And the first stress emerges: what if my determination weakens? I can't risk losing momentum. If I'm going to die, then I should be prepared at all times. At every new place, in every new room, I should look for potential instruments of death.

Starting here, I guess, if I'm serious about this.

4

The wedge of lemon comes dripping from my water. Leaning over the sofa, I switch on the lamp and jockey the plug slightly out of the wall. It has a spring mechanism that makes it pop out after a certain point, but I take magazines from the table and wedge them between floor and socket. This leaves a gap between socket and plug with power still flowing through.

I push the lemon in.

Whoosh. Crack! A throb shoots up my arm. Machines and lights click off across the building. I thud back in a swoon.

Darker quiet falls. Is it death?

Then footsteps past the door.

Health & Safety devices have intervened. I stretch my jaw open, move it left and right, blink a few times. And as my sense returns, a new feeling wells inside. I'm through another little door. Back in the limbo zone—but deeper, on a new level. That first limbo was barely a breeze against this lusty squall. Maybe because I've proven I have the courage for lethal risk and pain.*

---

* It seems the manner of our death concerns us more than death itself, allowing fear to form a barrier. A limbo can't really take off until you're secure in

Perhaps limbo throws up tests along the stair to its boudoir, in the way of a true odyssey. Looking around, I find myself even more detached from the object world, almost as much as wearing an iPod; surely this can only aid in dealing with my father, who noises at the door suggest is the next obstacle. It's clear limbo will have to expand. Maybe overnight—perhaps even to a day or two. Maybe Smuts and I even need to travel for last drinks. Why not—if nothing matters?

I park this thought in that cache of the mind where Enthusiasms find wishes to work on. It sits there alone; all my old wishes are gone. Alongside death it's the Enthusiasms' only project. We'll see what quirkiness they bring to the party—you'll know that wishes rarely arrive undecorated by the Enthusiasms.

Lights return, and after a few moments David steps in, frowning. "Are you smoking in here?" He sniffs the air. "Don't smoke in here, please. Your father wants you." He scans for cigarettes before handing me the phone.

My arm throbs as I take it. Still scanning around, David motions me into the corridor and shuts the door behind us. I hear fizzing as we leave the room, and a crackle. The lights click off again. An orderly hurries up the hallway.

My father says: "What's it all about?"

"I'm being held against my will."

"What? It's *because* of your will. Are you smoking in there?"

I let some silence pass to dilute his tone. Then I say: "It's not meant to be a prison."

---

managing the manner of death. This could account for a very low number of suicide limbos, as it calls for consideration in cold blood. Therefore, unless you plan to go under a train, I recommend a practice run—or at least a close romance with your chosen manner and its pains.

"You're lucky you're not in prison. Your commie pals are all over the news."

"Come on. And they're not commies, they're anticapitalists."

"Vandals, like that animal-rights crowd. Are you smoking?"

"Listen—"

"Charged, every last one of them."

"I didn't do anything. That's the point."

"What I find ironic is that it's always the parents who have to bail you out."

I pause while he vents at this and that, "parasites," "contribute to society," et cetera, and I reflect that age breeds conservatism, no getting away from it, unless you're Californian. Finally there's enough silence at my end that David steps away to excuse himself with the therapy group. I'm alone in the hall.

"I hit a problem," I eventually say.

"You did. I'm surprised you could even lift a projectile."

"Not that, I didn't touch a drink till later.* I'm trying to tell you I lost my faith. The building was too precious to damage. Capitalists restored her, this proud mid-Victorian monument with columns and flounces. Money restored her. It was an epiphany. I realized capital isn't the problem—I'm the problem. We're the problem. Nature's the problem. Why was I there to harm such a fine building?"

"Go back two," says my father. "You're the problem."

---

* Let's briefly state the obvious: drinking exists for the glorious purpose of loosening stays to this earth and ascending to the gods and Enthusiasms whence our spirits were born. When practiced with a fair heart, intoxication is a noble state of *Homo sapiens*, and the source of much divinity. While religious fervors, engorgement with sex, and certain drugs and foods can also achieve this state, remember: Jesus drank, and look how far he went.

"I held my cash card up to the door of the bank—and they let me in. The action group cheered, thinking I'd breached the defenses for them. But I stood inside and watched them being arrested on the steps. I'll never forget their faces. It just hit me: no matter who I align myself with, I'll always be outcast by a majority. My efforts to be at one with civilization were pointless. There's no single way. No single good. God's gone, replaced by the markets. Now they're going. We don't know who we are anymore because there's no *we*."

"What do you mean, God's gone? You're perfectly free to choose any system of belief you want, that's the whole point of our day!"

"Dad—there's a film out there called *Jehovah's Wetness*."

"You're raving. Have they sedated you?"

"A couple of weeks ago I started listening to Heart FM and it made me cry. Pop music. And I realized I'd spent my life saying goodbye to something without knowing what. We all have. It's not nostalgia, not retro fashion—it's the end of our flowering. Human progress is no longer a viable investment."

Guy Brockwell is quiet at first. Then, in emphatically spaced bursts: "What a load of undergraduate crap. In my day—"

"This is the result of your day."

"Oh, is it? And I suppose you'd have preferred something more totalitarian, a childhood like Gerd Specht's, with police filing your smell so they could hunt you with dogs."

"Nothing's more totalitarian than profit. And dogs are what come next, wait and see. Business has turned this country into an Afghan backstreet."

"My God. And to think you're twenty-six next birthday."

"In fact, every single global—"

"Stop there—let's talk narcotics."

"I'm—"

"Narcotics, Gabriel. Paramedics aren't stupid. They don't roam around looking for flounces in buildings. I could've driven a bus through your pupils last night. If you're trying to rally support for a binge like that you'll have to dig deeper than Heart FM. I'm telling you now—rehab is my last contribution. After this you sink or swim on your own."

"That'll be a change."

"Cinderella Boy: you lost a job reheating fries. And that's the best you've had, in case you wonder where the crowds of investors in your future went."

"Excuse me—that was a two-hundred-cover dining room."

"Gabriel, I drive past South Mimms every week. It's a truck stop. It's a damn Burger King."

"It may have shared a building with Burger King, but the dining section was spread over—"

"Don't make yourself look an even bigger ass. Now get the doctor back on the line."

"I'm telling you I turned a corner. I just feel rehab's the wrong response."

"On the evidence, what do you expect me to do? You may have turned a philosophical corner, but it's made you a mess. Last night was suicidal, Gabriel. What would people think? Now put the doctor back on, you're raving."

David West walks up the corridor, stopping ten paces away. He leans into the air, as if held by an invisible rope, stroking his chin.

"I just need to get away," I say to my father. "Put the usual triggers behind me."

"Nonsense, you'd run straight to Nelson Smuts, if he's not already dead."

"Ireland, for instance. Or Berlin—how about that? Away from this paintball-combat of markets. Anyway, rehab's hardly going to solve anything in two weeks."

"You can stay until they do. And don't get misty-eyed about Berlin, it's almost twenty years since we were there. Surprised you even remember it."

"It's the last place I was free."

"Gabriel: since then it's become the capital again, of the third most industrialized nation on earth. It'll be one big McDonald's. It'll be a parking lot. Nobody's singing Russian lullabies and fondling chunks of the wall. Things were changing before we left—I left a perfectly good business, remember. Anyway, if you've lost your job you can hardly afford to travel. My advice is: buckle down to your therapy. And if they can't cure your compulsive need to philosophize everything, then at least find an ethical model that moves you forward."

"I have the model—it's life that's moving backwards. Anyway, two weeks of therapy for a one-night bender is crazy. And let's say they uncover buried trauma—how is that helpful? Surely that's a workload for me across a lifetime?"

David hovers, ready to take the phone. I turn away.

"No deal," says my father. "Shedding light on some issues has to be the way forward. It's not just one night—you haven't been right for a long time. Light needs to be shed."

There he steps into a trap. Because the only issue I have in life is that he smacked me through a glass door. I stay quiet. It's a helpful feature of the guilty that their fears grow without outside help. I last saw him like this in the time between his divorce and my mother's death.

Hear him soften:

"Berlin, Berlin," he finally muses, like it's the first time he's heard of it. "You won't remember Gerd, my partner in the Pego Club. He never bought me out in the end. I should chase him for my bloody share. Massive, these days, it must be—can you imagine, these days? Unbelievable. Gerd Specht. Needed a kick in the ass back then."

"Maybe it's something I could look into for you. The old family business, eh?"

"With Gerd Specht? You must be kidding. Absolutely not. Very decadent man. Now put the doctor back on."

"He's not a doctor."

"Put him back on."

I hand over the receiver. David ushers me up the hall to reception, where I see Dalí opening lockers behind the counter. Asking my father to hold for a moment, David puts a hand over the mouthpiece: "Mineral water?" He smiles at me, and after I shake my head, he waves Dalí over and gently says: "Some water. And see if Roman's free to do a watch tonight. I'll need a watch room too, I think eight is ready."

He means suicide watch. I tense as Dalí Girl pads to the counter. A page turns on the desk. The intercom hoots: "Roman to reception, please—Roman."

I'm about to let gloom possess me when, in this lull between scenes, where one set of sounds dissolves into the next, a fire alarm shatters the quiet.

Whoosh. The Enthusiasms are with me. Running from the bottom of the hallway, an orderly peers through all the doors, slamming them shut, while David springs into action. Clients start to shamble up the hall, glad of the diversion, and even the kitchen cat—the so-called support animal—sashays up.

"Quiet Room!" yells the orderly. "Smoke!"

The alarm shrieks, David bolts down the hall, and while clients shuffle out to the forecourt I linger back and identify the key cabinet behind reception. Once Dalí Girl has moved out of sight, I locate my key, open the locker, and snatch my wallet and phone before hurrying out to join the others.

Drizzle swoops under spotlights outside, darting around like diamonds at the whim of the wind, while everyone huddles watching for signs of a blaze—rather hopefully, it seems to me. Once I'm sure of their distraction I duck into the row of trees that line the driveway, and slip away through shadows to the road.

My route takes me past the Quiet Room.

A window scrapes open, voices drift out:

"Looks like lemon."

"*Lemon?*"

"It's deliberate. We'll need the police as well."

"Fucking *lemon?*"

5

I stride a jagged line from rehab, writhing against weather like a worm trying to stay upright on end. I'm not concerned about being captured. My strategy is to head for the second nearest town. One advantage of our day is that you never have to be more than slightly smart. Remember this: there are no receptors left for smartness in the public domain. You need never be more than slightly smart or slightly nice. Anything more will arouse suspicion and rage, and confound the software that runs the country. This is because society's mechanisms are calibrated for stupidity and indolence—and to not be that way is now, by definition, antisocial. So I save myself the drama of scrambling through hedges and over fields. I simply set off not to the nearest town, but to the second nearest, which is smart enough. It wouldn't be profitable for anyone to search beyond the nearest town, especially when profit hasn't been disturbed.

I'm free to die. It's powerful to realize it. Every lick of wind, every crack of leaves is as emotionally stirring as the night before a fifth birthday. When you do something for the last time in your life, however small a thing, it becomes significant. And if you know it's a last thing beforehand—it becomes momentous.

No litter blew across the yards at rehab, but walking down this road trapped between hedges, litter blows again, and I feel at home. Twigs reach out like talons, I cuddle into them whenever a car speeds past, and I use this walk to start devising an ethic for limbo. Not to complicate a thing that's essentially free, but to see that I don't become buoyant and lose sight of my goal.

I start by defining seven reasons to die:

1. I come from an emotional Addams Family. I'm the lash end of a whip of ancestral and cultural psychologies which are miserable defeats that must be stopped.
2. I can see too clearly the dark motions of humans in action, and find these predatory and false. Neither can I be trusted to operate in a more ideal way. All I needed to know about human dealings I could've learned watching nine-year-olds in a schoolyard. After this, the process called maturity is simply one of disguise, community life simply an opportunity to learn that God dislikes the poor.
3. History's best thinkers eventually concluded that our flaws were too powerful to trust with freedom. Thus we've been groomed as hamsters in a wheel that benefits a laughing few. No more great works will be accomplished under the regime, because beauty is not democratic or profitable.
4. Owing to all above, the image of the person I want to be is one I could never achieve; and just pretending to be him will not suffice.

5. Love, touted as a principal reason to live, is just a Velcro of mental detriments which find an antagonist and stick to it. The result is a calcification of spirit. Love is an invitation to death, not life, and its flutters in the heart are as much the knell of an ending as the rattle in a corpse's throat.

6. High moments where our ideal selves heroically erupt into life, moments we're led to dream of and hunt, will never happen due to restraints in our characters. Only by choosing death have I found a nook where suppressed vigor might come out to play; and I say it's a fair price to see it flicker to life at least once.*

7. The Enthusiasms are clear about how things work. The rise of science as a source of wisdom—a science that attaches current feeble knowledge to all fact—has led us away from Fortune's most obvious truths: in thinking creatures all happiness not derived from intoxicants is false. Life is horrific without a drink. This has always been true. It's why intoxicants exist in nature. You can be moderate, a single drink will dampen two concerns—or you can follow me and blast all concern

---

* *Why die now?* The practical reasons for my death are as follows, and will be the same for you. We should admit that the knocking by these reasons on our doors has progressed to banging and smashing and jimmying with tools. In my commitment to death I've found the impetus for the life of sweet vigor and confidence I always wished for. With oblivion ahead, my angers and hurts are sated and quiet, and I am free. Life now has a predictable time, in the form of an elegant cone, and I can methodically furnish this time with the beauties and dares I imagined I might pine for in old age; because we never do the things we must, never foreseeing our ends—whereas if death had a date we would hurry to do them all.

from the landscape. Note, though, that the wages of excess is death. This tells us: be briefly happy—there is no long happiness—then step aside.

Approaching streetlamps light the sky like an aquarium at night, and clouds slink together like sea slugs to feed there. England's hum is pierced by rain, handfuls thrown in my face, and gusts of splintered noise. Before long a traditional English town unfolds before me. It comprises a Tesco, a Carphone Warehouse, a WH Smith, a Vodafone shop, a Burton, an Argos, a Boots the Chemist, a Burger King, a KFC, a Subway, a Halfords, a Shell service station, an Iceland, a McDonald's, two charity shops, three pound shops, a train station, and a police station.

A darkened Gothic church cowers behind trees.

I feel calm to be in my heaving land. Britain's empire might be the empire of modern capitalism, an invention of its quaintest loons, but I decide capitalism's grand flaw isn't Britain's fault. Rather it's plainly the fault, as with anything hopeful, of nature and her jokey craftsmanship. Stupid nature, which the church led us to admire as a perfect system, has crippled us as it cripples and kills everything, through shoddy design. All we have been driven by nature to achieve across history has today left us as soft as an infant's turd. And my beloved land, having so long been at the pinnacle of achievement, took the brunt. Some redress is surely due from nature.

We'll see about this, in a quiet moment, with wine.

A fire engine roars past with its lights flashing. I turn my back and stare at Burger King as if I might buy it. But whoosh—I find beauty there. The neon has dimmed on a corner of the sign, causing a delicate graduation of reds, from hot capsicum to dry blood.

The dimmer part is at the bottom, making dark matter seem to pool there, but that old blood sparkles with highlights thrown by other lamps nearby. There's no orchid or lily as rare as this fragment of sign, I reflect.

Certainly none spelling "King."

Arriving at the railway station, I find it droning with an alternating current of apathy and rage, buffeted as much between trains as when they rocket past without stopping. I switch on my phone and hear it ping a chain of messages.

"Single to London please," I say to the ticket clerk.

He looks up: "Forty-eight pounds thirty, that'll be."

"For a single? That's a pound a minute. And first class?"

"Fifty-five."

"I'll have a first-class single, then."

The clerk stares up through the top of his glasses. "I can do an Advance Saver for thirty-two, if it's a specified service you want."

"Then yes, please, the next service."

He squints at his screen: "That'll be the twenty-one thirty-six. Departing in ten minutes."

After buying the ticket I move to the shop, where I teeter for a while in front of the sandwich cabinet. This earnest national pursuit is worth savoring one last time, with its sweet dread of choosing badly and limiting personal happiness. I don't stand too close to the cabinet as there's a camera watching, which means I'm a suspect. In the same way a cliff can be scary in case some unstable reflex makes you throw yourself off, it pays to stand back from the cabinet because, as a suspect, I'm afraid they know something I don't. I might snatch one involuntarily, under pressure of scrutiny.

Ah, sandwiches—the beautiful game.

When it comes to finally choosing, I play safe and go for egg. I buy the one showing the most yolk, but having bought it, upon lifting the bread I see a row of yolk half-slices arranged at the front, with a single lonely lump of white on the expanse behind.

With my personal happiness limited, I make my way to the platform. It's too noisy with loudspeaker apologies to hear my phone messages, so instead I cock an ear to the variety of ways there are to apologize for chaos, which is one. The train arrives on time, but as I go to board, a platform attendant comes to inspect my ticket. She's pretty, beginning to show the thick ankles and hips that signal a journey north; a proud journey compared to the south, where pants are worn under a dress as if it cancels the ass outright.

"This isn't your service, I'm afraid." She points at the ticket.

"What? But it's nine thirty-six." As I say it, a passing officer slows his patrol, glancing over to assess the odds of a stabbing.

"That service is canceled, I'm afraid. This is the late-running twenty-one twelve. You'll have to catch the next service."

I look into the empty carriage. I can't afford to miss this train, at my back I feel the forces of rehab, my father, the police.

"Terms and conditions of the Saver fare are that in the event of cancelation you catch the next service. Which will be the twenty-one fifty-nine, though it's not due till twenty-two twenty."

"And how can I get on this train?"

"New ticket, I'm afraid—you'd have to purchase a full flexible fare on board."

"And can I cancel this ticket?"

"I'm afraid the terms and conditions of the Saver fare—"

"But I only bought it ten minutes ago."

"I'm afraid the service was only canceled just now. You can ask for a form in the office and write to Customer Services. You see, the terms and conditions—"

I wait through the sermon of small print, then look at her. She braces herself. The officer waits on alert in case I resort to threats or abusive language, while all around, from every gable and cranny, every tower and pole, the sproutlings of fascism, that state formed by decadence to mop up its mess, hum watching us on video: "Hm. Well." I finally scratch my head. "I don't blame you."*

She cocks her head sympathetically and wanders away. The officer also moves off, disappointed. This exchange highlights my problem with the war on capital: its criminal masterminds have placed themselves beyond reach behind blameless cogs, whose own lives are crushed between pincers and cogs.

It's a human shield spanning all society.

If I could meet the shadowy forces it might be a different matter. Bring me the shadowy forces! The ones who wore us down inch by inch till we accepted any outrage, put us in a room together and then we'll see.

I buy a second full-price ticket to London. Modern frustrations fan out in my mind like a hand of cards, not least that our language sets us up with its "I'm afraids" and "Sorrys." Surely no other language paves its own road to dismay. Then the twenty-

---

* When it's profitable to deny things to people, culture devises a reward system for automatons and spoilers. The attendant would otherwise see reason in letting me board the carriage, and would certainly be nice enough to do it—but instead of reveling in doing an innocent good turn, and wielding discretional power, she gains her reward from doing a "tough job," which means conquering logic and good nature, and finding refuge in those customer-management skills formerly known as meanness.

one twelve is late because tracks and signals need investment which is too costly; my ticket costs five times more than in Holland because the company has to support that crumbling infrastructure while simultaneously expanding its profit; the Saver fare is only cheaper because fewer holders will actually travel, having been foiled on the roulette wheel of delay or fallen foul of a trick in small print.

There it is: every flight and dash of hope, all rage and calm, the clatter and grind of every life owes its modern form to one thing—the profit of nameless others. In the instance of this robbery I take the Englishman's way out and simply resolve not to use the service again. My mood even lightens with the jokes this whips up. Over my dead body will I ever use this service again, ha ha.

As the train rattles through Stevenage I note that only bugs seem to be traveling. Ruddy blobs with spindly, grasping limbs. The lucky ones find newspapers abandoned on the seats or floor and read them, tutting while windows flash with industrial estates, with roads and roadworks, with trailers, and with cars that dodge and lunge behind them as if swimming with feces. So goes my last train ride, a hurtling montage of where things stand. Looking around, I wonder what it is that makes my fellows able to bear such a life. How can they face the day, when I can't? Is there some secret to living that makes its conditions irrelevant? A neutering of expectation, a mastery of the mundane? Or have they just grown accustomed to rape?

I decide the trip only serves as an example of how not to spend a limbo. If there was ever a time to seek comfort, this is it. There being no notion of future in limbo, it hits me that it's a naturally capitalistic space. Perhaps the perfect capitalist space, utterly organic. Limbo has no budget, no rating, no limit. It's a spend. I could've bought all the sandwiches at the station and picked the best one. And I didn't have to suffer the indignity of the Saver fare.

Finally I grasp the beauty of money: it elevates life into blue sky, above clouds of terms and conditions. It admits no term or condition except having. No stabbings attend the full flexible fare. And though it requires us to accept being robbed outright— can robbery even exist in a limbo? If a limbo has no future, then robbery deprives us of no future benefit. So robbery can't exist, unless it takes our whole bank at the outset.

A revelation looms.

I always wondered why the law allowed small robberies by companies from individuals, but not by individuals from companies. And why governments no longer promoted visions of future society, why promises only spoke of more good and less bad:

Capitalism is a limbo.

Not a structure but an *anti-structure*. Driven not toward a defined end, but hovering over a permanent present, harvesting a flow of helpless human impulses. It builds no safe futures, leaves no great structures, prepares no one for roads ahead. And why would it? We don't march through an age of civilization but float between Windows and Mac, treading water.

The revelation is a stroke of irony from the Enthusiasms. In finding the purest abandon before death, in fleeing the cult of free markets—I've become one myself.

Whoosh—a body blow.

I look around and things are suddenly dreamlike. I'm Ebenezer Scrooge on a moral tour of Culture Present. Even my countrymen on the train are perfect products, corpulent beetles comprising storage sacs for sugar and fat, with limbs just sturdy enough to navigate teller machines and stores—or else they are sallow and sphinxlike, having mouse eyes that glow with discontent.*

I must aim for a higher limbo. One that smells of hotel soap. A limbo where young Swiss strangers care for me. An evening more splendid than any since the fall of Rome—I ask for it now, as a newborn capitalist, looking up into the night through the window. Come, you Enthusiasms, manifest this wish.

And let us marvel at the style of its arrival.

In the middle of my reverie a robot calls to remind me I have voice mail. But here's a modern hitch: my calling credit is low, and if I call Vodafone to make a card payment, Lloyd's bank will instantly block my account. Mobile phone top-ups signal fraud, you see. Then I won't be able to remove the block because the phone will run out of credit listening to Lloyd's automated menus. And I won't be able to get cash to buy credit in a store because the block will stay until I call Lloyd's. I'll even be unable to call Vodafone—because it demands credit to discuss credit.

The phone is in its own dying limbo. Forced there by the markets. What a symbol. How alike we are. Suddenly limbo is the key to understanding all modernity. Anyway, I quickly decide this: I'll listen to one message and use the remaining credit to get Smuts pumped up to the night's bacchanal.

---

* *Human constructions only ever mirror the human body & its behaviors*: Look at any system designed by humans and you will see that it unconsciously copies a working dynamic of our own body. From governments to cities to restaurants to banks and instruments of credit—all are models of the supply and demand of oxygen and food, and of their transport, conversion, and removal. Then note the reverse: that our bodies come to resemble society around us. Is it healthy, is it fit, is it cheery or polite? Look around you on a train: there is culture laid bare.

I will never top the phone up again.

As long as I live, ha ha.

The first message is from Sarah, my girlfriend till yesterday:

"It's me," she says. "Just so you don't blame me for not warning you, Hamish is on his way round to your place tonight. He wants to kill you, for God's sake just do as he says. You have to sign yourself off the action group account, he's got the papers. Nigel's the new treasurer. And Yaseen wants your text for the new flyer. He's not happy either, they're both bailed to appear in court tomorrow. I've told them you won't have touched a penny of the fund. But it's the last time I'm vouching for you, Gabriel. I feel so fucking stupid. We all do. We thought you were so sensitive—but it's just weakness. Bourgeois inertia. All it'll take for the forces of profit to destroy this world is a few more people like you, all talk and no action. Anyway. Don't call back. If you found something for Douglas and Fay, just pass it on to Yaseen."

The message ends. Ah, well. How remote my old life seems. I'm as detached from it as if wearing an iPod. Even the political certainties behind our action group have been turned on their head in the space of a day—and flipped again on this train trip alone. And dear Sarah, the revolutionary, still fretting over a gift for Douglas and Fay's dinner party. Then calling me bourgeois!

I sit back and reflect on our relationship, here laid bare. You'll know that romance begins when we lasso a flying thing out of the air. Once snared, it can drop to hang as a weight or stiffen into rods of attachment that pass for love in the long term. But no flying thing started this romance. We found each other's lassos dragging on the ground, and stamped a foot on them. Her stretch marks never ached for my touch, my hollow chest didn't pound under her gaze. No crucible of fury contained us, no compulsions were vented in gasps. Our playground had just one game: "If it wasn't for you," playable on fields of any size. Ah, well. A lesson comes from this which you and I can peruse later, in a duller frame of mind, and with wine. You'll see that I've closely studied the dynamics of romance, but I tell you that this relationship was notable for its lack of qualities known to romantic love, including romance, or love. Of course, it had a fleeting hook one night, when by accident our perspectives were in harmony. Mumbled reference was made to our souls becoming one—that laughable dream achieved by none. Still, it was enough to ignite the pathologies that bound us. This is usually when nature invites us to think destiny must be at work, because what else could explain the mystery of such strangers growing attached? Well, no. Not destiny but pathology was there. Still, in these qualities our relationship was truly English, truly human, and I defend it, and her. Losing those defeating routines will be a blow to Sarah. I just hope, as our pathetic games were hidden behind a public face, that she can play out the loss as a tragic love and enjoy the abandon it brings. It's a kind of limbo, and so a fitting last gift from me.

Although I'm already a phantom, the loss jolts me nonetheless. It's another tie cut from the earthly plane. It may seem bleak, dear friend, to speak like this, and I don't do it having spurned visions of love, but rather having embraced them. I dreamt of serving some kindred soul, of course I did—some light, determined heart, one that engaged me in combat over things that mattered, punctured any part of me that set our bliss askew, and mastered me unawares to myself. One who undertook the workload of me and gave me her works to undertake. I even pictured her in a small, fine frame, with hair as black as jet, never sulking or dropping snide asides, but settling our spats with a pillow fight. Needless to say, I never met such a soul. In our time and place the souls I found were all trapped inside themselves, too busy at the mirror to feel me reaching out.

Ah, well. My mind starts to hunt things to look forward to, this is how it works, pulling itself along a rope of future comforts, ticking them off a list as they arrive. I see it now for the monkey device it is. Still I let it roam till it fixes on Nelson Smuts. What a party we'll have. I reflect that of the friends we collect over a lifetime, not every one fits all occasions. Each has their time, their seasons flourish and wither. But this night pummeled by gales, this odyssey on the rim of oblivion—this is Smuts's night.

Granted: I always wished I was him.

Smuts became a great chef, although his temperament makes him unemployable in the usual sense. Instead the epicurean underworld pulled him into its rarest bowel. Apart from those childhood summers when his foster parents brought him over from South Africa, we later set out to become chefs together. My father was indirectly responsible. With what remained of his swagger about running a club in Berlin, and with money mysteriously contrived from who knows where, he partnered up with a smug Canadian called Tattersfield to open a bistro on Kilburn High Road. The Coup de Gras, they pathetically called it. Nothing with enough character to erase the smell of fresh paint was ever cooked there, and even as it served its bilious pestos, their bickering over the name never stopped. They quarreled over whether the spelling "Coup de Grâce" would draw as much attention to their cleverness as "Cup de Grâce" or "Coupe de Gras" or "Ku-D-Gra," as the preening imbecile Tattersfield suggested just prior to making his asinine girlfriend pregnant. With that he added a screaming mouth called Lovey to the café's payroll, and a hammer blow to its plummeting fortunes. Throughout all this, Smuts and I haunted the kitchen.

Dreams sprouted there.

We would become genius chefs. Gastronomes would weep at our creations, kill themselves in rapturous despair. We dreamt of a restaurant called Nimbus, named for the aura around a saint— because our dishes would light a nimbus around our patrons. The place would have no signs, its name would be passed in whispers. It would exist behind locked doors, where couples weren't allowed. After signing a last will and testament, diners would be strapped into deep-sea fishing chairs and shrouded in linen with which to mop their tears.

We made such a fuss that our dads sent us to catering college.

But it was clear after a week that all I had was airs, and no talent. Plus I was timid around knives and flame. This slap of truth ended my time at chef school. I slunk home to help my father reinforce my worthlessness; a task we took to with all the gusto of model-train enthusiasts.

Meanwhile, Smuts really did have genius. To him a foodstuff was an alchemical element. He quivered around food, unleashed his senses upon it till no grain of meat, no stalk of spice kept any secret. Blades flashed like sunlight in his hands. Nevertheless, the hour of his final exam came and went without him. The absence was put down to his temperament, by then a known feature of the college climate. But later certain classmates and tutors found an invitation to a crematorium. Smuts had booked twenty minutes' burning time between funerals, and while the exam was under way had there blistered to perfection a suckling pig lifted straight from a sow's womb, unstressed by vaginal birth. Smuts was gone when the classmates arrived—but the pig was there, steaming under a serving cloche.

Back at the college they opened the animal up, at first heaping scorn on Smuts because the organs were still inside. Then a tutor saw that the gut was lined with pastry. The intestines were a black pudding of wild nuts, the liver a haggis of foie gras, the kidneys butternut raviolis, all anatomically exact. And when they sliced open the blue-maize dumpling that was the heart, a crimson juice spilled flakes of real gold across the tray.

A legend was born in the kitchen underworld.

And Smuts had other things going for him. He burst into his life with the tender musculature of a young dog, and with eyes and lashes that made everyone want to touch him and take care of him. As our young summers passed, nature took her chisels to Smuts. His hips ruthlessly narrowed, he sprouted shoulders and arms like the claws of a burly crab. By contrast nature paid scant attention to me. My eyes bulged apologetically, my whole gangling form was swept back as if against a nearby blast. I had no choice but to cultivate quirks for my character and peer out from the gloom behind them. Smuts meanwhile rippled under the sun, with all the symmetries that are an unspoken passport into society. Not that he was hacked in the way of hard and angry men, but rather strung and smoothed into a hallmark of nature, one of her boasts, like a hummingbird or a summer's day. The gentle rasp of his voice delivered simple ideas in blunt Anglo-Saxon words, and every action he took, even swallowing, set musculatures plowing over his body. As we grew up I felt girls get weak around him. They grew silly and forgot themselves. Whereas with me they remembered themselves—or worse, the powerful ambitions they had for themselves—and even honed their harsh caprices on me.

I suppose this is why my nerves headed inward, while his shot out to the skin where fingers and tongues fell to helpless obsessions. Smuts provoked intimacy by his very being. Modest girls would do things for him that prostitutes would refuse.

Despite this, he never saw us as different, which lifted me up. He shared those intimacies as if they were also native to my life. And by this arrangement they became native to me through him, and fed my boiling senses.

I feel Smuts even looked up to me. His temper could shift so quickly that his feelings were often left bewildered; and because his senses faced outward to be caressed, he hadn't much conversation with that inner traffic of feelings. I think my cerebral analysis of things was useful to him, and calming. This, I think, is why we're friends. We each have a quality without which the other is slightly futile.

I'm off to drink my last with Smuts.

I call his mobile number. He answers after five rings:

"Yo."

"Smutty," I say, "Gabriel!"

"Who's that calling me Smutty?"

"It's Gabriel."

"Wait up—what?"

"Gabriel. As in Brockwell."

"For fuck's sake. It's ten to six."

"Eh—where are you?"

"Tokyo."

"Oh. Well, Smuts—"

The line goes dead.

Ah, Smuts.

Smuts, Smuts. Hm.

6

It seems limbo isn't immune to disappointment.* I suppose the markets face the same lesson. The culture faces it. Things can seem rosy from inside a limbo. As detached as wearing an iPod.

Jolting into King's Cross station, I find it peopled by two races: the drunk and the frightened. Mobs decant to the trains barking echoes at the high glass roof, and many trains set off without conductors, presumably as none dare ride them. But I reflect what a glorious sight it is—society in its limbo, leaving a false appointment and making its own way to the feelings it was promised. Because it's worth it, ha ha. My only concern is that it's an ugly decadence, without mentors or finesse. Its wages are vomit and debt.

---

* The head of a pharmaceutical company admitted that only thirty percent of drugs work properly on thirty percent of people. And if you observe life you'll see that he merely identifies the mean threshold of human success in nature. The drug company was a working model of the mathematics of expectation, endeavor, whim, and fortune. Therefore abolish the notion of one hundred percent solutions so touted by culture. According to nature, thirty percent is a windfall.

We might see about this, in the course of tonight, with wine.

Meanwhile, stress mounts in limbo. My house is likely to be the target of a pinch, with both the anticapital action group and my father converging. Still I must regroup, after this setback with Smuts, and the place is where I live; or used to live. After I decide to mount a lightning assault by taxi, the scamp Enthusiasms send me a driver from that species of white-haired London cabbie who decided that in the time-distance equation of taxi meters, time pays more. So he waits for every light to turn red. Only eventually do we nose into my road. I suppose there are many things to say about the corner of North London where I lived, but they don't matter to the narrative anymore. One of its Victorian row houses is the place I shared with housemates Alan and Evelyn. I sputter past it in the cab, scanning for signs of trouble. All seems quiet. The television flickers through the first-floor window. I leave the cab waiting around the corner and let myself in, gathering flyers from under the mailbox, though as a technically dead person I don't have to. Courtesy is shown in my last hours. Light in the stairwell fades to dark up the stairs.

In the background I hear the television:

"I'm a housewife and mother," says a woman.

"And do you have any kids?" a presenter booms.

"Yes, three."

"Three wonderful kids! And what do you do?"

"I'm a housewife."

I go inside, collect some grams of coke, some hash, and some ecstasy from Alan's bag, and leave money for them. Then on an impulse as I pass Evelyn's room I grab the strongest perfume I can find on her dresser, and splash myself with it.

It wraps me in a citrus armor.

I pause, stunned.

"Guerlain," says the label.

"*Jicky.*"

Pure decadence. I leave a gram on her dresser in payment, then my reverie is shattered by a bang on the front door:

"Brockwell." It's Hamish, the head of the action group. "Come out! If you haven't touched the Action Fund, then we will not harm you!"

My heart starts to race, even as I ponder how stupid he is to think I might come to the door.* But before I can act I hear a ping on my phone. It's a text message. A warning about credit. Suddenly it occurs to me—maybe Smuts didn't hang up. Perhaps, consistent with our day, my credit simply expired, and the service provider, despite a fortune I've let them rob over the years, simply terminated the last crucial call of my life.

A receptive space clears inside me, between Hamish's thumping and the bloodsucking phone. And a moment later, in a drenching revelation, the night's answer comes.

I scribble Smuts's number on the back of a matchbook, then throw down the phone and smash it dead. Turning to my laptop, I log into the action group account and find nearly five thousand

---

* We're chastised for speaking badly of others, though we're born knowing that many are dumb. Of course, it's a hierarchy of stupidity, in which we also hold a stupid place, but it has a border, which is the point at which a stupid person is no longer humble. A person making allowances for their ignorance, and remaining polite, is a type of natural aristocrat. But beyond the border are the truly stupid, who also feel entitled. Worse, they don't suspect their stupidity, and can't imagine a greater intelligence than theirs exists. These are the dangerous masses which capitalism has empowered and set loose, sheep who respond to all things with the same bleat—and we should call them what they are at every chance.

pounds there, which I send to my personal account. I'm already a traitor in the group's eyes, so it's reasonable to think the fund is well spent on my destruction. And if I find the shadowy forces in the night, for five grand I can give them a good thrashing.

Next I look up Japan Airlines.

I throw on my Munch's *Scream* T-shirt and my military great-coat and gather the perfume, my passport, and a quick change of clothes, resolving to spend limbo at the airport overnight—not in the most obvious terminal, but in the second most obvious.

Then I carefully lift and weigh the laptop in my hands. I raise it over my head and throw it down—that vacuum of life, that cretin savant, that pilfering Latin maid, that predator's restroom.

As I kick it across the floor my housemate Alan bursts in.

"Ahh—depression's gone, then." He spins me around, searching my face. "When did you last sleep? Do you know what you're doing? Is it a whoosh thing? You have that pedagogue troubadour look in your eyes. Patronizing, glazed over."

I can't help but smile.

"Couldn't you just picket McDonald's?"

I sweep past him to the back steps, out to our alley, and around the corner to the waiting cab, where I huddle in the back.

With Hamish's noise still pounding along the road, the taxi grumbles away past my house shooting vapor into the night. Light glows in the windows where I once lived. Although it's an early twenty-first century English household—which is to say a tri-sexual household of unparented narcissists where, in the twenty minutes I was there, cash and products were transacted to a sum of four hundred pounds, and no fewer than five laws were broken—the sight of it disappearing makes me faint. I gaze through the cab window and realize no mark of mine is left here. In the end

I never even designed my prize artwork, which was to be a giant supermarket cart thrown on its side across the river. I look out on a world that won't know I've passed through. Starbucks napkins tumble and scud in the wind. Dudes swagger, blokes plod, lovers stroll head-down, smiling as if into the face of a bright Danish child, past pubs where beer mist swirls, through smells of pizza and yesterday's sick turned gentle; and wherever the lights are most dazzling, Euro-teens gaggle like piles of socks, each a hundred and sixty-five centimeters tall, approved by Brussels, oblivious to skanks and shanks and shit in the shadows. None see me pass. Their stupor isn't for me. Now I live outside stupors and delusions, looking in like a ghost from limbo. The clatter and chug of the taxi, its roll and pitch, its gliding blackness in the night make it a phaeton, a hearse led by a blustering team in black plumes, frisking and snorting a path through unknowing mourners. Goodbye, then, carbon footprint, farewell the Royal Mail, adieu lager louts, fish & chips, the Beckhams. Cheerio my dear, beloved place. Smaller lives than yours may come and go, and the seasons within them may flourish and wither.

But this night like a moonlit churchyard—this is my night.

TOKYO

7

My hair crests over my head like the dying wave of capitalism, molded by a corner of aircraft seat. As the flight cost much of the action group fund, I decide to leave the hairdo for my last day alive, styled as it is by costly Enthusiasms.

In other ways I fare less well. Though I managed the flight on less than a gram of cocaine,* dry air has chalked my throat to form cliffs that block my nose from behind. And there was no chocolate milk in business class, a scandal for nearly three grand. Instead eels and champagne siphoned blood to my gut and left my skin translucent. This under aircraft restroom lighting—truth lighting, calibrated for humility and submission—turned me into a working model kit: the Visible Capitalist.

---

* Ah, cocaine: this marvelous carbon-neutral alkaloid shares a family with coffee and tomatoes, and is famed for sharpening senses to a crisp and purposeful limbo. It aids missions, not random intoxication, though it can rescue bacchanals which peak too early. Still, beware: being also subject to markets, not much coke on our streets is cocaine. Check it: coke has a polystyrene sheen, sparkles with a pinkish hue, and should smell of either kerosene or ether. If your coke is floury and bitter to smell, if it's dull, or too sparkly, like glass, it could be poison.

On a brighter note: my drugs arrived safely in my trouser pocket. Guessing that the world would function differently from our derationalized zone, I carried them in the most obvious place—surely nobody would think me so stupid.

And so my funeral cortège reaches Tokyo, megalopolis by the sea, stamped like a pajama with notions of kittens and monsters.

Place where I am tall and strange.

It's daytime and the gods are with me. I have money and limbo-fuels, and Smuts is never far from sublime food and wine. My last drink will be the most splendid ever drunk. And after that brief and utter decadence, a perfect bonsai of our dimming age, by daybreak at the latest—I'll be gone, numb to my fate. It was a good idea to come, because clues to my physical life are behind me. Limbo is pure. Standing here naked at a window makes the scene at that window in rehab feel like a dismal previous life.

This window looks out of my room at the Peninsula Hotel. I gaze over all the beetling shapes, sharp folded edges, and up at the pearly sky, and say to myself:

"Rehab—Peninsula Hotel.

"Whoosh."

After savoring this hearty turn of events, I phone Smuts.

"Say again?" he grunts. "You're *local?*"

"Come for a drink."

"Get real, they're working me like a dog."

"Smuts—you know you want to."

"I'm not free till Wednesday."

"What day is it today?"

"Saturday."

"I propose a bacchanal that renders it irrelevant."

"A *what?*" Smuts pauses. "Oh, fuck me—you're in one of your Scarlet Pimpernel phases, uh. Watch out—Pimpernel in Tokyo."

"You're a hundred years out. Try nineteenth century."

"Putain," he groans. "And why?"

"They had a better decadence than we're having."

"Fuck me. And is it all whoosh? Do I have to bail you out with money?"

"I come as a capitalist, my friend. I've stepped into that fading light."

"Putain. Capitalist Pimpernel in Tokyo. Then you'll know why I can't come and play, markets are down, the boss is all over me. You should've let me know."

"I thought you didn't do bosses."

"*Wish* I didn't, uh. I *wish* I didn't. This one's a sour prick, one of those downer mouths like a fish. So miserable yesterday I almost called the cunt's wife to send his sword round in a taxi."

"I have the remedy," I say. "You know you want it."

"Mate—I'm being sponsored at this kitchen. Long story, but I can't blow it. Things are already stressed."

"What time do you finish?"

"I'm not going crazy tonight, I mean it. Come for a meal if you can behave yourself. But it won't be a late night, we've got inspectors coming. Yoshida-san's spraining a testicle trying to get a tank ready to move the fish to."

"Thought you didn't do fish."

"Not just any fish—*fugu.* Japan's finest, uh. It's the next big thing, poisons. Flavors aren't enough anymore. Come around six, I'll explain. And mate—Pimpernel can fuck off—uh?"

"You're a century out."

"Pu-*tain.*"

Smuts gives me an address to go to at nightfall. I'm dampened by the call; even asking where this urge springs from that demands company for my death. But I decide it's not a need for witnesses, or any such lurking psychology. Just a last good drink. And Smuts will surely warm to the idea of a drink, in the end. As to my end, I leave it to the Enthusiasms for now. In a perfect night I'd have a gun, the definitive suicidal tool. But for now, well. We'll see what instruments come.

I admit to flagging the word "poisons."

Ah, the Enthusiasms and their mysterious ways. We'll surely observe them, in the night's high moments, over wine. For now, to quell fatigue and seediness I pull the blackout curtains over my window and lie on the bed smoking a cigarette, while on television a *manga* rabbit-girl gets raped by a schoolboy. When she weeps you can see up other girls' skirts in the reflection of her tears. The Japanese like tears. By the time I lie back into the pillow, dreams come quickly and feverishly. I toss and crawl over the bed and finally wake with a start. A sense of knowing runs through me: that I've had my last sleep, my last dream. A ventilation fan hums in the room. Early night has fallen outside. Concerns come flocking: How will I die? How will I break the news to Smuts? Intoxication is the key. Our nimbus must be so shimmering and high as to be immune to outside reason.*

---

* This glow around saints is the crucial clue to humanity's mission. Recall the moments when drink, music, and good company lit you full of fraternal love, forgiveness, and joy, then think: according to every doctrine those are the highest states we can reach as human beings. Whole faiths are dedicated solely to achieving them. They are qualities of Jesus and a countless majority of prophets and gods. Therefore never has a ritual been more above argument than intoxication for the purpose of raising a nimbus.

I get up and do a line off the bathroom counter. As it sets about its frosty work, more key conditions come to mind for tonight: for instance, my mission must never come into contact with ordinariness. Nor will I entertain obligations or tangles or tedium, neither use my brain to compute routine or pointless things.

These must be steadfast rules.

I throw water on my face, towel it off, then throw the towel on the floor, to harm the environment. Splashing Jicky onto my wrists and temples, I go up in a decadent shimmer. Whoosh! Two miniatures of vodka even seem to go from the mini-bar down my throat; I only notice when I find the bottles empty. And because a night with Smuts can be unpredictable, I slip the remaining miniatures into my coat, noting there's even a full-sized bottle of red wine, a fine Pauillac, in the cabinet.

Surely for Smuts's rare palate.

With my hair remolded into a sort of shark fin by the nap, I carve aerodynamically through the lobby and out to a waiting cab, having to slouch in the seat to keep it intact.

So begins our night of nights, my friend.

The San Toropez Restaurant occupies the third floor of an office building in Shinjuku, a bustling, money-infested district of Tokyo. Stepping from the elevator, I find the dining room large and open, more landscaped than furnished, with poles of light beaming down on low tables: a sumptuous space, minimal, empty, and silent. What a resonant cradle of nimbus. I seem to be the first guest. Looking around, I see an aquarium spanning the back wall with a seascape of sand and pebbles, and a stone pagoda at one end. It's a tank you could stand up to your neck in and walk ten good strides through. Waves of green-tea light shimmer out, dappling the paper screens of the room while spiky fish, dumpy fish, and fish like mangled umbrellas hover inside with bug-eyes, and an octopus lurks in the pagoda. As I stand watching, a cook nets a fish and it puffs like a balloon, pimpling with little spines.

Smuts emerges from the back soon after. He winds toward me smiling easily, arms swinging loose, in a black Mao smock with its sleeves rolled up. I see his gaze as I saw it on the day of the glass door, like a set of headlights under his brow. He's leaner than he was, with a heavier shadow of whiskers, and muscles more veined, as if his bones had sucked his skin closer to him. Still, no sculptor of Rome ever imagined such a stern working animal as Smuts.

"Pu-*tain*"—he recoils—"d'you come from a whorehouse?" He waves a tunnel through my scent, flicks an eye over my hair, and nods at the wine in my hand. "And drink, to a restaurant? Did you bring food as well? Is it a fucking picnic?"

"A gift." I hand him the bottle as we hug.

"Fuck me." He checks the label. "Type of shit you drink with Doritos. Can't believe people still buy this crap with corks in."

I note that his accent has stopped commuting between South Africa and England, finally settling on the English side, with just an occasional flat souvenir.

"It's from the hotel." I frown at the wine.

"Mate. Times have changed." He pulls me through a galley separated from the dining room by a bar, where he thumps down the bottle. Three Japanese chefs hiss a welcome. As I nod back, Smuts's phone rings in his pocket. "Not again." He fumbles it out and kills the call: "Imprinted like a duckling."

"Who's that?"

"Never mind. Follow me, I'll show you a wine. A twenty-first century wine. Rare privilege for you tonight, uh, Putain. Then you can tell me why you're here."

"You've just defined it. I knew you wouldn't let me down."

"Let you down? You're going to grow wings. Decadent times call for decadent wines. Don't get used to it, though, it's the boss's private stash. Fucked-up little ninja." Laughter tumbles from Smuts's mouth in gentle barks, he dips his head to let them out. "Only wish we could drink together—you still around Wednesday?"

"No. But surely after you finish—?"

"Surely nothing, we work with deadly poisons. Serious business, harder than flying a plane. Then we're back at seven in the morning for inspectors. Envy you, though—this is a unicorn wine, you mightn't see it again in a lifetime."

"But surely—"

"Fuck off, Pimpernel, you're drinking alone."

"Hm." I leave the subject for now.

Smuts looks at me sideways: "Ever hear of 'travel'?"

"Is this a joke?"

"As a function of palate. Things have changed with wine, uh. We've identified another element of taste—called travel. Nobody understands it yet. A kind of propulsive length, a panoramic effect. You'll hear scientists speculate about ethanol re-uptake, but your romantics whisper about hormones. They say passions can imprint hormones—and as we know, hormones can fly. A grape can receive them. Anger, lust, despair. Love. That's why a true winemaker sleeps within seventy meters of his head vine."

A larder lined with shelves stands at the far end of the kitchen where boxes and packets sit like graphic artworks, tagged with ribbons and calligraphy, carefully dated and labeled with the place's name. Lights go on as we enter, and Smuts turns to me:

"Ever hear of Toque-Mesnil?"

I shake my head. Though I feel like a hundred yen, blunted by fatigue and philosophical locomotion, and now by the prospect of drinking alone—I revel watching Smuts in his world of unheard-of things. I can't see how his grand wheeze about wine can lead anywhere but nimbus. He takes me to a stack of white foam cases at the back of the larder and slaps a hand on top.

"First," he says, "get it out of your head that wine's just a drink. Real wine is like a missing human gene. It vaccinates you against mundanity, against bad life. And forget about your old-time wine tasters, a new elite has developed with high-octane senses. People who won't wait forty years to discover that a cork has reacted with their old vintage and fucked their evening." Smuts pauses to stretch his frame, stroke his face. Then he points at me: "They want a wine with a cap that locks like the tip of a missile. Those people drink Toque. There's evidence that up to three in ten bottles have the travel effect. Production's confined to ten acres of Mediterranean lava with a cemetery in the middle—locals say widows' tears cause travel in the grape. Whatever it is, the next five vintages are sold—and nobody knows who to."

My stare flicks between Smuts and the artillery cases.

"Then"—he draws back as if one might explode—"there's a world *above that*. A handful of palates who know of a decadent wine with travel in almost every bottle. Production limited to four acres of rare geology, a soil coincidence of a million and a half years, dating back to the first human ancestor. A unicorn vineyard, where the winemaker lives in the vines."

He lifts the lid from the topmost case. There, laid out like glittering projectiles, seductive and menacing, lie three black bottles.

"That wine, my friend—is *Marius*."

I stare as if they might rise up. Each has a simple white label headed in black, with golden capitals: MARIUS. The white of each label bears a different subtitle in script: *Symphony*, *Simpatico*, or *Symposium*.

The Enthusiasms are with me.

"Go for a *Symphony*." Smuts points. "The boss won't be in for a while, and I've got ten minutes before service—I'll show you something that'll pop your nuts."

He hides the used case under the stack and we leave the larder, picking up a wine balloon on our way past the bar. Across the dining room, up a stair, sits a corridor with restrooms where an attendant kneels polishing door handles. He stands to bow as we pass to the end. Smuts unlocks the farthest door, opening it onto a cubic room without windows. The ceiling is white, the walls are white, and the floor is white, neither glossy nor dull. The door handle is white, the door is white. A white table with two white chairs stands centered in the room, where hidden lighting throws no stronger shadow than a vaguely graying milk.

"The White Room," whispers Smuts.

Whoosh. The white of the bottle's label becomes a hole, its lettering hangs in space; and as the black wine splashes out, it tosses crimson skirts around the glass that flare in sparkling colors across the table. Smuts presses the balloon to his nose:

"So what are you doing here?"

"Visiting."

His brow falls.

"Drink with me, Smuts."

"Did you inherit a restaurant?"

"No."

"Then I can't. The time comes, Putain, when we have to get

serious. When we have to put something back. When our childhood is over."

I observe the wine for a moment. "Want a line?"

"*What?*" His brow crumples. "Where did you get lines?"

"Brought them from home."

"Mate, fuck." He shrinks back. "It's beyond Pimpernel now,
fuck me. You brought coke through Narita Airport? In Japan
they'll bang you up without charge, you'll disappear." He shakes
his head, hisses some curses, and eventually leans toward me,
clutching the glass. "Pimpernel, Pimpernel—what are you doing
here really?"

It's too early to confide. The secret's uncomfortable, but if my
plan's to survive it needs a tower of the loftiest nimbus. I shrug,
and nod at the balloon: "Can't I taste it?"

His jaw twitches left and right. He doesn't shift his scowl.

"Anyway, lot of noise for an Australian wine." I study the
label. "It's not even five years old."

"Shut up. You know nothing. Did I ever mention Didier Le
Basque? My sponsor. It's him who sources the wine. He'd tell you
about the winemaker. Unbelievable story, a man who abandoned
decadence to try and grow a grape with the answer to life inside
it. A guy who maybe discovered the secret to living."

"Oh, yes? And what is it? Ideology or product?"

"Don't know. I think it's more of a punch line."

"Hm. And do you know it?"

"No. Didier says you have to ask the man himself. Great story
leading up to it, though, about the moment when he understood
what things were about. I know this much: In the late eighties
a Maserati Ghibli Spyder was found abandoned on a bend near
Monte Carlo. Not far from where Princess Grace died. Pretty

sure the Basque said Spyder. It was traced to a pair of bikini models, sisters, from Paris—and an Englishman called Pike, a wild man who was seen driving one of them. Think about this: wine is always judged in little sips. It's always been about wine *tasting*. The bouquet, how it looks in the glass. They even spit it out afterwards. They spit it out! But what happens after a full bottle? What's the effect over a night? As the Basque puts it: you can admire an ocean from the beach—but to love it you have to swim out. Pike knew that. Drank European vintages to oblivion, logged their behaviors, met with their gods."

Fingers of gas rise off the black wine.

"Anyway, this car's abandoned. Nobody knew what happened. Pike was never seen in Europe again. He vanished. But years later a buddy of his, from Formula One racing, was invited to a castle behind Cap-d'Ail. A stock of experimental wines was there with handwritten labels. And he recognized Pike's hand. When he tasted the wine he knew things had changed. He went on to trace Pike to this hidden acreage. Found him bearded, living in the vines, driving an old truck. One of Europe's great rakes, uh. Fucking mystery to everyone—unless you know what it is he discovered that day behind Monte Carlo. Today he's just there in his vines, trying to put the secret into grapes. Production's tiny but he meets regulations, he can be openly traded, unlike Toque. Almost like he's trying to camouflage it."

I finally snatch the balloon.

"Didier'll tell you Pike had a revelation. Went searching for unicorn soil to settle his tab with Bacchus. Took him years, but he found it. Word got out to a few. Rumor says that virgins go to fornicate in the vines, that it's a pilgrimage for twisted convent girls and aristocrats. I met a man at the Kempinski who said a

Comtesse d'Auxonne conceived a child under Marius vines. Said since then the sound of crickets can make her cum. I wouldn't trust him, though, he was downing Léoville-Barton like beer. Still, uh. More than one sommelier's saving up for a tumble under the grapes. Didi's even advised them to do it under the Shiraz. Says the Shiraz thrives on passion but the Grenache prefers regret."

"So after a bad night under the Shiraz you could just roll over."

"Listen, Putain." Smuts draws himself up. "These pressings are from a geological fluke dated to the first human ancestor. They're a correction of nature. They grow on prehistoric minerals, passion, and virgin's cum. So drink the thing and shut up."

With my first sip of Marius a landscape rolls out, of black chocolate trees and tobacco skies, of cherry pastures where herb stalks tick in a breeze. After a deeper draught the panorama moves uphill. My sense of body weight and proportion subtly changes, muscles and organs recline on quiet alert. I look up to see Smuts grinning.

"Shut your eyes," he says. "You at the hill yet?"

There's a rising curve of warmth, a subtle lifting in all the body which coincides with the moving taste. The hill. "Yes," I say. "Yes."

"Good. See how long you can stay—take a smaller sip, then another one quickly. Feel the breeze? Feel the heat unfolding?"

It's there, a landscape where I'm alone, a living map that I'm propelled across.

"Might take a bottle or two, but Didier swears it can carry you back through its own vines to a porch where it's always summer's night. Where the correction to the first human ancestor lives. The trick is to stay there and be corrected."

Whoosh. Bottled nimbus. I blink, and look around, also entranced by the idea of this man discovering how to live.

Because, although it's late for me, I've come to realize that the notion is at the heart of my failure in life. Seeking ever-higher nimbus was how I defined "the good" in my ethic, and I stand by it, as in fact does my culture, simply seeking more and bigger and better of everything. But both the culture and I are on our way to die—whereas it seems this man found a mechanism to step back. Indeed, to step back at his peak.

I turn to Smuts: "And so this secret, this punch line you mention—is it about reaching for dreams, or just being happy with what you've got? Because it sounds like the man was having a great life before he walked away."

"Who knows, Putain, you have to ask him. Even Didier won't say. Anyway, don't get too fucked up with the idea, it'll drive you crazy. Enjoy the wine, look around, and ask yourself—do things get much better than this? Uh?"

"They don't get much better."

Smuts looks on proudly. "Tell me that's not an armament for the modern day. Yoshida's only good feature—he's got taste. He built the room for Toque, but then had to test every bottle in case it didn't fly. A pricing headfuck—he couldn't charge the full bottle, and you often don't get travel till the third or fourth glass. If there was more than one White Room party in a night he'd end up wasted. Marius solved that, though he doesn't bring it out much anymore. Japanese don't have the booze gene. Last month some Yakuza cunt hurled all over the walls. Had to repaint the whole room."

"It's a temple," I say. "A temple of nimbus."

"This is nothing, you should see one of Didier's events—not that you ever could. Nobody's even allowed to talk about them. But they put this shit in the dark. Fountains of Marius is what

I've heard. Fountains of it. That's why I have to behave myself—with some *fugu* experience Didi might pull me into his European operation. Nowhere to climb after that. Didier 'Le Basque' Laxalt is the godfather of high-octane catering."

"I wondered what got you into fish."

"The deep end of fish. Ever eat *torafugu*?"

"Can't say I have."

"Poison blowfish. Very sweet. The trick is to slice it leaving just enough poison to buzz your lips. A little kiss from death. Fine art, though—if your lips go numb you're fucked. No antidote. Takes years to get a license."

"Is that all you serve?"

"With a twist: *fugu*'s farmed now, without poison—but ours are wild tiger-blowfish, caught off a line in the Sea of Japan. Massively toxic. Illegal, ex-quota, sourced quietly through the Basque—hence we have to switch fish in the tank tomorrow, put in regular ones for the inspectors. Yoshida's been having a baby over it."

"Not a love child of yours, by the sound of it."

"Midget prick, he's just a businessman, it's all about the money. If he could make more selling supermarket *fugu* he'd do that—but people pay a premium for the really edgy stuff. He's raking it in. Opening his second place next month, a bigger one, where all the walls are saltwater tanks, like dining under the ocean."

I reflect for a moment, hovering on a ridge of Marius. I've fetched up in a salon of limbo. A place where patrons come to touch the shadow of death. My mind boggles. Death by gourmet pufferfish, what a rococo flourish by the Enthusiasms, beyond anything I could've dreamt up. I'm dining with fellow limbonauts. Whoosh. Of course, for me it's also a chess game, to navigate all these factors without hurting Smuts. But the Enthusiasms have shown themselves to be end-players, take note. With Marius in my veins I feel I can trust them with the night's arrangements. For now I'll settle back and unfurl my senses.

I become aware of Smuts watching me. "Hm," I muse, "so if you poison a customer do you have to kill yourself?"

"Once upon a time, uh. Fuck that, though, nothing to do with me—Tomohiro, the tall one, is the chef. He's the only one tonight with a license."

"But do they monitor how much you order? Can you just eat too much?"

"You'll see how it is. Most of the dishes aren't toxic, and the poison sashimi's so thin you could watch porn through it. Minimal danger. The scary deal is the offal. The liver, and especially the ovaries. But offal's not on the menu, it's totally banned. In Japan it's even illegal to sell whole fish. And we can't even trash the offal, hobos have died on the streets. I don't think you can even incinerate it. One ovary can kill thirty people, uh. But they still love to mess with it. Macho deal, kind of Russian roulette. Nibbling the organs is as far as you can go. There's a few deaths around the country every year."

"So how do you get rid of the offal?"

"Fuck knows. Gets collected. Probably buried under the seabed or something, dropped on fucking North Korea. We have a special icebox for it, you'd think it was nuclear waste. I've only seen it a couple of times. Anyway, come get a table." Smuts unfolds from his chair. "And Scarlet Putain—hope you're not on any medication."

"Hm—why?"

"Because I'll order for you."

8

A hostess in a kimono tends me with the hesitant grace of a stork, crossing paths with her shadow as she moves under the light. Patrons arrive, and the salon's canvas comes alive as their creases, colors, and smokes smudge and stir it. Pufferfish watch from the tank along the wall, sometimes traveling to the kitchen in a pagoda box, heads and tails poking out, gasping and flapping. This is the scene, and every so often Smuts beams over the counter where he's in motion with the surgery of rare food.

Over a sashimi of sweet *torafugu* I monitor the kitchen for clues about poison. Quite a few minutes pass this way, till finally I catch myself picturing chefs tossing offal over their shoulders and losing ovaries like marbles on the floor. I have to laugh. Planning a death at a banquet shows bad grace, and mistrust in the Enthusiasms. Opportunism is called for. I leave it for later nimbal moments, which will surely come. What's important now is to make the most of limbo. As it's heightened my senses to such an extreme, I simply bask in the goings-on, smoking, drinking, feeling this voluptuous salon around me like a silken coat. What a salon of thrills, a training-limbo with its lethal hors d'oeuvres. What a civilized culture to think of it.

At one point Smuts brings me a sliver of fish on the end of his finger, a sort of *amuse-morte*, and motions me to take it with chopsticks. He watches like a cat as I eat it, and swells with pride when I react. What a dainty expression of hunter-gathering. Among other subtleties is a moment out of the blue when a fish breaks surface in the tank. As it splashes down, all the diners refer to each other across the room, nodding, smiling, and gasping. They use the opportunity to inspect each other, as diners do, and to create rapport. I join them and am bonded, even opening my mouth and pointing at the tank, which is too much, I admit. But in such a tranquil place the jumping fish is a highlight, and highlights are the pixels of a life. We're all witnesses together of the jumping fish, nobody else in the world is. The same pixel is added to each of our lives, and we'd feel more comfortable now to be survivors together of a plane crash, or stranded in a raft at sea. Who would be the leader? Who the panicker? The sly one? The martyr? Such are the outermost ripples when a fish jumps. This is humanity, in its little ways, and I feel a fleeting nostalgia. Note how in our wildest nightmares it's not necessary to see a friend at a window, nor a doctor, nor a rich man—but just another person. Looking at it, it's not such flawed behavior, this constant reaching out. Perhaps it compensates for the flaw of our being here at all. Perhaps it's even a sense that together we should be able to man this drifting boat of life.

Such musings are a delightful pastime until I start to muse on the act of musing itself. Then I realize food and time are making Marius fade from my system, and that the *sake* is in too small a pot for a steep nimbal climb.

I pull some miniatures from my coat and find the restroom.

Smuts walks in while I'm there: "Tomohiro says the boss isn't coming in. Halle-fucking-lujah. And just so you know, I've told them you're a big-deal international food writer. Try and look professional. I'll put you on my tab."

"Cheers." I pull out two miniatures of white rum and separate them between my fingers, pointing one at Smuts. He likes rum.

"Fuck off." He turns away. "Just think about it—I have to work next to a man who slices sashimi so fast it hits the plate wriggling."

I shrug, and stand looking at the bottles, I suppose in a bovine sort of way. They become glossy under the light. Smuts rubs a hand over his face. He stifles a yawn. And finally his shoulders slump, resolve being like an inner coat hanger, and he swipes the bottle up. We toast with our left hand, as always—because it's connected to the heart.

"Where are those lines?" He eventually pats my pocket.

Whoosh.

I needn't say much about the sanctity of a restroom cubicle where drugs are shared.* While Smuts cuts lines on the cistern, herding and chopping with the speed of a chef, a graphic chart comes to my mind of our friendship: I see two spheres of very different colors, our individual lives beside each other—and in the slim vagina of their overlap a third color appears, which is where we meet.

I snort my lines from the bottom up, while Smuts takes his straight down. We have another shot of liquor each, and a nibble

---

* People in a restroom with substances occupy the most principled ranks of camaraderie. In our time there's no greater treaty of discretion, no more widespread code of honor.

of MDMA. Finally Smuts straightens, sucking a lungful of air: "Pu-*tain*!" Then he bustles out and I'm left alone licking dust from my bank card—a refreshing bitter chaser, after which I waft back to the table like a cloud.

More rice wine has arrived, and now has the effect of a foot bath after treading a winter lawn. I'd like here to draft a recipe for the nimbus all this raises; but like some of the best things, it comes from intuitive and unpredictable sources. I'll lay out certain recipes, of course, in a quieter moment, over wine. But for now, if you follow me, there's only one master recipe for a limbo:

Have some more.

The evening takes on a rhythm, proceeding in verses of fish and *sake* with a chorus of drugs in between. These are triggered by Smuts with a nod to the restroom. As a note of research, hot *sake* seems to act as a balm between sharp and soft substances, blending them in the way a painter joins sea and sky. *Sake* and MDMA make a fine sky for spirits and cocaine in this way, a masterpiece of nimbus, like a Dutch port scene, busy yet bathed in tranquil light. As I think about it, all things in life are this way, a question of fusion, just like a fragrance; even our experiences seem to have three notes of flavor: a high note, which is the immediate slap of an event; a middle note, which is the average effect while it's under way; and a base note, which stains you after the experience passes, and contains its memory and truth.*

After a number of these choruses and musings, some of

---

* Note that in planning the perfect debauch, an innocent party, or even a lunch, or a life, these three component notes should have attention paid to them individually. Had I realized this earlier my life would have been a fragrant symphony indeed. Ah, well.

which I write down for you, the house starts to empty of diners. In inverse proportion to my soaring nimbus, the fish in the tank slow down and swim low, maybe grateful to survive with their toxins. Smuts's colleagues wipe sweat from their faces, while Smuts moves up and down the kitchen on trivial missions.

My attention drifts back to poisons.

Clearly I'll have to smuggle some back to the hotel, because in these elegant surroundings it becomes clear what a brutal trick it would be on Smuts, no matter how bright our nimbus. Really savage, and my intoxication deflates somewhat with shame. It highlights a problem of limbo: that the untethered mind can lose its civilization. It becomes self-absorbed and incorrect. Curious, then—some things *do* matter. Limbo needs a constitution. In fact it's a riddle, because if deciding to die means that everything ceases to matter—then dying ceases to matter.

Whoosh—some things *do* matter.

The last of the *sake* flies down my throat, and I bite off some MDMA right at the table, to see if I can avoid the fallout from this question: which things matter? Thankfully I have suicide to fall back on. Yes, and the hotel is the obvious answer. Poison to hotel. Dump passport and wallet. Anonymous dead. Found on the street, or on the beach. In the Sea of Japan as a denizen, or like seaweed washed to the shore. Even my shark-fin hairdo points to the sea. And as seafood's the cause of death, who's to say I didn't meet the fish in the Sea of Japan? It cuts Smuts's employers out of the equation and unless it was front-page news, even Smuts wouldn't find out for ages.

Ah, Smuts. This idea is just sprouting branches when, some distance across the room, the last table of gentlemen grows loud. Hisses and grunts arise from their table, sounds you'd expect with sword thrusts. Looking over, I see that one man wears tartan trousers, and two have ponytails as shiny as plastic. The eldest sits alone at the head of the table, and seems to be the agitator. All are drunk. Rising smoke absorbs the tank's glow, making the salon a setting for an epic with beasts and fire.

I'm transfixed—but Smuts's colleagues avoid looking at that table. I watch staff prepare to leave and see that when a noise erupts that might make them look, they turn to each other instead. Tomohiro, the licensed chef—a taller, gentler-looking man—dons an overcoat and comes to bid those last patrons good night.

The oldest gentleman responds with a commanding slap on the table. A shiny grey suit hangs off him, and his mouth seems poised to express shock. Not as a gesture; his mouth is that way by nature. Man born on the edge of shock.

Bang: he slaps again. The chef stands with bowed head.

Finally the old limbonaut spits out some words, whatever you'd say at a stabbing. Groans erupt from his henchmen, but the elder dismisses them with a wave, a hysterical flap of his hand, like an infant. He's the table's boss. Infant boss on the edge of shock. He stares at the chef. Tomohiro addresses the floor. In reply the gentleman hisses, reeling back as if gripped by a lethal rage. He smacks the table again.

Chopsticks jump.

In the middle of this drama, looking more like Kabuki theater, there comes a moment when Tartan Man glances sideways at me and smiles. The tension of my voyeurism suddenly breaks. We're bonded now, in a club, and I settle back with a cigarette to watch things unfold. It seems the limbonaut is asking for something which Tomohiro is ashamed to refuse. And although my nimbus makes me just want to hug them all and confess, with some effort I manage to chill with the introspective quiet of the lone diner, groping the scene invisibly.

Smuts soon sidles up. "Bizarre." He sets another dish before me. "Yoshida usually deals with them personally. He's like a virgin bride when they come around. Now they're giving Tomo a hard time."

"What are they saying?"

"Fuck knows. 'Why do those fish look like us?' probably. 'How did you get our families into the tank?'" Smuts stifles a laugh.

The gentlemen hear it, and turn.

Smuts quickly covers his gaffe, announcing to me: "The first course was *fugukawa yubiki*—that's a *fugu*-skin salad with *ponzu* and red pepper."

I smile at the gentlemen. They squint back, and in the time their attention is turned, Tomohiro gives them a token bow and marches out to the elevator.

"To finish I recommend *hire-zake*," says Smuts. "*Fugu*-fin-infused wine, flame-broiled in its cup. Will you take it in the White Room?" He leads me swaying up the corridor and calls the last waitress to fetch the *fugu* wine.

In the White Room he thuds into a chair. "Pack of cunts. It's nearly midnight."

"Can't we stay out there? I'm enjoying it."

"First get some lines out. Bit obvious if we're both in the restroom. Anyway, maybe the old fellas will take the hint and fuck off."

With the fastidious air of bomb defusers, the air of all drunks performing dexterous tasks, we cut the rest of a gram on the back of my wallet, so as not to lose it in the White Room. I also keep one eye on Smuts. His nimbus has stuck at a festering level. One thing I'd forgotten—after a certain point Smuts can fester.

"Pu-*tain*." He slurps a line up his nose.

Far from taking a hint, the limbonauts grow louder on the other side of the door. Smuts decides to outwait them, but between three rounds of *hire-zake*—aromatic and generous in its nimbal favors, with a charred fin sticking out—his eyes turn red and begin to flash. At one point his phone rings in his pocket, and he rips it out and throws it across the room.

Finally the waitress knocks with a message: we're to join the gentlemen for a nightcap. I'm pleased to return to the salon. My nimbus is lofty, my body numb—it's time to prepare for a finale. Leaving the room, I send a pulse to the Enthusiasms about poison, which is surely their end-play, as this gathering of elements is too organic to be coincidence. But in attempting a whistle to accompany the pulse, I spit all over Smuts.

"What the fuck?" He wipes himself with a sleeve. "Pull yourself together. Let's neck a quick toast with these boys, then get them out. Don't worry about the language. Have you got any calling cards? Japanese love calling cards."

"What would I put on a calling card?"

Smuts pauses to chew his lip. "True. Then just bow a lot."

We reach the table through a thicket of rising smoke. Infant Boss sits nodding as we slide into the group, and up close I see a twinkle behind his edge of shock. In fact there's a better-than-expected feeling at the table, the noises are just a theater of men playing men. Nimbus is rising, in its local way, with smells of hair gel and rice. In between nods and bows I ponder how remarkable are seekers of nimbus. We spot each other like beacons across any distance. We're an aristocracy, able to move through all strata of culture and connect through sheer spirit. Yes—nothing less than a natural aristocracy.*

Smuts calls the waitress for whiskey. She brings a bottle of Suntory, and as Tartan Man charges the glasses Smuts nudges me rather obviously and raises a toast to the old man: "Boned your wife on Tuesday," he says. "Dry as a brick."

The man falters, looking to his cohorts for clues.

"And I find she uses her teeth too much. I'd check yourself when you get home, probably down to a stub by now."

Tension grips the table. I'm about to elbow Smuts when one of the ponytails lowers his glass and says in polite English: "In Japan, what we say with a drink is—'*Campai.*'"

It's an opportunity to correct the moment. I duly smile, and raise up my glass. But Smuts can't resist a smirk.

The elder studies him. Weighs his demeanor. Then he stiffens and slams down his glass, unleashing a phrase of such terrifying resonance it can only describe babies at play with a chain saw.

We flinch.

A gauntlet has been thrown. The henchmen nod as the Japanese seem to nod, whether they mean yes or no. After a

---

* Tonight it's plain: humanity isn't divided by race, creed, color, or wealth; one thing alone makes humans unequal, and it is energy. The gift of Enthusiasmus. Those endowed form an aristocracy, and recognize each other in an instant. As for the rest of humanity, though we can as a mass be written off in a democratically useful sense, some nonaristocrats can also be honored: the insecure who have not built defenses of false confidence; the humble and straightforward who accord respect; and the bingers and revelers who at the height of a bacchanal remain true to the spirit of nimbus.

pause the English-speaker turns to Smuts: "Yoshida-san always allows it. Of course, as the challenge is yours—you will join us."

Smuts gulps his drink and nudges me: "Watch me score points with the boss. Tomo was too chickenshit to feed them their favorite treat. That's what the noise was about."

"What is it?" I ask.

"Offal," says Smuts. "They're challenging me to some liver."

My senses sharpen.

Smuts's breath is a rag of fish and cocaine. He steadies himself on the table and sets off on a zigzag to the kitchen. In his absence the gentlemen make a ceremony of refilling my glass, resuming their chatter of gasps and grunts. They alternate flattering and scolding each other, which in their drunkenness makes them as charming as old ladies playing poker. The three cohorts are of a lower class than the elder, who tries to project cunning at all times; soon his rebukes grow comically fierce, and before each he catches my eye to join him in the joke of his cohorts' appeals. Though it's plain the men are gangsters of some kind, they've let alcohol turn them back into children—a glorious function of nimbus. I warm to them, and raise a toast:

"Here's to us, and others like us," I say. "Though they're all dead."

The elder squints up, studying each word in the air. Then he laughs, and all the table nods and laughs along. Nimbus inflates to new heights, and I ask myself: is it a trick or a gift of the Enthusiasms, a push or a pull, that these hours bring such a welcome from strangers? Here across the world I'm with souls of equal whimsy, we understand each other in nimbus, and we're brothers for the night—which tonight means forever.

Am I being tempted back to life or bade farewell?

Because things rarely get better than this.

All I can do is kneel and make a ceremony of the next drink. I think I see hesitation in the elder's face as I pour. He sways slightly, the worse for wear.

Then Smuts returns. He has a bowl and fresh chopsticks on a tray. As he puts the bowl before the elder I see it contains a range of slimy globules.

Silence descends. Smuts and the elder sit facing each other, chopsticks armed and raised. They peer over lumps no bigger than large peppercorns. The old man struggles to stay awake, eyelids drooping, head swaying. He takes a breath, looks into Smuts's face. And brings the lump to his teeth, nibbling it, slurping noisily.

The henchmen gasp.

Smuts sucks his lump onto his tongue, rolls it around where we can see it. Then bites it through and swallows.

After this, they sit still.

The duel is over. I join the cronies in monitoring their faces, which stay blank, downcast, blinking, running tongues around mouths, over lips. Then, as tension reaches its most brittle height—they both look up, and grin. Applause erupts. The pair retire their chopsticks, bow deeply, and shake hands. In a flood of those chemicals that dissolve adrenaline we loft into the sweetest nimbus I've ever known, intoxication, danger, relief, and newfound brotherhood soaring in clear, blissful skies. Another drink is quickly poured, and for this we all chatter and grunt and gasp at each other, without understanding but in perfect comprehension.

Of course climaxes on this scale are taxing on the flesh. By the time the drink is finished, the elder limbonaut has nodded quietly off to sleep.

His henchmen set about helping him up. Their formation into a single lurching mass makes the octopus swoop through the tank behind us, scattering wrinkles of light across the room. Finally, with the smiling elder lifted between their shoulders, the group moves off as one creature to the elevator, and we follow to say good night.

Looking around, I note that every last staff member has vanished from the restaurant. I see Smuts swaying and he sees me searching the room.

"Nobody else would deal with them," he says, guessing my question. "They're the boss's pets, everyone else is scared."

"But—surely they haven't left you in sole charge of a *fugu* restaurant? You're just the apprentice."

"They obviously left these boys in charge. Different thing. The old fella probably runs the protection racket for the district. Anyway, Tomo knows I've got keys, and someone will have to be back soon to clean out the tank. What could possibly happen?"

Smuts opens the lobby door: *"Oyasuminasai!"* he waves after the men. "And boys—don't let him operate a Japanese toilet, we'll never see him again."

Two arms reach out of the mass to wave goodbye.

As the elevator doors close, Smuts turns to me. "They had a great night. Didn't they? The boss'll be in my pocket, they're like his homeys."

With that, he goes to the table and spits out the lump.

I follow and peer into the bowl. "You didn't eat it?"

"Get real, I don't have to do that. These fellas probably have immunity. If a *tora* bit them, the fish'd probably die."

I stand looking into the bowl. Tiny condiment dishes also form part of the table setting, and I flag a pair as containers for smuggled offal. I lose myself gazing so long that Smuts takes up chopsticks and picks a lump from the bowl.

"Open." He brandishes it at my mouth. "*Torafugu* liver. Once in your life. Open up."

"Do I get a last drink?"

"Don't eat it, just taste it. Open up, Putain."

I open my mouth. Smuts doesn't let go of the liver but pokes it under my lip, running it left and right. Then he removes it, watching me. A tingle jolts my gums. Whoosh. A compelling thing. The Enthusiasms have advanced a taste of my death.

I hope you observe this, last friend—look at the nature of Fortune, feel its dynamics at work. See how artistically the night's ingredients fall into place. Surely this also paints a valuable guideline for life, in case you plan to stay back.*

Smuts returns the liver to the bowl. "Hell of a buzz, isn't it? Electroshocked my mouth, holding the thing in. You can see why Yoshida took me on—it's my contact who supplies the wild *tora*. Did I mention Didier Le Basque?"

A bad sign from Smuts. Forgetting earlier sermons means he's fallen out of the nimbus, like an eagle falling from a thermal tube. Although it signals a good time to raid the liver bowl, I also resolve to pull him back for a last private drink.

We sit down at the table and I toy with the bowl, edging it close. "Funny how, as a name," I say, "Didier Le Basque doesn't evoke the Sea of Japan."

"Uh?" Smuts sways. "In this business it evokes all rare pro-

---

* Articulate your wish, watch for signs, then snatch opportunities as they're delivered—this is the clear and practical guide from the Enthusiasms to navigating a life, or a death, through nature's world.

duce. If I can get a job with him I'll be made. Especially on one of his banquets. Doors fly open everywhere after a Basque event. And he's watching me, I can feel it. Testing to see how I stand up. What I need now's a massive gig in Europe to really win him over. If I was just conveniently there I'm sure he'd call me in."

I pull a pair of vodka miniatures from my coat, and with whiskey from the table prepare two Golden Bullets—thin floating layers of whisky over vodka, known to repair the most punctured nimbus. Then a stiff line, followed by Drambuie on ice, to nurse and savor. In this way we soon sit in clear intoxication again, in the crystalline state of late drunkenness that ends at a high plateau, the savannah all drinkers try to return to. It's the nimbus I aspired to for tonight, one without fear or consideration, a place achieved after hard but fortunate excess, where peaks weren't reached too early, or if they were, a dose of helpful substances, or tactical vomiting, opened an upward path again; a place that most often exists two or three tries after the state you thought was your last; a place whose climb is helped by dancing but not by food; a place often stumbled upon by accident, you having collapsed just under its crest.

Here we pass the time like picnickers, drinking and chain-smoking, as the plateau is that final approximate state where more or less of anything doesn't matter. A glycerine Tibet where you whirl under stars, arms outstretched, free from your self.

Only the gentle bubble of the tank is up here with us.

In this state I take possession of the offal bowl. With each tiny liver I remove to a condiment dish, my limbo nudges its tastes closer to the sea, to the cold, to gray water and salt, to the clang of waves on the ear. And as the tastes grow into lusts the wisdom befalls me to confess to Smuts. To leave a note in his mind, for the future. Let him know that my death is but another of our adventures—and for all we might know, not the last.

But as I turn to him, the elevator clunks and whirrs in the lobby.

There's shuffling. The lobby door clicks.

After a moment Tomohiro comes in lugging a foam ice chest. He staggers past without seeing us, but as he takes a fishnet from beside the tank Smuts starts and turns. The chef looks over.

"Uh?" Smuts stands. "Is it seven already?"

"I think it's barely three," I say.

Tomohiro drops his gaze. Seeing the bowl and dishes of offal before me, he approaches to look. His face falls even further and he walks to the kitchen, returning a moment later with a small security flask, as might be used for medical specimens. Inside are some larger organs—and as they become clear, Smuts starts to frown.

Tomohiro takes up chopsticks and collects a lump from my bowl, holding it beside the flask for comparison.

"Fuck me." Smuts snatches up the bowl. "Were these ovaries?"

9

"The old guy's on breathing equipment," hisses Smuts. "Tetrodo-toxin paralyzes your muscles. Sodium channel blocker; you stay lucid but trapped inside. The boss once told me it took forty-eight hours to know if a client was poisoned. This old fucker was flat in less than three."

Air stops circulating in the restaurant.

Tomohiro says nothing more to us. With the substitution of fish complete, he turns off the lights and walks out with the ice chest, shuffling like a zombie to avoid spilling water. The offal leaves the building with him, including my specimens from the table. We listen to the elevator doors close as if their whirr and clunk described the unstoppable grind of destiny. The elevator goes down. Our nimbus flickers—then descends. Smuts hunches forward with a sigh. His head rolls into his hands. "I'm so fucked," he croaks.

An impulse takes me to just throw myself in the tank. But I'm frozen here. Some things do matter. "Look," I say, "the man was thoroughly refreshed when he left here. He might just be sleeping it off. The others may've told the hospital he'd eaten *fugu*, and they simply presumed—"

"Can you just fucking talk normally for a minute? 'Thoroughly refreshed,' what the fuck! It's like being stuck on death row with fucking Frasier Crane!"

"Sorry. He was off his face when he left—"

"You don't get it—I couldn't tell an ovary from a liver! How smashed is that? I served him an ovary from one of Didier's Tro-jan *toras*. And Japan's the wrong place to get blamed for anything. High conscience, not like back home. I'm so fucked."

"But he could barely keep his eyes open to eat it."

"Now Tomo knows. And he knows I'm wasted."

"Hm. Well, I tasted some too. Was that an ovary? You even sucked some."

Smuts grunts. His hands stay over his face, as if longer blind-ness will pull a brighter reality after it. "Fuck knows anymore. Best have some lines, that's supposed to open up the airways. Best keep the lines up tonight and see what happens. I don't know if to drink or fucking kill myself, uh."

We sit in silence for a while, smoking. Even our smoke is too weak to make plumes, it just crashes to the floor. As for the Enthusiasms, well—what can this mean? A farewell, a tethering back—or just a callous trick? The night's been devoured by death themes. As if death themes rode here on my back, then bumped into another swarm and lost their bearings. The night's just death, death, death, death. I've become a magnet.

I ponder the ironies while Smuts's jaw clenches and crackles.

"But then," he says, "he ordered poison. Ordered it!"

"Exactly. Forced you with threats."

"In a noble establishment specializing in deadly poison, where the customer's always right. A place that serves risks. What am I going to do—not serve him? If he comes to a place that serves risks, and orders risks—of course I'll serve him risks. Is it my fault if he's unlucky?"

"No two ways about it."

Smuts struggles to kindle hope. But after a moment his head falls back to his chest.

"Yeah, like they'll really see it that way."

I stare at my friend. Only now is it clear why I instinctively sought him out: because he spent much of his life in a limbo. My father always spoke of Smuts's carelessness, because he was— orphaned, because he lacked the anchor that can chain us away from the abyss, the anchor of a first stable parent. But it wasn't carelessness my father saw; it was independence. Baby Smuts, before he could think in pictures, had to decide whether he was alone in the world or in a compact of care.

He was alone.

And in life we always rush back to the state we first know.

"I'm so finished now," he says. "And if the Basque's name gets dirty over this—fuck only knows. There won't be enough ovaries in the sea." His jaw sets hard with the thought. Seeing my greatcoat on a chair beside us, he leans over to rifle through it for miniatures. None are left, all he finds is the bottle of Jicky. Still, he unstops it, sniffs it, and carries it to the bar, where he uncaps a bottle of chilled vodka, pours two shots, and knocks a drop of Jicky into each. I smell the drinks approaching, almost see them trailing starlight.

"Angel's tears," says Smuts.

They take our breath away. When I eventually recover my speech, I feel it falls to me to say: "Sorry if I unhooked you tonight."

Smuts nods, looking up at the tank where the new fish hang

in limbo. "You are a cunt, Pimpernel. We don't seek you here, we don't seek you there. But I also have free will. Typical, the situation was stacked too high. Not just that Didi sponsored me, and everything hangs on it—but I also told him I'd find it a bit easier. A lot easier, in fact. I'm just getting sick of myself, to be honest. I didn't know a *fugu* license can take ten fucking years. I thought I'd be in and out in six months—and that was six months ago! All this big talk to Didi, like I was starting from the finish line, like it was a formality. And you know I don't even like fish. Hate fish, so I came to a place where the boss even looks like one. And then there's this other little thing brewing. Typical little hitch of mine. Fucking stupid. Just brewing away."

"What's that?"

"I don't even want to hear myself say it. Anyway, uh. This was my last try. I'm twenty-six. Too old to be a fuckwit." He hangs his head so low it almost folds into his lap. I see a squall of feeling pass through him, tightening his back, forming a pearl in his throat which he swallows. "I'm at the end of the rope. After this, I don't know what."

"Perhaps if you met the boss with this man Didier? A reminder that you're part of a package of benefits?"

"Listen to me: Didi's above all this. He just pulls the strings, fuck knows where he actually is. France, or somewhere. I could tell you rumors about the Basque that'd make your heart stop. He can shut down a high-end kitchen in under an hour, with just a phone call. Shut it down. He can leave hundred-meter yachts rusting at the dock for lack of crew and supplies. Didier supplies the suppliers who supply the world with special things. Has the best chefs in his pocket. He could fill a stadium with Michelin stars and still find somewhere better to eat. And I know chefs who've worked on his events who turn and walk away when you ask them about it. They don't smile and change the subject. They don't say, 'I can't tell you.' They fucking turn and walk away."

"Then isn't he above caring about one restaurant's fish?"

"Not when his name's involved. Wild *torafugu* are strictly controlled here. They keep track of them. Huge risk."

"Hm. But it's still just a fish, I mean—"

"Fucking Pimpernel, I'm not in the mood to teach you how things work, uh. Wake the fuck up. It's not just a fish. That old guy tonight will have spent two hundred thousand yen to end up on a ventilator. See how your Africans eat rare monkeys for status? See how your Asians eat tiger and rhino? What we put into the body isn't just calories. It's medication, spirit, symbol. It's divinity. Billionaires and princes and sheikhs eat weird shit. They take it deadly seriously. Imagine the clout you get doing favors at that level. That's Didier. The man doesn't need a passport. Anyway, it's all irrelevant now. This was it for me."

I nod, and chew the inside of my cheek. Smuts's phone rings faintly in the White Room, but he ignores it.

"We'd better fuck off before the place turns into a crime scene." He lurches up, scattering chopsticks over the table. "I'll grab a laundry bag and stash some Marius. We might never see any again. Can't get any more busted than I already am. Call it severance pay. Then let's run somewhere I can't be reached, like your hotel. Maybe try calling the Basque, before he hears it all from someone else."

We slip back to the larder, where Smuts retrieves the Marius we opened earlier. He takes a long swig and hands it to me. As I drink he sets about filling a canvas bag with bottles, replacing their empty cases at the bottom of the stack. He's almost finished when a sound filters into the larder.

A gentle knock on the lobby glass. A timid knock.

"Uh?" He freezes. Then his face droops: "Ah, fuck me—not now."

Peering through the darkened kitchen, I see a small figure at the glass. The dining room is mystical from here, washed in a catarrhal glow, the silence brightened by the bubbling tank.

Another soft rap at the door.

"Fucking *maguro*," hisses Smuts.

"What?"

"Tuna. Dead fish." He pushes the door open another inch. "Remember that other snag I mentioned?"

"Who is it?"

"Boss's little girl. Ah, mate, fuck. Pass the bottle."

"What—how old is she?"

"Fuck knows. Well, I mean—she'd have to be eighteen, look at her. She'd have to be seventeen or eighteen." He snatches the bottle and swigs from it, squinting out through the doorway.

"Hm." I peer at the form. "If size is anything to go by—"

"She's Japanese, remember."

"Even taking that into account, she looks about—"

"Plenty of smaller adults than that, uh."

"Ten."

"Piss off, she's in college! Eighteen or nineteen, at least. I've seen parts that prove it." After another knock, Smuts pulls me to the back of the store where he can hiss more freely: "The kitchen's supposed to feed her after school. College, you know. And—you know. She started coming around. And then. It's like that. Now she won't stop hassling."

"Her name's Maguro?"

"No—Keiko. *Maguro*'s what they call your traditional girls—who just lie there, who you don't know if to fuck or resuscitate."

He empties the bottle upright into his mouth.

"Does the boss suspect?"

"I've still got ten fingers, so probably not."

Another rap at the door.

"I can't deal with her tonight." Smuts goes for another bottle. I watch him misjudge his reach and almost topple over.

"Just wait quiet," I hiss. "She'll go away—won't she?"

"Ah, fuck, that's the thing. She's been waiting longer and longer. Like it's love or something. She's imprinted like a duckling." Smuts shakes his head. "That's why I've been volunteering for morning chores, getting out early. I mean, she's a good girl, uh. I'm not saying she's not. Smart girl. And really hot. But—ah, fuck. I just get sick of myself, I should know by now."

We decide to wait quietly. In the bubbling half-light a revelation comes to me: that a person's life is nothing more than a finely orchestrated circus of rats, always on the brink of crisis. Never with fewer rats in play than make chaos a certainty if one of them breaks step. Smuts may have more rats than most—and I've tonight flung open his door and blustered in, waving cheese. My heart sinks. I say nothing, but all this runs through me. Still the girl waits at the door, knocking every so often.

Smuts starts to pace. When he realizes he can't pace without making noise, he teeters on the spot, lunging this way and that. Twice I stop him grinding his teeth. Smuts is the worse for wear.

"Told you I wasn't off till fucking Wednesday," he finally hisses. "Now look at it. We have to get out of here."

The hiss is too loud.

"Neru-san?" comes a little voice.

Seeing him quake with foiled energy, I grip his shoulders and try to calm him. "Smuts," I whisper, "listen—"

But it's too late. "You're like a sawn-off fucking stalker, Keiko!" He explodes through the kitchen: "What the fuck, uh! Nerusan, Nerusan, Nerusan!"

Keiko shrinks back as he blasts into the lobby. I watch the pair clatter into the dining room, Smuts raving, the girl trying to stroke him from afar, pawing the air, tossing squeaks like a kitten. Light from the tank plays on them. The girl seems a third his size, though watching her in three dimensions I note she has the figure of a young woman, a perfectly formed miniature.

Smuts throws her facedown over a table, snatching up her skirt at the back. She giggles and flails. Her boots fly through the air.

I'm frozen at the larder door, feelings racing to catch up, stumbling through a day that's yet to be understood, of unleashed forces, of ambiguous notes from Fortune. With a shiver I realize these visions won't be sorted at all, I have no time for sequels, nor analysis, in my life. As for the scene before me, well, with your ardent mind you can imagine the havoc it wreaks on the senses of a young sphinx watching.

"Is this what you want! Nerusan, Nerusan, Nerusan! Following me around like a fish on the fucking tide!" He rips off his shirt and his form grows unreal in the light, abdominal strakes welling like biceps, arms crawling like rope.

I move out to the bar, electrified. All Smuts's passions ignite at once. "Fish, fish, fish!" he shrieks. "Toxic fucking fish!"

I slip behind the bar, crouching. From here the tank shines as green as a winter sea, framing the pair, adorning the scenario with pufferfish, chilling it with the knowledge of an octopus hid-ing in a temple. Smuts yanks one of the girl's legs off the floor, snatches her by the waist, and hoists her over his shoulder. As Keiko kicks and writhes I see white cotton twist and bunch over her loins till spider-legs of hair poke out both sides, and finally darker skin. Smuts turns to the tank. Fish flee to the back.

I hold my breath.

With one explosive thrust, a mighty baring of his figure, he tips her over the edge.

Her scream becomes a chime as she smacks the water. Waves fly up to breach the tank's rim and clap to the floor. But as she thrashes to the surface, a second, more enchanting life blooms underwater, where her clothes rise off her with chilling calm, where her skin shines and shimmers and her panties turn filmy like semen, clinging till her mysteries all appear, well at home in the deep.

Smuts vaults into the tank.

I recoil as tidal waves set off up and down it, smashing to the floor, spattering over the nearest tables. Reflections burst across the salon in shudders and shards. Fish panic and swarm, bristling with spikes, and as churning water swirls to the bottom and starts to raise sand, the octopus scoots up, menacing through its skin with flashes of color.

Smuts snatches it by the bulb and mashes it to the girl's ass, where it sucks itself astride her. She gags and screams. Clamping a hand over her mouth, he pulls her to him, rasping into her ear, ramming her close by the small of her back. In the pedaling of her legs, her vulva appears for an instant, green-gray frills and folds, in their element, mingled with tentacles.

Then the view's gone. Smuts is inside her. He lifts her legs around his waist and thrusts, grappling and grunting till a rhythm takes hold, the speed of a resting heartbeat at first, building slowly as his feet sink foundations in the sand. Her head throws splashes down the tank, hair whips streams into the air. Smuts grits his teeth and pumps. Eventually the pace sends the octopus to its shelter, and with this relief Keiko's eyes pop open and lock on to Smuts, first in shock, then fluttering until their lids surrender and droop. And as the cold hardens their skin and tensions are gradually spent, the girl's cries break apart, and moans rise up which Smuts echoes back. The pair caress, and when they kiss it's in the same slow motion as their bodies underwater, touching, tracing each other with fingertips. Until without a word they each draw breath and sink, entwined to their full lengths, mouths sucked together sharing air. Their form revolves to the bottom, and they buck there, softly, fondling in a cloud of black hair. After a moment I see, or fancy I see, fluids puffing from their sexes, smudges and gnarls and wisps curling up.

So compelling a spectacle is this, so entrancing a theater of nature, the merman Smuts and the *fugu* succubus—that I miss the lobby door opening.

The first clue is a sense of not being alone. I turn and find a man in the gloom to my left. Sour-faced, in a black suit. Behind him come three uniformed shadows, then a shadow with a briefcase and clipboard.

They skid across the salon floor, arms swept back in alarm.

Smuts and Keiko have absorbed each other. They float to the surface as one, eyes shut like infant dead. A tinkle as their heads break the surface. A gasp, a puff of breath.

Water laps and drips into quiet.

After a minute—cloistral tranquillity.

Then the lights click on.

Whoosh.

An officer leans smoking outside the police station. He squeezes a cigarette beside his cheek and watches us descend like a monstrous circus, the leviathan Smuts, the shark-finned sphinx, and their teeming wranglers. Fish samples are first to enter, borne in a bombproof chest, flanked by officers.

Marius clinks time from the rear.

The bag of wine has been attributed to me, and an officer has been appointed to carry it. I savor the distraction of its clinking as he tries to avoid Smuts's trail of water, setting a course left of it, then right, as though it were infectious. I lose myself in this as we lose ourselves in our holidays from the platform where we depart them. I suppose because the next stop is my pocketful of substances.

As we step into the building, a policeman ropes Smuts's and my handcuffs together, sitting us on a row of chairs against a charge-room wall. Two local types slump at the end, similarly crushed under Saturday's mallet. While I reflect what a coarse occupation policing is the world over, with its tattered fixtures and decor of maps and flyers, Smuts's mouth forms the turtle beak it does when he thinks hard. It's usual to imagine the brain as a circuit board flashing with notions and answers, but with Smuts a notion is like a ball in a wooden bagatelle: you hear it echo all the way to a slot, where it clicks and stays forever. This is what happens now in his brainatelle.

"I'm so fucked," he croaks.

A lengthy pause follows, during which officers strut around pointing at things and frowning. Apparently an interpreter will arrive, and the evening's first witness. In the meantime I hear Smuts answer the occasional question in Japanese. It sounds like his kitchen French, he slides and bumps over it running.

When we're alone he hisses, "I think the octopus bit Keiko. They have beaks, you know. That's why the boss hasn't arrived. She must be at the hospital. Look at the symmetry: everyone's either in hospital or jail. Some night, uh. Some coke. Have you still got the coke?"

I look down and scratch my head.

"You're so fucked."

The sergeant's desk, or that of his local equivalent, stands facing us and draws our gaze in default of anything more hopeful. After another long silence Smuts says without turning: "Hope you can pay for your own lawyer and your own food in jail. I'll be struggling to look after myself."

"Hm. And your sponsor—?"

"Get real—he did me a favor. Doesn't mean he sends pocket money. Doesn't mean he's going to bring me up, and sew fucking labels into my school clothes. Pimpernel twat. Wake up!"

Needless to say, our nimbus has crashed.* And in that way

---

* Stress chemicals kill nimbus. They must be like a slurry that enters the blood-stream. One effect is to diminish the bravery that attracts good fortune, and

the spirit has of sampling outside conditions from time to time to refresh its decor of metaphors, this limbo that began as a glance across tanning beds has turned into bad sex in a Travelodge. All things, it seems, have a life span of innocence hurtling to dismay. All creation is a first clay vase made at school. Ah, nature, that vicious turd.

Wistfully I look back on earlier times.

"Surely mine's the worse position," I say. "My crimes are still in my pocket, and as a tourist I'd be unlikely to get bail. Whereas your only proven offense is a romp in a fish tank. At home you'd get off with a warning and be a legend for life."

"Immaterial. Here they can hold you weeks without charge. Meantime, Sardine Face'll get me for the poisoning, and whatever else. I'll get a sword through my eye in jail over Keiko." Smuts turns a filthy gaze: "I just wish you'd tell me what the fuck you're even doing here. This morning I had things under control."

The moment's bleak. Never did a comrade more deserve the respect of truth. But against gray daybreak my plan looks foolish. I face the hardest choice of a friend: to be brutal or to humor. Being brutal means exposing the limbo, which would show its absurdity in this context, and set Smuts's stubborn mind to dismantling it. I have to keep it safe from the absurd, safe from anything that might erode it—it's all I have left, and its momentum grows by the hour. Death wishes like this may even be self-propelling, they may throw a switch at the outset, unleashing a juggernaut of Fortune, making it impossible to maneuver or change your mind.

---

at the very moment it's needed most. Surely then the world of this slurry, its management and disposal, is at the heart of the human mission to discover.

Pondering is called for. My diagram of Fortune has collapsed. For now, though, I'm aware of Smuts watching me, waiting for me to answer why I'm here.

"Just came for a drink," I finally say.

"A *drink*?" His mouth falls open. "You were just going to get off a plane in Tokyo and have a drink? Mate"—he drops his head—"mate, Putain."

An officer approaches and unties us, leading Smuts away down a corridor beside the charge desk. Smuts doesn't turn to me. I watch him move off with a sticky gait, shining in wet trousers. "A *drink*," I hear him mutter down the hall. "Tss."

My body cringes into a fetus. So much for Enthusiasms. Limbo was too rampant to unleash on others, or even to bring near them. Too despotic by far, a maelstrom of mayhem and death. And it was an airtight sealing of my fate, because limbo, with its sense that I had nothing to lose, coaxed out things that I still did have to lose.

And lost them.

After a while an officer comes for me. Behind him walks a wiry older woman, who is the interpreter. Her gaze slides around behind glasses. She explains that I'll be searched while statements are taken elsewhere to clarify the night's events. I move off down the corridor, noting that limbo had a form after all—it was a passage to a goal, a narrowing cone to it, and because the goal receded out of sight, the form itself dissolved. Enthusiasms aren't sucked to it anymore, nor luck, because death has for the time being become impossible.*

---

* All dynamic things seem to be conical in form. No matter where you begin an endeavor, or what nature it has, it sets off from a yawning gape and either

Whoosh. It's gone.

We enter a small interview room. Although a table and chairs are here, I'm told to stand. The strangeness of our gathering strikes me—the sphinx, the lady, and the officer, somehow together in Japan. The officer motions me to spread my limbs.

A hand goes into my left pocket, fingers brush my leg through the cloth. They pull out my wallet and toss it onto the table. Then, after my cigarettes emerge from the coat pocket, there's a wait while he inspects and sniffs each one before lining it up alongside the others. After pulling my passport and notepad from inside the coat, checking my face against the passport photo, and flicking through the notes—he moves to my right.

Just as I feel his hand at my leg, the door opens. A face peers in. By its pallid, froglike appearance and ill-advised haircut, I judge it to belong to a plainclothes policeman. "Nerusan Smatosu?" He looks me up and down while this sinks in as "Nelson Smuts."

Behind him in the shadows lurks another figure, and as the view between us clears I see it's Tomohiro. He first sees my notebook on the table, then recognizes me, leaning in to point and hiss to the officers.

"Ah!" exclaims the plainclothes officer.

"Oh!" My policeman steps back.

For a moment all stand and examine me. There's an exchange between them, followed by nodding as Tomohiro pushes into the room. And with this their frowns start to thaw. The interpreter blinks, and says: "You're a guest—of the restaurant?"

---

unravels at the rim, or propels you to a narrowing point. Space itself may be conical. Life may be conical. Be prepared for cones.

My scalp relaxes as a revelation looms. It's a massive one, a breeze already flies off its towering and nacreous form, patrolled by bats.

"This is the master of the kitchen," she explains.

"Yes, I know," I say.

"He asks that you forgive the incidents tonight. The man responsible is not part of the usual team. He hopes your meal was a strong example of their work, which has been called the finest in Tokyo. If not, he begs that you return and allow him to treat you as you deserve."

"Assure him I'll remember the meal in the highest terms."

Tomohiro smiles at this answer, which anyhow is true.

In the corridor behind him an officer passes with the canvas bag, stopping to ask a question. Tomohiro reaches for the bag and looks inside. For my taste, he looks too long, and I begin to tense. But he eventually hands it to me.

"Perhaps this can balance some of your inconvenience," interprets the lady. "Perhaps, the master respectfully asks—it can help you to recall good things."

The chef looks me in the eye, and as we bow my revelation crashes in—I've just been rescued by the parallel limbo of capitalism. Passing like a ship in my own waters, it widened a course to pull me off the swell into its humming interior. The free-market limbo—not a rustic single-celled limbo like mine, but a behemoth wired and plumbed across every inch of its hull with avenues and protocols of escape and reward—has taken aboard a sphinx, even though I'm a cohort of the suspect, and at very least complicit in the night's events.

It has done this thinking that I'm a food writer.

And therefore able to influence profit.

Whoosh—I've been taken up by the Master Limbo.

Who knows how long I stand absorbing this, but I must look dazed because after carefully replacing my cigarettes, passport, and notepad, the policeman taps my shoulder and nods at the door.

"You're free to go," the interpreter says with a smile.

My limbo reinflates in an instant, its cone re-forms, Enthusiasms flood back. And I step from the room with a formidable ally—a mentor limbo on which to model my own.

None less than the Master Limbo of capitalism.

On a pretext of clarifying the name of my hotel, I ask to see Smuts, and they agree to allow it, briefly, in the company of an officer. I jot down the interpreter's number before she goes, so I can contact the police station through her—then I wait in the corridor while Smuts is being searched in a neighboring room.

I wait and savor the pain.

It doesn't sit well with me to leave people behind.

One confidence I can share with you which might explain the strength of my feeling is this: when I was little my grandfather stayed with us for a few weeks. Tommy, as we called Grampa Brockwell, had a laugh up his sleeve at all times, one that sharpened his tongue to a wicked point and made it poke like a cuckoo from a clock. But when he was old his body started disobeying him, and his face grew unsure, and then frightened.

He took a fall one day at our place.

My father's generation was the first to stop looking after its elders. My father decided it was modern to look after ourselves, you see, and not to get too weighed down with Grampa's problems, because Gramps wouldn't have wanted it. This was his modern approach. Except Tommy wanted caring-for. He took a fall and lay on his side, twitching like an insect. He looked up at us. But my father, on his new psychological health drive, had booked us seats at the cinema. A friend of Auntie May's who used to be a nurse, was dropping by to mind Tommy while we were out.

She hadn't arrived when he fell.

My father looked at his watch, asked Tom if he was okay, propped him against the bed, and left him there for the lady to find. Because otherwise the film would have started without us—and Tommy wouldn't have wanted that. I remember looking back from his door. His eyes followed us out. It was true that in the days he had laughs in him he wouldn't have wanted us to make a fuss. But those days were gone.

Later that night we followed a quiet ambulance up the road to home. It spilled spotlight beams, checking house numbers. I knew it was for Tommy. He never opened his eyes again.

The Piano was a glutinous and muddy film to me. That's what we abandoned Tommy to see. And the same feeling is with me today. Crushing pain. I can't leave another soul behind. I have to get serious. Standing here I resolve to confess everything to Smuts, right now, and to offer myself unconditionally for any mission he feels might help his cause.

Limbo will have to stretch a little more.

When an officer finally ushers me into Smuts's room I find him sitting barefoot, huddled on a bench under a fire blanket.

I sit beside him. The silence is heavy.

"They let me go," I say. "I'll be better placed to help."

"Yeah, great help," he grunts.

"If you need a sworn affidavit or something—whatever you need, just tell me. I'll call later when the dust's cleared. Just tell me—whatever it is, I'm yours."

"You tell me—what the fuck you're even doing here."

"Well." I sigh. "I was in rehab. Actually this all started beforehand—but I ended up in rehab, and had to get away."

"Right, and Burger King pays enough for the Peninsula."

"It wasn't a Burger King, it was a two-hundred-cover—"

"You're fresh out of rehab, burning someone else's money. The only thing I can say: Tokyo qualifies as getting away, all right. My workplace in Tokyo qualifies as getting well the fuck away."

"Well, Berlin was the first idea. I thought we could go together."

"But you didn't know anyone there you could mess up enough."

"I'm dismal with it, Smuts. I'm sorry."

"Doesn't add up," Smuts's thinking-beak returns. "Tokyo or Berlin."

"Berlin adds up, you know my history. Remember Dad ran a club?"

"So the choice was—clubbing, or mess up Smuts."

"No, no—Berlin was—"

"Club—or Smuts." A ball starts rolling in the brainatelle. "Clubbing or—"

"It's nothing to do with the club."

"So why say club? I didn't say club, you said club."

"No, no, it's just that my father—"

"Berlin, club, your father." Smuts's lids flicker.

The ball approaches a row of holes. The ruthless mechanism will decide something come what may, and I find myself running after the ball, trying to steer it:

"My father was reminiscing, that's all—said it must still be there, the club, run by his old partner. Massive, these days. The point is, he didn't want me to go because the partner's a very decadent type. I barely remember him. So anyway, I was in rehab, and—"

Smuts holds up a hand: "Now you're making sense. Was that so fucking hard? Big club, decadent man—he does food—uh?"

"Not that I know of."

Smuts frowns. A fleet of balls sets off behind his brow: "Decadent club, no food, Smuts, Berlin—you're launching food!"

"No, listen—"

"Massive decadent club—Smuts—food."

"Smuts, Smuts." I shake his shoulder, but my tone calls the officer from the door. He checks his watch and waves me out.

Smuts's stare follows me off the chair. "I'll do it. That's what this is about, isn't it? My move back to Europe? Mate—Berlin, executive chef. Fuck, that'll move the game up a notch with the Basque, that'll put some pressure on. The symmetry's perfect! Why didn't you say something?"

"Smuts, we haven't heard of this man in twenty years. Look—"

"Mate—uh? Putain? You're unbelievable."

Conflict rages between my spirit, too touched by Smuts's wild hopes to crush them, and my brain, too shocked at the delusion's scale to let it pass. My voice falters trying to break into the bagatelle.

Smuts's gaze darts here and there. "No question, I'll do it. Sell him on banquets, sell him on decadence. I know his type. Sell him on Michelin stardom. Masquerades, lobster tails. Sell, sell, sell. Mate? Mention Didier's name if you have to. If I line up an awesome gig in Europe, he could intervene here, pull some strings."

"But listen—"

"Fuck me, I'm back in the game. Can't believe you let things get this far! Puts everything in a whole new light. Okay, so the night went to shit in the fish joint—but it's because a scout came to pull me into a much bigger deal. An awesome gig in Europe! Of course it was messy, we're not just talking any scout—it's the son of the founder! Didier will understand that!"

Before I'm able to mount an adjustment, the officer takes my arm and leads me out, pulling the door shut behind us.

"Putainel," Smuts calls after me. "Fix it up."

"Smuts—"

"Yesterday I had things under control. Uh?"

The officer points me to the bag of Marius and escorts me to reception. Tomohiro stands half through a doorway, watching. I look at him. A gentle clamping of lips is the only comment I can make. He returns it, and bows.

With that, I leave the scene.

Light floods the window at the Peninsula Hotel. I peer down through it as far as I can, checking, as all creatures do, how far there is to fall. My head slumps against the glass.

It frosts with breath.

Checkout time approaches and vacuum cleaners are at work in the halls. Nimbus has turned to nausea, Smuts is under arrest, an old man fights for his life, I'm not dead.

And now I need a club.

11

While squirrels charm the parks of London, and *karasu* birds sprinkle Tokyo with cries—wild pigs threaten joggers in Berlin. This is the scale of whoosh we're dealing with, my friend.

Berlin has nothing to learn from anyone.

From all I've read and watched in the years since I was there, sniffing news like a puppy, this is what I sense of her position: That if today London is a drinker on the verge of losing her keys, Berlin is one just woken to find herself still alive, and on a Sunday. That while her tallest hill will always be artificial, built from the rubble of some four hundred thousand bombed buildings, the new era that sprang from her bullet holes and bunkers is real. I sense that wherever trees and flowers didn't grow, art and ideas sprouted in their place, till her iconic graffiti, her recent decor of Porsches ablaze at the curbside, her clubs that refuse entry to stars, her seething countercultures, anti-cultures, and stolid everyday folk now shout one thing:

Berlin is not for elites—Berlin is for people.

And their limbo is over.

Marlene Dietrich's city-state assembles out of forests and lakes beneath me as the flight shudders down through dusky cloud. I tingle inside. As we fall closer it becomes an orderly maze like the best foreign train set, a maquette of buildings, boxes, containers, and rigging that twinkles across marshy hinterlands toward the Polish border, still supervised by the blinking spire of the television tower at Alexanderplatz, a giant eyeball on a toothpick, once raised to taunt the West across the wall. Watching with my face pressed to the window, I reflect on the odyssey so far. In fact how mysterious that having called it an odyssey it then became one, complete with monstrous contests and decadent talismans, the likes of Jicky and Marius.

I wonder what this stage will bring. As Berlin's air fills the cabin, I'm rinsed in a mixture of dread and hope.

Smuts's brainatelle called the Peninsula before I left. I knew it was the brainatelle, the call was a monologue, sounding hopeful in the way madmen sound hopeful at the scene of a fire. It dictated this schedule: I'm to go direct from the plane to the decadent mogul's club, whence I'll call Smuts with offers he can relay to Didier Le Basque. Two hours is how long he allows, including time to explain the wine to customs and for the mogul to chuckle over how much I've grown.

Smuts's boss Yoshida still hadn't been interviewed when I left. It means Smuts could be freed if the right enticements came to bear on the boss, for instance from Didier Le Basque. Despite such pressure I was buoyant about the mission for the first hour out of Tokyo. I foresaw Smuts and me laughing in the tumbledown alleys of East Berlin. Then I had a line in the restroom and my visions went away. An intoxicant reversal happened. Reality suddenly shone more than hope.

With this shock I set to examining reality and hope, those

treacherous riverbanks of existence.* Because in reality I'm landing without much money to find a man I met when I was a child, and talk him into opening a restaurant for a friend in jail. Whereas in hope, a vast hospitality empire awaits where I'm fondly remembered by a back-slapping grandee who makes deals on the toss of a coin.

These shades of potential filled the long flight to Munich, and much of the shorter one to Berlin. Somewhere between those potentials lay possibility, but I had trouble deciding where, and that indecision, that loss of bold face, shifted me from phantomhood into a simple category of deranged person who travels around at random on someone else's money with a single change of clothes. This is the lens of reality: watch out, friend, I warn you. I became a type of person usually seen much later in a Hawaiian shirt with more than one Thai marriage behind him.

All this took a while to get over. It took some Courvoisier and club soda, and a few idle screaming matches in my mind, over money, with someone called Thong, before I felt I could afford hope. And in reality I feel there are hopeful signs. While my father's calling the club massive may or may not be accurate after twenty years, his reluctance to let me come on account of the partner's decadence—that bodes well. Why else would he be so

---

* Reality is a lottery of horror whose chaos led humans to develop an alternate world of hopes and plans. Human existence is what we do in the gap between those worlds. All joy and failure arise from managing that fragile duality—and unhappiness from trying to live too far above horror. Life is most bountiful when we stay low and expect little. As with limbo: decide to die—then live. But protect your gap, as regimes will seize it to fill with their ideas, controlling your fears for their gain—and none more than commerce, assuring us we're different, and should expect more. This evening's vital message, then: Mind the Gap.

reluctant? It speaks of real excess. It speaks of a rich and venture-some libertine, exactly who we need to find, someone at least in sympathy with our position. And maybe it's not such a crazy posi-tion. Perhaps within a context of limbo it's pure commonplace. Because aren't the greatest inspirations brought to life on a whim? Aren't they a snatching of chance from thin air? Such an arena is native terrain for Smuts. Perhaps our debauch merely sharpened his instinct, made him see these possibilities around us. After all, the zigzag of his career came entirely from whims like this. Why not Berlin? It wouldn't be the most miraculous thing to ever hap-pen to him.

All this had to churn through me before I could return to the question of my death. Then that brought new qualms. Surely I couldn't die leaving Smuts in jail. Under normal reasoning it would be unthinkable to die leaving a friend in jail. But under an inverse ethic it would be desirable—because if my living causes such harm to others, even landing them in jail, then my death prevents further harm.

A eureka moment. And most powerfully, having found a way to move forward, I regain limbo's reckless tools, the better to actually help Smuts.

It is, to quote from the market itself—a win-win situation.

I quickly copy the ethic's wiring into my own limbo. Suddenly it's a toddler limbo, with its first little sophistication.

And with this in place I step from the plane in command.

Ah, the Enthusiasms. Why not Berlin? For Smuts's sake I'll give the performance of my life. I'll use limbo for all it's worth. And, thinking about it, there's even my father's share to barter with. He did say he abandoned a share in the business, you can vouch for that. Yes! I'll commandeer his share—surely this Gerd

Specht will feel the debt heavily, and go along with any plan. Banquets in Berlin—why wouldn't he agree? And for Smuts's purposes the scheme doesn't even have to be running, it just needs a nod, a few details, an interim pedigree to impress the sponsor.

How stupid were my fears in light of reality!

I sweep off the plane and fidget, waiting for my bag. It doesn't take long, Berlin Tegel is a sensible airport shaped like a doughnut, where every gate has its own immigration, baggage reclaim, and customs, barely a few steps from the roadside, without a hint of threats, abuse, or shopping.

As if someone simply wanted me to pass through.

So it is that within five minutes I stand on the pavement under an evening sky, earmarking a bottle of Marius to impress the voluptuary Specht. Over a cigarette I even consider taking wallpaper to erect a makeshift White Room. That'd show him what we're about. While I ponder where I might find wallpaper at this hour, an old cabdriver heaves my bag into his taxi. I climb inside, watching him with that awe that can attach to the first locals of a mythical place.

"*Pego Klub, bitte.*" I study his Prussian jowls.

"Where? Piko?" He halts his entry behind the wheel.

"Pe-go. *In der Brunnenstrasse?*"

The man stays hunched at the door, as if we might best abandon the mission. I'm not too put off by this; he's from a generation retired from clubbing, and realistically, in a city riddled with venues, I allow for the Pego to have moved since the early nineties, even to have changed its name.

For now I direct the driver to my old stomping ground, Prenzlauer Berg, home of the original Pego Club. Once nuzzling the Berlin Wall, this area's stark decrepitude was a beacon that brought adventurers flocking after the German Democratic Republic collapsed in 1990, around the time I toddled into town. Postapocalyptic grunge became the cradle for a club scene still famous today, and still owing its spirit and style to the no-man's-land between East and West, between past and future. Heady times, when I think about them; times when I wished I'd been older. What I now know is that history didn't let Berlin catch her breath between eras. That's why the district looked the way it did. Much of her battle damage went unrepaired after the war, and when communists then closed her to the West, ownership of buildings fell into a limbo as owners and tenants didn't or couldn't return. It's no wonder that after the wall fell these borderline quarters of Prenzlauer Berg and Mitte became a playground for the likes of my father, with his acrylic shirts and bad teeth. At that time you could start a club by kicking out a factory window and phoning your friends to bring beer.

A lump sticks in my throat as we pass into the old East. Cruising along, I see that stealthy proletarians have been replaced by stylish bohemians, goods carts by ergometric baby carriages, ruins by biological food marts. Whereas in my time it wasn't unheard-of for balconies to snap off buildings and crash to the street with revelers aboard, today's skyline is mostly sanitized, with shops and cafés bustling where shadows once lurked. What a feature of our hurtling age, and of Berlin's, I reflect, that at twenty-five I can already say things were so different in my day.

Even so, it still looks like a place for Frederick the mouse; though he'd now do as well with an espresso machine. All these sights prompt me to reflect on how mistaken our impression still is of Germany—although I grant that any German will call Berlin a special case. Nevertheless, it seems to be in the British interest to regard it as a dour, mechanistic, unromantic place, its peoples without humor or style. Yet the German language today is a softer one, a surprising one, vast and flexible, even whimsical, and the people meek and thoughtful, far from the Huns we'd still like them to be.

Kastanienallee was my nearest thoroughfare as a child, a long and straight incline eventually dipping towards the center of East Berlin, where the blinking spire of the Alex stands. The driver slows halfway up the street, catching my eye in the mirror to ask instructions. I recall the club being somewhere on Brunnenstrasse, but he tells me it's a substantial street, and rather than waste my money I'd do better to confirm the address and proceed on foot. The reasoning is sound. As I'm barely thirty minutes off the plane, and spying the Kastanienhof hotel up ahead, I tell him to drop me there. It makes sense to take a room, ask directions, and freshen up before meeting the über-sybarite Specht.

"So then," grunts my First Genuine Local, lifting the bulk of Marius. "Around here they'll know more about the clubs."

"*Danke*," I say.

"At least more than me, I'm from Hanover."

With my local utopia thus slightly punctured, I step into the old hotel-pension. Of course, it's not the Peninsula, but it's clean, modern, and unusually comfortable in a way that suggests the staff have been here for years. It means they're at home, their hospitalities have been tested over many a winter's night. I learn, for instance, that I can borrow a chessboard from reception, buff my shoes while I wait for the elevator, and even smoke at breakfast in a dedicated smoking breakfast room.

Pure civilization.

But they know nothing of the Pego.

Fear comes prickling when the phone directory doesn't list
it either. At least not under Pego. Then a minor revelation blows
in, bearing good news and bad. I stand absorbing it at reception
while another local man wafts in who hasn't heard of the club.
The good news is that this is Berlin—the more awesome a club,
the less it seeks to advertise. In fact, just as I recall this, the local
says there are still clubs around that only admit holders of tokens
given out in the nineties. The bad news, however, forming the
bulk of the revelation, comes from the same fact: the best things
don't advertise, the rare ones don't seek members.

East Berlin isn't a client of the Master Limbo.

I'm without an ally.

A pang of reality grips me. On the East Berlin club scene,
massive can actually mean bleak. Best can mean poorest, with the
tiniest basement, and the least choice of drinks. A reverse ethic
operates here. Specht could be a purist. And though I hold this
to be a zenith of progress—it doesn't help Smuts.

I have slightly over an hour to call him, and now a master revelation starts to dawn. A format begins to emerge to these limbo
days, a symmetry, as Smuts would say, which is this, just look: the
fallout from my decadent limbo demands a wholly decadent solution. A capitalist solution. No amount of grunge or purism will
help us; we need a vast hospitality venture, we need a capitalist
who opens restaurants at the drop of a hat. We need the sheer
grunt of the markets. I was helped by them in Tokyo to get this
far—but now I need more, much more.

Look at the symmetry.

Ah, the markets. Finding the club is suddenly more daunt-
ing than not finding it. What if it's a purist dive? I drop my bag
in the room and step onto Kastanienallee, bringing along a bot-

tle of Marius for either the purist or mogul Specht. My nerves settle somewhat with the sting of night air. In any case, mogul or not, after twenty years in business the man should at least be well connected. All we need is a good lead. These thoughts rebalance me as I dodge a tram and cross over the street. But looking up and down, I now have mixed feelings at seeing no Starbucks or McDonald's. We don't need Frederick the mouse, we don't need purism. We need rampant consumption, we need excess.

We need the Master Limbo of modern capitalism.

On Kastanienallee the wandering population is in the process of dissolving between evening and night dwellers, and I scan them looking for vestiges of the old East—a plastic jacket worn too tight, a trouser too short—and though there are signs of Eastern chic, the air mostly hums with design projects on drawing boards. Designer stubble twitches with them in cafés and bars—not burning, obsessive projects, already seared by madness and solder, but projects fit to discuss over a cappuccino. Projects that harmonize with the modern soundtrack of Prenzlauer Berg, an endless wistful replaying of the *Gulag Orkestar*, of Gnossiennes, of Gymnopédies—of any melancholic lullaby that helps the new bio-bourgeoisie imagine its baby carriages amid rubble and daisies.

Contentment fuels no excess.

Ah, well. Passing a beardie who reminds me of my father as a young man, I enter a bar on the corner of Kastanienallee and Zionskirchplatz. Strains of the Deutsches Requiem seep from the church across the cobbled square.

In the bar I order a beer, using its first exhilarating draughts to prepare an inquiry into the Pego. I don't rush to the task in case Specht is too well known. Spies might report to him that I seemed too keen. This is my level of focus—witness it, will you—after the tumult of earlier. It even stretches to deciding that when I find the club, I'll spend five minutes quietly scoping it, trying to catch sight of Specht. With his image and manner in mind, and having seen the space where our hopes lie, I can withdraw for a cigarette and muster a stance for an official pitch. Meanwhile, its clientele, the nature of its door staff, the music and decor will embed in me, inoculate me, like hormones in a Marius grape. Enthusiasms are a force that attracts like to like, so carrying a dose of the Pego is bound to help.

The Enthusiasms can be exciting, I muse. Like wearing a cape. I nurse my beer and order a schnapps and, when the bar-maid returns with it, begin my inquiry in German:

"*Entschuldigung*—"

"What do you want?" she snaps in English.

"I'm looking for the Pego Club."

"Piggo?" she says. "Piggo Club?"

"Pego. Pe-go."

She shrugs, throwing the question to another waitress, who stares blankly back.

"There's still some hot clubs around," a shaggy man calls along the bar. "But you really had to be here in the nineties. Is this your first day?"

I look at the man. Though clearly German, he speaks American television English, and has the minor good looks, the studied unkemptness, of the full-time barfly, the career seducer of budget tourists.

"I was here in the nineties," I say. "Do you know the Pego?"

"Dude," he says with a laugh, "you weren't clubbing in the

nineties. How old are you? You were in bed with your teddy bear in the nineties."

I find myself bristling, and pause. How curious—I'm already possessive of Berlin. How dare he lay more claim to her than me? And to the nineties, for that matter. I churn for a moment, marvelling at this territorial quirk. With some discomfort I finally identify it as a quite British foible. It's the jealousy of the Joneses on holiday, when a new ginger family pays too much attention to their waiter Miguel. Here they've carefully groomed him over a week between Saturdays, made his laughter theirs, and suddenly:

Horrible fat new gingers calling him Manuel.

"Is the Pego still around?" I stare into my schnapps. "Somewhere on Brunnenstrasse, I think it used to be."

"Wow, you studied your map, huh? Brunnenstrasse. Except we put more accent on the 'unn,' like 'Br*unn*-en-sh-trasse.'" He shuffles up to join me. "Dude, if you're looking for girls—"

"I'm not, thanks." I pay for my drinks and walk out.

"Hey, my friend!" he calls after me. "My friend!"

But I step into my own Berlin, spacious and tranquil, whining with trams. My lifelong Sunday, my stern old Frau.

Two more bars and a kebab stall haven't heard of the Pego, or of the colossus Gerd Specht. Four students I stop haven't heard of them. Halfway down the street I find an Imbiss still open, and reason that this type of small shop, selling confectionery, cigarettes, and drinks, must be as good as a concierge's desk for the district, news must surely gather here.

But the man inside knows nothing.

Ah, well. The time can come to any endeavor, as it does to believing in God, when your world hangs without factual support of any kind. I become aware of it just as my two hours are up. It's early morning in Tokyo, and Smuts will be waiting. The Imbiss-keeper sells me a phone card. He seems to nod sympathetically as he hands it over the counter, maybe sensing that no laughter will flow from it. And curiously I don't have the instinct to snort lines before calling. Perhaps uncertain news is never best delivered crisply. In fact, I haven't felt the urge for oblivion since I landed. Even though limbo doesn't seem to muffle me here.

Even though I feel reality's steel on my skin.

Finding a phone booth nearby, I dial the police station in Tokyo, resolving for safety's sake to drink more from now on. The duty sergeant answers, and after some grunts Smuts's voice echoes through as if from the long past:

"Putain?"

"Smuts—I made it. Are you okay?"

"Just tell me the deal—name of the venue, how many covers, et cetera. Things are hotting up over here."

"What's happening?"

"The old guy's pals say he didn't order offal. They say he was too drunk to order anything. Yoshida hasn't given a statement yet, the lab's still testing fish. I told the lawyer that you witnessed the guy ordering, but he says you're not a Japanese speaker so it doesn't count. Fuck knows what'll happen. Balls are in the air. Things look fucked. I'm just keeping my head down, sketching up menus for Berlin. We managed to get a message to the Basque, he's calling tomorrow."

"When exactly?"

"Just tell me about the thing! Putain! What the fuck!"

"Well, Smuts—I haven't been able to see the man yet."

"What? Don't tell me that. Don't tell me that now."

"The thing is—"

"I'm fucking begging you."

"Smuts, I'm on the case—it's a Monday night, I'm fresh off the plane."

"You have to fix it up. And I mean fix it up. According to the lawyer a professional domicile in Europe is critical. Things are different for a visiting specialist than for an itinerant kitchen hand. I told him about Berlin. And he agrees that if we can get the Basque on board we should be fine—he supplied the fish, it'll be in his interest to pull me out. But on both counts we need a venue by tomorrow. And Putainel—"

"Hm?"

"It needs to be fucking awesome."

12

Morning is unwelcome. I find my blanket twisted in a pile.

When I first step outside, yellow leaves blow up the street. The truth dawns on me that the Pego is dead. Gerd Specht long gone from the scene. Reality comes in the way it most loves, on a wind. Of course, there's an outside chance the club might still exist somewhere—that's Berlin's nature. I know that besides this Eastern vestige she has quarters as charming as Paris, badlands as stark as Siberia, shopping as rich as New York.

So it is in Berlin. A club could move and not be heard of again. Or it might simply die where it sits.

Passing an outdoor table on Kastanienallee, I see a blackboard offering Big Breakfast and Little Breakfast. My gut forces me to stop. I choose Big Breakfast, hoping to fortify myself for the day, but when it comes I sit staring at the plate.

Nearby is Choriner Strasse, where I stayed as a boy. I can't bring myself to look for my old building. I should feel charmed to be in East Berlin again, hearing bicycle bells on the street. But I haven't the luxury of charm. Under this cool morning my death wish seems like masturbation. This feels more like a city where if you want to die, you just put out the recycling, water the herbs, cancel your *Süddeutsche Zeitung* subscription, and die.

In any event, I spend the day going through the motions of a hunt. The sky stays overcast. After trying all the Spechts in the phone directory, I mount an assault on Brunnenstrasse, Rosenthaler Platz, and Torstrasse, sweeping up and down in my greatcoat, drinking coffee and smoking, because in Berlin you can smoke. At great length I've been told that Berliners don't ignore the European ban because they smoke more; rather because nobody again will tell them what to do.

Still, twenty Gitanes Blondes bring me no closer to the Pego. I find a Soviet army surplus shop where I thought it used to be. After this the day quickly passes into night.

I shiver. Futility comes to me in one of those floods that can seize a mood. Among the short residential streets that run like spokes off a square is Swinemünder Strasse, and I head down it. In my mind the word Swinemunder translates into Swine World, and for that bitter omen alone I take the route. Barely a hundred steps away it hits Granseer Strasse—Grand Sneer, in the same monkey tongue, surely describing the veal-like lips of nature. The street runs beside a small park, charming but with nothing unusual to recommend it, past typical five-story blocks standing one behind the other with a garden in between, the *Vorderhäuser* and *Hinterhöfe* where Berliners mostly live.

Then up ahead I detect a spill of light and noise. One of Berlin's delights: a café-bar nestles for no good commercial reason in the ground floor of a quiet residential block. Whereas in Britain this would be an outrage to business modeling, a lethal snub to targeting and demographics, in Berlin the idea is simply this:

If you feel like a coffee, we can make you one.

Drifting toward the light, I realize I've been strangely relaxed in the capital of the world's third-largest economy, notwithstanding my mission. Despite its being a larger and healthier economy than Britain, I find that my guard is down, the perpetual buzz of frustration and fear is gone. Perhaps because no business I've entered has been founded on a need to expand to fifty outlets by next year. No staff member has been primed to manipulate more sales from me than I intended to give. No cameras suggest I might flee without paying. No signs warn that I'm about to be affronted in a way liable to make me resort to threats, violence, or abusive language. No unit of my space or time has been seized under a philosophy that the tiny fraction of people who respond by weakness or mistake to a trick are a valuable target group. That work of bacteria in suits, involved in nothing but the business of themselves and of human decay, seems largely absent here.

I'm not part of a sales curve.

I'm not presumed a thief or a fool.

And a coffee's not a lifestyle choice.

It's a coffee.

Three figures sit smoking in front of the tiny bar. They watch me approach, drawn like a midge to the light. A Latin American man smiles and stands to greet me.

"No, but this was a seriously big business," goes his conversation with two grayish men. "Really one of the big banks." The two men are locals of roughly my father's age, though still wiry and strong. They wear modest clothes, neither colored nor uncolored, that say nothing about them. Our host brings three shots of Peruvian *pisco*, courtesy of the house. I order a beer before he goes inside to tidy, leaving me with the pair of sand-blasted faces. We hunch smoking, watching shadows play among the trees.

"Is this still Prenzlauer Berg?" I eventually ask.

"No, Mitte," says the craggy man. "Though it depends what you're thinking, because if you mean the Prenzlauer Berg of the famous Berlin Wall, then this is still considered it." He raises his beer and points across the park: "A couple of blocks down is the wall. Those buildings at the edge were only for Stasi agents and other trusted officials. They could see the West from their apartments."

"But if it's old Prenzlauer Berg you're looking for," says the comrade, "you're a few years too late. You really had to be here in the nineties. Are you American? Your German is quite good."

Ah, my secret Miguel. I suppose a foreign sphinx in a great-coat is as unusual here as a sausage, it's just another weekend raver with forty euros in his pocket and two new friends called Andreas.

"I'm English," I say, "and I was here in the nineties." I also wonder how soon into the decade Berliners started saying this, or if before that they said eighties.

"Really?" says the comrade. "But then as a baby."

"My father started a club here in the nineties. I think on Brunnenstrasse."

"Oh? The Kim Bar?"

"*Nein*." Craggy slaps him on the cuff. He chews the inside of his cheek for a moment, rolls his eyes up, thinking—and finally shakes his head: "*Kim Bar hat nach den Neunzigern geöffnet. Wenn du die Neunziger meinst, zumindest an diesem Ende der Brunnen-straße—dann muss das der Pego Klub gewesen sein.*"

His Eastern brogue hits me jumbled, only assembling after a short delay.

Then I reel back in the chair.

The men recoil, thinking language has confounded me. After a moment the speaker waves an apology, and says in English:

"If you mean nineties, at this end of Brunnenstrasse—it had to be the Pego Club."

13

The alternating Klaxon of a Notarzt van bounces off winds in the distance. It's a sound in black and white, an ambulance from a newsreel, resounding through bygone streets.

For me its souring blasts describe a passage from dread into hope. I let the quiet unfold, the ambulance waft away, till the men lift their sagging faces into the night. Then I lean in, peeling strips from my beer label, rolling cones in my hand:

"And—what happened to the club?"

"Well." Craggy turns to his friend: "Wasn't it the tall one, from Leipzig—?"

"There used to be two, remember. One of them was Bernd—Bernd Specht."

"*Gerd* Specht?" I prompt.

"*Ja*, that's it," says the comrade. "Gerd Specht." Both stare up a little higher, blowing smoke into the lamplight.

"So—what happened?"

"The place closed," says Craggy. "I think he went to Kreuzberg after that."

"*Ja*, to Tempelhof." His friend turns to me: "Did you ever see

Tempelhof Airport? Biggest single building in the world. One of Hitler's projects from the thirties."

"*Nein*." Craggy shakes his head. "The second biggest structure in the world after the Pentagon. Or the third. Top three, anyway."

"*Ja*, well—you should see it. A masterpiece of architecture from the Third Reich. Fantastic monument, over a kilometer long. Three and a half million square meters in the middle of Berlin. Almost empty now. The airport occupies a small part of it, but I think that's closing soon. The city wondered if to put apartments, or a hotel. But they could put twenty hotels and still have space."

"And Specht moved there?" I nearly whimper. "With the club?"

"*Ja*, his business must be there, and who knows what else? Nobody really knows what's inside. I think there's a dance school there somewhere, and also a bowling alley put by the American forces. There may be parts not even touched since the war."

"There's even a fish farm, I think." Craggy nods. "Sounds like a joke but it's typical Berlin, we just don't know what to do with these places. A good move by Specht, though, going there early. Can you imagine having such a building as your premises?"

As the men speak I feel the warmth leave my fingertips.

"The walls are like five meters thick," says the comrade. "Solid stone and concrete. You could stand next to it and not hear a club."

"*Nein*, three meters thick," Craggy corrects. "The beauty billionaire, Lauder, from New York, wanted to buy it and make an avant-garde clinic, where jets fly to the door. But you see, typical Berlin government, they only saw the symbol of the super-rich using their monument. They didn't see all the jobs it could make. And Berlin needs jobs, we still never recovered from reunification."

"Now you talk like a capitalist," tuts his friend. "Berlin doesn't want to be a playground for the super-rich."

"Well, look at Hitler's big dreams," says the comrade. "He wanted visitors' mouths to fall open when they landed in Berlin, that was the idea. They get off the plane and their mouths fall open. From the air it has the shape of an eagle, and the airside even has a roof, so planes park underneath like in a giant garage."

A serene smile grows on my face. The breeze no longer bodes ill, now it smacks of beginnings.

"Gosh." I drift back to the moment: "And have you seen Specht there?"

"Oh, *ja*." The comrade nods. "Last year I met the Brussels flight, which is the last international service into Tempelhof. Specht was in front taking a delivery of drinks."

I sit absorbing this till exploding vistas make the conversation sputter and fade. One vista in particular becomes a goal: a sphinxlike figure alone at the head of a banquet table, in the middle of a monumental salon—elegantly deceased.

Yes: the furniture of my death is here assembling. You might think such an uplift of hope works against the interests of suicide. No. I can tell you from here that it has the opposite effect—pressure to get on with it. All my ties are cut, I'm a wraith in waiting. Because, though it may have escaped you in these musings so far, with all my talk of this disconnection or that—the fact is that only one thing underlies a death.

And that is an absence of love.

An absence which I have in abundance.

After some last words between the men, we bid each other goodbye and disperse into the night. Turning back the way I came, I note that Grand Sneer is now Grand Seer, Swine World is

Wine Mounts. When a taxi rounds the bend at Zionskirchplatz, I fight an urge to hail it to Tempelhof and sit watching the building till dawn. Because the possibility now exists that Specht has a venue unlike any in the world, unlike any in history. A kilometer-long monument where planes fly to the door.

I shiver imagining it.

In light of this breakthrough—because possibility lifting its skirt can still be called a breakthrough, even more so when it serves a desperate hope—I snort no lines and drink no drinks. I carefully walk to the phone, looking both ways for the tram.

But in Tokyo there's a problem. Smuts doesn't come on the line. The duty sergeant has a lot to say, but I don't know what it is. When I repeat Smuts's name he answers more insistently, and when I try to read out the Kastanienhof's number he just gives the same answer louder.

In the end, with both of us grunting, he hangs up.

I don't know what to think. Perhaps it's already too late—though Smuts did say that weeks can pass before charges are laid in Japan, and I suppose charges are the next possible hammer blow. When I try the interpreter's number it goes to voice mail, so that in the end, for peace of mind, I have to decide that Smuts simply used up his morning's phone privilege. I should get some sleep, set off early to Tempelhof, and call from there with more concrete news. It'll be the same day in Japan. And perhaps in the meantime the sergeant will report that I called.

Just look at my lively schemes. Watch the human mind weave perfect sense from chaos and failure, turning mysteries into contraptions where one thing leads fruitfully to another, till a problem has been tunneled clean through. Such is the fantasy of control. For one thing, it's a lie from children's literature, perpetuated by weary parents, that sleep must bring refreshment. Because it doesn't. In my situation a child would better have a nice wine and a cigarette, and play cards with his parent, than sleep.

Obviously that would be a hippie parent.

For me the short night passes like an itch, till I'm forced to crispen a nimbus with substances. While it's still dark outside I sup a full poet's breakfast of seven cigarettes, three lines, and half a bottle of Marius. As it's such a big day I also shampoo my rusty mop, letting the shower jet pummel my spine. I blow-dry my head, and sprinkle myself with Jicky. Then I sprinkle myself again to widen the aura into a net, against the pitiless mesh of which the arch-profligate Specht will fall helpless.

While birds make good their callous agenda, I wrap a bottle of *Symphony* in a laundry bag and head for the mystical airport, struggling to expel an image of Smuts hanging from the ceiling by his belt. In the end I'm unsuccessful at this. Other notions unsettle me, swarms of them, and as the U-Bahn train nears Tempelhof, I'm forced off a stop early, afraid that the doors might open onto Specht's office.*

I stumble back to the earth's surface and find myself in Kreuzberg, at the foot of a long avenue. This seems a realistic part of town. A working part, still with its sights, its curiosities and bars, but also with older people, with more Turks and fewer babies. Its stately buildings are less recently refurbished than Prenzlauer

---

* Sleep depletion has a fragmentary effect on notions. See how they can shatter into swarms of notionettes, till in the end I'm not so much dealing with an image of Smuts hanging as trying to banish the urge to discover the Japanese word for belt, in case I can recall it from among the sergeant's words. This is too dramatic and roundabout a way to experience concern for Smuts. If you encounter this: back to bed.

Berg's, its shops less inhabited by concepts and whims, given more to the everyday.

While I finish a cigarette at the intersection of two broad avenues, Yorckstrasse and Mehringdamm, the Enthusiasms toss me a choice. On one side of Yorck sits a Burger King; and on this side of Mehringdamm, a couple of doors up, is a secondhand clothes shop. Both have implications.

It's the way of the Enthusiasms to work like this.

Burger King might ballast me for the crucial day ahead. But after a moment's consideration I feel the charity shop must be the right choice, and as I move to the window the reason unfolds in this question: which of these clothes would Specht wear? What type of decadent is he? A garrulous Peter Pan? A brooding Dr. No? I enter the shop, which is the largest charity shop I've ever seen, and look across rack after rack of old fashions, including uniforms, fancy dress, leather and latex. Because whatever Specht's nature, it must be true that any mogul would be unimpressed with an ex-weasel in a military greatcoat. It's a serious matter, and an interesting thing happens that leaves me frozen under the spell of a revelation: in wondering what to wear, I realize I'm asking who I am. Who is this sphinx in his limbo? How does a phantom dress for his business? Because in the midst of all this laundry my clothes are suddenly wrong. They belong on a person I no longer am. In a time and place I no longer haunt.

Like waves, revelations break in sets, and the next one knocks my thoughts back to center: while I can reflect on who I might be, and take the risks I must in being him, I should focus most on appealing to Specht. If he's a contemporary of my father, for instance, and was friends enough to open a club with him, he must also have been a beardie with bad taste. But then: decadence comes from overabundance. And a club on the scale of the largest building in the world, or even the second or third largest, speaks of flamboyance and self-love, of acumen and admiration of risk.

All my powers of judgment are tested. I stand scowling between racks till my only resort is a simple process of elimination:

First and easiest to disqualify—clubbing clothes. Because just as a good drug dealer won't be a user, a club owner won't be a clubber, and may even despise his clients. I consider evoking Specht's East German roots, which means bland and ill-fitting clothes. Completely wrong, because his ascent to magnate suggests he won't recall his roots very fondly. Everyday business wear—no, because that's what his suppliers will wear. Black mogul-wear—possible, though such a man will have either an ego or a compensating mechanism for low self-esteem, in either of which cases he might despise his look-alike. Gangster wear holds some promise, though I must remember I'm a returning child already known to him, so any attempt at menace is crippled from the start.

I'm exhausted by it.

The morning marches on till I've eliminated all options but one—a wild card which I can't even find arguments for, let alone against.

I finally leave the shop as Die Sphinx.

Die Sphinx wears a Bavarian Miesbacher coat—short, gray, with staghorn buttons—over a shirt embroidered with edelweiss flowers and alps. A whoosh for Specht. A risqué counterpoint to his laser-light world, a Volks-comment, a gesture, an irony, sailing close to the breeze without invading the absurd, the border of which, in this instance, I judge to be lederhosen.

I manage to avoid the traditional Miesbacher hat with its feather ornament until the shopkeeper explains that in Bavaria the hat is the sign of a free man. As a truly free man I must buy the hat, though it stays in the laundry bag with my old clothes—because mine is an occult freedom.

Ah, the protocols of limbo. These locomotions propel me light-headed and sweating to a bar up Mehringdamm, where a beer rebuilds strength. Strangely a line isn't called for. After this my walk to Tempelhof is up an incline, not steep but long, which becomes a kind of ascent to Castle Dracula. It seems impossible that an airport will be here in the middle of town, much less one of the world's greatest structures; but as the avenue steepens, a curious limbo develops in the space of a block, where clouds swirl lower and grayer, buildings cower back from the road, and businesses catering to any sort of comfort melt away, forming a cappuccinoless no-man's-land between Kreuzberg and Tempelhof where no charming persons gather, nor baby carriages, nor birds.

I half expect circling bats.

A block farther up there's still no sign of a monument, and I feel mounting pressure to call Smuts. The morning has come and gone. Avoidance is seeping into the calling routine, despite my best intentions. It's because the calls have fallen victim to reality-creep. The brainatelle has fallen victim to it, and the delicacy of Smuts's situation means I'm not using the force I should in harmonizing it with grim fact. For instance, I'd be overjoyed to call with news about any kind of club at all; whereas Smuts would feel I'm already late with a contract. Our different backgrounds partly account for this—he's a man of international networks which he swings across like a monkey, networks of alleys behind kitchens where the bidding of genius is done. He assumes I'll spark opportunities as he does, pluck him from one alley to another across the world.

Whereas I never had networks, or bidding. Or genius.

Well: I once had an alley.

We've also become separated on a graph—look at it: he's forced to live high above chaos in a stratosphere of hopes and dreams, while I'm here on the floor, grinding away at small, hard-won victories. Between us we form a chart of all existence. Every day of limbo is suddenly a working model of life.

Pausing to straighten my staghorns, I realize we've even come to illustrate the Master Limbo's engine: see how its milking action uses daydreams to lure our grasping up from horror. And now I must follow its example. I must milk the wanton Specht. Instead of harmonizing Smuts with the facts, I must lift reality to meet his needs. One explosive performance is all it might take to equalize fact with the brainatelle.

Pulling myself together, I sweep up the last few meters of the incline and finally reach the crest, where I stop dead.

My breathing slows, and deepens.

The hulk of the old airport slams into view across a small memorial garden. It doesn't fully unfurl its scale, but rather teases above trees. No vast grounds attend it, no acreage of parking; it stands beside the sidewalk like a sudden mountain range. With growing wonder I walk a block in each direction, struggling to gain a sense of its mass. Hitler's monolith hugs an airfield within semicircular wings which are a rhythmic arc of towering sand-stone slabs and cascading glass ribbons that stretches out of sight in both directions, ending who knows where, probably Poland. Clean, resolved, symmetrical; a deco behemoth, a beautiful, untouchable thing, surely impossible to erase from the landscape. And jutting from the bottom of her arc toward me, at the junction of Tempelhofer Damm and Columbiadamm, stand two quadrangles of sandy buildings, as big as hospitals each, that make up her raptor's talons; tiny within the scheme of the whole, but forming between them a parking lot and entrance square where the legend "Zentral Flughafen" perches above main doors.

Last night's locals were wrong; she could fit a thousand clubs.

From here I see no movement around the buildings, as if their gravitational force repelled anything smaller than a church. Then, setting out across the small parking lot, I eventually spy two men loitering by the entrance. Their clothes recall old freighters and tugboats, and billow tersely, no doubt from gravity. They watch along with stone eagles that scowl off the walls as I mount a few steps and pass inside. The glass doors rattle to equalize pressure behind me. Then stillness. A narrow stone lobby stretches left and right of me, empty of souls. Two *Terrorist Wanted* flyers are taped to a wall. And ahead a chamber unfolds to the size of a cathedral, a titanic expanse set down some more steps, with sailplanes hung from its ceiling. Down the left of it sit empty glass locales, and along the right a neat row of check-in desks, seeming like miniatures from here, and all empty but one, where a girl slumps onto an elbow. If it weren't for glass plunging between elegant ribs, and light flooding through recesses high above, the concourse would make a tomb for someone Cleopatra would have served on her knees.

After a moment there comes a soft click-click-click: an old woman appears up the steps with a little dog on a leash, as if on her Sunday promenade. The dog wears a red coat, and trots clicking along beside her.

"*Tag*," she says in passing.

I nod. "*Guten Tag.*"

At the distant end of the concourse a globular gentleman

is sweeping, and when he sneezes—*kaff, kaff*—the sounds flap lazily through the air toward me. I stand frozen by the place; and this is but one room in a structure that curves for more than a kilometer left and right of me. A terrace of cathedrals in a single construction so empty and still that you can hear a terrier's claws on the floor.

Specht takes on new proportions.

I shiver.

Rather than hike all the way to the gentleman or the check-in girl, I turn back to ask the men outside about the club. Then on my way through the lobby I spy a handful of empty bar tables to the right. They face a kiosk window which appears to be open. As I approach, a woman's voice drones out:

"Look at this one coming if you want a laugh."

Then another: "Pff—little Ludwig. Looks like he escaped from *The Sound of Music*."

Nearing the window, I see that it's a tiny Imbiss, purveying the driest kinds of cakes and rolls and the least colorful confectioneries. Glass cabinets on each side of a cubbyhole feature soft drinks, beer, and curling souvenir stickers.

A woman leans heavily at the back, arms folded. She's dark-haired, in gaunt middle age, her features molded by inconvenience and bitter fate. After a moment a younger, smaller woman moves past into a back room.

"*Entschuldigung.*" I ask the Frau: "Is the Pego Club here somewhere?"

She looks me up and down without moving her face.

"Someone said it might be here. Or a certain Herr Specht—is he known here?"

"Hnf," she grunts. "If we're to list everyone who's known here we won't reach the letter B by Christmas. Better idea: you look and tell me if you see any Herren around."

"Well"—I glance up and down the lobby—"not just now, no."

"So, then."

"Hm." Miserable cow. Remembering that there can be a certain sport to rudeness in Berlin, I bide a few moments, then try a different tack: "Do you have coffee?"

She turns her back.

"If not coffee, I'll have—"

"One?" she snaps over a shoulder.

"One what?"

"Coffee."

"Ah—yes, yes. *Bitte*."

"Then you'll have to ask the attendant." She disappears into the back room.

Seeing ashtrays on the tables, I pull out a stool and light a cigarette, now fascinated with the woman's insolence, which is on as grand a scale as the building itself. I hear sniggering from the back room, and a moment later the other figure emerges, which is a girl, also dark-haired, and stern in her face.

"*Mit Milch*?" She goes to a push-button machine.

"No, thank you very much."

"Pff," she scoffs.

Now some other nuance of my person has struck a wrong chord. I follow her with a frown: "Excuse me—did I say something wrong?"

"I haven't given you anything yet."

"What?"

"I haven't given you anything and you thank me. Is that how you are in Austria?"

"I'm English." I move to the window.

"One euro forty."

Now vexed with the pair, who must be mentally deficient, I slap down the coins and take my coffee to the table. After a moment the older woman emerges from a door along the wall, clacking past me to the entrance. Through a window I follow her bobbing head down the steps outside. When I glance back to the kiosk I find the girl watching me. She drops her gaze and switches on a small transistor radio. Music echoes out from that evergreen wavelength only ever found by older drivers.

After tidying behind the glass for a few moments, she finally looks up: "What business do you have with Herr Specht?"

I gulp my coffee: "Do you know him? I'm an old friend."

"Friend?" She examines me. "I don't think so."

"Look, can you just tell me—"

"I haven't seen him. He probably won't come till after four."

"Four? This afternoon?"

"Pff—did I say something else?"

Whoosh. She vanishes into the back.

Against all logic the news sends me to the restroom for a line. I set my teeth grinding with positive stress before heading to a phone booth on the street. While it's too early to report the situation's full potential to Smuts, and I caution myself to keep things low-key, still I'm excited to let him know I found our man.

A different officer answers the phone in Tokyo. Then comes a lifeless monotone:

"It's late, Putain."

"Smuts—I found him."

"Yeah, listen, the fish tests came back, uh. Negligible toxin.

They say I must've milked offal for weeks to get enough to hurt the old guy."

"Eh? Those fish were deadly. We tasted them ourselves."

"Not the ones Tomo substituted. See where things are headed? They're saying it had to be deliberate. The lawyer's been here all day. This morning he was softening me up for an assault charge. Now he's talking attempted murder and asking for a check."

"But wait—I witnessed the substitution."

"And I suppose you've got a fish to prove it. Without the original fish it's immaterial, we're two wasted tourists against a local institution. You wouldn't believe the moves going on right now. Suddenly Tomo's in Okinawa and can't be reached, the boss is naming the new restaurant after the mayor, the Basque changed his trading name in Japan. Big fucking chess game going on right now."

"But Smuts—"

"The Basque's in a phone conference with the boss, then he's calling me. And d'you know what I figured out, you there, Putain, full of coke because I can hear you sucking it down your throat? I figured this out: he's deciding who to sacrifice. He's talking to us both, then he can either stick with me and drop Yoshida in shit. Or he can go with Yoshida and fuck me off. And d'you know what? Yoshida buys a hundred covers of produce from him every week. And I buy none."

"But wait—who's to say he won't supply you here? I found the place, found the man. It might end up a better proposition than Japan. Look, in a few hours I'll be—"

"Wake up! I've just said it's happening now! And nobody's just strolling out of the way! Putainel! Cunts are running!"

My hands twitch. Along with my nose and heart they go

numb with a cold that squirts from inside. It's a hallmark squeeze
from the Master Limbo. Within a second I feel carefully guarded
hopes rush up my throat:

"Smuts—the place is over a kilometer long."

"Uh?" The line hushes to a crackle. "Fuck off—you went to an
airport by mistake."

"It is an airport. Hitler's airport from the thirties. Once the
biggest building in the world. Most impressive chunk of architecture you'll ever see. Virtually empty. Over three million square
meters in the heart of Berlin. Planes fly to the door."

There follows a silence only broken in my mind by the sound
of tumbling balls.

"You wanted awesome," I add, and as I say the words they
echo through me like fireworks—because all I've just said is basi-
cally true, and all of it describes a venue more splendid than any
since the fall of Rome.

Here, my friend, is the place of my death.

"Fuck," Smuts eventually hisses. "Tell me again, I'll write it
down for Didi." He repeats each detail in a whisper, jotting so
hard that I actually hear his pencil striking paper: "A mile long,
thousand clubs, district of—can't spell that, can't spell that—Berlin
airlift, millions of meters, jets to the door."

With each scribbled hope I feel the Master Limbo throw a
spell over us both, Smuts for his salvation and me for my demise.

"Mate," he says, "it looks sensational on paper. Putain, Gabriel.
You sure about all this? Think of it in dining terms—how many
tables fit into a kilometer? Jesus Christ. The Basque'll cream himself. Listen, I'll get off the phone, he's about to call. But give me
a number to reach you, I'll put you down as the contact. Call me
again later, uh? And Putainel—thanks. I mean it."

I hear him softly whistle as the line goes dead. Then I stand for a while with the phone pressed to my ear, boggling under a granite sky, teasing myself with glimpses of the building at a distance through trees.

It seems the cone of this endeavor is at its point. Its end-play.

The moment calls for many cigarettes lit one off the other.

Because I must whip up great forces of nimbus.

I must milk the mogul Specht.

And then I must die.

Whoosh.

Hm.

14

Cocaine, tobacco, and daylight are an honest mix, three of very few honest things in nature,* and known to reset priorities in a realistic way.

First of all, my clothes are wrong. My appearance should make Specht hope the bank is still open, not wonder how the lyrics go to "Edelweiss." I hurry back down Mehringdamm to the clothes store, where I find a retro-stylish suit, a black one which gives me an older air; and as a decadent flourish I add a gray faux-fur overcoat, which also serves as a buffer against the object world. Thus insulated from horror, I wander the streets of Kreuzberg until four, setting off along Yorckstrasse with my swollen laundry bag. I think about eating, and actually enter three places to eat; but in the end only have coffee and lines, trying to sharpen myself to a lethal point. A hyper-genius is what I try to become, a cutting torch of reasoned determination; and strangely, although tremors

---

* You might conceive arguments against this, but no. A tiger is fluffy and will kill you. A snake is designed to be invisible until it strikes. This is nature.

and grinding of teeth attend it, I do soon possess a mercurial acumen and find myself winging decisions with ease.

The first comes on Yorckstrasse, as I'm passing a video store whose storefront isn't occupied by videos but by a golden Labrador snoozing on a beanbag. Hardly an embassy of the Master Limbo. The dog seems oblivious to profit and loss. I decide to find quieter residential places to roam, where capitalist spirit might be less brutally snubbed.

Duly rounding the next corner, I find myself on Grossbeerenstrasse, a graceful street where decisions come as plentifully as leaves tumbling up her curbs. Here I decide to throw out the notion of reality-creep. Because in reality we have a kilometer-long venue. We have the debauchee Specht. Therefore things are bright. At worst I'll forgive my father's share in return for a month's trial of decadently themed banquets, which Smuts would oversee. Didier Le Basque could provision them, and I could handle their publicity and front-of-house. Specht could hardly disagree. It's a windfall for him, and finding clientele would be as easy as handing flyers to his patrons as they left the club in the small hours. Enticements could also appear on bar menus, drink coasters and the like. Masquerades, lobster tails.

I stop as the truth blows in: my wishes are being delivered.

The first banquet will be my farewell.

Whoosh—the Enthusiasms. See how their cone spiraled to a point in the city of my free childhood, home of last innocence. What an end-play. And what a high note to leave on, seeing Smuts and Specht off on a grand new venture.

Just look at all the symmetry.

Grossbeerenstrasse is an everyday street, some of whose late nineteenth century buildings are unrefurbished. One is under a scaffold, and a couple of doors past it sits a bar: the Piratenburg. A sign in the window reads "Smoking," and I duly step inside, where an affable West Berliner pours me brandy and coffee and lights my cigarette across the bar. A pair of older locals hunch alongside me, and after nodding to them I turn my hyper-acute mind to the question of the farewell banquet.

Now, well: the artifact of my life is poor, let's agree. Of dismal quality, ludicrous to celebrate. A wasted life. Still, and here's the crux of my message to you across these strange days, these earnest pages, and the crux of my limbo itself:

Inside me were unexpressed forces.

Because surely self-respect comes not from what we do, but from what we *feel we could do*. It's this reserve power, these unseen strengths that I will toast farewell. Forces within us like the gases of the sun, whose burn we occasionally feel, whose barbarous and perfect edge we sometimes see at play in a nimbus; whose wholesale unleashing might have led us anywhere but where we are.

Forces weakly called potential when a child dies.

Forces which are the only part of me I will miss.

Because look at it, my friend: all that has ever been called love of life, is a love of things that won't happen.

A love of dreams.

And so I will toast unspent forces in both of us. I will toast and shed a tear for all that we were not. For this reason, and not for simple exuberance, our farewell dinner should be as splendid as anything since the fall of Rome. A Feast of Trimalchio. A night of the *Satyricon*. A limbo that burns all restraint, a cone of nimbus so high and clear that stars are sucked inside it. There, last intimate comrade, we will live. There we will rise up, free for once from our cage, in honor of all that we were not.

But could have been.

I stifle a tear. It's nearly four. Although the host isn't looking my way, something draws him over to ask if I need more brandy. I take another quick glass and find that it has a parachute effect, cushioning my fall to composure. Then, maybe sensing that I came from nowhere in particular, and might be headed nowhere nearby, the man offers to mind my laundry bag while I wander. I thank him, and pull out a bottle of *Symphony* to carry in a pocket.

"For a friend," I explain.

"Lucky friend," he says.

Afternoon sun lights the town outside, and I walk to the end of the street where a waterfall tumbles down a storybook parkland hill. A languid society dots the space between trees, chirruping and clapping that distant soundtrack of all parks, where hybrid dogs with bandannas meet apartment dogs straining to escape from huffing Fraus, and one lonely hippie with a bongo shows the world why he's lonely. On top of the hill stands an impressive monument like a church spire, and I climb to it, not wanting to meet Specht too early and seem too keen. As I climb I ponder why I'm suddenly so full of nourishing feelings. So full, perhaps, of life. I have every reason to fret, and crucial tasks to perform; but instead I wander in a limbo before them, knowing they can't yet touch me. Yes—it's a limbo before them. A moment before them. How sweet life would be if all its moments were like this.

Putting it down to brandy and sunshine, I wander over Mehringdamm to Bergmannstrasse, where Berlin, so routinely gashed by history, leaks antiques from certain basements like blood from dripping punctures in her flesh. Centuries of furniture, rugs, furs, chandeliers, bronzes, china, books, music, and jewelry flow up to the street through doorways, a perpetual flea market that leaves me whirling with possibilities for the banquet. Because I'm savoring these, the walk to Tempelhof seems quicker than this morning, the neighborhood more familiar and friendlier, full of new potential.

I dab myself with Jicky as the airport looms, deciding not to hunt the Pego by myself, as poking around a kilometer of empty monolith might look suspicious. Instead I'll take some coffee with Hard-Faced Frau or the girl, and maybe if one of them softens, as Berliners can suddenly do, they might point me to the venue.

The Frau is there examining her nails when I arrive. A customer sits reading a paper, the radio crackles weather reports for the Baltic coast.

"*Ein Kaffee, bitte?*" I ask at the counter.

Frau looks up slowly, halting her gaze on my suit. In any other person this would come with a comment, a raised eyebrow. But she just stops and stares. It's a subtle attachment of scorn. I already quite dislike Hard-Faced Frau.

"*Mit Milch?*" She eventually slumps to the coffee machine.

"*Nein, Danke.*"

I take an empty table and feel a jolt of nerves. The mission now reaches its point. *Milch Specht.* I'm glad to pause for a few moments, composing myself before the kill. Even Sauer-Frau is a minor comfort, a sort of human base camp before my ascent to Gerd Specht. Over a cigarette I'm also heartened to see that I'm not her least favorite person, as an approaching local makes her grunt and disappear at the sight of him. It makes me feel sorry for the man, a rustic, slightly moth-eaten character who would appear more at home carving marionettes by candlelight.

He turns to click his tongue at me. I tut back in sympathy. We're in a club now, of Sauer-Frau victims. Still, he waits patiently at the cubbyhole, in his late middle age, resigned, as if the kiosk itself had leeched his youth away.

"If you're lucky there's another girl in there," I venture.

"I hope so," he says, "or else we might as well go home."

Moments pass, and I reflect on the things that sap a life, here embodied in this mustard cardigan of a man with his long face, his furry ears, and scrubbing-brush mustache. Floes of skin under his eyes seem to gather weight by the minute, until finally the Frau reemerges, handing an envelope over the counter. With that she grabs her coat and leaves the kiosk, clattering past in a swirl of scent.

And so my moment comes. Seeing that she didn't soften, and before my club-mate shuffles away, I finish my coffee and turn to him for directions:

"Excuse me—would you happen to know of the Pego Club?"

"Eh? *What?*" He flinches.

"Pe-go. Pego Club."

The man stiffens, leaning in to squint at my face: "Who's this? *Mein Gott!*—it can't be little Gabriel?"

Whoosh. I turn to stone. "Herr Specht?"

His hands wave around like a minstrel. "Anna! Anna!" he calls. "Is this who came this morning? How can you say he looks Austrian? Fetch coffee!"

The girl shows herself at the counter. I suffer a passing away into nothingness, a reeling, as Specht takes my arm and settles me back at the table, sitting himself opposite.

"*Haa.*" A reedy little whine escapes his throat. "*Kleiner Dichter*—little poet! Remember? And what was the name of that rat?"

"Frederick," I hear my voice say. "The mouse."

"Frederick, Frederick. *Haa!* And what are you doing in Berlin? How long you stay?"

"Hm. Not long, I think."

"*Mein Gott.* All those years. You must be—?"

"Twenty-five."

"Twenty-five. Haa. *Mein Gott.* And still understanding German!"

And so, with nods and whines, Specht's long, yellow, carious teeth bob around till the first awkward silence arrives: that deflation of reacquaintance, when after a minute it becomes clear that all has been said.

I toy with my cup, sifting through rinds of hope in my mind. He could still be a magnate—look at Warren Buffett, an ordinary man in spite of his billions. There might still be a club, he might've passed it on to a next generation of libertine, even to a son, for all I know. This would be consistent with Berlin, with modesty, with his Eastern roots. He might be living a homage to survival, a homely retirement after his wild excess.

But then: a smell of unclean laundry wafts off Gerd Specht.

"You see the changes." He nods out through the window. "Everything clean and commercial. But Berlin's still poor. 'Poor but sexy,' that's what our mayor says. *Haa.* Of course, nothing like before reunification. That was really something, I guess you won't remember. Do you believe your father was the first Westerner I spoke to? And a week later we had a business. That's how it was. Of course, he needed a local person to sign legal papers in those days."

Gerd leans back as the girl serves coffees. Having found a topic to erase awkward silence, he chats away with that wistful vigor of older people who mostly reminisce to themselves.

"Bah, well"—he frowns—"when the wall came down, don't think everyone was here waiting to be rescued. In fact we were quite insulted. The German Democratic Republic was an idea we believed in. Many still do. Of course, like any government it had its problems. Communism is ambitious for a society, much more than capitalism, and not a fast system to arrange. But don't believe all the stories about Stasi control, it wasn't so bad. We believed in our state, and we were all in it together. Over the wall you could get a hundred types of cheese, while we could only get three—but we could only get them together, that was the main thing. That's what the West never understood. They treated us like refugees, and it wasn't that way. The collapse of the wall proved to us that they were exactly as we had thought—individualistic and arrogant. For them it was just a chance to be patronizing and to advertise global capitalism. But now look. Reunification wasn't so good for us. Don't think East Germans fell into jobs and went shopping. Even today we're treated differently."

"Still today? I didn't realize that."

"No, *ja*, it's mostly East Germans who stayed unemployed."

The theme stirs sediments in Gerd. He stops to savor them with a chew of his lip, then slaps his thick hands on the table. "So—how did you manage to find me? When you mentioned the Pego I nearly fell over!"

There comes a time in certain nightmares when it's best to find the end and let it kill you. This is such a time. I draw breath and play my only shot: "Well—my father said he left behind some unfinished business."

The words just hang between us.

After a pause, Gerd slowly nods. "So, and it's true. I never thought I'd see you again. But it's a long time ago, those were old deutschmark. Tell your father to keep his money, I couldn't take it now. Bah."

I look down into my empty cup.

"Though I admit he left me in a bad position. What he took wasn't profit, it was operating capital from the business. After a week it was a desperate situation. He didn't say where he went. The club was in my name, but there was nothing to pay the suppliers. The Pego had to close. After that I couldn't open anything in Prenzlauer Berg or Mitte, nobody would touch me. When I got married, Gisela's father helped us get started again, and we put the next business in her name."

"I'm really sorry. I didn't know that."

"Ach, don't worry. Nothing to do with you. I wouldn't have mentioned it if you didn't bring it up yourself. Young adventures from long ago."

"Well"—I look around—"you found a great home for the club."

"*Haa*—" His whine curls out of hearing range. "I mean the next little business." As he says it, the girl catches his eye from the kiosk, holding up a packet.

"How many today?" he asks her.

"Two," she says.

"Then leave the rest there, they'll be fine. My mother used to eat them after a week, so four days is fine. And how many *Würstchen*?"

"Three—plus one for Gunnar."

"Eh? But you didn't give him bockwurst? We had to get those from Kaiser's, remember, they're like sixty cents each."

"There's nothing else," says the girl.

"No, yes there is, there's wieners in the tray, look again. Anna, that's like sixty cents you give away! Next time he gets wiener.

Take the bockwurst out of sight if you see him coming around." Gerd frowns before turning to me: "Sorry—this is Anna, who helps us before taking her holidays—to where, Anna? America? A literature thing?"

"Pff." The girl gives a joyless smile. "Galápagos Islands, an ecotour. To see the giant tortoises, I've only told you ten times. Don't you remember the video, about Lonesome George? Did he look like a literary figure?"

"Ah, *ja*, the famous turtle." He nods, turning to me. "So that's Anna, and here we are. No more club. Now it's our little Café-Imbiss. Well, a kiosk, really. But soon the airport closes. We'll have to find something else. Gisela wanted a flower shop. Perhaps I would like that too. Flowers instead of coffee—*haa*."

I stare numbly at the kiosk.

"Gisela," he prompts, "my wife—who was here before."

"Ah." I nod. "Really? I'm sorry if I seemed rude."

"Ach. She has her days."

"Well. It seems a shame to close the airport."

"*Ja*, isn't it? When we arrived there was lots of hope for Tempelhof. Services were growing. For years it was doing fine—did you see the old Billy Wilder films? That's Tempelhof in the old days. Bah, but now it costs the city nine million a year just to keep the building alive. Not profitable. Also the Green Party doesn't want it. We had a vote in Berlin, even Angela Merkel wanted to keep it—but not enough Berliners came out to vote. So it closes just now. *Kaput*."

I nod at my cup, hunting words to fill this void left by plummeting Fortune.

"*Ja*, so." Gerd taps his fingers. "Tempelhof. Imbiss. Gerd Specht. If your father wants to visit, he can come. Let's forget the past. What's he doing these days?"

"Hm. Good question. He also had a café once, but it didn't last."

"Bah, food. Did he tell you we tried it in the club? Sent us crazy after a week. Mustard all on the floor. Bah. Forget it."

Ah, well. Here, posthumous friend, we descend to Fortune's most bitter, ironic crypt, its lowest one, deep beneath the Valhalla trodden by the merely blighted. Reaching this rock bottom, my heart just lies down to die. And note: though it owes its descent to a loss of hope, its terminus is a worse place still—my shame at having blustered here to get heavy with this mild and wistful Geppetto.

Ah, Gerd Specht. His little kiosk and his Frau. His transistor radio burbling evergreens. A timeless portrait of all that redeems a cardigan and makes it heartbreaking.

I doubt I've felt so low in my life.

"So." He rises with a grunt. "Time to clean the mighty Imbiss, it won't clean itself—*haa*."

I hoist myself after him, ready to slink away. New images come of Smuts hanging from a ceiling by his belt. And in the midst of this stifling ballet, Gerd pauses, looks at me, and says with a gleam in his eye: "Oh, but Gabriel—if you're still around on Friday, I invite you to a special party. Something you can't believe. And with some real food. Here at Tempelhof, in the evening. Well, you might be busy—but you're welcome if you'd like to come."

"Thank you." I slide some coins across the table for my coffee.

"Bah." He waves them away. "My contribution to the arts. I hope you're still doing your poetry? And tell your father to call if he likes. Pego Café-Imbiss—I even kept the name, for old times' sake."

I smile sadly at Gerd. "I never asked Dad what Pego meant."

"It's how Paul Gauguin sometimes signed his work." He checks for Anna before lowering his voice: "An old English sailor's word for cock—*haa!*"

Watching his cardigan hover into the kiosk, I wonder if there was ever a youth, in the sense we know it, in Gerd Specht's life. Would his "special party" throw new light?

Who knows? It doesn't matter now.

I'm almost out the door when I remember the bottle of Marius, and turn back to present it to him through the cubbyhole.

Gerd takes it, beaming like a grandfather: "*Nein!* For me? Too much!"

At this instant the radio launches into John Denver. "Annie's Song." Gerd freezes, looking down at the bottle. I watch his face grow taut with feeling, and I turn and walk away, buffeted by sentiments from this most cloying of songs.

A cloud of pathos and shame follows me from the building. In my ridiculous suit, with my fur. I turn to see Gerd's loose-fitting hand wave goodbye from the kiosk, and it stirs me like a wave from a train of children fleeing war.

Then I slither out of the monolith.

Outside, all is massive and built of stone. None of it will ever move again. The sky is still, and newly clouded. Trees without leaves are black against it. They don't move either. And beneath them, in a space the size of a bathroom, lies Gerd Specht's world.

The real world.

Trudging down Mehringdamm, I know what I must do. Whether under a train, or off a bridge. Whether by poison or drowning. It doesn't matter. After collecting my bag from the Piratenburg, I find an Internet café and immerse myself in helpful information, to cement my mood, to install the right mindset.

The Web is useful in this respect, even throwing up academic papers from a seminar entitled "Death, Decay & Disposal after Post-Modernity." Among the papers are some succulent gems which I read like holy scriptures, even mouthing the words to myself, themes such as "Stillbirth: An Argument in Favor by the Aged and Dying" and "Beyond Hygiene: Crematoria and Cremation as Statements of Post-Facto Suicide." I wallow with these and other morsels until I'm a clean machine, empty of whim and desire.

I don't know what to tell Smuts. Probably best not to call. Rather I should dial my father and call him a cunt. Because once again my future founders on the wreckage of his selfish past. My situation stinks of his being here before me, him and a generation of larcenous babies that never grew up.

A state accompanies hopelessness which removes the urge to even drink. A sort of kill switch, I suppose. I pass the bars on Mehringdamm without stopping, pass the curry-wurst stall over Yorckstrasse where patrons stoop against the chill with their *pommes* and wurst and beer. And from here I take a cab to the Kastanienhof, where I lie blank-faced on my bed, watching nothing happen in the sky through the window. The Enthusiasms have shown their hand. An end-play indeed. This was them removing obstacles to death, bursting the hopes that are most ludicrous in retrospect; the ones that are always last hopes. I pull out my notepad and pretend to scribble some last tips and anecdotes from limbo. These very notes, in fact. But thinking about them, maybe they don't matter either. You'll be the only judge, unless they're crushed under the wheels of a train, or washed down the River Spree.

It turns dark outside. At some point the phone rings in my

room. It takes me a few moments to identify the ringing, and when I locate the receiver I find Smuts on the line:

"Gabriel," he hisses.

I sit up. Hearing my given name is rarely a good sign.

"Listen carefully—I'm on the lawyer's mobile. Take down this number, we won't be able to talk anymore."

"What?"

"His name's Satou, take the number."

I rummage under the sheets for my notepad.

"The case is going to shit—but listen, the Basque's hooked on your venue, hooked like a fish. Not on my original plan but on some event of his, probably one of his high-end deals, maybe even a banquet. His ears pricked up big time, uh. Naturally I told him it was our club, he had to work through us—you know, son of the founder, decadent situation, et cetera."

"Hm—well, actually I've some bad news on that front."

"He's always looking for rare venues, hunting the unicorn, and I told him everything you told me, kilometers long, planes to the tables, et cetera. I've never heard him so quiet, fucking incredible, just listening, and hey—"

"Smuts—"

"No, listen, listen—if it turns out to be for one of his banquets, he'll sacrifice Yoshida in a second. He lives for those events, I'm telling you. Keep your fingers crossed. Fuck, you wouldn't believe where my head's at, I'm living in dog years over here. It's like being nailed to the fucking wheel of Fortune. My head's raw from the little rubber clacker thing!"

"The what?"

"You know—on the wheel of Fortune. The thing that clacks over all the pegs. The money, the sofa, the fridge-freezer."

"I'm not sure Fortuna's wheel has the clacker thing. Not as classically described."

"Shh, anyway, listen—one last job and we're home safe: the Basque wants you to meet a man there. A trusted German contact of his, just to confirm what you've got."

"Smuts—there is no club."

"Not an interview, not a pitch. Just a drink, and talk to the guy, who's local, and he can give Didi the thumbs-up. I've given him your number, so stay by the phone, those boys will move fast."

"There isn't a venue. It ended up being a kiosk."

"It's a first contact, that's all. Only fair to get a local opinion. And you'll have an excellent drink, Didi's people are always high-flyers. Rich boys, most of them, seriously decadent. But listen: you'll have to play him like a fish. Dress the part, play it cool."

"The club's gone. There's only a kiosk."

A ball finally rolls in the brainatelle: "Uh?"

"A kiosk."

"What? Kilometers long?"

"It fits three people, standing."

"*What?* What are you saying? Putain?"

"I'm sorry."

"No, no, listen—don't pull my chain, uh? All you have to do is tell the man what you told me. Never mind three people—tell him what you told me, exactly. Uh?"

"The problem is—"

"No! No problems! Did you make the building up?"

"No, but—"

"Then meet the fucking man! Tell him what you told me!

Shift the game to the next level. You have to do it. And find a fucking venue, borrow one for a day, do something. Gabriel!"

"But have they just abandoned the investigation altogether?"

A pause hisses down the line. "Putain—the old guy didn't make it. He passed away in the night. They're moving me to a prison. This is for real now."

15

I stir in the early morning still clutching my notepad. Bird cries pelt the window on nature's behalf, designed as they are to trumpet her rule. Babies must also be waking in their boxes, hungering together with businessmen and bankers to assert their tyrannical grip.* How is it, I wonder, that those creatures most given to puffing themselves up and crowing their worth revere the early morning? Surely such behavior shows not an ascent but a descent, from civilization to crude zoology, there to join strutting cockerels and gorillas beating their chests.

In fact differing only in that gorillas save on the suit and tie.

Raising myself onto an elbow, I go to work on a booger turned

---

* No better evidence exists of nature's trickery than childbirth. Witness the towering arrogance of new mothers for proof that nature uses Rohypnol-like drugs to achieve her ends. Watch them unleash a teat in a café, control the width of a busy sidewalk with a carriage—because in their drug-addled minds they bear not cousins of apes but tiny superiors of infinite entitlement, whose eminence bathes them by association. If it weren't a deranged phenomenon, why would nature trick us into it? Why don't we find the blissful dell of family by a process of reasoning? Because there is no blissful dell. Only the stranglehold of callous nature.

hard in my nose. After painstaking excavation I manage to pull out a diamantine latticework sleeve, a perfect little cast of my nostril, still candied with cocaine and set with tiny rubies of blood.

I pop it into my mouth and jolt into the day.

Feelings and schemes load inside me, but I find them a turbulent mix, calling for decisions and bravery. Again we see inverse proportion at work, demanding maximum bravado at the point of least hope. Ah, these wretched cones. What's clear is that I must die before this wormhole of a cone gets any deeper or darker. Before another morning like this one comes jeering. I fall back onto my pillow, exhausted with it all, and for some reason as I start to doze I'm visited by an image of my mother, as best I remember her gangling softness and quick, humble eyes. There she is, grinning through a crowd of teeth, in the days before learning that her husband's whims counted for more than her, for more than us, before learning that a pressing, unfinished matter would pull him away, and that the unfinished matter was simply his childhood. There she is before all the things she was raised to care about were no longer fashionable, before they were scorned because scorn sold more products, before she herself was scorned for having no greater ambition than to fill a house with love. There she is, that beautiful soul, smiling.

In the moment before it all turned to dust.

In the moment before dismay.

In the moment before.

How I wish I could hug her. What I wouldn't give to hug her now, that smiling, woolly person. And how important are the hugs we never had. Because some things do matter. Some things matter very much.

While others don't matter at all.

My eyes grow hot, and I wrest myself back to the moment. I must speak to Smuts's contact. Perhaps he'll be satisfied with a few vagrant words, a promise of something in progress. Anyway, death is a moment away if things get too hard. I could leave a sworn statement about the fish. I could attribute my death to the injustice of it, or even take the sword on Smuts's behalf, avenge the old man in the Japanese way. Make the ignoble noble, trade suicide for hara-kiri. All these myriad tools are at my disposal. All these countless devices, numbering one, which is death.

Still, these hopeful flurries don't quell my main concern: that the call will be a date with the Master Limbo. And though I've wished for as much since reaching Berlin—the Master now wants something from me which I don't have; and I can only imagine how it deals with nonpayment of its wants.

I reach off the bed for my kit bag and pull out a bottle of wine. A palliative therapy. *Simpatico* I choose, as the name seems more fitting before breakfast. But I've barely emptied the neck of it when the phone starts to ring. I light a smoke before answering.

"Good day," says a man in German. He has a soft, crisp, well-modulated voice. "It seems we have friends in common."

I wait quietly on the line until he adds: "And according to one of them, unless I have a death wish, I should avoid drinking with you. Could it be true? I like the sound of that. Will I pick you up in, say, an hour?"

"Ahh—hallo," I reply. "But I'm afraid I'm engaged just now. Perhaps we could meet another time? Or I could give you a call?"

"Unsatisfactory. Because I understand we might also have an interest in common—and we need to establish in the very short term whether we do or don't have that interest. Though we can deal with one preliminary question right away, which is: I presume you know that certain public parts of the interest in question can be legitimately hired from the city for private functions?"

"Hm? Of course," I lie.

"Good, good. Then we're talking about something out of public bounds. Something, shall we say—extraordinary. Something 'awesome,' as our friend in Tokyo puts it."

"You could say that."

"Excellent. I think I can guess what you're proposing—and if it's what I hope it is, I'm impressed. I salute you. Actually, from the moment I heard where you were staying I reported to our man in Paris that things felt good. You know how he is about discretion. It shows real discipline to keep this business out of the Hotel de Rome or the Adlon—you must be dying up there with the cappuccino communists, you must be sick of the sight of pasta. It definitely calls for a drink. But can we at least say this evening? We must move quickly, our friend will be waiting for a call."

"May I ask who's speaking?"

"It's not important on the telephone, I'm sure you understand. For now it's your friend in Berlin. Can we say nine o'clock? In front of your hotel? You'll know who I am. We can be candid in person, it's tiresome playing cold war on the phone. I'll look forward to our drink, very much. It's been a while since I plugged into—the network."

"Ah—the network. Yes."

"And you know—I sense this could be its finest hour."

After bidding the man goodbye, I sit for a moment watching smoke curdle the light between curtains. And when I finally replace the phone I can't help but shake my head. Ah, Smuts and his culinary al-Qaeda. Smuts and his kitchen KGB, with its shadowy myrmidons. Who knows when any of them find time to cook or eat amid intrigues? They probably spend their time at Burger King, plotting overthrows. I take a long draught of Marius, settling back to ponder it all. But after a while my mind starts to boggle. The realization dawns that Smuts's fate may really hang on this underworld, or overworld as it more seems. His plight is far from a purely legal one, tainted as it is by commercial interests. It's natural to imagine those interests holding the key to his release. But to the extent that I can even help, my problem is twofold: firstly, no deal to free him is actually offered. It's only implied, and then only by Smuts. Which makes it a chess game, of wholly unspoken interests, between strangers meeting over a venue. Secondly, and no less crucially—there is no venue. Which makes it a bluff.

And the Master Limbo will be better at that than me.

The situation is ominous and suddenly very real. Of course, if I'd had such a call at my old flat in London it would've been easy to dismiss as bad theater. London has an immune system against the ominous and resonant, probably because public servants wore us out over the years with sinister language.

But then, I'm not in London. Oblique interests do exist in the world, of sufficient scale that those who deal with them learn to behave in guarded and unusual ways. People do exist who roam in secrecy, who beat around bushes, hunting only the rarest prey. Hunting unicorns, as Smuts would say. Such people do exist.

Perhaps nowhere more than in the limbo of modern capitalism.

A chill soaks through me. I've blindly thrust a hand into its wiring, into a tangle of practices and protocols so rare and aloof that it remains unknown to all but a lofty few in the world. A comment of Smuts's comes to mind: *"I could tell you rumors about the Basque that'd make your heart stop. I know chefs who've worked on his events who simply turn and walk away when you ask them about it. They don't smile and change the subject. They don't say, 'I can't tell you.' They fucking turn and walk away."*

Whoosh. The overworld.

All I have to offer as it tightens its cone around me—is a kiosk.

And if Gerd's wife has anything to do with it—not even that.

For a moment I consider changing hotels, or putting myself under a U-Bahn train. But there's really nothing for it—if I'm committed to Smuts, I'm committed to meeting the man and painting him a castle in Spain. All the better then that he proposes a drink—I'll just paint him the necessary castle, and make the night my farewell.

With this decided, I spend the rest of the day the way a budget tourist might spend his last day alive, which calls for a sandwich in the café downstairs, followed by drinking and watching television in bed with the curtains shut. Here's a thing, though: at a certain point I could swear I feel the fabled Marius correction take place inside me. I actually pause while prehuman minerals and energies seem to flick a loose switch in my genes. And from this, perhaps also from intoxicants generally, I soon find myself preparing to meet the Master. I don my suit and fur, splash myself with Jicky, and pack a bottle of *Symphony* in a plastic bag, till at nine o'clock two things converge outside the hotel. The first is a tramp who sees the bottle and staggers up: "For me?" He reaches out. "You great, great man. You great figure."

Behind this scene comes the whine of a turbine, then out of lamplight a moment later a black Mercedes which lunges to the curb, sparkling like liquid, and sends the vagrant reeling.

I take a breath. Already I feel a hangover looming, but this needn't be bad news. Rather it might help me rehearse the lesson of maturity, and shut mostly up.* Tonight's mission doesn't call for logistics, no, no. It merely hints at a venue. After Smuts is free the truth can unfold as it will. Because let's be realistic: such a schoolyard wheeze as this can only come from that family of Smuts deals that never happen. That are replaced as quickly as they arrive, by hotels on icebergs, bistros in Baghdad—by anything from the carousel of maybes that buoys a brooding genius between smokes behind a kitchen.

Fairly wise, this approach, I feel.

Surely flowing from genome-corrected grapes.

I step up to meet the car, then falter when I see a girl behind the wheel. She looks immaculate, with hair so clean and black that it competes with the limousine for sparkle. I pull back, thinking I've mistaken a shampoo model for the kitchen overworld; but in a flash, and without a sound, the rear door swings open and a hand calls me in. Across a central console I find a trim, dark-haired man dressed in black. Perhaps forty, with the boyish good looks of an actor. "Thomas," he says with a smile, offering me his hand.

There's nothing sinister about Thomas, although he's smooth

---

* Learn to love a hangover. Nurture and adore it like sad music. This Cinderella of debauch is a hidden boon, perhaps its greatest one; because wise decisions are made there. A good hangover, a few hours into its term, brings hunger, and gratitude at survival; it resets the human condition to its default, admittedly wretched but also realistic and serene, disinclined to mayhem. It's a window from the deathbed looking back, where we wish less jarring choices had been made. Therefore make no decisions while drunk—but use the hangover to make them at your most prudent, human calibration.

and charming. I warm to him as the car surges off, pressing us back into a nest of soft leather.

"Gabriel," I reply, handing the bag across the seat.

He peers inside: "Ahh, *Symphony*—the 2004!" His face ignites, and he pauses before looking over to say: "You know—I think we're going to get along."

Another pair of eyes glances back, almond shapes in the mirror, then a button nose and a smile. "Cool fragrance," says the driver. "Jicky?"

"Bettina," says Thomas. "She has an amazing nose."

"And," she says, "you applied it just now—the citrus is strong."

I look into the mirror: "Yes, it is a beautiful nose."

And at this the ice, which anyhow was very thin, breaks in the car and we all laugh, and a sort of day breaks inside me. We motor like friends into the heart of Berlin, clear night flashing past, voices softly ticking like watches; and when occasionally Bettina's gaze appears, fantasies arise in which I master her vanity.

Surely a sign of returning hope. Ah, this insane limbo.

"So, then." Thomas takes my hand: "Tonight's agenda is simple. I have a question and a request, both of which, having seen your style, I'm sure you can easily satisfy. But let's not rush into things. If you'll indulge me, I'll savor the mystery over supper." He pauses before adding: "This may be a long night."

We reach the River Spree as it rolls under Friedrichstrasse, where the giant flags of the Reichstag ripple the skyline. The car stops beside stairs leading down to the riverside. "Grill Royal," says Thomas. "Hope it's okay for you. I'm known here, but they're discreet. Still, we'll save any serious talk until later."

Thomas's entrance into the restaurant calls a crossfire of glances, and though service is busy we're quickly assigned a table with a prime view. I watch a tourist liner glide past the window leaking mercury and gold across the gelatinous whorls of the Spree, and here, under flattering light, over linen and silver, I find a plane of well-being where I must pause, my friend, and call you in. Step close to these glowing linens, this sparkling glassware, snuffle this scent of hot food and vaporous wine, turn your ear to this elegant chatter between pleasant minds, and admit with me:

The Master Limbo gets some things rather right.

How can frail creatures resist comfort? And why should we? As wine, rustic breads, and chilled butter appear before us, these are questions we must ponder—also asking why comfort brings such poise, how it brings generosity of thought, peace of mind, how its light removes blemishes from the skin, till in the end we're as proud as shining starlets—even possibly because we're worth it.

This is the Master Limbo. Observe and contemplate.

Because suddenly the night doesn't look hard at all. Suddenly it looks like pure civilization. How absurd were my fears in light of this reality! I recall now the first and most welcome effect of the Master: putting one at perfect ease. How could I feel uneasy in such a setting? Granted, I'd feared an interrogation by a master chef or hired ruffian, but something about Thomas, his shine, his breeding, suggests he's not involved in the catering industry at all. Moreover, it suggests that as a person he isn't given to interrogations of any kind. I wonder if he's a just previous guest, or a friend of the mysterious Basque. However it might be, he seems a layman to the process, just as I am, and therefore probably thinks I know more than I do. The night simply calls for me to sit back, shut up, and observe the goings-on.

With the appearance of oysters and finger cakes of black bread, he turns to chuckle: "Did you hear about the fish, in Tokyo?"

"Hm? I was there. Tasted it myself."

"Just now—this week?" He stares, laughing. "And you're still alive? You get better and better. Tokyo, Tempelhof, Marius—I've been trying to guess your connection to Berlin, but honestly, after this I give up."

Ah, the Enthusiasms. Or could it be that I finally swim with my natural school? Has capitalism merely plucked me to where I should be? I'd never considered the world of smilers, of fluent talkers and sharp dressers, to be my school. Though I admit there's something about the habitual smiler that can make life smooth, my problem with smiles is that the markets seized them to use as fronts for sodomy. They can't be trusted anymore, for all that goes on behind them. And so I find myself in a curious position, between worlds. What different worlds they are. For instance, I trusted the scowls in Gerd's kiosk—because they promised nothing.

And then, I suppose—nothing is what I got.

Thomas catches my eye. "And is it true he entertained a girl in the tank? Your chef? When the Basque called he almost couldn't speak from laughter."

"Hm. I think it'll be a while before Smuts is laughing."

"From what I know, it's typical of Didier's boys. There must be something he can do, don't take it too hard. I'm guessing you have a similar orbit in the network as I do—arm's length, with occasional contact. Probably the safest position. At first I couldn't believe what went on. But that's just how things are at this level."

"I'm certainly in a safer position than Smuts."

Our gazes break apart, but Thomas leans in to shake my arm. "You know the Basque respects a maverick. All his best people are like that. Probably why they work so terribly together. My first event with him was at a Prussian hotel, the Schloss Neuharden-berg, a castle near the Polish border. He flew in three genius chefs and six great sous-chefs. By the end of the fish course there was a stabbing in the kitchen. And by the time the main was served, two cars were on fire and three people were missing who we've never seen again. I'm still embarrassed to return to the Schloss."

"Sounds like a police magnet." I sip some wine.

"That was definitely his last hotel event. And the last with multiple chefs-de-cuisine. After that he went underground, things got serious."

Settling into this chilled Chablis, taking our time over oysters and bread, my comfort grows with Thomas, and with the situation, till I find myself scouring my memory for anecdotes from Smuts that I can use in conversation.

"Still no less vulnerable," I say. "I mean—how do you explain a fountain of wine to a local cop?"

Thomas nods, peering over his glass. "As far as I know, he never had a problem. Well—look at the scale of venues he's used. Fountains are the least of it. And from the very beginning, an event's first and most important tool has been the warning pistol. Everything's designed backwards from that. It's a holy tradition now. The first employee is always the lookout with the blank gun. The *alarum*. And the first consideration for any venue is the evac-uation. I think it's only been tested once. They found that the shot drew attention from the evacuation to the lookout, so it actually served a double purpose. And because it's obviously a blank gun, things aren't so serious for the lookout if he's caught. Needless to say, he gets paid extra in that case."

We pick over oyster shells in their beds of ice, dip bread into puddles of seawater and lemon, bathing our fingers.

"Unbelievable planning goes into the events these days." Thomas slides a last mollusc over his tongue. "The ones I've seen, anyway. Typical Basque, he's like a rich kid doing jewel robberies."

We laugh, but as Thomas draws breath to continue I become aware of a chubby, gray-suited type swaggering over.

"Brandy!" He waves at Thomas. "Brandy-boy!"

"Werner." Thomas nods. "Get fired or what?"

"How can I fire myself, I'm the boss?" The character sits without invitation, leering around nearby tables. He doesn't greet me.

"It's a joke. Seems late for you to still be out."

"Please be gentle—I've just lost my woman."

"Oh, no, the giggly one? Or the Mexican?"

"The other one—with my home and children."

"Uff, sounds expensive—very sorry to hear it."

"Don't remind me, I'm at the Adlon a week now. She won't let me in the house. Give me some wine—let them bring another glass."

"Have mine." Thomas fills the glass with wine.

"Hear who fell down the chute from Lehman's?"

"Shh, Werner, not here." Thomas looks around.

"What? That's not news, the dealing room's full of it. Anyway, Madoff will draw the press. Meanwhile, see the back doors flying open everywhere? I hear there's even a time bomb at World Bank ticking toward 2012. Know how I know? Their back door flew open. Who knows where they'll run?"

"Depends how rich the bomb is," says Thomas. "Anyway, it doesn't concern us."

"What do you mean, it doesn't concern us? The theories end here, Brandy. These first crashes are just drops in the ocean. Try getting a phone signal in Zurich today, you won't get one—lines are totally jammed with inbound cash."

"It's a renewal, let's just say that." Thomas gently folds his napkin onto the table.

"A renewal! Back to subsistence farming, maybe. Back to fucking hunter-gathering. Let me tell you what I heard about Bank of Scotland."

"Actually, we're just leaving." Thomas rises. "This is Rufus, by the way—a friend of a friend I bumped into. I'll go splash my boots."

"Leaving already?" calls Werner. "Do I stink now?"

When Thomas doesn't reply, the interloper gets on with quaffing our wine. "Rufus," he eventually grunts. "How'd you get a name like that?"

"Don't ask me."

He pauses to stare. Then returns to munching our bread.

There's a disturbed feeling at the table. Thomas's instincts are correct. Civilization, which must be a delicate substance, even a vapor, has vanished. After minutes listening to Werner slurp like a pig, watching him help himself to the rest of our bread and wine, I make an attempt at conversation:

"Did I hear you say Brandy?"

"Yeah," he grunts. "Life's too fucking short to remember his whole name. Thomas Georg Philip Frederick Florian von Brandenburg Stendal Saxe fuck-knows-even-what-else. Needs a business card about a meter long. The *petit prince*, who never met a woman with hairs around her ass."

Thomas returns in time for this, motioning me up. "You mean, who can tell the difference between the ass of a woman and the ass of a man."

"Get out of here." Werner empties the last drops of wine, and we leave him smirking at a mother and daughter nearby.

Staff nod good night as we move to the entrance. Passing a service trolley, Thomas plucks out a full bottle of Rochelt Vogelbeere and tucks it under his arm. "Herr Bauer has invited us the bill." He smiles. "With this, to take away."

"Of course, Herr Stendal."

As we step outside, he stabs a key on his phone, and by the time we reach Friedrichstrasse the Mercedes is there.

"One downside of the business world," he says with a sigh, climbing in. "You have to be civil to assholes. Shame about supper. Unusual for Bauer to show up here, normally he's over at Borchardt. More his temperature. Took the Basque there once, bad move. The captain thought he didn't speak German, and blamed him to his female companion for a mistake with the table. Really bad form, unbelievable."

"Wages of sin," I ambiguously say; in fact not even understanding it myself.

Still, Thomas looks over. "Exactly, that's Bauer—all money, no class. Typical Berlin to bump into him, you know how it is. Twenty years since the wall, and at our level there's still only a handful of places to go. Otherwise it's pasta or kebabs. Or up where you're staying, yogurt and Bionade. Amazing you survived it."

"My luggage weighs twenty kilograms and it's all Marius."

Thomas nods before turning to me. "I like you, Gabriel."

We cruise down quiet streets, finally purring up to a baby skyscraper tucked behind buildings on Stresemannstrasse.

"Solar Club," says Thomas. "Now we'll talk."

We take vodka martinis to a smoking area, where king-sized leather beds line a wall overlooking the city. Couples and three-

somes stretch out on two of the beds, and we take a third, where
red light, smoke, and gloom give the air of an opium den. Settling in, I scan Berlin's low skyline through the glass—and after
a moment am taken in by a patch of darkness, a hole in the view
quite nearby. It looks as if an entire city block has vanished into
space. I point it out to Thomas.

"The Topography of Terror," he says. "Don't you know it?"

"Is it a park? Seems awfully dense, light doesn't even make it
in from the streets."

"That's Gestapo headquarters. Also the Prinz Albrecht Hotel,
where the SS were based. Himmler, Heydrich, Eichmann—that
was their address."

"But wasn't that all destroyed?" I crane to see into the void,
but no light escapes at all, not even a cigarette tip. It's an absolute
deletion from Berlin's twinkling map.

"Of course, but at the end of the war. Next minute the Russians arrived, and history moved on. The GDR didn't know what
to do with it. What do you do with the most evil address in the
world? Rent office space? Put a children's playground?"

"Wasn't a kindergarten built over Hitler's bunker?"

"Yeah, but that was deep underground. On top all you see is
a mound of grass. This is a whole city block of ruins. Even after
the wall fell nobody knew what to do with it. In fact the Berlin
wall still runs down one side of it, untouched. I think it's the only
section still standing. A tradition just grew of avoiding the place.
The city threw a fence around it and nature claimed it back. After
sixty-five years it's like Tarzan's jungle in there, even has lianas
growing. But underneath you'll find foundations and rubble, and
bunkers will be there, and tunnels, I guess. Still today. You can
walk out of a luxury hotel, go to a jungle in the city center, and

pick up a piece of Gestapo headquarters. Only in Berlin. You've led a sheltered life here, my friend."

"Perhaps. Though only till now, I fear."

The evening's intoxicants start to mill at the foot of the next climb, which is the trek to the high nimbal veldt, there to roam wisely under stars. I decide to press it into my service lest the evening slip from our hands.

"Smuts has been moved to prison," I say.

Thomas reclines, squinting through his martini. He idly converts "Smuts" into the German for smacking lips: "*Schmatz*," he says. "*Schmatz*—good name for a chef. Look, the Basque knows we're meeting tonight. Obviously the situation's difficult. Japan's difficult, and a little out of his territory. But he stands by Smuts. You should know that. He once told me how he found him at the Kempinski in Bruges. Did Smuts tell you? He may not have realized the impression he made."

"He has a few stories from the Kempinski."

"The Basque heard something on the grapevine and went there posing as a diner. Arrived late, demanding only *amuse-bouches*. Ten courses of *amuse-bouches* he ordered, and apparently Smuts poked his head from the kitchen to see who this French asshole was. But he didn't refuse him, or send *amuses* from the list. Instead he took a cart of ingredients to the table, grabbed the prettiest waitress, and invented little poetries on the spot. Right there at the table. And for the last one he took a sliver of fish, pulled out his cigarette lighter, and flame-cooked it hanging from his finger. He hand-fed Didier Laxalt like a baby. Can you believe it?"

"Sounds like Smuts."

"Yeah, listen, Didier doesn't tell stories about every chef he meets. He captures that kind of talent, grooms it for himself. The kind that isn't confined to the teachings of the kitchen. It's why the Basque doesn't look for Michelin stars, almost always disqualifies them. Because a star calls for consistency over a period of time. It's for the married, who can do the same thing over and over. Bu t in turning a part of their talent to the question of routine, they lower their ceiling. Basque looks for the autonomous genius, the wild and free naïf—he takes a risk, naturally, that they spectacularly fail. But when they don't, they extract from nature an experience so breathtaking that nobody can forget, or even find words to describe it. And this, I believe, is the case with our friend in Tokyo. I wanted to say it aloud so that we understand what brings us together. And so you feel reassured that he has powerful friends. Basque came from the Foreign Legion, remember. As a hard man he might laugh at a few days in jail—but he also understands brotherhood." Thomas gives me a slap on the leg. "So relax. Take heart. Nobody will let him disappear."

A flood of high feeling runs through me, a kind of hopeful determination. Ah, this Master Limbo. Peopled not by complainers or theorists, but by creatures of action.

Thomas empties his martini into his mouth, swirls it, swallows it, then catches my eye: "Which brings us to the crucial question."

His face is obscured for a moment by my upended glass. But when its liquids have gone, all savored at length, along with droplets of frost that follow them down to my mouth; and when my tongue has stopped stirring, and lays still, and the glass stands back off my lip—I find his black eyes boring through me.

"I've guessed the obvious for myself," he says. "But let's recap and understand each other. Firstly Smuts cites a decadent club at Flughafen Tempelhof. Now, as you must know, there is an old cabaret among its odd enterprises—but for the purposes Smuts describes, I discount it. And as the airport will close this month, I also discount any permanent venue. Meanwhile, you and I have agreed that certain public spaces can be hired for functions— the terminal, for example, after hours. And we both know the building comprises working spaces and historical spaces, some untouched in years." Thomas's smile begins to flicker. "So it all comes narrowing down to a point. Something which, when the Basque called for my opinion, initially made me laugh."

I feel myself pressed into a corner of the lounge.

"But after his call I thought again. I thought about the claim Smuts had made. The unbelievable claim. The frankly ridiculous claim, which was this: Smuts claimed he had several kilometers of Tempelhof Airport at his disposal."

My pulse starts to bang.

Leaning in, almost whispering, Thomas goes on: "Then, thinking about it afterwards, I called the Basque back to say there was a single conceivable chance that this could be true. One negligible fraction of possibility. But that if it *was* true, it would represent the most electrifying opportunity he and I might see in our lifetimes. And if we acted fast, the most perfect timing of anything we might ever do again. So then—Gabriel Brockwell— one small question."

My heart stops.

"Don't name it out loud," he whispers. "But do you have access to the complex? The only one Smuts can be speaking of?" He stares without blinking.

My tongue darts over my lips. I begin to nod as if conceiving of that very place, as if conjuring its picture to mind. "Yes," I finally hear a voice say.

Thomas slumps back, blinking left and right. "How the hell did you do it?"

I sit quiet for a moment. "You said only one question."

We stop perfectly still, watching each other. Then he lunges, wrestles me down, tousles my hair, punches my arm. "You star. Let's drink."

Whoosh. We ride the elevator down to the waiting car, where Thomas pulls out two fine cigarette cases, handing one to me: "Survival kit," he says. He also grabs an iPod, two sets of earphones, and the bottle of Rochelt, before setting off scampering like a boy with a kite. We fly around the corner onto Anhalter Strasse till the black hole of the Topographie des Terrors draws alongside, its woods twisted and creaking, tendrils seething out to the sidewalk. Near the block's far end, a slim no-man's-land of tall grass pushes the jungle back off the fence, and we stop here, panting. Thomas checks the street up and down, but only his Mercedes prowls some distance behind. Our attention turns to the fence, which stands lower than shoulder height, and is flimsy considering that it quarantines a kind of hell. Thomas finds a spot where it's also bowed, and shakes it. With a grunt he vaults the wire, and presses it down for me to scramble over.

We vanish from the modern day.

As we make for the heart of the wilderness, our contact with the city fades, dark presses in till we have to feel our way through the tangle. It's a setting from a witches' tale, branches writhing with filaments, roots clawing out at our feet; as if to warn us away, a wind even rises to shake the canopy overhead. Thomas shines the screen of his phone, making monstrous copses reach out, hinting of coiled snakes watching from branches and spiders as big as your head.

A fear nimbus comes from all this, but inside it I detect a core of something else, a virginal buzz that's quite intoxicating. My mind turns to wondering what, and I realize it's this: the place has cut intellect off from perception. We fly on instruments, because only the brain knows we're in the heart of a capital city—the senses have no evidence to support it, if anything being swayed the other way. This inner struggle produces its own sensual voltage, a touch of what parachutists must feel. It seems the senses distrust the brain, crudely improvised as it is by nature.

In addition to this our airways were blasted open by the run. Now we vacuum up jungle mists, and the buzz is so clean that it makes me wonder if the run was part of a plan. Looking ahead, I see Thomas lighting thickets with his phone, and I weigh the odds of his being a grand wizard of nimbus. Proof frankly mounts for it, here alone with liquor at the world's most heinous address.

"Achtung." He points out a hole up ahead.

An opening leads underground through a wreckage of vines and rubble. We stop to adjust to the dark, and after a few moments symmetries of brick and concrete appear. It's a glade amid foundations, enclosing a rug of fallen leaves. Somehow it invites us to sit, and we do, pulling up our collars and hugging our coats around us. I reflect how rare it is to see nature as untrained as this, in its purest cannibalism and chaos, with parasite upon parasite upon parasite; except of course in the free market. Shining the phone on his cigarette case, Thomas points out a tiny jar of cocaine, a razor blade, and some joints, or cigarettes. I pull out my case and find the same, but he stops me from opening the cocaine: in the bottom of the case lies a cellophane envelope holding a square of blotter acid. He takes the blade and slices a corner for each of us.

"Coke will keep us cold," he says. "This is also speedy and lasts longer. We don't need much, just enough to make a base camp."

A base camp. Surely the words of a wizard. We chase the tabs with fruit brandy, and he lights one of the cigarettes, from which a bitter smoke pours out to mingle with ground mist. Serenity comes over us, and warmth, as we smoke. I sense that it's heroin. I sit in Gestapo headquarters doing smack and rowanberry brandy with a nimbus wizard. How can it be? In my mind I see that a rope of history stretches here from the bistro kitchen after school. Smuts took up the rope and pulled this moment in; a moment in a life of geniuses, voluptuaries, and wild fortune.

But I sit at the end of his rope without him.

And now it's for Thomas to pull him back.

He passes the brandy and lights a joint of hash. It dawns on me that my limbo is weaker than these men's everyday lives. This is how reduced my spirit is by culture. Oblivion for me is just a Thursday night for Thomas. I fall back spinning onto the bed of leaves, feeling consciousness tug on its bindings. And I ask myself which is more terrifying: to lack the spirit to soar—or to have it. As a gust rustles overhead, Thomas's eyes flicker at me like the black orbs of a crow. My mental arguments must have seeped into the air, because he then mysteriously says: "Economy in pleasure is not to my taste. Divinity is achieved through the senses—whether you abstain from sensing or indulge in it, life exists in relation to how deeply we sense."

Nimbus flares at this. Acid starts to peak. He lies back and I catch his face in profile, see his lips resting open, the tip of his tongue poking out. It's the default human, his body turned instrument, without pretension, without psychology at all. Intoxicants have disconnected us, we're empty tunnels for gales to blow through. He turns to see me watching him, and we smile know-ing we've met for real. A cage crackles over us, and all around churns with dark. At some point his phone rings. He moves it to his face, lights himself ghostly green, but I can't tell what he says. I'm trying to dodge splinters falling from its ring, but end up hit in both eyes.

My attention turns to nature.

She has me in her boudoir, lying down. After all my nasty comments. Vengeful destiny delivered me, or Smuts's rope, or my father's bistro, or limbo, or Himmler. There is tonight a feeling of perfect connection to some system or another—but to which never grows clear. This is as sure a sign of nature lurking near as is the smell of shit around the devil. And sure enough, leaves and stems start to lunge at me, they jerk and twist and choke, and the earth rots to liquid beneath my head. A revelation comes—that hell isn't hot, but heaven is: hot and liquid, while hell is cold and rotting.

Thomas passes a cigarette and I clutch it like a life buoy. But its tip burns holes in the dark, it leaves flaming blobs wherever I stop it, that don't go away. Such is this workload of nimbus. I try to keep the cigarette still over my face, try to suck without looking. But in the process I hear voices. Gasps and giggles in the dark.

After a moment Thomas presses earphones into my head.

"Rammstein," he simply says. "Bye-bye."

An electroshock jolts me stiff: the crunch-crunch-crunch of massed troops on the march, *"Links, two, three, four,"* making the canopy rage overhead and the ground shake beneath me as they pass. Then comes a hellfire of guitars. My eyes roll back in their sockets. I leave my body and join the air. Two women arrive, and one squats to plunge her hands into me, scattering my essential gases across the ruin. She stabs them with her tongue, and the reek of earth joins vaginal sweat and kiss-smell to baste us, suction us, squelching till our juices run sour to the ground and we die together, here to decompose with nature. Ah, this dreadnought nimbus.

My component parts will never fit snugly again.

The fitful sleep of the cold dead finally takes me, the sleep of worms, till some time later, in a different life, I'm roused by Glenn Miller.

Moonlight Sonata.

Light prickles the canopy. Imperious nature relaxes her grip, night being her manor, the better to kill and harm. Now her toadies the birds mock the souls who died before morning. A girl is here with me. I cuddle her, reaching for buttocks to wedge a hand between, someplace where softness and warmth still hide. Thomas is spread-eagled beside me with another woman slumped over him, stirring. We're trouserless. A polka-dot panty blows from a branch in the canopy above.

Needles of sunshine flicker through it.

Thomas's girl has thick lips. Her mascara has bled onto her cheeks. She reaches to drag a wicker case through the leaves, from which Thomas pulls intravenous serum bags with hoses. He hangs them overhead on a tree, and peach nectar flows through which makes us blink when it hits our mouths. Then an Armenian brandy appears, and like an emergency-room procedure a sequence of therapies unfolds which forces our bodies to scroll through expressions of nausea, headache, drowsiness, anxiety, lust, and hunger, at which last condition Thomas spoons cocaine for each of us, starting with the girls.

"Here," he says, "because you are just objects to us."

"Thank God," snorts a girl, "or we'd have to pretend to respect you."

Sunlight dusts this plateau of recovery. It gives the air a freshly rinsed taste. We feel like Berlin itself, woken alive after a heavy bombing. Then ginger-and-lime Lauenstein chocolate gives us hope, cigarettes awaken humor, and I finally note that my lady friend has piercing blue eyes. Life's faculties mount a provisional government with these agents, enough to prompt canoodling until beer appears from the basket, perfectly chilled by nature. And this decisive therapy soon sends us swirling from the underworld like nymphs and satyrs, the aristocrat, the sphinx, and the lissom maidens a-swishing.

It's early morning on Anhalter Strasse. City and sunlight hit us together like a cymbal crash. Up the road our car sits waiting with a new driver. And here I'm struck by an epiphany so monstrous in its scale, so blinding in its effect that I feel my skin has turned inside out under the sun, that my innards possess magnetic qualities able to call vast fortunes together. And it's this: anything can happen if I want it to.

The Master has blasted all my doubts to hell.

A decadent banquet at Tempelhof—why not?

"Gleisdreieck!" sing the girls. "Gleisdreieck!" And we leave the basket and fly across empty streets until prairies of sand and scrub roll out of nowhere, then woods, overgrown railroads, and crumbling stations, abandoned since wartime, somehow forgotten in the heart of Berlin. The city disappears, replaced by these lands of the *Gleisdreieck*, once the main rail junction for the Reich. With our senses off their leash, our shoes forgotten in Himmler's jungle, we swoop chattering and laughing on abandoned relics, over dunes, between tracks, following signs to places long vanished, till the morning becomes a montage, a sundance caper where we finally collapse panting in a vast chaparral, dusty as cowboys, there to caress till we're damp again with sex.

Lying after a certain time under a grassy ridge, feeling the breeze, watching it stir the hems of skirts and tousle hair—one of the girls suddenly yawns.

And the night clicks off as if by a switch.

We quickly age in the light, denizens trapped in the shallows. Long shadows warn us off the chaparral. Skies grow blue, nature's agents must surely be gathering to kill and maim each other. We pick our way along the tracks, past old freight warehouses, until finally, down a last sandy bank, the city reappears. An avenue passes ahead and I see that it's Yorckstrasse. We're in Kreuzberg. Within a minute the Mercedes purrs up and we fall inside, the girls sprawled giggling across us; and in the hush of the car their decaying scent makes me want to take one home and doze with a box of cakes. But I feel it won't happen. A sadness. They're girls who can just come and go.

I rest my head against the window, looking forward to my bed, till after a while I feel the car slow and turn, as if snaking close to an address. I open an eye. The Zentral Flughafen looms beside us like a battlement, still unlit by morning.

"Remember I'm staying in Prenzlauer Berg," I croak.

"Eh?" Thomas's eyelids flicker: "But let's see our complex."

My pulse bangs to life.

"We'll call the Basque from here. You have keys, don't you?"

16

"I never said a wiener cost nothing. I'm saying if we get nothing for it, then better wiener than bockwurst. That's like eighty cents she gives away."

"And this is the bockwurst that last week was sixty cents? They get more expensive as they turn green, then, that's how things must work in Gerdland."

"Ach, Gisela, *Gott*."

Through the door I see Thomas waiting in the car, a girl dozing on each shoulder. Necessity is the mother of folly, and I told him to wait ten minutes while I assessed the safety of an inspection. If I don't return in that time, he's to drive away and we're to make contact late this evening. This was something he accepted, maybe even a little chastised for having imagined we'd barge in like a frat party.

I tremble out of sight by the entrance. Sickness drenches me inside, my bare feet siphon cold from a kilometer of stone. My hair's damp and plastered down my face. My coat has bonded with nature, collecting leaves and twigs. Some of them crawl. And the only brain functions open at this hour are the Jesuits that inhabit the border between bacchanal and hangover, spinning nightmares from innocent things. They point out what's happening: a collision of worlds. Absolute worlds unto themselves, but incoherent to each other. In the Mercedes one world, in the kiosk quite another.

And me in between, with growing issues.

"Come on." I hear Gerd across the empty lobby. "If you cook them they're perfectly okay. My mother would still eat them for days yet."

"She should know, after twenty years dead."

"Ach, *Gott*. Why are you being so difficult?"

"Difficult? I'm calculating how much they'll be worth next week, these bockwurst. We might retire to Italy."

"Please face the facts: this is our last month of employment, we have to make the most of these last days. They should be big days, as the place closes down, full of tourists and who knows what. We could really make headway. Anyway, why should we give our best stock to Gunnar? Don't policemen get paid? Is it a Mafia arrangement? Will he bomb the kiosk if we give him a wiener?"

"Such a wurst tycoon. No wonder you can afford holidays."

"Ach, don't say that. The trip is a treat for you, a break from everything. I thought you liked Kühlungsborn? It might not be Venice, but still the Brauhaus is lovely and we can walk on the seafront, have a beer. After this month it won't be so easy, I thought we should live a little, while the kiosk has turnover. It'll be romantic."

Bile rattles up my throat. I decide to chance crossing the lobby to the lavatory. But with my first step Gisela's voice turns especially harsh, and I shrink back to the wall:

"Oh, *ja*," she spits, "so romantic, with Gottfried on the Baltic. For old times' sake we even bring our own Stasi agent to monitor us."

"*Gott*, Gisela, *shhh*—he's having a bad time. It's not like he'll be in our room, we're just giving him a ride to the place. You know he'll spend the whole day in a *strandkorb* with some brandy and a hunting magazine. This break was meant to cheer you up."

"And see me grinning like a honey-cake horse."

A whine works its way into Gerd's voice: "I'm very sorry it's not the night at the cinema you wanted for your life. Still, you seem to have survived. Life's not over. The cinema's still there, we can still try. I worked hard to see you had all you needed. Life's not a dream, Gisela! Times are hard for the workingman!"

"Oh, the big workingman, with his investment wurst. Fifteen years I spent heating *Würstchen* and washing cups, and now that it's finished I have nothing. You have nothing. Not even the toaster, the oven, or the cups."

"We have a coffee machine. They're not cheap."

"My father bought the machine, Gerd!"

"But you're not blaming me? Business is a risk. That's how business is. A risk! Do you think I planned for us to get nothing? Is it my fault they close the airport? It could have been the other way—maybe Berlin decides this is the greatest airport and fills it with planes until we're rich. Then what? You'd be every night at the cinema!"

"Are you blind now as well? Look at the place! It's a tomb! Do people get rich in a tomb? Or do they get buried there!"

"Bah, come on."

"Come on? Come on! I took my risk too! I could have been out of here! You wish the wall was still standing so you could hide behind it in the East! Where you wouldn't have to get anywhere in life! You and Gottfried and all your gray cronies could've just stayed there hissing about everyone else without having to prove yourselves any better!"

"Don't start with old times again."

"Old times? *These* are my old times! *These* ones! *They* were *new* times, and I was on my way out of this place like a bird!"

"Bah." Gerd's face falls in the tone of his voice. "Well, why didn't you just go, then?"

"I should have done!"

"You should have just gone, then. Why blame me years later for something you should have done, I can't do it for you."

"Because *I felt sorry for you!*"

Whoosh. Silence follows in shock waves.

In the pause between this and the sound of cheap heels, Gerd's eyes appear in my mind, perched on the edge of their sockets. "Where are you going?" he calls after her. "What about the trip? Should I just cancel it?"

"Do what you want!" Gisela clacks out of the kiosk. I hold my breath as she passes. The Mercedes is still outside, but so fearsome is Gisela's energy, such is the friction of her entry into the earth's gravitational field, that it pulls away before she sears any paintwork. The figures in the back don't stir. I watch the car turn onto Columbiadamm, a donkey's ear of steam poking from the exhaust.

With these departures a weight lifts off me. After some deep breaths, tuning my ear for sounds of Gerd, I set off across the lobby. In the terminal only a few moving forms mill about, older sorts waiting for something that mightn't come. I descend the few steps, glancing around. The restroom is down some more stairs to my right, but as I turn for it something hot trickles to my lip.

I touch it, and it's blood.

Stopping to dab my nose, I see a small figure cross the concourse. I only notice because it cocks its head in that questioning way of parrots and dogs. While I try to lick blood from my face, or wipe it onto my hand and lick that instead, the form moves into focusing range. It's a young woman in a red coat and beret. She lowers a mobile phone from her ear and pockets it.

It's Anna from the kiosk.

I go to draw my overcoat around me but find my fly broken open, my underwear missing, and my belt still undone. A lump of sick heaves into my mouth. When I try to swallow it, my nose starts to pour like a faucet. I spit the lump and hold an open sleeve under my nose, pretending to fuss with my hair, moving strands with a finger.

Anna slows a few paces away, expressionless, finally stopping to look me up and down. She eventually points. "You missed a hair."

I lower my sleeve. Blood pours onto my foot.

"Do you need an ambulance?"

Before answering, I suck a wad back up my nose. It crackles well enough, but blood still splats to the floor and runs to my mouth. One drop hangs off my lip for a moment before falling. "I think I just need some cakes," I croak.

She nods slowly. "To eat—or to put up your nose?"

Now adrenaline calls drugs back to life. I start lightly tripping, and end up absorbed in the spatterings on the floor. She stands staring till I begin to sway.

"Is that a normal Thursday night for you?" she asks.

"Pretty much. Though sometimes I go out for a drink."

I detect a minuscule rising of eyebrows. Not mirth. But not

not mirth. And she says: "Gerd might have a cake for you. Can you find the bathroom?"

"Yes, thank you. Thanks, Anna, for that."

"Pff." She turns away, coat bobbing daintily like a bell.

I stumble to the conveniences. They sit clean and empty in their underground domain, a cool oasis where you and I can regroup. The splash of my emptying body decks them with echoes—forgive me for that—then cold water stanches blood loss, and more or less cleans up my face. I sit for a while on a toilet, spinning, until the lack of cakes becomes an emergency. Gerd isn't familiar with me day-to-day, I reason, so he mightn't think my state unusual. He needn't see me barefoot, if I approach along the wall. I button my coat to its full length and make my way upstairs.

"Frederick." He smiles through the glass—then: "*Mein Gott*—what happened? Where are your shoes? Come, come, sit down."

"I just need some cakes."

"*Haa*—already training for our little party? It might be a wild night tonight, eh? But you're about twelve hours too early."

I see Anna smirk from the back.

"In fact we'll have another special party in a week or so, if you're still around." Gerd busies himself making coffee. "A bigger one, the last one before we leave Tempelhof. A farewell. Did you ever eat *Berliner Kartoffelsalat*? Gisela's going to make some, totally authentic. Gisela's a great cook, you know."

Sugars from a sixty-cent cake usher my system into a stable hangover. But one symptom is sentimentality, and my chest soon aches with Gerd's attempts at lightheartedness, knowing all that just went on. I feel dirtied by knowing because I secretly pity him; the most weakening secret a person can have, and the most necessary to keep. In any event, unable to bear it, I make an excuse and limp out to a taxi.

"Haa," calls Gerd. "Hopefully we see you later, then!"

I wave a hand and slink back to my bed, where a last feeble sugar in the brain resolves to attend the party. Because you never know. A wild party, you heard him say it. And that will call for more splendor than a kiosk. No?

Still, I pray before laying down: "O Son of God,"* I croak, "great nimbal prophet, support this thy bacchanal. In your mercy let nimbus rage, let the party shatter all probability, let it swarm through palatial salons unseen since wartime and free for us to borrow on a whim." My pathetic words soon crumple me onto the bed, where I plummet to sleep.

Dreams touch down like tornado spouts.

In one it seems I'm a nineteenth century patriarch with enough character to have made a family with Anna. She sits prim and reserved, the way those women do who were formally schooled in the conjugal arts. We must have engaged in polite intercourse, probably through an embroidered slit in a bedsheet, because two small babes lie in her arms; one is Smuts, the other is old Gerd.

It falls to me to see about a holiday.

---

* Let's also admit the obvious: if a spiritual force underlies human life, it seems best described by classical gods, that is, a council of capricious portfolios governing the spectrum of natures between kindness and cruelty. To those of orthodox faith we must gently but firmly ask: does life really suggest the existence of a single caring force? We just can't ignore the lack of providential intervention in the vast majority of sufferings. And if there were such a power, be pragmatic: would resurrection from a peaceful grave to join smug and raucous evangelists be a fate we should rush to embrace?

"What nature of vacationment were you contemplating, sir?" the travel agent asks.

"An oceanic vacationment," I reply.

"I see." He opens a huge ledger, using fully outstretched arms to turn a page. "A crossing by steamship? There are some notable sailings coming up, both on liners and—well, if I may be so bold—freighters, sir."

"Freighters, you say? Merchantmen?"

His gaze narrows over his spectacles: "These can sometimes furnish a more—shall we say 'intimate' crossing experience. For those who perhaps more seek the solitude of the deep itself. So to speak, sir, of course."

"Yes, yes." I slap the counter. "That sounds the sort of thing. Indeed. And would you by chance have any passages that don't— how can I best put it—"

"Don't—return, sir? Don't come back?"

"Hm. Yes. Passages that might not, in a manner of speaking, entirely quite return, in the way that term is normally understood."

"I see." The agent leans closer, blinking for a few moments. "I see, indeed. So really a—*sinking*, then, is it, sir, you'd like to book?"

"Well"—I draw myself up—"in as many words, I suppose. If you put it like that."

The agent cocks his head: "Of course, this considerably narrows our choices. But, for instance, I can offer a sailing bound for—Maracaibo, sir."

"Ah—Maracaibo!"

"Yes, sir. Maracaibo. Of course—it's merely *bound* for there. If you catch my drift. The vessel will *embark* on that course. After which embarkation, by the grace of God, the Baltic being what it is, well. *Ahem*." He clears his throat.

"Yes, yes." I stroke my chin. "Quite. And so all souls—?"

"Yes, sir. Everyone, apparently. Quite tragic to say."

"So we'll all just—hm?"

"I'm afraid so."

Whoosh—when I wake it's nearly dark again. This will be a dream that's hard to shake, whose memory will riddle me for a while to come. In addition I wake knowing that it's the eve of my last chance. My end-play. After a few dodges, feints, and false starts, the cone finally reaches its point: tonight is do or die.

Stirring onto an elbow, I lay out two lines, and ponder the question of prayer. Logic establishes that it's wiser to acknowledge deities than to not. Salvation may or may not be probable, but it costs nothing to have a ticket, this is what the great thinkers decided. Anyway, the marvelous prophet Jesus was a living figure in history, it can't be denied. As proof of a force above humankind he brought the best wine to the wedding of Cana—in fact this was the very first sign of his supernatural gifts:

"*'Everyone serves the good wine first and the inferior wine after the guests have become drunk. But you have kept the good wine until last.' Jesus did this, the first of his signs, in Cana of Galilee, and revealed his glory; and his disciples believed in him.'"**

Yes: Christianity sprang from a wine nimbus. The prophet was gifted with such unearthly control that he let pass an entire wedding party, till the lightweights went home, the boors collapsed, and the hard core went scrounging for beer—before pulling out the best bottle. And lo, did they rejoice, and follow him.

Deciding to wear the fur as a talisman, I flatten my hair and dab myself with Jicky before assessing my form in the mirror. The

---

* John 2:10–11.

vision is unmistakably that of a phantom between shindigs. Gerd might be a modest man, I reason, but a party's a party, and a wild party—indeed a special party, as he said—must be a debauch in any language. I take a slug of wine in the prophet's honor, and prepare for this last gambit—but as I inspect my nostrils for snow the phone starts to ring, and I tense. After watching it tremble for a few moments I hurry out before it can ring again.

Frosty night has fallen by the time I reach Tempelhof. The airport rises still and black against a lamplit sky, with few lights burning in her windows, just enough to give an emberlike glow. I pause, listening for pounding rhythms or laughter, or any wild hubbub at all. But there is none. Gravity sucks me swaying up the steps, and I find the lobby even quieter than usual. This means that the rasping breath of an older person, or even the creasing of clothes, can be heard from some distance away. And it just happens that such rasps and creasings can now be heard. They draw my attention to the kiosk side of the lobby. A handful of people are there in the half-light, older types, men and women, hunched at the tables. There's no sign of Gerd. I stand wavering at the doors, ready to write the affair off. Even more so when Gisela Specht appears in the kiosk; she wears a leather jacket with a denim cowboy skirt and has a reckless crimson slash across her face, roughly where her mouth used to be. Her appearance brings the same mixture of wonder and disgust as the sight of our teachers did when we saw them in casual dress at a sports day; at once a fascination that they could so closely resemble real people, and a distaste that they should think fit to try.

Nobody turns to look at me. Perhaps a refinement of the old East, where eyes grew in the side of the head. Present are an older, probably Turkish couple; a tall young man in a large urchin's beret;

and a waxy old monolith of a man with bulbous features and a cigar. His eyes are challenging: bulging milky blue eyes that sit facing the kiosk like marbles. They must be able to transmit messages without moving, because Gisela tosses her head at the nuisance of them and gives the man a beer. At this, in isolation from the rest of his enormous head, the bottom lip dips open to grunt.

Gisela spots me as this goes on. Although I can't say she acknowledges me, much less shows me any warmth—she doesn't show contempt, and I feel it a small triumph. I step closer to the group, which makes the Turkish couple look up and nod. We're in a loose-knit club, then—a dismal one so far, given the needs of the night, but still. It has at least one younger member, and in a beret, which suggests something more jaunty than sitting around the kiosk all night. Also I reason it's early for any truly wild bacchanal. I'm no sooner thinking this when another, even younger figure appears through the door along the hall. A petite young woman who wears jeans under a woolen coat, and has her black hair in a bob. She carries a tiny bag, in contrast to other handbags around,* and her steps are short and quick, almost squirrellike in their levity. It's the girl Anna. A reflex makes me blush, as if she might guess my dream of this afternoon.

I watch her through the corner of an eye, because classmates also come under new light at a sports day. She's a girl whose features border on the plain—despite large algae-green eyes and small, well-cut lips—but they're features rescued by a kind of

---

* Note that handbags come sized according to the age and concern for things in general of the carrier. An aging person must need more support from external accessories as their inner powers decline; plus their sensitivity to that decline must lead them to imagine even more dismaying contingencies. Thus in Gisela's bag you could fit a plumber's toolbox, in Anna's merely a chocolate éclair.

determination, the kind you see in certain six-year-olds stoically queuing among adults. This sense of purpose, seen in a lack of coyness, a straightforward gaze, mingles with lip gloss to make her appearance here like that of a firefly in a cave. But as I warm to these beginnings of potential, thinking it won't take many more such arrivals to meet the minimum for a small party, she smiles at the lad in the beret, they wave at the group—"*Tschüss!*" they sing, "*Tschüss!*"—and step away into the eve.

"Have a good night," calls the Turkish Frau. "Stay warm."

After the hissing has subsided which always follows the young—"Where will he take her, surely he's not into poetry as well?"—"No she's taking *him* to some showing of old pamphlets up Karl-Liebknecht-Strasse. I can think of better ways to pass a Friday, he must be keen"—"He's hardly a kindred soul, poor girl—she's so earnest, but I feel it must be loneliness, I'm sure that's why she's so aloof"—only rasping breath and the creasing of clothes remain. Within minutes a new couple arrives, also older, with centers of gravity up near their chests, then another, shorter pair, of identical height and girth like salt-and-pepper shakers, and with square heads.

And following them comes a chubby man. While I take in his balding head, his blond, rather sparse mustache compared to Gerd's, his shining face—one thing about him rings the final bell of the night's endeavor:

The man wears a sailor's fancy dress costume.

He also carries an electronic keyboard of the type producing little rhythms and chords via buttons labeled "Samba," "Bossa-nova," "Quickstep," and "Foxtrot." His sailor's cap hangs from the keyboard, trailing ribbons.

My spirit has mostly fled by the time Gerd enters.

In fact I must pause here, friend, and frame the scene that follows. It makes no sense to note my sinking heart, my plunging fortunes, as instances would be too numerous and their tenor too bleak for words alone. Instead, and as you well know my position, I recount the following just as I watch it unfold:

Gerd enters in a naval captain's outfit too small for him, and with too small a hat, which perches on his head like a pie. He grins with his long, yellowing, bristlelike teeth, to a murmur of approval from the gang around the kiosk.

Within nations and societies, in cities, districts, streets, and even buildings, it can sometimes happen that human groups form a backwater which over time comes to fester with a nature of its own. This has happened here. With perfect clarity I realize that nothing I might witness next is necessarily common to Germany or to Berlin, nor to Tempelhof or even to humanity itself; but rather that I have stumbled into a small and brackish pool outside life's tidal flow, where drips occasionally echo, where shapes lurk, and where warmth in the water can merit suspicion.

"Frederick, you made it! *Haa*—and with your shoes!"

I watch Gerd's cap bob down the steps while Gisela closes up the kiosk. At this our motley band files across the concourse after the captain, not to a vast colonnaded venue but to a small canteen tucked into a far corner of the terminal. Its counter is shuttered, its chairs are upended on their tables. Against a wall stands a trestle sideboard with some bottles of cheap wine, a bowl of pasta salad, a plate of cold sliced sausage, a basket of bread rolls, a small tower of plastic cups, and a waste bucket.

Gerd sits me next to the stony man, who I now suspect was the man sweeping here on my first visit. "Gottfried Pietsch," he says, and to the man: "*Gabriel, von England.*"

"*Ah, so,*" Gottfried grunts. "*Er sient aus wie ein Walross.*"

"*Haa*—he says you look like a walrus."

I look down at my coat: "Hm—ha ha."

Gottfried smells strongly of body odor and beer, and gives a sense of being able to take in all the world through the edges of his gaze. After a few moments, finding the other tables taken, an almost spherical old doll comes to join us. Her name is Magda, and she perches on the edge of her chair like the dutiful widow who once followed a husband around, probably for decades after uncovering the full horror of his character, because she's now able to convey her body to a place without admitting being there. She neither stays nor leaves, neither smiles nor doesn't.

Neither sees me nor not, nor probably cares to.

I soon excuse myself to feign interest in the keyboard. As Gerd sets up a small stage, measuring lengths of cable between his hands, I note a relaxed swing to his movements, not despite but because of older age; his body doesn't arch and torsion up its length anymore, but rather pivots from the pelvis like a crane. Maturity supposedly has its rewards, and maybe pivoting is one of them, though I've yet to hear it described.*

"Gabriel, this is Dieter Strassmann." He presents his fellow

---

* Should you ignore my example and choose the path of physical decay, perhaps not all of it is bad news. While the body withers off the bone, the process we call life still seems to take place inside. What seems to happen, I've discovered by observation, is a process of reduction, as in a meat stock. By deathbed time, only the primal salts and essences seem to remain. It appears any life distills character like this, no matter what one's pot starts out containing. So the dissolute, the infirm, the addicted will all distill; and therefore have we any business imposing standards on them or on anyone, whether for charity or social order? No, because life is that distillation alone, and it proceeds heedless of anyone, with what ingredients it has.

seaman, then leans close to hiss: "Tonight we're watching out for Gottfried, in case you wonder—he has a hard life at the moment, and no real friends. So he needs a drink, but not too much of a drink, you know?" His gaze shifts over that lonely figure. "If you get talking to him he might try converting you to socialism, I tell you now. But otherwise he's fine, a really clever man, you should see what he builds in his workshop."

"Ha," says Dieter, "old Gottfried, still recruiting."

"Shh." Gerd looks away, loudly adding: "And later we try your wine, eh? Great. An Australian wine, Dieter, from Gabriel. And look—something special." He points out the pasta salad and, seeing Gisela skulking near the back, calls out: "*Was ist das—?*"

"*Italienisch,*" she calls back.

"Italian," he proudly says. "Gisela's a great cook."

Liquid slowly pools in the salad. The keyboard launches a squelching accompaniment of tuba blasts, knocks, squeaks, and drumrolls.

"Did you ever hear of *Klaus und Klaus?*" asks Gerd. "Famous duo from Hamburg."

"*Nee.*" Dieter frowns. "Klaus Baumgart is from Oldenburg."

"*Ja*, okay, but the duo is from Hamburg. Or else why are they dressed in sailor clothes and singing about the North Sea coast?"

"Oldenburg is next to Bremen—what coast do you think is close to Bremen?" Dieter rolls his eyes and shakes his ruddy head at me.

"I was going to tell you Dieter was in a famous *Klaus und Klaus* tribute band in Leipzig. But suddenly he's also a professor of world geography."

"*Ja, ja,*" scoffs Dieter, "as if Bremen is such a far-world place."

Taking pity on my foreignness, a gentle old lady at the nearest table clears her throat to say: "Quite beautiful, Bremen—you must have heard of the university? Famous even as far as China. Bremen's really become a center of excellence."

"*Ja*, they make Beck's beer," says her man. "After two of them you feel excellent."

"Well, anyway," says Gerd, "we're a *Klaus und Klaus* tribute band—*Gerd und Gerd*. Sounds more credible than *Dieter und Dieter*, don't you think? Although it takes us ten minutes of the act to explain why Dieter is also called Gerd."

"And," says Dieter, "we're not from Hamburg."

A stodgy rhythm takes hold, of tubas blasting left and right with drumrolls in between. As I return to the table both Magda and Gisela look at me strangely, I realize my face has twisted with horror, as if watching a puppy die. I straighten it and take my seat next to Gottfried. He grunts as I sit down.

Then I set off drinking as heavily as I can.

Through this blank face I watch a nimbus slowly rise in the terminal, which brings a problem of philosophy on top of everything: is a nimbus of small pleasures equal to the most ruthless debauch? What separates we who crave substances to lethal excess and those who relax with tuba blasts and wine? Who is more the master of their nimbus?

The sailors explain in banter why Dieter's also called Gerd, wine flows, and everyone sings along to "There Stands a Horse in the Hallway," till the once-most-colossal structure on earth quivers with jollity. I turn to find Gottfried swaying economically, mouthing the words with a scowl. A security guard pulls up a chair and nods along, Magda's brow rises between verses, and even Gisela's boots step left and right, no doubt knowing that leisure aids health as much as tofu or an enema.

Nimbus is nimbus and I struggle not to be swept up.

Ah, the brutal Enthusiasms.

There comes a break during which Gerd invites me to open his Marius. As I pour, Gottfried reaches for the bottle to examine, and his eyelids flicker quickly when he takes a first sip. He seems to freeze for a moment, and I freeze beside him; then his gaze swivels up. "*Sehr gut—Dankeschön.*"

And so the evening passes, chatter rises and falls, food is picked to scraps, wit grows blunt, and jokes turn lame. My body glows with wine, buzzes with most of my last gram of nasal amusements. For everyone else, nimbus peaks and hovers for a while; not loftily but authentically, as if touched, like life, with the sadness that it must die before the morrow. And at the first couple's departure, a milling of guests and a limbo of long good-byes begins at the buffet. A flurry of whispers about who'll see Gottfried home, or if he needs another wiener.

And here I close the frame for this scene, dear comrade, yearning as I am for death, even wondering where to leave a last note. So ends the decadent Gerd Specht's special party. You and I will feel much the same about it, I needn't add anything else. And in any event a much more interesting thing happens next.

The night delivers a stunning end-play.

"Poet!" Gerd waves from the stage: "Come help me, I'll show you something."

He folds the trestle table, bidding me help with the amplifier. Dieter grabs the keyboard and we cross the main hall, past a departures board that's stuck on a flight to Saarbrücken, and into a stairwell where stairs descend three stories to a security door. Here in the monolith's bowels Gerd pulls out a bundle of keys.

The door clangs open.

An underground highway stretches ahead of us, and beside it a railway, cobbled between its tracks, curving into the distance out of sight. I sway at the door, staring.

Shivers run through me.

"See?" says Gerd. "More than five kilometers of bunkers and tunnels down here, built for the Third Reich. Who knows where they go? Huge complex."

We drop the musical equipment in a store near the stairwell, where with my mind racing to digest what I've seen I scan the store's shelves, trying to regain calm. The room is dotted with expendables for the kiosk—sachets of sugar, plastic forks, some mops and brooms, and a box with Chinese texts and starbursts.

"Looks like fireworks," I say, as much to hear if my voice still works as for any interest in the box—because it dawns on me that this can only be the complex Thomas expected to secure. Kilometers of sublime Gothic underworld.

"*Ja*, fireworks." Gerd nods. "For the airport farewell party."

"Rockets?" asks Dieter. "I'll beg some for Heide's birthday."

"I can't split them, it's a self-contained pyrotechnic show."

"Ah—where you just light the box?"

"Exactly." Gerd switches off the light. "Linked in series, they go off timed like a ballet. Really clever, there's about sixty euros' worth in there. We'll set them off at midnight, as the airport's finale. Have a last drink to the place."

"On my street a few weeks ago the Leftists lit one of these inside a Porsche," says Dieter. "Jesus Christ, you should have seen it, blown to pieces."

"A Porsche? Just from fireworks?"

"No, *ja*, unbelievable, I didn't expect it either. What I figured out is that the car is so well sealed that the booms caused a pressure shock and blasted everything out. Then the whole thing caught fire. Some serious booms, we all came out to see. In ten minutes it looked like a nuclear strike, you wouldn't believe it."

Gerd pauses. "And weren't we supposed to be Leftists?"

"Well—I thought we were Marxist-Leninists."

"And what's the difference?"

"Who knows? Maybe just the Porsche thing."

"*Ja*, well. If you don't meet any Leftists before Heide's birthday, Gottfried knows where to get rockets cheap if you need any."

"Ha—he could get a tank if we wanted."

"Though I have some crackers here left over from May Day." Gerd locks the store and leads us back out into the bahn tunnel.

"Thanks, I'll look for rockets—size matters to Heide."

"And she ended up married to you? *Haa!*" We tramp up the highway to another metal door, which Gerd swings wide open.

"And see"—he flicks on overhead lights.

I reel on my feet. A mall stretches ahead through rows of heavy archways, arch after arch after arch, as if bounced between mirrors to eternity. Shadows off to the side promise more passages, more salons, out of view.

It's an underground Alhambra.

"From 1935," says Gerd, "a bunker for airport staff. Then you have the Lufthansa bunkers, women's and children's bunkers, American forces command centers—it's an underground town, the complex even has its own waterworks and power plant, independent from the city of Berlin." He leads us through a warren of salons. "Look—see the painting of the man getting drunk? See the lettering? Originals from the 1930s. Nothing touched here in seventy years."

On the wall a man is painted in profile, head back, almost vertically emptying a bottle into his mouth. I look without breathing.

A nimbus icon.

We return to the first mall, where archways form vaulted compartments leading one into another, on and on into the distance, each spacious enough for a dinner setting, a lounge setting, a dance floor, or whatever you will. Mythical underworld decadence, a Gothic palazzo, empty, soundless, windowless. As still as death's mansion.

With a nimbus idol.

Whoosh.

A wonderland.

17

The early bird catches the worm, thus quoth the *Limbus Magister*. So this morning I rise with birds, babies, baboons, and business-men, even donning my suit to join these agents of unfair advantage in bending the day to my will.

The mission: to secure the keys to wonderland.

Because something occurred to me in the night: that these aren't just the keys to an underground Cockaigne. They don't simply open the way for a secret banquet, a friend's release, a luxurious death—but also unlock the limbo of modern capitalism at its deepest, most gaseous sphere. At its heart and soul.

Market forces may have trapped Smuts and me, but angels, demons, Enthusiasms, and limbos now crowd to the point of this odyssey's cone, arriving to stage an end-play. The keys open nothing less than a vein of Western God.

Over a palliative wine I can't see why Gerd wouldn't loan them. I imagine three scenarios, depending on his response. If he gladly loans the keys for an indefinite period, I can call Thomas over and show him around the complex. That will seal my part of the bargain and secure Smuts's release. If Gerd is more hesitant, loaning the keys for a specified while, I'll rush to make copies in Kreuzberg, showing Thomas around later when the kiosk is shut. And if he only loans them for a moment, I'll open the doors and foul their locks, prop them with cardboard for later entry.

The phone also woke me this morning, after a few tries during the night, hence you see it buried under bedclothes and towels. This seemed preferable to unplugging it, which might have somehow signaled my avoidance. Suddenly I'm a young man on the move, as the Master chases its wants—but with today's strategic model adding new confidence, at its next ring I dig up the phone and answer.

To my surprise it's not Thomas, but a certain Toshiro.

Toshiro Satou in Tokyo, making a polite introduction.

"We are going before the court on Monday, October twenty-seventh," he says. "Then the case will be decided. Mr. Smatosu tells me you were present at the scene. Perhaps you can tell me: did you see the victim pay for his meal?"

"Hm." I cast my mind back. "I don't believe he paid."

"Oh, no." Satou sounds crestfallen: "I hoped you saw."

"Well, I don't think the men paid at all; they just left."

"Oh, no. But you saw the person ask for parts of fish?"

"Yes, I did. He ordered livers, I observed him closely."

"Ah, good. And which words did he use to ask for it?"

A silence comes with a sinking feeling, then: "Oh, no."

"Listen," I say, "it's very simple: all night the restaurant served deadly poisonous fish, not farmed, but from the sea. And after the incident I watched a man substitute the fish in the tank, and take all the poisonous ones out with him."

"And Mr. Smatosu knew they were deadly poisonous?"

"Well, of course—that's what the restaurant is famous for."

"And still he served them to the man, knowing of poison?"

"Hm. Well—"

"Oh, no."

"Look—can you just tell me what will help us win the case?"

"Ah. It's only needed fish, and the proof it came from there."

"Well, that's not going to happen. Are witnesses not useful?"

"Oh, no. You see, in Japan the court is most shameful matter."

"But surely it's shameful to send an innocent man to prison?"

"Yes, yes—but an innocent man. In this case, if the man knows some fish parts are deadly poisoned, which are in a safe box, under a key, and with deliberacy he opens the box to bring the deadly parts to the client—then is not innocent."

"But the client was drunk—he insisted on ordering the fish!"

"No, no—the client is in restaurant, where he can safe be drunk. Instead our problem is that Mr. Smatosu is drunk! In a place of careful service! How can it be! Very serious matter in Japan! What can make him think to get drunk!"

"Hm, well. Never mind that, I don't see how the kitchen's master can avoid responsibility—as the licensed chef, he abandoned a *fugu* restaurant to a complete beginner while there were still clients inside asking to eat livers."

"Yes." Satou pauses. "And left them safe in a box, with key."

"Well, it sounds as if Smuts can be imprisoned for simply doing the job he was meant to do. The substitution of fish doesn't seem to matter anymore."

"Oh, no—fish are important. If fish is illegal strength, then Mr. Smatosu couldn't know it can kill. Responsibility passes to the owner of establishment. But with evidence of only soft-flavor fish from farm, it seems he deliberately poisons the man by using such big amount that a reasonable person can see it's too much."

"Hm. So our only hope is a sample of that night's *torafugu*?"

"I think so. And with the restaurant connection clear to see."

The call doesn't improve after this, although I learn that I might have a chance to speak with Smuts via his prison phone card in the coming days.

A pall descends. The twenty-seventh is barely ten days off.

Only the Basque can save us, and even then it seems a tall order—not only does he have to provide a sample of *fugu*, but he'll also have to implicate his client. Even break the law to implicate him. Weight bears down on the mission. I lug it out onto the street with my hangover before the phone can ring again. Because as slim as chances seem, there'll be no chance at all if I don't get the Master's quid pro quo.

Jesuits in my mind send a warning to watch out for Thomas's car—not only here but around the airport, even though we have no appointment to meet in person. With him being a man of action it seems a fair precaution. If he's grown impatient, any more excuses about the keys could damage my credibility beyond repair.

Holes in the cloud cover drop beams of light on the city. I hail a cab under one of them. By the time I reach the airport the ground shines with rain. The sound of it hissing under tires, lights wavering in puddles, the forward lean of wandering people, all lift my pulse to the resting state of a limbo: excitement under dread.

The airport is busier than I've seen it before. I have the taxi drop me at the small monumental garden facing the entrance talons. Blocked by its bushes and trees, I scout the scene for black Mercedes-Benzes. Cars come and go around the front, and the parking lot is more than usually full. And sure enough, halfway down a row sits a sparkling black Mercedes. I crane for a better look—and there it sits.

I peer and pause, but then—there's another one. And as I step back to light a smoke, a third black Mercedes sails into the parking lot. Make note for your own odyssey: there are no days off in limbo. In fact, the success-measuring device of my brain, only ever active near the absurd, now pits the scene against my dying wishes, asking if ending my days in a monumental garden in Germany was what I had in mind.

Enervation comes over me. In fact, I wonder if I'm still tripping, if there's a car-multiplying factor at work. I decide to approach the terminal with my head down, and even then, glancing over my shoulder, I see another black Mercedes. I scurry up the steps and throw myself into the building's vacuum, letting it rattle me in through the doors.

Gerd sees me entering from the kiosk. "Boom, boom," he sings through the hatch, "there stands a horse in the hallway—*haa*! Eh?"

"Ha ha, yes." I step up to the window.

"You know, I heard from Gottfried. He almost never phones, but suddenly he called to say he liked your wine. If you tell me which supermarket has it, maybe I'll get some."

"I doubt you'll find any. But I have a bottle I can give him."

"*Nee*, you shouldn't give it, then. It's only Gottfried, he can drink Chianti."

"There's more to him than meets the eye—that's a real unicorn of wines."

"Bah, typical Gottfried, you never know what's going on with him. Half the time he's like a statue, then you suddenly see something else." Gerd flicks a look around the lobby before lower-

ing his voice to a hiss. "Real Stasi man—did you hear about the
security police of the GDR? That's Gottfried's old job, probably
at a high level too. In Germany we don't speak of those things
anymore, times have moved on. But he saw some sights in his life.
Dieter knows more about him. He always jokes that Gottfried
still keeps his work socks and gun next to his bed. But it's only
half joking. He lives every day like he's waiting, maybe to score
his master stroke for socialism, give one last good punch from
the GDR. He still quietly monitors, watching the horizon for
comrades. Watching like a Doberman."

"What does he work at now?"

"He repairs bicycles in his workshop and does maintenance
work here part-time. But things are bad, I feel sorry for him.
He lost his wife a couple of years ago and the color went out of
his skin. Now his business goes downhill, and the airport soon
closes. He loves this place, even though it wasn't part of communist Berlin. I think he feels it a bit like himself—solid and full
of hidden tunnels. Gottfried has a better security clearance than
me, you know, he even gets to help on the airside, around the
planes. He has a sharp mind, very rational, people always recognize it in the end. He soon makes himself a fixture. You should
see some of his little inventions."

Anna emerges from the back, making Gerd return to his
doings on the counter. "*Nein*, Gottfried," he mutters. "Let him
drink Chianti. Why not?"

As conversation begins to falter, I draw breath and step up
to the mission's front line: "That was an amazing basement you
showed me after the show."

"*Ja*, isn't it? Must be as much building down there as on top."

"Really? You must lend me the keys, I'd love to look around."

"*Haa*—but no. Under federal law we can't allow tourists. Until the end of the month it's still an international airport, and the tunnels also reach airside. Strict authorization required. Even I have no business going down—the kiosk usually has its storeroom up here, but the airport is using it while they move things out. Routines are changing as the place closes down. Bah, well. Don't know what we do after that."

"A real shame." I try to keep my face from falling.

"Ach, I guess that's life. Anyway, the city is full of bunkers if you're interested. Abandoned subway stations, breweries, tunnels—even highways. Hitler was going to replace Berlin with a super-capital, Germania, like a new imperial Rome. They say that for every building on the ground in Berlin there's another one underground. The Berliner Unterwelten company makes tours, you should call them."

Picturing Thomas on a guided tour, I excuse myself and crawl back to the hotel. The strongest man couldn't sit through another act of my life. As the taxi passes over the Spree I recall my evening with Thomas. Already it seems like a month ago. The distance seems greater because I look back from another world, the world of horses in hallways and fights over bockwurst. This slipping in and out of worlds is exhausting, I reel trying to bring the two together.

In fact, I'm reminded of the parachute cadet who asked an instructor: "If the main parachute doesn't open, how long do I have to deploy the auxiliary?"

To which the instructor laughingly replied: "The rest of your life."

There does not exist in human design an answer to the forces now exerted on your servant and illustrator. For a few moments I lie paralyzed on the bed, reflecting on the forces I've unleashed. I ponder how tiny were the seemingly insurmountable forces of yesterday. Ah, this cone. How roomy it used to be. Croaking to myself as I stir, I lay a generous line that makes me bleed through both nostrils. Then, plugging them with tissues that grow heavy and wet, I gather together my worldly belongings, I suppose as a sort of gauge of self-worth, and stop to peer at them over dripping tusks. What decadent luggage. What have I become? I ask. What became of the luggage of vitality, the smiling soft toys, the fruits from an auntie's orchard, the sandals just in case?

I never had that luggage, is what became of it. I was merely led to believe I had it. The dreams and equations of my life were orchestrated for me on the basis of a life I never had. By executives called John for whom I don't exist.

Here is my fucking luggage: a dozen bottles of wine, a flask of perfume, a Miesbacher jacket and hat, a faux-fur coat, and an alluvium of drugs.

I move to the pile and straighten the feather on the hat.

After ten minutes back on the bed, taking in this sum of my life's work, the phone rings, and before I know what I'm doing, I snatch it up off its cradle.

"He lives!" booms Thomas. "My God, for a while there I worried that I'd blown the deal—sorry if we were indiscreet towards the end, of course it was dumb to show up at the venue. Hopefully there's no harm done?"

"'He lives' is a bit optimistic," I sniff.

"Ha, still suffering? Then at least I was a good host. And maybe this will brighten your day: I reported to our friend in Paris that your proposal was just the one we'd hoped for. He's on cloud nine, especially as this is the last month in history we'll be able to use it. It's like a banquet on the *Titanic* the day before it sailed!"

"Oh, yes?"

"He has the mother of all events brewing. The mother."

"And what of Smuts? Have we the mother of all cases?"

"Of course—Didi's in conference right now, don't worry. There are some strings to pull, and naturally he feels bad about his client there. But really it was a case of 'buyer beware' for the old man, we can't let any of our people take the blame for his unlucky gamble. Rest assured that things are happening in the East."

"That's very good news."

"As for our event, we have to move fast. After I gave him the all-clear about the venue, Basque set a provisional date of Friday, October twenty-fourth. The end of next week, the last weekend of operations at the airport. It'll be by the skin of our teeth, a lot has to happen between now and then. I won't say any more on the phone—but boy, are we going to drink on Monday. Save yourself."

"Oh, yes?" I stir off the pillow. "Well, but there's still a hurdle or two to get over."

"Don't worry, it's all in hand. The crew will arrive Tuesday."

"Oh, yes? Which crew's this?"

"You know, Basque's people from Paris—surveyor, electrician, decorator. Security people, et cetera. By the end of the day everything will be under control."

"What? But I'm still trying to get keys!"

"Excellent, get me a set too. Grab a bunch of them if you can. Listen, I won't hold you up on the phone—let's meet tomorrow for brunch, I'll collect you at either place. We haven't spoken of remuneration, and also I have a small favor to ask: Basque will

arrive incognito on a commercial flight through Tegel, so won't
be checking any luggage—and I thought what a nice touch if we
had a bottle of your 2004 to share with him, I haven't been able
to find any in over a year. I thought if you're in the cellar this
weekend, perhaps you could grab one to give to him?"

"Hm—and which cellar's this?"

"Ha, don't be modest. I like you more and more, Gabriel."

Whoosh. My hand drops with the phone. Across the bed,
through its tiny speaker, I hear Thomas like a faraway hornet:

"You just get better and better. 'Which cellar'—ha!"

18

What conceivable thing among these libertines' chattels might benefit from the cool, dark, unfluctuating conditions of an underground cellar?

Oh, yes. And as the taxi glides back over the Spree I pat the bag of Marius, even unzip it to caress one of the bottles. Perhaps beauty can be useful after all. Because Gerd surely balked at loaning his keys after I mentioned exploring the bunkers. But if his own store is there, presumably also accessible to Anna and Sauer-Frau, then the issue isn't with possessing the keys as such but with roaming unauthorized parts of the building. Thus I need a more workmanlike reason to enter the bunkers—like a need to store something in his basement. And after all, even Gottfried is with me if the question comes down to the health and safety of a remarkable unicorn wine.

Ah, Thomas, you genius. You concierge of Enthusiasmus.

I find Gerd putting on his cardigan when I step into the terminal. And somehow, even though my situation hasn't materially changed, the bluster of shifting Fortune and the clink of wine in my bag usher in an energy of free passage, that energy of certainty above confidence. Puffing with the bag's weight, I explain to Gerd that this rarest of wines needs a stable home for a few days. He looks to Anna, who tidies in the back room, then pulls out the keys and hands them to me: "Do you remember which doors? The green key, then the yellow."

"Thanks, yes. I'll be back shortly."

"*Ja*, give the keys back to Anna." He pauses to stare on his way out the door. "And Frederick—at least down there it'll be safe from Gottfried, eh? *Haa!*"

My pulse grows sharp as I near the basement. Something more than just excitement. As I open the door to the bahn tunnel, it hits me: I descend into a limbo. A real one, in an abandoned underworld. The thought makes me stop and sway. Tempelhof: a limbo. Gabriel: a limbo. Security lights shine off cobbles between railway lines, and I stop to look forward and back. The bahn stretches into the dark in both directions, lights curling away around bends. Behind me my past, in front my future.

My eyes grow full and hot. A tear drops onto the road, falling in a spot where light makes it glisten. It's the only sparkling thing underground. The space is suddenly a model of my unconscious. Dark, festering, tunneled through.

With one tiny sparkle inside it.

Soon to close down forever.

After removing a bottle for Thomas and leaving my bag in the store, I can't resist going to the bunkers. The key slides into Wonderland's door, I switch on the lights. And there I stare through the arches as if peering down a well. The space is momentous. A habitat of Pan, steeped in emotional shadows from all who passed through on a knife edge of life. If grapes absorb yearnings, then these walls must tremble with them, ooze them, shriek them out in the night.

A curious breeze hurries me back up the bahn tunnel. New ideas swirl in its wake. Thomas now suggests payment might flow from the venue. I hadn't considered this, being so concerned with my death. Perhaps, if it really goes ahead, the caper might fund Gerd's recovery. A little capitalism for a good cause, strictly managed, of course. The symmetry, as Smuts would say, is perfect. A redistribution of wealth. My death can still follow, and in the style I wished for: a banquet unlike anything since the fall of ancient Rome. No risk attaches to Gerd. If I copy the keys, then his set remains safely upstairs with him. The kitchen overworld will take possession of the complex for a night, and be answerable for itself. Why not some regulated profiteering? As Gerd milks his last sales of bockwurst upstairs, a nest egg might hatch underground.

A repayment of family debt. Just look at the symmetry.

Although a sensor inside me flags this as a final plunge down the Master Limbo's throat, I ask myself: why not?

Righteous plans seem to summon the energies needed to carry them out. In this case I sweep up the stairs and onto the street, taking care not to be seen by Anna. Dialing Thomas from a phone booth, I ask for assistance in a low, secretive voice, without explaining why or for what. He responds well to this, and in the burning of a cigarette his Mercedes appears flashing through the traffic.

Only Bettina is inside, hair drawn up inside a chauffeur's cap, a vision so ravishing, so bold and modern, that I must pause at the door, my friend, and call you in close: step up with me, hear the throaty hiss of a perfect turbine, smell leather mix with musk, see this spotless maiden masquerade as a man, as a servant, toying with it, with us, flashing dimples and teeth and clear eyes, and admit with me:

The Master Limbo gets some things rather right.

I sink back into the seat as Berlin speeds past the window, as silent as a film, descending night painted purple and orange on coated glass. The car's acceleration describes things to come. The beginnings of a whoosh. A final, decisive whoosh, because little is more proven than that the Master Limbo of modern capitalism makes things happen—and makes them happen yesterday.

After three calls Bettina finds a locksmith prepared to open his shop. We race to an address and I climb out with the keys.

"Hmm." The locksmith scratches his whiskers when he sees them. "This red one we can't do. You see? Nor this one, nor this one. Because they're high-security keys."

Through the window I see Bettina leave the car.

"But you see this one? With the sort of hollow leading edge? A different matter. We certainly can't do it. You have to take it to the company that made it."

"I just need the green and the yellow, and this brass one here."

The man nods doubtfully. "They look like institutional keys. Some are very old, look at this one. And I mean, look at this here, see? Where are they from?"

"Uh—my institute."

"Ah—the one up here, what's it called?"

"No—the other one."

His eyebrows poise for an answer, and I smile, blinking as if the German will be a problem to speak. But he waits. His fingers close around the keys.

"*Das Institut,*" I finally say, looking up to jog my memory: "*Das Institut zur Optimierung menschlicher Angelegenheiten.*" I think I've just named the Institute for the Optimization of Human Angelhood. His brow hovers up, he stares at me.

A bell tinkles as Bettina steps in.

The locksmith shrugs. "And this other one here, well—I doubt anyone could do it."

"I only need the yellow, the green, and the brass ones."

"Hmm." He strokes his chin again. "You need it for Tuesday—or can it be later?"

Bettina barges up: "Why are you wasting our time? Cut the keys, we're in a hurry!"

"I beg your pardon? I'm only doing my job!"

"Are you totally stupid?" She jabs her head: "Do you think we'd come onto the street on a Saturday night to leave a job for Tuesday?"

The man recoils. "What? How can you speak to me like that? I'm doing you a favor even looking at the job! We do good work here, of course I have to examine the keys! As it is I'm inclined just to shut the door on you!"

"I'm sure you'd love to shut the door!" She moves into his face: "You're here taking jobs for Tuesday and certainly still meaning to charge the out-of-hours rate. Isn't that right? Standing here pushing up the price by making it all look so difficult. Show me your trading license! Show me your license and tax documents while I call the police! Is there a family upstairs? In a trading premises? Get them down!"

"Madam, it's outrageous! Unbelievable, now! I'm doing my job correctly and you insult me in such a way? I should call the police on you! On you I should call them!" The man slinks away into a back room, muttering oaths.

After a moment we hear the whirr of a grinder.

"My guardian Berliner." I give a smile of relief.

"I'm from Hamburg. And he's a Turk, he just fell into the rhythm. They must drive you insane. You're so lucky in London, the shops here are barely starting to open on Saturday afternoons, never mind Sundays. Try finding a supermarket tonight in Berlin."

"Hm. There's certainly a mellower pace of life."

"Fine pace for him," she tuts. "Times like these you need things to happen. And the lives of people like us are made of times like these."

Within twenty minutes of this poignant truth we purr back into the airport, where one lonely figure stands outlined at the main doors. I see that it's Anna, checking her watch. As we approach, another, much larger shape emerges—Gottfried. It's too late to halt the car. We coast up to the steps, where Bettina jumps out to open my door, pausing to salute me with a cheeky laugh, the peak of her cap flashing under lamplight. Only now does Anna recognize me. I see her face harden, though she says nothing, turning instead to bid Gottfried good night as he trudges off.

"I'll collect you tomorrow for brunch," chirps Bettina. "Here or the hotel?"

"Hotel's fine," I quietly say. "I'll leave you this bottle to give to Thomas."

The car roars off and I turn to Anna and Gottfried, fumbling out the keys. Gottfried nods without a word and steps away into the night. Anna stays watching me on the step below her. "Pff, well, well," she says after a withering pause.

"Sorry—bumped into an old friend on the way back up."

"You certainly did, so I see."

"It's not like that." I hand her Gerd's keys.

"But it's like something. You must at least be a spy. Gabriel Bond, and they sent your orders. To vomit on the airport. To bleed on Iran."

I look at her, catch her eyes briefly sparkling. We stand for a moment in silence.

Then: "Pff—bye-bye," and she walks away.

I take the train back to Kastanienallee, lolling in a trance as girders and lights flash by. As I turn over the day's equations, it occurs to me that I'm not as happy as I ought to be. A bottle of *Symposium* and ten cigarettes in bed help me sift through the facts: I have keys to Wonderland, the Basque and Smuts are conspiring his release from prison, the banquet of my death is set to take place within a week. My new ally of capitalism does nothing but throw solutions and comforts my way. Like Smuts I feel that life proceeds in dog years, I feel nailed to the wheel of Fortune.

And maybe it does have the clacker thing.

But still there's discomfort deep inside, and as the last tram whines past the window I wonder if it's this: I've stepped between worlds all week, comfortable in each, with friends in both, but the scene on the steps this evening felt like a door slamming shut on one of them. Though I know little about Anna or Gottfried, a part of me identifies with them, and felt the knowing in their looks as a goodbye. Particularly Anna, who strangely, even disturbingly, seems prettier every time I see her, and extracts more respect with her cool, sphinxlike stance. My arrival in a limousine might've unlocked the heart, or at least the legs, of many a girl back home—but with Anna it felt like a betrayal, not only of her but of myself. Has so much nuance passed between us that she can now deliver such truths without a word? And if so, what other intricacies might be passing through her gaze? Do I also detect a new coquet, a twinkle as these discomforts find me out? Has she found my measure, across so brief a time? Why would she want my measure at all, and what judgments had she made that I can now even betray?

Pff, who knows what? For now I put it down to fatigue and the imaginings of a guilty mind. Perhaps also a realization that she's someone who in my previous life might have excited my interest. Another irony from a limbo.

However it is, by early morning I feel the affair as another disconnection, a kind of iPod in each ear, and I fall asleep long after the dawn, waking again with just enough time to throw on my clothes and meet the car outside. Only one synapse is active: the one that tells me I'm today joining capitalism's world.

Reaching the city center, I find that world waiting like a bride, with a welcome buffet that explodes through a corner of the Adlon Kempinski toward the Brandenburg Gate. Iranian Imperial caviar glisters between oysters, sweetwater crayfish, buckwheat blinis, Maine lobsters, king prawns, chanterelles, duck livers, truffles, stingray wings, pigeons, artichokes, frogs' legs, muscat grapes, fig mustard, passionfruits, and rabbits, while thickets of tarts, puddings, petits fours, pastries, and cakes gesticulate using the same shameless devices as rare birds peddling sex in the wild.

"Do you have peanuts?" Thomas asks the waiter. "Unless"—he turns to me—"you'd prefer to join me in some champagne and strawberries?"

"Beer's fine." I rub my face. "If not just some sleep."

The aristocrat settles back, smiling across the table. After a minute he reaches out to make space on the linen for drinks, strawberries, and mixed nuts. We toast, and he bites the tip off a plump strawberry. "Thanks for the wine, I'll send it to the Basque's room. He arrives tomorrow, so be prepared for things to pick up speed after that. And here's a proposal: I trade you the key to a junior suite upstairs for your keys to the complex. We need to get the ball rolling, time's incredibly tight."

"Sounds a bad deal." I swig beer. "History's largest wine cellar in return for a cupboard here. Where will I land my plane?"

Thomas laughs and reaches into his pocket. "As you put it like that—" He motions me to open my hand under the table, and drops something into my palm. I peer under the tablecloth and see that it's a brilliant yellow diamond.

"A small thank-you." He leans close: "You'll know that no cash, plastic, or electronic instruments can pass between any of us from now on. The hotel tab is safe, but only use your Christian name, don't put your usual signature, and stick to room service." His gaze flicks around before he adds: "At the corner of Kreuz-bergstrasse and Mehringdamm is an exchange if you need to cash the stone."

"Second time in a day I've felt like James Bond."

"I know it's theatrical, but think about it, it's perfect currency. Travels easily, trades well across the world, has a single exchange rate. Bewitches everyone who sees it, bails you out of situations on the street. Hides in your mouth or up your ass. A fraction of the weight of gold. A cigar tube holds a fresh start in life."

"Do you think they could fetch one of those cake stands to the table?" I nod at the tumbling mass of tarts, flans, and pastries.

"I'll have it sent to your room—I can see I'm losing you. Get some sleep, it's all in good hands. We'll start creating a presence at the venue."

"Hm—a presence?"

"Legitimate covers around the building. Too much suspicious activity goes into setting up, we need locals to get used to us gradually. By the night of the event we shouldn't raise an eyebrow. You didn't think we'd just turn up and throw a party?" Thomas stays looking at me, and a smile grows on his face: "Sometimes

I think you don't grasp the scale of this." He presses a key into my hand: "Other times I think you're cool as ice. Though you can drop the disguise now."

I look down at my matted fur. "What disguise?"

"Don't crack me up. Get to bed."

I sketch a map to the bunkers and hand over only the green and brass keys, as the yellow is for the kiosk store with my last hoard of Marius in it. After agreeing to meet tomorrow evening to collect the Basque, I cross the hotel lobby in a heavenly light, one that gives the glow of childhood back to the skin, turns eyeballs to ivory, lights collars the white of fresh snow. Thence to my suite to collapse.

The sight of pillows makes me quake with fatigue. As a cake stand arrives with champagne I survey the room's woods, its chaise longue, its desk, sofa, minibar, and king-sized bed. I take off my clothes and lay my tubular white body down. It's pearly under the light, translucent to a short depth, sort of marbled. Here it is already cadaverous, this body, ravaged by ill-advised life. A reticulated maggot lolls halfway down in a shrub of coppery hair.

A last glum witness, wondering why.

Sunlight is gray and cold through the window when I stir on Monday. The sky doesn't swirl or flow, it just hangs. The morning brings starkness. The frameworks and casings of my body have come untethered from my skin in the night. Now I scrape and rattle, and my heart wobbles as if suspended in a sac of fluid. Just look at nature. The device she assigned to deal with a simple drive to the airport is the fight-or-flight mechanism, a one-size-fits-all panic button assigned to deal with everything from shopping to imminent death. I'm crushed by our rudimentariness. No amount of intellect, no cut of clothes can disguise how ill-conceived we really are.

Seeing the flacon of Jicky poking from a coat pocket, I snatch it up and take a swig. Whoosh: it defibrillates me, leaves me gasping, and, curiously, after a moment I even find it quite palatable. I splash some over myself, just as a commando will fry and eat the tail of the scorpion that stung him—then take another sip. The effect is even more harmonious, shocking my senses with fragrance. After this, a few cigarettes and some German television; and finally I'm ready for the day.

My first task is to call the lawyer Satou and have him give Smuts my new number. With some excitement I wonder if I might see him again. The thought propels me under the shower and, after making a note to collect my things from the Kastanienhof, sets me off to find Gerd, another friend, I suppose, which is important in a person's last days. Yes, another friend, because I look forward to seeing him, am glad to go to the kiosk, and only wish I could share these crazy times with him, tell tales from a limbo like a pal just back from vacation.

I find Gerd alone in the kiosk when I arrive. Although the terminal mills with passengers and staff, the kiosk backwater is deserted. Sadness comes with seeing Gerd. He's a man whose ambitions come at no cost to anyone. How perfect if the banquet left him a gift. It seems set to go ahead, this event, so all that's needed is a redistribution of wealth that doesn't foul his pride. I watch him before he sees me. He moves things under the counter, seals lids, shuts boxes, as if preparing to close.

"Frederick!" He brightens.

"Are you closing already?"

"Ach, nobody came all day. I don't know what it is, not even our usual taxi drivers came by." He spins away to fuss with something at the back. "And Gisela went to her sister in Stuttgart. She really needed that, it's great. Trading new recipes with her sister. Gisela's a great cook, did you ever try *Berliner Kartoffelsalat*?"

I'm too taken with watching to answer. After a moment he shows his head at the window: "On Friday is our farewell party, eh? Then you'll try it."

"On Friday? This Friday, the twenty-fourth?"

"*Ja*, of course—it's the last weekend of the airport. Serious food and drinks, and also fireworks. You'd better start training—*haa*."

Now comes the inner plummeting so central to a limbo. Ah, this workload. All I can think to reply is: "And where's Anna today?"

"Anna? Getting vaccinated for South America. She's so excited to see the giant turtles. I guess they're really something— the famous one, Lonely George, is supposed to be nearly a hundred, and bigger than a desk."

"Bigger than a desk? Gosh." After helping Gerd lower the kiosk shutter, I walk outside with him, scanning for a taxi.

"Which way are you going?" he asks. "Maybe we've time for a beer at Piratenburg?"

"Thanks, I'm moving my room. I'll take a cab from here."

"Bah, rich man," he says, squinting across the parking lot. I follow his gaze and spy a familiar shape at the other end, beside Columbiadamm. Gerd ambles a few steps up the pavement, craning to see. Then he stops, looks at me, and we squint ahead together.

Gottfried's lumpen form slides into view.

He sits perched with some other men at the bar of an impressive catering trailer, all white Duco and gleaming steel. It has

music and bistro lighting, and is watched over by stylish young
attendants who chatter and giggle with patrons. Aromas of grill-
ing meat and fresh-ground coffee sweeten our approach.

"Gottfried?" Gerd steps through a portal of palms at the curb.

"Ahh." Gottfried turns stiffly. "I was now coming to see you."

"Coming to see me when?" Gerd's face falls. "What's all this?"

"Oh, *Gott*," says a policeman. "Four beers ago he was coming."

"*Gunnar?* I saved you a wurst all day! What's going on here?"

"Well, I didn't want to bother you. Anyway, here has schnitzel."

"Eh? What?" Gerd takes in the scene like a man arriving
home to a burglary. "Schnitzel will cost you. We'll always heat
you a nice wiener, you know we will, compliments of the house.
Or even a nice bockwurst, if you prefer."

"Actually, here is free." Gunnar sips froth off a stiff cappuccino.

One of the attendants, a pretty girl in a powder-blue uniform,
leans over the dazzling counter to beam at Gerd: "Everything's
free today for friends of the airport. What can I get you? The special is Wiener schnitzel with warm *erdapfelsalat* and lemon-thyme
salsa, and the soup is a seafood bisque with baby dumplings and
dill."

"This is Laura." Gottfried points with his beer. "From Leipzig."

Gerd stands looking around, fingers twitching beside him.

"Lovely Laura from Leipzig." Gottfried chuckles.

"So sweet!" the girl pinches an imaginary cheek.

"Don't forget intelligent. Sweet and intelligent."

"I want to take him home!" squeaks the girl.

"It can be arranged."

"Ha ha ha."

"Ha ha ha ha."

"Bah." Gerd nudges him. "Piratenburg, eh?"

"Not now," grunts Gottfried.

The kiosk magnate looks down for a moment. Clenches and unclenches his hands at his sides, gazes over the row of patrons. Then he pats my shoulder goodbye—two soft little pats—and steps away by himself.

I watch his cardigan hover off down the road.

19

"You saw the wagon?" Thomas sits texting in the back seat. "Nice, don't you think? By Wednesday we'll have another two trailers there. We'll keep that one open to the public, and for the event it can double as a reserve kitchen."

I stare bleakly through the window. Although I'm not inclined to discoveries tonight, I can't help but make one from here: the world is a glossier place through the glass of a limousine. "But are you allowed to just park and serve food like that?" I ask.

Thomas doesn't look up: "The city licensed it. Tempelhof's last days are a special event. Less than a week to go. Exciting."

"You'll kill the small businesses in the terminal."

"What?" He turns a gaze on me. "Whoever didn't make their money there in the last seventy years isn't going to be saved by this week." Thomas finally slides himself up in his seat and puts down his phone. "You're not getting sentimental over the old cobwebs in the building? They're mostly East German, you can't even call them businesspeople. They're plodders, they're cogs. And we're not running for profit, we're giving food and drink away. We're doing the right thing by everyone."

"Seems harsh to say. Some very smart folk in there."

"*Ja, ja.*" He laughs. "Every Eastie's a nuclear physicist. But what's the point of a nuclear physicist who sweeps floors for a living? A rocket engineer who can't peel a banana? A neurosurgeon who can't hold a conversation?" He hangs his mouth open awaiting the reply. "My friend, your English sentimentality's showing. A charming quality, but trust me—they'll be fine, and we'll be fine."

"Are we going to General Aviation?" Bettina peers back.

"No, he's coming discreetly, Air France."

"General Aviation?" I look at Thomas. "For private aircraft?"

"Three or four jets will be involved before the week's out. The runway is the venue's equal most attractive feature. Produce can be flown direct from source, and the guests can land right beside their table." He sees me blink at this, and reaches over to slap a leg. "I tried to tell you: it's the mother of them all."

"Sounds like it. And who are the guests?"

"Ha—even I won't know for sure. And if I did, I'd have to kill myself. But I can guarantee you this—they eat jets for breakfast."

At Berlin Tegel I make an effort to show a good face. Who knows what to expect from this character Didier Le Basque? I should be overjoyed at his arrival, on paper, at least. In any event, I'm saved from much wondering by the appearance of a thickset, bottom-heavy man through the arrivals gate. Black stubble covers his face and jaw, spreading up over his head like burnt lawn. A strange and massive nose precedes him, then eyes glinting quickly through an unspoken no-man's-land around his overcoat, a force field common to all whose power blares from inside.

The Basque doesn't look at me, but offers a finger of his left hand to squeeze before moving past in a wave of cologne. Only when he sees Thomas does his brow lift off his nose. "Look at this one"—he points—"the looks of a movie star give him a soft life, uh? Me, I have to work double hard to compensate my ugliness."

"Oh"—Thomas grins—"and you consider it compensated?"

He receives a punch, the pair kiss on both cheeks, and we stride out to the car. The driver's seat is empty, and I see Bettina in a taxi queue ahead. Instead Thomas takes the wheel with Didier beside him, leaving me to loll in the rear.

We first head back to the Brandenburg Gate, with Thomas and the Basque hissing across the front like boys digging a tunnel to China. I soon find myself intrigued by this Basque; his spirit is somehow sudden, passions thrust and dodge inside him as he talks, making his body bustle with inexpressible force. And though his fast-shifting gaze warns not to ask questions, you feel that any offense of his would come from fervor and not malice.[*] It takes no time to identify his echo in Smuts's voice, not least the "uh?" at the end of a sentence, and the constant "Putain." But then fine-dining kitchens are known to breed dialect, so it says nothing about the pair. Likewise the Basque's swarming energy, which I've observed in other powerful types. As he drops his bag at the Adlon I watch staff around the door react to his presence,

---

[*] *How to recognize good people:* Scrape away the liberal dogma, and the obvious is true: you recognize good people by their faces. This truth is shunned, even presented as unfairness, but only because those doing the shunning want to be recognized by edited histories rather than the clear facts that their eyes are greedy or that they look like assholes. And there's a companion truth to this: assholes find each other's faces good, and hence congregate. This is the mechanism by which governments come to be formed, along with other zealot groups and committeelike structures. Remember: a good person will only want to interfere with their own life. You need do nothing more than this to be good—and your face will reflect it.

and after a moment I detect a hook in his demeanor—a disdainful gaze he gives everything at first, then a measured assent which comes as a relief to the recipient. In this way he hooks them by their self-esteem, pulling them more gratefully into his service.

"So, Gabriel," he growls into the back, "you have a girl? Or did we disturb your hunting tonight, in which case I'm sorry."

"No, broke up with one not long ago."

"All the better. Berlin is fine hunting."

"Hm—frankly, the only one I've met here seems difficult. Just a glance from her is like a smack with a mallet. Hard case."

"Putain, but that's why they're spectacular! You have to chase them! Maybe Thomas lends you one of his fancy cars—once a girl doesn't burn her panty on a plastic seat, she quickly sees reason in everything you say."

"Ha ha—I think this one would see the opposite. Anyway, I'm not interested in her, she's just someone I see around the place."

"A little socialist? My friend, when it comes to ass on plastic, no girl is a socialist. Give it rich leather and the panty falls off."

I laugh at Didier and he growls a laugh back, playing a combination of dirty uncle and soldier, prodding man to man, testing my humor, softening me.

"In any case it's all academic," I say. "A tortoise beat me to her."

"*Quoi?* A tortoise!" the men exclaim.

"She's leaving for South America on a wildlife tour. The giant tortoises of the Galápagos. She's smitten with Lonesome George."

"Ahh," says Thomas, "that's the famous one. The animal's like a hundred years old."

"Uff." Didier rolls his eyes. "Then don't feel too bad. You simply have to say she prefers an older type." Laughter fills the car, two tenors and a basso growl as the Mercedes surges off into traffic.

Not until we head for Tempelhof, when this banter is over that sorts men into hierarchical packs, does Didier open himself up to my view. After some chat about failing banks, he looks over his shoulder and I chance at saying: "Ironic, isn't it, a high-rolling banquet in such a climate?"

Before answering he softly says: "In case it hasn't been assumed, what you see and hear from now on belongs to us. You won't find our secrets heavy—in fact they're light and rare like stolen kisses. But we must keep them. Nobody has ever broken trust with me—think and you'll know what this means. Uh?" He stares until I nod, then goes on: "*Bon*. As to your comment, you're wrong, there's zero irony. The middle class might see the economy failing, but the truth is that we live in the richest time of all human history, an abundance the Romans could only dream of. You don't notice because of capitalism's success—real wealth has moved up into the hands of very few. There never has been such wealth concentrated in individuals, uh. Never."

"But surely—"

"Listen to me: the so-called economy is meaningless, don't be distracted by that. It was never a device for societies. Here's the analogy: think of a space rocket. Ninety-nine percent of the rocket is just a fuel can—and when the fuel is used up, it falls back to earth. What you see now with the economy is just that—the can falling down empty. The people who built the rocket are way up in space. Nothing will ever touch them again, not for five hundred years. Large or small is the only choice in human life, my friend—and they made a choice."

"Then it's the perfect time for a banquet."

"Exactly. It's the best time in history for a banquet—though it also presents a big challenge. Accumulators of wealth often have no palate, no higher senses. Some only come from camel herders, or from the ruthless bourgeoisie. Many aren't particularly inspired or intelligent. They often have no tuning for nuance. People think the powerful bask in a world of exquisite subtlety because they see them owning sublime antiquities and artworks. But the two things are mutually exclusive. You cannot have painful sensibilities and be powerful. The two destroy each other. Most own great pieces of art because the pieces themselves are powerful. So it's a challenge for us because it's hard to satisfy dull senses—and that's why we work with big ideas. With locations and experiences they can't buy for money. Naturally the wealthier they get, the harder it is to find things they can't buy. We're working above the margins of possibility. Also such banquets often celebrate special occasions, which doubles the challenge because the location must reflect the occasion. You can't toast a shipping tycoon in a shipwreck, uh. This banquet, for example, is a passing-out ceremony, a change of life at the highest level. So as a motif the airport is perfect because of its role in the famous Berlin airlifts. It was like the River Styx—craft not only passed through to another destination, they passed through to another life, another history. See how it fits? Remember, beauty must be surprising—and so the truly exquisite must really shock and be strange in its proportions. Guests have to leave wondering if the occasion really happened. And this building is a perfect launching pad for that. The best I've had."

"Must keep you busy, finding locations at this level," I say.

"We're not a catering outfit, we don't do this for a living. We're just showing off. We do the impossible because we can, because we have testicles, because in life we choose the large over the small—though naturally it doesn't hurt our business to create legends. When you're the richest man, or the second, or even the hundredth richest, you want to feel that you own the world and everything in it. And when you serve those people like we do, you have to occasionally show them that you have the keys, that you can deliver it, if only for a night."

With this we turn onto Columbiadamm, where the hulk of the airport rises into view. "Look at her, my God," Didier gasps under his breath. "Ernst Sagebiel's masterpiece. Norman Foster called her the mother of all airports, uh. We're driving half a kilometer already and the building still goes on out of sight. And look, look"—he nudges Thomas—"eagles still guard the outside."

Thomas has uncovered another route downstairs, through a utility room accessible from outside. We descend to Wonderland.

"*Pu-tain*," Didier hisses as the lights snap on.

For a time the only sounds are the scuffing of shoes and the swish of breath in still air. And when we slowly gather in the middle of the long salon of archways, more time passes before minds go to work, before ideas come in whispers:

"What about kitchens?" asks Didier. "Any still exist in here?"

"Better mobile," says Thomas. "Film catering vans outside."

The Basque nods around the vaulted ceilings, measures distances up and down the concourse in his mind. "First things first: the blank gun must be outside in the railway tunnel. Evacuation can be through the end down there—do you know if we can access tunnels to the airside? Are there direct routes out to the planes?"

"At least two routes," says Thomas, "though we still have to reverse-engineer one more security lock to get a key. Did you figure out a flight plan?"

"Of course—we'll file a nonstop plan from Paris to Helsinki, which brings us directly overhead. Then we make a precautionary landing due to instrument failure. Paris can set up something noncritical with one of the cockpit lights."

"Smart. So the plane is on standby all evening, ready to roll."

"Exactly, open for all to see, stairs down, interior lights burning, systems left on. Friendly, friendly, friendly; and even anonymous luggage inside."

"Perfect. And if we take on fuel, use some ground services, the airport will love us. The field usually shuts at eleven, but if we pay our fees and keep within noise limits we can be cleared for takeoff round midnight, especially from a precautionary landing and given that it's the last Friday of operations. Though I warn you, because of the date they might suspect we're joyriding—Schönefeld is the all-night airport, and just as close by. But it's nothing some charm from the crew won't fix. Who's flying?"

"Actually the lead guests will fly themselves, without technical crew—we'll need a couple of dummy pilots, just to hang around the plane and upstairs."

"I can fix that—we're using a friend of mine to supply another jet for produce, and his company's known at Tempelhof so has good clearance to airside."

"*Bon.*" Didier nods. "And did you rent some cover space upstairs?"

"Confirming tomorrow. I think we can get any amount of hangar or office space, and also some of the main terminal for singular events, after-hours though."

"Singular? Then book one for every day. Possess it all right away."

"Won't it waste too much time, running daily cover events?"

"Tell them it's a film production, just stand a camera there. We have to possess as much of the building as possible, there has to be activity in every corner until they don't remember what's normal anymore. Throw new faces, new activities, new furniture at them every day now until they're tired of wondering what's going on."

"And what of the menu?" asks Thomas. "Refrigeration is an issue."

"You know how it is, uh—it's according to what we can get. What we still need is a signature dish, and the scale of that won't be known until the end. I'm working contacts day and night. So far, in actual possession, we can probably do a tiger."

"A *tiger*?" Thomas blinks.

"Clean one, uh. Little one. You have a problem with it? It's an animal. If we didn't eat it, another animal would, or it would eat us. You think it's enlightened not to eat? That's the logic of our death."

"Hey—I'm not arguing."

"Good. There's no argument there. I thought maybe you joined the campaign to save cute things, and things that beep underwater. For this guest list we have to be symbolic, don't think we're going to break our balls like last time, growing hybrid crops, making stem-cell cappuccinos. Especially not from a catering van and with a walk through open air before service. This time it's bold and simple, with unique, full-flavored ingredients, exquisitely treated, and served under cloche. And actually, the more I think about the open air between kitchen and table, the more I suggest we set up a theatrical cover. A film production upstairs which can then spill out to the trailers and so on. You get the picture, uh? A cover where anything goes."

At this Thomas and Didier step away down the salon, muttering, pointing around the arches and walls. And a realization comes to me: that Smuts's and my seminal dream is here unfolding—Nimbus. Our restaurant from so long ago.

The dream seems to flood back through the arches, assembling in all its details as if this were the space it was meant for. Shrouds to catch tears and sauce, last wills and testaments, no signage, no couples, its name passed in whispers. Will there be shrouds at this banquet, I muse, or deep-sea fishing chairs with straps?

And what of the dress code, must I find my own clothes?

Seeing the men return, I catch Didier's eye. "Is there a dress code?" I ask. "Should I keep an eye out for anything? Evening wear? Or is it masquerade?"

They stop, framed between archways, and stare for a moment. "What?" Didier peers down his nose. "Dress code for what, for who—you mean guests?"

"Yes, for me—at the banquet. Should I find my own costume?"

The air suddenly grows heavy. Didier takes another step toward me, I watch his lips slowly load like a gun. "My friend—this is strictly a closed event."

I stand silent, looking from one man to the other.

"Perhaps"—he shrugs—"there might be something you can do when we set up, if you like—I don't know, maybe help in one of the trailers."

"Ah. Hm. I just thought that, after—"

"Listen, no, let's be clear: our business is concluded—uh?"

20

I find it impossible to rise the next morning. Instead I lie with a vague sense of foreboding, clearing my throat and scratching myself for no other reason than to prove I still exist. It must be afternoon when the phone rings, chirping little shots of adrenaline. Behind Smuts's voice I hear the clatters and cries of a prison; a groan here, a yelp there, echoing off surfaces of iron. It takes him a moment and some words in Japanese before he's alone. I nudge my cold breakfast tray aside with a knee.

"Gabriel," he finally says, "you cunts forget me or what?"

"Eh?" I stiffen. "Of course not, what makes you say that?"

"I know the Lord works in mysterious ways, but at least tell me what the fuck's going on. I'm living in prison years, which are made of that last hour before the school bell. I keep waiting for Didi or Satou to bail me out of here."

"But—haven't you been in conference with the Basque?"

"Have I fuck, not since that one call at the police station. All I can think is he's at the Peninsula playing with himself. Most likely in your room, uh."

"Well, no—he's over here. His colleague said you were in

touch, said a plan was in hand. Everything's full steam in Berlin, moving in dog years."

"Uh?" The brainatelle loads a ball. "Well, did he say what the plan was? If it's about me it'd be fucking amazing to hear what it is before I go down for murder on Monday."

A chill soaks through me. "Smuts—I heard that everything was under control. They're over here organizing the banquet."

"Well, I guess that's something, at least he's still hooked on our place. Thank fuck for that! Did he mention me in connection with the menu? The only good thing about here: I've had time to sketch up some seriously plush menus."

"Hm, well—he's hardly going to discuss any of that with me." An icy glimmer still spreads through me, the room even starts to pixilate—not from what I've heard, but for what I sense is to come. It's a slow dawning on a cataclysmic scale. "All I've heard thus far is that they may possibly get their hands on a small tiger."

"Uh? Tiger? Bad move, that surprises me—cats are crap."

"I think he said they weren't going too haute cuisine, they were looking more for symbols. Simple, full-flavored produce."

"Putain, if it's a cat we might only be able to work with the tail. Unless it's a cub, a milk-fed cub—is it a cub? If it's a cub tell him to start milk-feeding right away, it'll need eight to ten weeks at least, I reckon. The quicker I can get on to it, the better—tell him to hold back on the menu for now. What's their proposed date?"

"Hm—quite soon, I think." I fall back, feeling sick inside.

"Okay, listen, Putainel—if they're that fired up about the venue, and already thinking ahead to the menu, then the trick now is to *close the deal*. Close it today if you can, it's getting scary over here. But remember who you're dealing with, play it cool. And whatever you do, for fuck's sake don't give them too much access to the place! Not until we see things start to happen over here! Uh? This is our only move left in the world, don't blow it. The power rests with us—but only as long as *we control the keys.*"

Whoosh. Thus in earnest, showing unarguable, even perfect reason, Smuts delivers what must be the end-play of them all— the finale in a tome of finales, the terminus of a sphinx and of all hapless enough to cross his ill-omened path—for I have given, as give all small persons who would woo the Master, the keys to salvation in return for a patch of sunlight on linen, a feather pillow, and my breakfast in bed.

Only one message can come from it: go the way of all earth. Embrace the pale priest of the mute people, yield the ghost, find the Stygian shore, answer the final summons, pay the debt we must all pay, put out to sea—fuck off and die.

The ensuing night sees me finish off all remaining substances, empty the minibar, and weep till my ducts stick shut. And come Wednesday, in the wake of this solitary binge, I step out to face the world a last time. A different world than before. Now it's the Master's world, trod by parasites, usurpers, and sundry germs.

I step out feeling like the primary source of this infection.

When I reach Tempelhof I find it swarming. Massive service doors sit open along its length while trucks with flashing lights beep urgently up and down, attended by pods of men on missions unknown. In the midst of it all the kitchen wagon sits pumping modern beats—and there at the counter stands a figure dressed in black.

He wears his collar up like a film-noir spy, almost touching a rakishly dipped homburg, and rocks gently on his heels to the rhythm.

Drawing level, from a distance, I see it's Gottfried Pietsch.

My physical state is equal to that of any person undergoing their last day of breath after a long illness; one leg has turned stiff and tries to drag, my arms have become stuck to my ribs at the elbows, and my hands curl inwards like claws. I try to pass the wagon without being seen, and feel I've succeeded until a voice behind me grunts: "*Englander*—if you're looking for Specht, he's not inside." Gottfried hasn't turned, but rather sniped me through the back of his head. I approach him at the wagon.

After I've watched his beer glass tip to his lips, its elegant paper cravat spinning on the stem, then watched him land it back on the bar, he says, still without turning: "Would you know something about a film production happening here?"

"Hm." I cough. "Can't say I would, no."

After a stony pause he swivels to stare into my face. I manage to withstand a moment or two of his ice-blue rays, which have the same effect as looking into the sun—then I squint, and drop my gaze. After another moment's silence he makes a small ceremony of removing a fat cigar from his breast pocket and pointing with it up Columbiadamm, where two figures sit on the curb under a tree. One is Gerd, head in hands, with a phone to his ear. I thank Gottfried and wander up to find Anna sitting beside him, tracing spirals on the ground with a twig.

"Bah! What?" Gerd's voice quavers out as I draw near. "But they also killed the kiosk, and that's not a matter of who has the most money, it's a matter of fair practice in the territory of a small business. Eh? Well, I know it's the airport's business too, but you tell me if giving fair warning isn't a part of their duty to tenants."

Anna rises, brushing off the bottom of her jeans: "What do you want?" she hisses. "This is a bad time, they're trying to cancel Gerd's farewell party."

"Oh, no, I'm sorry—who's trying to cancel it? How can they?"

"Some last-minute event hired the terminal. Gerd's closing down the kiosk early. Things are bad enough today without you here prowling for cakes."

"But surely they can't stop you from trading? I thought the terminal space could only be hired after hours, for special events."

She narrows her gaze. "That's true—but whether we open or not, the van over there is giving food away, so what's the point? And how do you know about terminal policy?"

I stand quietly swaying, finally stepping up to the nearest tree, where I prop myself like a tripod. "Hm, well—I must've heard it around the place."

"And," she goes on, "because of the events we're not even allowed into the building on Friday night. Gerd's talking to a lawyer, it's just not right."

I nod and look away, trying to fight this welling pain. Here's the Master Limbo of capitalism, a firestorm, not only consuming all in its path but sucking oxygen from the world around to feed its ravening vacuum, even draining lungs far and wide of its estates. A van reverses nearby, beeping insistently, and in its beep I hear the voice of that limbo crowing: "I win, you lose."

"Ach, Frederick"—Gerd looks over—"did Anna tell you? They're trying to stop the party, but I haven't finished fighting yet. No, sir. Not as long as there's air in my lungs." He nods to himself for a moment before looking at the wagon. "Did you see Gottfried? Someone told him they're making a film—*haa*."

After this spike of levity his face falls into a state of determined mourning, and he fixes a stare across the avenue. Anna checks her watch and turns to him:

"I'll go now," she says. "Shall I get the same as before?"

"*Ja*, the cheapest." Gerd nods. "Maybe the poet can help you carry them."

"Pff." Anna looks me up and down. "Poet? That explains something. Though maybe I end up having to carry him." She turns to me: "Are you fit for a walk?"

"Yes," I say, "if I can be helpful." And frankly I'm glad to get away, with everything around here beeping and buzzing like predators swarming in for a kill.

Anna's éclair-sized bag hangs from her shoulder, and I find myself wishing it contained the éclair it was designed for. Instead she pulls out a tissue and hands it to me. Blood starts to poke from one of my nostrils; I dab it.

"And where should I leave them?" she asks Gerd.

"Put them down in the store—here, take the keys."

We set off on this mission for Gerd, who knows where to or for what, but it's the least I can do for him, and anyway it can only be to a less taunting place than here. A walk might even stabilize my condition enough to summon wisdom, because traipsing behind Anna, watching her buttocks locomote in denim, I'm reminded that life is behind me. Only death stands ahead, where nothing locomotes. I scrape along as a wraith, and as the airport's clamor fades behind us I know I must use the calm of these hours, use the space of Berlin's broad, pragmatic streets, the lack of intrusion by profiteering limbos, to plot a swift death—one without a banquet.

Anna is quiet until the traffic lights on Schönberger Strasse.

"Were you always this way?" she asks. "Or did Gerd's 'special party' ruin you?"

"We missed you at the 'special party,'" I say.

"Pff—I cried my eyes out not to be there."

"Hm. I felt that way about my family's parties."

"I don't have a problem with them." She scowls. "Except they're in Dresden."

"Ah, sorry. I assumed Gerd was—"

"I'm a distant cousin of Gisela's. Incredibly distant."

Crossing the road, she takes pains to keep a space between us. Only when a massive building looms ahead do I think to ask about our mission.

"Storage trunks," she says. "To pack away the kiosk."

My gut heaves.

What looms up ahead is IKEA.

The place is monstrous, it's a *Flughafen* of commerce. The parking lot alone seems to take us hours to cross. My heart beats thinly as the building's shadow falls over us, and dialogue fizzles out as I search for exits and places to run. Left of the entrance a bank of checkout tills stretches to infinity like an international border, where hordes of antlike shoppers bob with their goods. Traffic only passes out. Doors to the right give onto a lobby with an elevator going up one short level. Anna takes me to the elevator, and upstairs we pass into a marked channel that twists into the distance through waves of furniture and chattels. A cold sweat breaks over me. The path cuts through shallows, tides, and drifts of basic furnishings, past ladles and shelves, pots, cushions, sofas, and tables.

There's only one direction of travel. I come to feel unwell.

"I might just duck out for a cigarette." I stop in a cluster of bathroom solutions, a sort of backwater out of the tidal flow. A couple of other shoppers eddy here briefly, but are soon swept out into deeper furniture. I watch them whisked away on a flotsam of cup holders, soap dishes, and waste bins.

"What's wrong with you?" tuts Anna.

"We seem to have walked miles."

"Pff—we're not even halfway."

My persona faints dead inside me.

Prongs of icy panic set the scene spinning until finally I turn and flee, back past ladles, past bookshelves and sofas, arms flailing in a headlong fall toward the elevator.

But its doors are shut.

There's no button down.

Over the railing I can see the world through the window, see people wandering in freedom, chattering, smoking.

But there's no escape for me.

The store has been made escape-proof.

I catch my breath. A Swede has trapped me in a store. With a hangover. Somewhere at a distance a vicious, cashmere-clad agent of the Master Limbo has perfected a trap for humans. We're rats to him, mere units of profit, of such low intrinsic worth as to need a one-way elevator in case better judgment stops our passage through a maze to his tills.

It's a laboratory of shopping. A vivarium of human weakness.

The work of forces who'll stop at nothing in their lust for gain.

And in Berlin! Town of the People! The pain is too much. If it has reached here, this infection—it must have reached everywhere.

I glance around for bodies. Surely not every rat had the fiber to get through. Then I bolt back through the store, flash past mile after mile of Nordic pine, slowly mastering corners until the ground floor opens out before me like a harbor mouth. Ahead on the shore goods trolleys roam a chaotic dock, and I aim for a bank of tills behind them. The power of miracles propels me there, strides lengthening, arms thrusting like pistons, gaze darting across queues to judge the shortest one.

But there is no shortest one.

The tills are jammed with walking wounded.

I flit this way and that, but my hands are empty, consumers can't understand my lack of products, it's a club for those who have them, they're bonded by them, I'm a heretic, a rogue cell, and in that way of organisms meeting deviants they mass together to obstruct and repel me. My abduction is complete, it's a scene from Orwell's worst nightmare, of rats stupefied and milling with goods that aren't even fucking built.

The Swede has even calculated the immune system effect of crowds!

In terror for my life, through a flak of exclamations and jostling, I finally burst through a loosely packed queue and vault an old lady's trolley to freedom.

Sometime later Anna finds me twitching beside a hot-dog van in the parking lot. "Don't tell me." She sets down her boxes. "A man who doesn't like shopping."

"It's unlawful detention, remote-control sodomy."

"Pff." She tosses a gaze to the sky. "Without IKEA Berlin would be sleeping on the floor. It's perfect for here—simple, inexpensive, and cool. It's the people's store."

"They must've gotten a taste for mass rape."

"What are you saying? Did they point a gun at you? It's just a shop! You get your things and come out! If you don't want to come, then don't come!" She chases her words with a stare, then looks halfheartedly around, as if someone else might walk her home.

"You don't like me, do you?" I light a cigarette.

"Do you have any likable qualities?"

"I think so."

"What are they?"

"Well." I take a long drag, blow a trumpet of smoke.

She waits till my silence becomes an answer. I look up and see her small, sharp teeth smiling down, her hair hung over her forehead in strands.

"Hm," I say, "then I suppose we agree on something."

"Ha ha, yes. You're dreadful, and completely self-indulgent."

I have to laugh at such breathtaking effrontery. "Ha ha, well," I say, "you're judgmental and rude. Miserable German girl."

"*Dankeschön.*" She gives a scornful curtsy.

We can't help but laugh again, a laugh ringing with the relief that comes after truth, and I muse how little truth has graced my life, also wondering what gives her the front to grace it now. Maybe she's the opening act of my life flashing before my eyes, a precursor to admitting my sins, to meeting my Maker. It would be consistent with the Enthusiasms to send someone like this and, come to think of it, to send me on this Ghost of Christmas Future shopping tour, to witness the vibrant human world reduced to a maze of milling rats. Death is surely near, then, and when I look up at the girl I find her watching me, as if making sure that her truths have hit home. I can't recall ever having such a frank exchange with a stranger, and feel it as a slap.

"You're a mess," she finally says. "Do you need some *pommes* with mayonnaise?"

"Thank you, if it won't harm your opinion any further."

"Ha ha." She makes for the van. "Nothing could do that."

One euro buys a little tray of fries, which confirms to me that the van must be sent by a charity to this place where it knows innocent victims will gather. A cloud rises off the fries into my face, and the tubes and nozzles of my body sweetly ache as they slide down. I eat watching a stream of hostages gurgle out of the store with their loads while birds loiter nearby, threatening our food. It truly seems that between nature, the Nordic date-rapist, and the despicable sphinx, all modern life is here in its horror.

"I don't think Gisela's very fond of me either," I muse.

"Fond of you? Gisela really *hates* you. *Loathes* you."

"Oh? Hm."

"You haven't worked that out? That's why she went away! Huge fight between her and Gerd. After you came to the party they started fighting, she didn't think they should pay to feed you. All Gerd could say was, 'He brought the best wine—Gabriel brought the best wine,' but the fight never stopped, it went all the way back to his club-owning days in Prenzlauer Berg. Did your father once steal from him?"

"Well—according to Gerd, at least. I was only a child."

"Ah, then that's why." She pauses for a moment, staring. "So your father steals from honest men, and you turn out quite awful and self-indulgent."

"Don't you ever lie even just slightly, out of politeness?"

"What, you mean like this: maybe there's hope for you."

"Ha ha ha." My head tumbles into my lap.

She bursts out laughing as well, watching it all hit home.

"Ha ha ha." I stumble to a trash can, lift its lid, and hose it with a froth of fries.

Anna turns away, nodding confirmation to herself. When I've finally composed myself, I lug her boxes back up to the airport, my day unraveled, my body ruined, my character reduced to what it is, i.e., apparently nothing.

"That was fun, then," I puff as the airport appears.

"For you maybe. You seem to have time to wander around bleeding and breaking up marriages. Why are you really here?"

"I could ask the same of you. You're not an obvious choice to staff a kiosk. Are you a sort of truth patrol? A free-range blunt instrument?"

"Pff, I do what I can. I'm saving up for a vacation."

"In the next millennium, then, if the kiosk's paying."

"I'm just helping Gerd before I go. I've been working at Potsdamer Platz for the last year. When the airport's closure was finally announced, Gerd was sure these last weeks would bring a boom. He bought a mountain of stock."

"Hm." I set down the boxes. "I'm sorry, you know."

"I don't say you're not. It's also typical of Gerd to panic over the party and close the shop down. I understand why he's upset, he's been planning it all year. But he could hold it somewhere else. Suddenly he's territorial about the airport. Herr Pietsch is the same, hanging around like an old lover." She looks up at me through clear green eyes. "I'm only worried in case Gerd sells his car or something stupid like that, trying to fight in the courts. He doesn't have money for lawyers. He's just exhausted after Gisela left, and now with this competition from the trailer. The airport ended before he expected it to, it was his only security in life. Gerd relies on strict routine."

The hiss of a jet threads a breeze from the airport. We pass by the tree where Gerd sat, searching the wagon up ahead for signs of him or Gottfried. But they don't appear. As I pause to catch my breath, Anna sits herself under a porch in one of the service entrances, monitoring the street with a frown. I join her between worlds, between life and death on the one hand, tigers and bockwurst on the other.

"I wish I could make things up to Gerd before I go," I say.

"You won't find it easy, he's a proud man and he hates debt.

I shouldn't tell you, after the trouble between him and Gisela—but Gerd is very fond of you, in case you didn't know. He never had his own kids, couldn't afford them. But he remembers you well from your childhood and defended you strongly against Gisela. So you paid him back in a small way just by coming around. He's a man who values the people and things he's known for a long time. I'm sure that's how he tolerates Gisela—once the shock wore off, she was just always there, he grew accustomed."

"Hm, well, thanks. Touching that you mention it."

"Pff, don't get excited—you're still disgraceful."

Only silence can follow this, but when it does the tendrils begin to emerge that tie strangers together, barely smokelike at first, and probably growing to nothing more than cobwebs over the length of this pause. But I wonder, if I weren't on my way to die, how long it would take this girl to inspire a household ivy of attachment, of the kind whose fronds flow curling off a mantelpiece. Perhaps not long.

"Must admit, I didn't expect you to open up," I say.

She ponders this for a moment, nodding. "It's just strange that you show up without any visible reason, and then things start turning bad. I don't want to see Gerd hurt, he has enough going on without your mysterious agendas."

"Hm. But honestly, I'm sorry about all that's happened—and when I came I had no idea how things had ended between Gerd and my father."

"Pff—let me stop you before you turn it into some tender, innocent mistake." She turns to scowl. "The issue which Gerd can't see, but which I can, is that you came here to self-destruct. And I've seen self-destruction before. Berlin has seen it too. Coming from England you probably find us all so meek and quiet, you think we never tasted decadence. But did you ever ask why we might be this way? Because we tasted decadence like you've never tasted it. We tasted it so much that in the end Hitler seemed a welcome relief. And now you come with that same flavor on you, a smell that took us a century to wash out of our clothes. That smell of a vacuum, of a selfish chaos. Because what selfish people like you never realize is that self-destruction is a team sport, pulling everyone in. It's not a cool game, and it's not a game for the stupid. So forget about your father, forget about whatever you blame for your position in life—you are successfully achieving what you decided to achieve. And all I ask is that you don't recruit us into the game, because we already had our turn. We don't need your smell around to remind us what started it."

"Whoosh." My gaze falls. "That's pretty strong."

"Life is pretty strong."

"Hm—I guess I should take your frankness as a compliment."

"You should take it as a favor that I go so easy on you. If you weren't an artist, as Gerd seems to think, I would have to put it in very plain language."

Whoosh, just look at her, friend, come in close—because here on the edge of death, oozing pain wherever I go—I still have to stifle a smile at this hard little nut beside me. God only knows why, after a hammering like that. Such is the cut of her razor that I have to clamp my lips shut to keep from giggling at the sheer force of her.

She sees it, and her face grows even darker. "Pff, and now what?"

"Hm." I turn away. "You actually quite like me, don't you?" The words hang for a moment, watching us; and then I look up and see her also struggling, in that state of a child being teased from a sulk against their will, squirming in the face.

"Don't try to escape. You admitted you have no likable qualities."

"But do you think so? Or why would you waste your breath?"

"Because like all successful destroyers you have the heart and intellect enough to formulate an ethic based on your experience, which is clearly one of betrayal and pain. But you've formulated the wrong ethic. Nobody can like or respect that. And what I'm telling you is that while decadence might have come to your town, we've moved past that. Berlin isn't at the end of a cycle, it's at the beginning. You should get back on easyJet and go vomit with your friends."

"Whoosh," I say, "that's strong. EasyJet, eh? Sounds like something I needed to hear quite a while back. Like something I needed back at the very beginning."

She turns to snarl into my face, baring her sharp little teeth, shaking her head as one might at the filthiest of children.

An old wish floods back to me. Ah, this limbo.

Silence settles after this, there's no answer, and it's too late in my game to reach for her. Though I check her face for good humor now and then, my mind eventually sinks back to other matters. I set about scheming: I have a yellow diamond in my pocket. If I can make a reparation to Gerd for his losses I might die a vaguely redeemed man, not least in Anna's estimation, which suddenly seems a valuable goal. It's curious how people come to be admitted to one's mental jury, that tribunal to which we plead and present our mitigations.

My first thought is to cash the diamond; but I suspect Gerd is embarrassed by debt and would much rather forget it. Then it strikes me: if I give him the diamond itself, let him find it thrown somewhere—because after all, this new commotion around the airport makes it a plausible find—how could he refuse? And if I help to identify it, congratulate his good fortune, call witnesses—then surely it's bingo.

Going downstairs I roll the stone around my pocket.

The air shudders when the security door swings open. Although we don't venture far into the tunnel, I longingly peer up it and spy movement some distance away beside the tracks. Anna spots it too and we pause, craning to see. A pair of men in overalls appear pushing a cage on a trolley. Then as the lead man glimpses us, hastily throwing a blanket over the cage—we catch something buzzing around inside.

What appear to be tiny hovering birds. Hummingbirds.

Anna looks at me.

I shrug and am about to make light of it when I'm saved by Gerd's voice echoing down the stairwell: "Eh?" he calls. "Anna?"

"We're just dropping off the boxes," she replies.

"You took long enough." His head appears on the landing.

"Because your poet was vomiting."

"Thanks, Anna, for that." I cough.

"Frederick? Are you okay? Actually, I'm not feeling well myself—finish with the keys, Anna, and I'll go home for a while. Enough for one day, bah."

"I'll walk with you to the corner," I say. "I'd best be going too."

I fondle the diamond in my pocket as Gerd and I amble away. Between the terminal entrance and the monumental garden sits a large bronze of an eagle's head on a plinth—apparently the remains of a whole Nazi eagle that once crowned the terminal building, until American forces dismantled it, shaving its head to resemble the bald eagle. Pausing to admire the bronze, I wait for a family to pass behind us; then, as Gerd points out where the eagle used to perch, I plant the stone on the pavement.

"Gerd." I point: "What does that look like to you?"

"Eh—what?"

"Down there. Like a diamond."

"Bah." He reaches down. "Glass. How could a diamond be here?"

The gem sparkles in the palm of his hand. We prod it.

"First of all, it's yellow," he says. "Diamonds are white."

"No, there are yellow diamonds."

"Ach, but incredibly rare. This must be costume glass."

Nonetheless his fingers close around the stone, and we set off walking again. My mood lifts, as although there are no witnesses, on his way home he'll surely stop at the Piratenburg where all-knowing pals might confirm the find.

Overtaking the young family who passed us, I watch Gerd linger to smile at the parents. Then, in slow motion, he reaches to a little girl dangling off the mother's arm:

"Here, little one." He presses the stone into her hand: "For a princess."

21

So dawns the day before the banquet. I've done all I can—and can undo none of it. It's my last morning. From my bed at the Adlon Kempinski, because there's no seaside nearby, I resolve to walk into a lake and drown. I lie wondering whether to do this in daylight or darkness. Then the phone rings, and I flinch:

"Gabriel—are you awake?" It's Thomas.

"Apparently." I hear hubbub around him.

"Do you know KaDeWe—Kaufhaus des Westens? Come upstairs to the oyster bar."

"I thought our business was concluded." There's no way to say this other than frostily. I recall the pain of vanishing dreams.

"Don't be like that," says Thomas. "If it makes you feel any better, Didier and I won't be banqueting either. It really is strictly closed, they don't want we lowly caterers around. But we have a little proposal, do come."

After a shower I take a taxi to West Berlin and slump in the back trying to piece together my failure as a limbonaut. In finding a party venue for Smuts I've so far been instrumental in the collapse of a marriage, the destruction of a small business, and my exclusion from the party itself. Still, no more. Perhaps Thomas's little proposal will be a lever for Smuts before I go. Beyond that, I'll cast a last eye over the mother of all airports and over my curious friends there. And be gone.

The view through the window distracts me slightly from my pain, as driving up Kurfürstendamm we seem to enter a different city, with glossy storefronts and flamboyant old buildings behind café awnings and trees. Trees, I muse, seem to prefer the affluent to the poor in cities. Still more evidence of God disliking the poor. As we pass these extravagances it's clear what a thorn West Berlin must have been in the communist flesh. And I recall that this affluent enclave, for which John F. Kennedy declared himself a jelly doughnut, was the very one saved by the Tempelhof airlifts. The Soviets tried to starve her like a tumor, but hadn't counted on the Master.

KaDeWe is a lavish department store. I take the elevator up to its food hall, where the rudest, most pristine specimens of produce cram every inch of the view. Around a few corners I come upon a seafood section, and there find the oyster bar. Didier sits hunched over a table in conversation with Thomas, gesticulating wildly.

Thomas nods me to a stool as I walk up. "We're down to West of Ireland oysters on the menu." Champagne quickly follows, but my body must have regrouped against me in the night because the first sip burns me like battery acid.

"Impressive place, uh?" Didier nods a greeting. "For me the most incredible store in Europe. It also has the most restaurant seats of any venue in Germany, and the most oysters move over this bar. The only thing I could ask more is a bottle of Elgood's Black Dog with the oysters. A beer from your country, uh—a little secret of connoisseurs." As the next oysters arrive he turns back to Thomas, who explains:

"Didier's just reminding me about Pike, I hadn't heard the end of that story."

"Ah," says the Basque, "he has to tell you the ending himself." And to me: "Thank you, by the way, for your bottle—that's what started us on Pike." Didier lines up an oyster and tips it into his mouth with all the solemnity of a burial at sea. "But I guess the rest of his history is known on the grapevine. I lived by the idea ever since: Pike was at the peak of his powers in Europe. He was with this one girl who was a model. And it turned out she had a sister who was even more beautiful. So he had her as well. And the moment came when he had to drive one of them to Monte Carlo—"

"Was it in a Ghibli Spyder?" asks Thomas.

"Yes. I even think I know where it is today. Worth a fortune now. Anyway, the other sister was already in Monaco, they would drive and join her. Of course, Pike was going to have them both that night. And so the moment came when he found himself on a winding road with a model next to him in a sports car, on their way to meet an even more beautiful model. The sea was blue, the sky stretched tight, the air was hot, and he could smell the girl, the leather, and the sea. Ecstasy was guaranteed. And at that moment he said to himself: '*It doesn't get any better than this.*'"

We hold our breath, oyster shells poised in midair.

"So he stopped the car, got out, walked away—and never came back."

"*What?*" Thomas recoils. "Not sure I could've done it."

"He discovered the power band of pleasure lies in the moment before. He realized there is no present tense, things don't exist until captured by memory. Pleasure can only die in a past, however recent or far it is. When he stopped at that moment, he captured a perfect future." We sit suspended with the implications until Didier shrugs: "By these discoveries you learn to truly live."

"Remarkable," says Thomas. "Except for—"

"Uff, Jesus Christ—now you're going to ask me what it actually means? It means that your best moment isn't with the twentieth beer, but with the first beer in front of you. It's not on your hundred millionth dollar, but on your nine hundred and ninety-ninth. It means that human pleasure comes from opening a door, not from walking through it."

"So it's a philosophy of restraint? Acceptance?"

"A philosophy of adulthood. Only babies reach for everything. Pike spent his youth drinking Europe dry of fine wines—then came the moment he went to grow it instead."

"Ironic to serve his wine, then—the idea goes against all the banquet guests stand for."

"Naturally it's way over the head of the guests," scoffs Didier. "But then money by itself has no pleasure attached, they just eat it like sharks eat fish, without feeling."

"And there's still a punch line to the story?"

"Oh, yes." Didier grins. "Ask him yourself one day. Now we should talk with our comrade, in case he feels bad." He turns to me.

"Well," I say, "only that Smuts is still in prison, with a court date in four days' time. He feels we've forgotten him."

At this Didier's brow descends to his nose. His eyes turn to slits and he leans back, spreading out his arms, baring his chest; he scowls at me like this for a moment, then folds himself back to the table, gliding his face toward mine. "Do you doubt my word when I tell you we have the case under control?"

"But you must admit: time's slipping away."

He watches me, motionless for another long moment: "Please appreciate that the question here is to make Smuts's hands clean without getting our hands dirty. Uh? And only one thing will do that. Tomorrow we'll see."

"But tomorrow's the last workday this week."

"*Bon.*" He thumps the table and rises. "Thank you, gentlemen, I must go. Thomas, see if you can make a proposal to Gabriel for me—and I see you both tomorrow. Big day, uh?"

With that he vanishes into a maze of produce.

Thomas and I spend a minute adjusting to life without the Basque's electrical pull. Then, after a sip of champagne, Thomas leans in: "Are you familiar with the position of *pursuivant* at these events? Technically the *alarum pursuivant?*"

"Can't say I am, no."

"Very important. The position of *pursuivant* addresses one of the forgotten arts of a party, which is the beginning and end. The greatest event will be damaged if at the end the guests are allowed to drift away—so a perfect event starts and ends precisely. It must end slightly earlier than guests would like—in this way it stays freshly picked in their memory, keeps the excitement of unused potential, as well as the necessary drop of regret. These elements together make the heart of what we look for in pleasure—just like Pike's story, now that I think about it. The job of the *alarum pursuivant* is to signal the beginning and end. We'd like you to consider accepting that role for tomorrow night. You know the *alarum* will be posted outside the banquet hall with a starting pistol, as a first warning. And the *pursuivant* is the agent who traditionally delivers the guests safely to and from him—so it involves meeting the guests at the aircraft, leading them in; and at midnight signaling the end of the event by putting the lights out in the venue and leading the guests to the *alarum*, who will cover their exit back to the plane. You will be masked and wear a cape, which will be waiting in the administration trailer before the event. Didier and I will be behind the scenes too, monitoring."

Thomas pauses to finish his champagne, then leans closer, lowering his voice. "We feel you would be particularly useful in the role, not only because you're familiar with the complex, and of course discreet—but also because of this: you must be acquainted with some of the locals from the airport?"

"I know two or three of them, sure."

"A fat man in black, who wears a hat?"

"Hm—that must be Herr Pietsch, yes."

"Because that man has been spending his day at the wagon asking questions. And not purely innocent questions—he's a man who knows what to ask, if you get my drift. We're a little concerned. One of our people also saw him underground yesterday, so we know he has clearance into the complex."

Thomas sits back, watching me while this settles in. I try another sip of champagne but soon abandon it, trying not to squirm.

"So in your position as *pursuivant*," Thomas goes on, "which will keep you around the entrance to the venue, you could perform a valuable task in managing this man, and any others who might happen past. Yes?"

"I'll give it some thought. See what we hear from Smuts."

At this we sit watching each other for a moment. Then Thomas steers the talk to informal matters, and the meeting ends.

I exit through the jungle of foods feeling tired and confused.

On top of this the absence of intoxicants brings another flood of feelings and thoughts. As well as a ravenous hunger, I now yearn for some kind of home.

And feel a pressing need to escape exquisiteness.

My room at the Adlon doesn't quite satisfy the latter, but still I repair to my bed to let my mind comb through the options now crowding the point of this cone. First comes the question of whether to trust the Basque and Thomas. One thing I've learned about the Master Limbo of modern markets is that you're never off the hook—just when you think you're home and dry, a situation fails and the Limbo offers a next solution. That is happening here. First the promise of a venue was enough for Smuts's release. That situation collapsed, to be replaced by a condition where the keys to a venue would secure his release. And as that situation proved false, another condition now seems to be offered, which is to decoy Gottfried from the goings-on.

All the Master Limbo's fees are being paid while none of ours are. This is the basic equation, take note—this is how the Master works. It keeps us in hock while promising release upon payment of a next condition down the line.

But are the Basque and Thomas part of the limbo itself? Or are they merely pirates, surfing its edge for the sake of adventure?

This is the crux of my position: if I can trust the pair, I should attend the banquet in good faith, for Smuts's sake. And if I don't trust them, I should find a lake this evening.

My mind wanders from this to the nature of these worlds I stand between, and will soon leave behind. An overworld and an underworld were my estates, though I proved pointless in them both. On evidence gathered throughout this odyssey I think I can say the underworld is my world. I spend a few moments paying it mental homage. I suppose every creature should die knowing where its heart once lay.

The idea makes me think of Anna, Gottfried, and Gerd.

Recall Anna's empty face, my friend, unmoved by any challenge or surprise. I wish I'd mastered the poker face before death. When a strong reaction isn't called for, there's no reaction at all, and I feel this more honestly reflects life's workload. A sense grows in me that these aren't dour people, but that they hold themselves in reserve. I think of my ex-girlfriend Sarah. She doesn't really like her friends, but they fit the template of who she should like and have the right accessories, so she pretends to like them. She has taken this to be a duty of friendship. I think of myself, pretending to like them for her sake, and them probably pretending to like us, because we seem to like them so much. I think of everyone I know just pretending. It brings this revelation: it's dishonest to expect life's base condition to be happiness; and in maintaining that lie, another lie is needed, then another and another. How could such a detour have arisen in our thinking? Who benefits from the idea that anything less than happiness must be a treatable condition?

Only the markets. Only the Master.

I'm blasted from this reverie by the phone.

"Gabriel," says Smuts. "What's the game? I'm just calling to say don't give those boys the venue, looks like they boned us."

"What? I've just come from the Basque—he assures me everything's well in hand."

"Mate: what's in hand is his dick. Satou's entering a guilty plea first thing Monday. Says it'll go easier than arguing about fish."

"Eh? Surely we have a business day left?"

"Oh, yeah? What business day's that?"

"Tomorrow—today's only Thursday."

There's a dull silence, and then: "Putain—it might be Thursday there. But it's already tomorrow in Japan. Wish me luck."

22

An October sky like a pane of frosted glass sits over Kreuzberg. I make my way to the airport to say goodbye. The end-play only pointed to one thing—the end.

I catch sight of myself passing a shop window. My skin is yellow, my hair as stiff as hay. Just look at me, will you? My clothes hang off me like a tramp's. This is the wages of limbo. I buy a half liter of chocolate milk at a Turkish Imbiss, and with this august sustenance limp away up the street. It's a fact worth noting that a derelict person can attract suspicion and fear from passersby, but not if he carries chocolate milk. The passing eye always looks for alcohol or drugs on a derelict, and so is pleasantly disarmed by chocolate milk. With this urban white flag, then, I continue up Mehringdamm to the *Flughafen*.

Approaching the kitchen wagon, I see another two trailers parked beside it. One is fully enclosed, with mirror glass. Gottfried's hat is nowhere to be seen, so I make my way toward the terminal. As I reach the steps Anna hurries out in her coat:

"Gerd's missing," she says. "I'll check Piratenburg—can you go and find Gottfried?"

"What? Of course—what's happening?"

"Gerd lost the fight for his party. Now he owes four hundred euros to a lawyer and his car is missing. He wasn't looking good when I saw him, I'm afraid he might do something stupid. He's taking things way too hard."

"Hm—sorry. And where will I find Gottfried?"

"Have you been to his place? The little bicycle workshop around the corner from Piratenburg. See what he knows and meet me at Gerd's, I'll use the phone there."

"And where's Gerd's? Are you able to get in?"

"Grossbeerenstrasse, just past Piratenburg, third floor. Of course I can get in, it's where I'm staying until I leave for the Galápagos."

I find Gottfried's shop in the basement of an old apartment block. Bicycle parts languish behind a dusty window. The shop looks closed, but a few moments after I ring I see Gottfried's shape stir inside. He doesn't open the door but cracks it an inch, peering around his feet. Then he reaches down with a grunt, hoisting up a ginger kitten:

"Come in—she has more spirit than wisdom."

He strokes it with a chubby finger and shows me inside. Dozens of beer bottles line the wall nearest the door. On a table at the back I spy an empty Marius bottle, a souvenir from Gerd's party. And I'm struck by a smell of chain oil and unwashed laundry. Still, Gottfried is shiny, his hair's combed, he wears a checked flannel shirt. He shuffles around muttering to himself under his breath, stroking the kitten. "Where's the thing?" he tuts. "Here it is—no, no, it's the other one," and during this time certain shapes begin to emerge from the clutter. Contraptions here and there, his inventions. Among the bicycle parts I see a rotating shoe tree made from a wheel, and through a door I see a small device beside his bed combining a cigar and a traveling clock.

He spots me looking. "You like it? Cigar alarm—wakes me with a lit cigar every morning. Anyway, today we're watching out for Specht, in case you wonder. He has a hard life at the moment, and no real friends. So he needs a drink—but not too much of a drink, if you know what I mean." He steps to a cabinet in the darkest corner and scrapes open a drawer, pulling out a beer wrapped in cloth. I watch him unwrap it, handling it as one handles the tools of a busy youth gone by. "Here," he says. "Let's walk with it and check the *Flughafen*."

"You've refrigerated the wardrobe drawer?"

"Ah." He winks. "Come, just bring the beer."

We wander past Victoria Park to Mehringdamm and at a certain point, for no visible reason, he says: "Did you get the girl?"

"Which girl?"

"Don't be coy."

"Anna? You're joking."

"I never joke." Gottfried swigs from the beer. "From the questions she asks me I give you a fair chance. Her mind is looking for ways to explain you." He sees fit to stop at this juncture and stare into my face. "All men have madness inside them. And some have much more than others. I know it too well. A man without a strong woman is a ship broken off its anchor in the night. Things can turn dangerous."

"Hm—well, it's good of you to mention, of course. But really I think she's disgusted with me. I hardly know her, and she already told me as much."

"And I hardly know you. But perhaps she might be disgusted with what you do to yourself. Which is a different matter. If, let's say, her father had been a fine East German writer who had a strong romance with alcohol—and as a consequence left the world too young, and left her alone—hm? The picture suddenly changes."

Whoosh: a beam of new light hits the arena, new depths appear that make me hush on the walk up the hill. How curious, I muse, for life still to be throwing revelations, still flicking lights and opening doors. The picture changes indeed.

With this significant exchange, which I sense is as unusual for Gottfried as for me, born in the shimmering vapor of unexpected change that every so often rises between chapters in life—he relaxes back into himself, growing still in the face, reverting to the eye mechanisms of a crocodile; and we enter the airport's lobby. Gottfried seems unhurried to find Gerd. In fact, I wonder if the mysterious hubbub around the airport somehow invigorates him, if he finds the vapor of change attractive and rejuvenating—because after a while, he suggests we promenade outdoors. Strolling through the parking lot toward the wagon, I note that he now holds himself taller, thrusts himself out that bit more. And twice now I've found him scrubbed and fragrant, his clothes crisp and clean. Something in vaporous limbo favors Gottfried.

Something in adventure is good for him.

Before reaching the wagon we spy an open service door. A painted creature takes our attention from the gloom, and we move in to have a look. There a horse-tailed satyr glances wickedly off a large wooden flat, maybe a section of sideshow hoarding. It's not badly painted, rendered in oils, sunlit, in throes of high merriment against woodland depths, with boughs and leaves and fruit in a fringe at the top. Other creatures run off the edge of the flat, and I pull it forward to reveal more panels behind. There's Pan with his pipes, head thrown back in ecstatic abandon, and beside him a Medusa whose serpents coil and tangle, baring their fangs through branches above her head.

, "Nineteenth century," says Gottfried. "Maybe an old freak show."

The last flat is the headboard, a mayhem of nymphs and sprites exploding from trees, tearing bites from ripe fruits, scaring birds from the boughs, while grand sideshow lettering ominously reads: "*Launen des Schicksals*"—"Quirks of Fate."

As I turn from the flats I see Gottfried watching me. He doesn't move or blink. After a long silence he simply narrows his gaze and asks: "Are you unwell?"

"Hm—I've felt better." I sense him measuring my vital functions.

"Because I see you here quite pale." He pronounces the words softly, in a whisper whose stronger notes also growl: "With uneven breathing. So your heart is diverting blood under stress. Here, looking through the cargo door, at the paintings. What is it in that action, I wonder, that makes your body divert blood under stress?"

I try to meet his gaze, but only last a moment.

"Is it," he says, "that these freak-show paintings attach to a situation that is known to you? Could they be for a mysterious 'production' which may or may not center around the mobile kiosk over there? Some questions have arisen to ask."

Only now do I start to feel my blood diverting under stress.

"Has the time come for us to share a secret?" He continues to stare. "Because another little story is running here, isn't it, under-neath this one? Sudden mysterious English boy comes to Gerd. Sudden mysterious film production. A game of chess has opened up underneath. And I know that you are aware of that game—because you are one of its players. I know that to you, in fact—it's probably the main game."

I look around without answering. No blood remains to divert.

"We live in peaceful times," he says more casually, "hopefully we're dealing with youthful exploits, not threats to civil order. And I don't mind some adventure. I don't mind a game now and then, believe me. But there is a viewpoint from which you may have deceived and manipulated everyone within kilometers of this cargo door. People who've done you no harm. There is a viewpoint from which you may have set loose a decadence on our peaceful place. From which you may have unleashed real pain, even against your will, on people you actually like. And all with a selfish plan that somehow attaches to these paintings, to that wagon, to all these new people."

My gaze has fallen. The only heat left to feel is from his stare.

"Our talk makes you uncomfortable. I don't like to discomfort a friend. Whereas"—he sets off walking again—"the Frenchman wouldn't think twice."

I have to shake my head: "How do you know of a Frenchman?"

"It was a bluff." He glances sideways. "You've just given me another piece of the story. Though the French are always in there somewhere."

There's nothing I can say to Gottfried, and as I walk I feel my plans crash and burn around my feet. He slows after a moment's quiet, saying:

"The reason I chose to speak to you is that I'm familiar with many human situations. Even extreme situations. Each has its scent, its feel. And they each have satellites, other people or situations attaching to them. Very often you can judge a situation's nature by looking at the relative position and quality of its satellites."

My head stays down but his sails up, musing skyward.

"And one of your satellites is my friend Gerd Specht. Which indicates two things—one, as he's quite fond of you, that you must be of sound basic character. And two, that he stands to get hurt as your satellite. So then, looking into your situation, into this unfolding scenario at the airport, and putting it all together, I formed the judgment that you're a bright and sensitive man, perhaps a little too ardent, often ambivalent due to a complicated worldview, slightly dissolute—who has set in motion a series of events which now spirals out of control." Gottfried pauses, searching my face. "Spirals to such an extent—that you now even feel disposed to kill yourself."

He gives this time to sink in, which it does with the sound of his wheeze growing louder and starting to echo. But still there's more:

"You're not a brutal man, I can see that. You wouldn't contemplate any violence. In fact, you're a romantic, a dreamer, and I rather think you would walk into the sea. In which case it's a good thing we're not near a beach."

A pause follows which is an invitation to answer, and I look up, struggling to form a denial—but before I can even open my mouth, Gottfried has reached into his coat and pulled out my notepad, opening it to the first page:

"'There's no name for my situation,'" he reads, handing me the pad. "You should take more care of notes like this."

My veins melt to water. Gottfried takes me by the shoulder and walks me away from the airport, speaking softly: "Life is a strange animal, with none of the boundaries we think are there. Situations can turn at any time. Of course things will spiral out of control, in fact they're meant to—look how many industries depend on the spiral. So what I say to you is—you have comrades. I've worked out most of what's going on, though your precise connection is slightly vague, the game is missing a piece somewhere. But that's not important. We both know that a finale takes place here tomorrow. And I think we should talk before then. Things don't have to go the way they seem. We're a new force in the game—and we're the one with the most power, do you know why?"

Gottfried's face seems to grow.

"Because we're the only unseen force." And at this, after a pause, he softens: "Go check on the girl, she must be worried."

"And what about Gerd? If he's not around here—"

"Don't be too concerned. I've known him a long time, he's not an inventive man. That's the beauty of Gerd Specht."

Gottfried sends me to find Anna, and I walk to Grossbeerenstrasse shattered by his speech, struggling to gather fragments of my world as I knew it. Past the Piratenburg bar I enter a dark old building with frayed rush matting up the stairs, and on the third floor Anna answers the door to Gerd's apartment.

"No sign of him at the airport," I mutter.

"Well. Who knows, then? You get one credit of good character."

"Thanks. How many to reach average?"

"Ten thousand," she says.

No smile accompanies the comment, so I quietly step into the apartment, entering as all people enter strange places—tentatively—and gaze through the windows onto the street, absorbing smells of dish cloths, dust, and old cooking. It's a sparsely cluttered place, recalling that ilk of older people who collect souvenir spoons. On one wall is a color photocopy in a wood-effect frame of Gerd in his sailor's suit, smiling out. On a dresser sits a wedding picture with exactly the same smile. I muse how much pathos there is in seeing different pictures of someone in the same pose, with the same wooden smile. In the garden, on the beach, looking this way or that—they've decided over the years that a frozen grimace is their best feature. Pathos and quite some human beauty live in that portrait of the blind and fragile self.

Anna only speaks when I ask to use the bathroom.

"Down there." She points to the hall: "On the right. I'll make tea."

I pad down the hall, slowing past an open bedroom door. Above a pile of clothes, a poster of a giant tortoise is pinned to the wall. "Solitario Jorge," reads a caption beneath. Everything in the apartment seeps into me and weighs me down with feeling, until finally the smell of economy soap quashes me flat. Worse, it's Gerd's soap, a six-pack from the discount market. Not that economy itself is dampening—I'm glad to wash my hands, and do it thoroughly, as if my troubles stained me. But the scent combines with gray light through a window to smack of hard reality.

Which is the smack of defeat. I hurry from the bathroom.

"Sit." Anna pulls out a chair at the kitchen table. Cakes have been put on a plate, and she passes a mug of steaming dirty water.

"What is it?"

"Sage tea. It's what you need."

I pick up the tea box: "Says here it's for symptoms of menopause."

"Exactly. Gisela won't mind."

And so we sip, and toy with our mugs. Our exchanges come roughly the same distance apart in time as the apartment's knickknacks sit in space. A clock ticks somewhere, and in the general quiet, watched by those knickknacks, conversation becomes irrelevant. Slurps of tea mix with soap smells and despair to boom juicily through the air. Economy soap is too intimate a thing for daylight, I decide. I kill an impulse to imagine Anna under her clothes, lest a small romance of the mind take hold, which would be a bitter taunt at such a moment.* In fact, unable to salvage any workable plan from the day's developments, and even foreseeing a ruinous collision of worlds up ahead, my life's horizon has shortened to minutes. One more setback, one more untoward revelation is all it will take to wrap up the odyssey. This, after all the false endings, all the dashed hopes and sudden twists—is the point of the cone.

"I might have to go around nightfall," I say. "Will you be okay?"

"Pff—better than watching you drink."

"I'm not going to drink."

"Then I definitely don't need to know. Anyway, better here than with Herr Pietsch."

"Gottfried? He's suddenly quite a character. His face is even starting to move."

"Lately he comes every morning for coffee. I'm the one who opens the Imbiss in the mornings. He just monitors you."

"Old habits die hard."

---

* As a general rule watch out for silent romances. At only twenty-five I already have two indelible welts of passion and regret from people I never met, and only saw once in passing. It's a testament to the barbarous artworks of nature. A fleeting silent romance still touches the source where all feeling is born, and is strong precisely because we know the romance will never be. It's the highest romance—because only the ones we never have are perfect.

"I wish they would die. Have you been to see Stasi headquarters? Not to say anything bad about Herr Pietsch, he can also be sweet, and I know he's just lonely. But at the Stasi museum they all look like him—scary old farm boys with animal eyes."

"They're still there?"

"In photographs! And the headquarters are just as sad. When you see the quality of things they made in the GDR it's pathetic, like schoolchildren's work. There were no incentives. If you tried to do better than the lowest comrade, you'd make him look bad and everyone would hate you. So you worked to the lowest common denominator."

"The free market does that for profit."

"*Ja*, and of course that's worse, and only sends wealth to the top. At least under socialism you got a high education and some kind of job. But there has to be a better collective model than the GDR. So depressing. In the museum they still keep the pads they used to put on chairs during interrogations. They bottled the smell of your nervous ass, so they could send dogs to hunt you down."

"So," I muse, "poor Gerd slipped through that education net."

"Eh? 'Poor Gerd' is a physicist. Particle physics, I think. Gottfried has a degree in engineering. Gisela is a speech therapist."

"*What?*"

Anna's gaze slowly narrows to a glare. "Oh, I see—just because you don't find us laughing in a Porsche you think we must be peasants!"

"No!"

"Look at you! First you're surprised to find personalities behind our straight faces, then—oh, my God!—you find education under the sausages and coffee! Soon we start to look equal to

you! It's a crisis! Eh! Mr. Superior Decadent Vomiter! Eh! And I
suppose you come with a Nobel Prize in medicine?"

"Honestly, no—I just wasn't thinking."

"Eh! Or a triple doctorate in molecular biology! Or are you
too big to study?"

"I studied classics, but listen—"

"Pff, you see? A lady's degree, doesn't even get you a job as a
teacher."

"Well—I never quite got the degree."

"You see! Oh, my God! Now the empty-faced rabble start to
look even better! So what do you do? You must curate the national
museum! You must direct the state theater! You must play concert
piano!"

"Hm." Things dawn in rather a new light. "Nothing at the
moment. I was a cook. Mostly sausages—ironically enough."

"Ha!" She throws a cry to the ceiling: "*Ha!* O Doctor Vomiter
from England! O Professor Bleeder from the Great West! You
make the GDR look like high civilization!"

"God, you're a hard girl," I eventually say. "You don't actually
like me, do you?"

"Do you have any likable qualities?"

"I used to think so."

"What were they?"

During this pause, one I suppose is always destined to sit
here, I foolishly decide to fish for a softer ending:

"And why doesn't Gerd practice science? If someone works in
a kiosk you don't immediately take them for a particle physicist."

"I think he couldn't afford to. It's a specialist field, and you
can guess that East Germans didn't bring a reputation for high
achievement. He came into his marriage direct from a crisis with

the club, with debts, and couldn't spend time building a career. He stayed owing his wife's family. The kiosk was meant to be a short-term solution, a launching pad for better things—but it never took off."

"Well," I say, "surely you know I never put myself forward as better than anyone else."

"*Oh, no!* Making theories about the natives and their facial expressions! Discovering they might be little 'characters' behind their hard faces, with their folkloric little ways—do you even know who this 'character' Herr Pietsch is? Let me tell you who this is, your new little friend from your holidays—this is the product of his mother's rape by a Russian soldier after the war. Who was left in the toilet of a hospital, and raised with a shaved head by the state. As a boy he played chess, and people noticed him, because chess mixes young with old, men with women, rich with poor— in chess the minds of players meet each other alone, in purity. And his mind was clear and brilliant. He worked hard and got a scholarship to study engineering. He won prizes for his thesis. He worked in Moscow and it's said that nobody there could beat him at chess. He impressed enough people with his mind that he started to mix with senior communist officials. He was a committed Marxist. When he returned to East Germany his party liked him and they moved him into a trusted position in the Ministry of State Security. And there they discovered that your little 'character' was the most gifted interrogator. Every secret that was locked in a room with him came out. He knew the corridors of the mind! His was always a long, slow game, an end-play. And he always won. For years he was responsible for determining the truth at the highest level. And at that level interrogation is the greatest spontaneous oratory art. It uses the maximum of timing, composure, acting, and argument. It takes down the walls of a man's reality brick by brick, and builds them back in a way he will accept. And an interrogator at Berlin headquarters would also be dealing with intellectuals, with equally great minds. So don't think he was interested in collecting smells. He was the right kind of socialist, he believed in people. But towards the end of the German Democratic Republic a new kind of bully came on the scene. Your little friend said something wrong and for his last years of service was moved back to listening duties, sitting all day and night alone in a hole, switching a tape recorder on and off. With his gigantic mind. And to stop himself from going crazy he memorized great works of German and Russian literature. Even today you can play a game with him, just mention a sentence from a work, do it anywhere, suddenly, across a room—and without thinking he'll continue to recite from that sentence, forward or back, as you wish."

Anna pierces my gaze, makes sure I feel it pierced. "When the state collapsed he was too old to compete for work. He turned his mind to fixing things. He made his shop where he repaired bicycles. But then bigger shops with money and shinier bicycles came, and he was forgotten. This is who you had the honor to meet. A man with a life, doing exactly what he should do with it—create an environment where his gifts can serve what he believes in."

She leans closer: "And you? Can he possibly match your high achievements? He never had a week in Spain. He missed every series of *Big Brother*. He never learned to send a text message, never even got a mobile phone. He doesn't vomit when he drinks. He doesn't bleed. A person consists of what she or he actually does. Herr Pietsch doesn't need to make a theater of his face, he's not out to seduce you or misrepresent himself."

"You read me all wrong. I like everyone very much, and look up to you all. Rather *you're* the one judging *me* on first impressions."

"They're the impressions you give us! If we can't trust them to be accurate, then why do you give them? If that's not you, then what is? It illustrates exactly what I say—your world is reversed, facial tics are all you have left. You come from a cult of appearances, and underneath is a chaos that can only respond to medication."

"Pff, look—"

"Pff? *Pff?* Now you make fun of me!"

"Sorry, unconscious. Ach, but listen—"

"Ach? *Ach?*" She glares.

"Sorry, sorry—but listen, these are very wide-ranging accusations, come on. You have shops in Germany—look at IKEA."

"It's a question of need and want. Here few people ever own an apartment, for example. Why would we, when the law protects us to rent? What's the point of an apartment after we're dead? We don't live on credit, the economy doesn't run on shopping, we don't accumulate things to make us feel worthwhile. If you take away what we have, we don't change. Can I say the same for you?"

"But I don't have anything."

"Exactly—*and look at you!*"

Whoosh.

23

A wind has risen, sending hands of water into my chest which gently push me back. I loosen my tread in the sand and let them push. At first the cold is a problem, then I grow accustomed. Then it becomes a problem again, then I grow numb. Soon the shivering will stop. How gentle it all is.

Ah, well, my friend; every wish I made came true and this is the result. But at least I got to know who I am before the end: I am the Master Limbo. Every protein of me is a market force, hungry to be filled. I am the Master Limbo and here I am with nature, with weeds lapping my shirt, crawlers at my shoes.

Parasites upon parasites upon parasites.

Because we are one and the same force.

Glorious, perfect, innocent nature, doing all that life does, which is simply to do all that it can, no matter how it finds a way.

Whoosh: a wave dies on an outcrop, clapping over rocks to punctuate the moment. Not a mighty breaker, incensed and roaring, out to punish the shore; but just a ripple, straight and meek. This is the truth of my death. A lake pays no tribute to unexpressed forces, though they might seethe and boil inside

me. I suppose because nobody knew they were there. As Anna
would say—because no seething and boiling were ever actually
expressed to pay tribute to. In fact, nothing ever issued from me
to pay tribute to, though I lived feeling there were forces that
could have. Things are as they should be, then, in the end. Just
a minor sphinx, once a weasel, up to his neck in a lake. The lake
meekly laps, swirling things painfully slowly.

I had the foresight to beg an airtight freezer bag from Anna,
so my notes might survive, for what they're worth, also swirling in
slow motion, really more like simply turning. And if nothing else
there's a drink recipe in here somewhere, and a warning about the
Advance Saver fare on trains.

I step farther into the lake till the sun's last juices shimmer
under my eyes. As it sinks so I sink, we die together as one, and
the lower my viewpoint sinks, the more of the world I can see, till
my vision takes all of it in, speeds across the surface of the water,
across lush miles, over all its creatures and plants, its colored furs
and mottled skins, its glistening seas and smoking peaks, and
I see the truth unfurl in a flashing sky—that no grand design
underlies us, neither perfect nor flawed, but that each thing tries
to make its way as best it can, against harsh odds, under a thin gas
wrapping the earth. All anything did throughout my life was feed
off me, and our currency was money. My father came to Berlin
because of it, left Berlin because of it, left his wife because of it,
damaged me because of it. The action group formed because of
it, was corrupted because of it, shunned me because of it, rehab
admitted me because of it, chased me because of it, the train was
late because of it, the policeman was there because of it, sandwiches were watched because of it, the taxi was slow because of
it, Smuts is in jail because of it. Now the airport dies because of it,

Gottfried languishes because of it, Gerd is unemployed because of it, his wife has left because my father came because of it, and left because of it.

Then I came back.

Because of it.

I let myself fall, hear the tide clang over my ears. Life surely was a strange animal. I feel the lake break through my lips, feel my breath start to bubble.

And whoosh.

END

PLAY:

On this side, where cold turns to warmth and pink to gray and blue, I hear a voice, faint at first, maybe the voice of that god we carry within, perhaps even an objective god, an Enthusiasm come to attend my journey:

"You worked it all out, then," it says.

"Yes, I worked it out," I say, "finally."

"Finally, eh? That's good, very good."

"Yes, it feels correct, after all," I say.

"So is the answer to live or to die, in the end?"

"Well, to die, I'm afraid—I'm just an animal."

"Really? Well, shame. Just you, or is that all animals?"

"Well, I can't speak for anyone else. I think it's me, for now."

"I see, I see. You don't like it here anymore, then, no?"

"Well, no," I say, "things have gone downhill."

"Aha, yes, they have. Other animals, eh?"

"Exactly—it's wholesale carnage."

"But then—where are they?"

"The other animals?"

"Yes, not here?"

"Well, no."

"So?"

The dialogue seems perplexing, for a god; I shake my head, coughing and gasping. But after a moment it comes again:

"Nothing else is swimming in its clothes. What does that suggest to you?"

"Well—this isn't swimming, the clothes are irrelevant."

"It suggests that animals don't do this. Only you are doing it. What separates us from all creatures is that we have the choice to be like them or not. As a person yourself there are things you can do. In fact, there are things you must do, for honor's sake."

At the word "honor" I feel my ear clang to the surface.

"Tomorrow night, for example, two types of creature will gather in the caverns under an airport: one will be on a plate being eaten; and the other will be eating them and laughing. The critical question of life—which type are you?"

"Do I have to be either?"*

"Then go make a third space at the table."

"It sounds to me like you're trying to talk me out of the lake."

"No—you're trying to talk yourself out of the lake. Do you really think someone intent on killing themselves would still be dragging through such an agonizing charade? You describe it as a limbo—well, let me tell you something: what you've snagged on here is simply adulthood—the most terrifying limbo of all. And make no mistake, all the notions of adults are limbos like yours—capitalism, communism, all are just weightless ideas. Still, you must choose one and work to improve it, or design an even better one. The moments before this shock were a sweet point in life, a childhood. But now it's time to cross over. In case you hadn't realized, crossing over is what you're here for today."

"What? But this is a drowning. Do you mean to say—?"

"It's precisely what I mean to say. You are now at the sharp end of a ritual spanning every age of history, reaching every person,

---

* Life is abject and stupid when deeply scrutinized. The evidence from all who've felt or thought too deeply is that understanding brings disillusionment. Moreover, I vouch to you from that state. Very few can live to a certain depth alone, where mysteries glow beneath them enough to form a sumptuous backdrop to otherwise simple lives, without having to taste poisons from below as well. While it's the job of artists to roam these depths and reflect their madness, it isn't recommended in order to have a good life. The conclusion: don't dive—merely float and swim. Delight in stupidity. And where the deep sucks you down, run to that sanctuary for all victims of the deep: intoxicants.

with a choice to make that can't be reversed. Make that choice: do you want to die an infant—or an adult?"

"Well—which one would it be if I stay here and drown?"

"Infant."

"And to be an adult would involve—?"

"Getting out and taking your chances."

"But half the reason I'm here is all the shit I've caused. My prospects are all in tatters, I can't come back."

"Of course you can. In nature nothing ever dies. Leave your childhood in the lake, that's what this moment is about. Rise again fresh and strong."

"But I'm exhausted. Where would the energy come from?"

"Unexpressed forces! Don't be so tragic! Express them! If you feel the species has an enemy, gather comrades and go after it!"

"Hm? Unexpressed forces?" I feel a prickle of heat in my chest, a spark growing into a flame, and before long, fed by a gust off the lake, a ruthless blaze. "Unexpressed forces!" I cry: "Unexpressed forces!" I shout it again and again till I hear the other voice come with a different tone, a stronger one now, and I feel the quality of numbness change in my limbs, as if a weight falls off them.

"Watch out for him, now," says the voice. "He has a hard life at the moment, and no real friends. He'll probably need a drink—but not too much of a drink."

Then comes another voice: "I win, you owe me a brandy."

"A brandy?" I try to open my eyes. "A brandy?"

"Shh," goes the voice. "I'm talking to Specht."

"A brandy?" says Gerd. "Or was it just a beer?"

"Don't try and get out of it," says Gottfried. "I bet you for a brandy—that an Englander like this won't pick the closest lake. He'll pick the second closest."

WONDERLAND

BANQUET

A different kind of bond exists between men who pull each other out of lakes. Within two hours of Gottfried hauling me out I confess my life to him. Confess the banquet to him. Make a comrade. Make a pact.

It's October twenty-fourth.

Enthusiasms have spoken.

The leading edge of the banquet arrives like the slap of a storm. Gottfried and I step from his workshop into a flying drizzle, minding the kitten at the door.

"Typical Gerd." He stops to button a jacket over his work clothes. "Whole day in the Rubens Café, then he calls us bad friends for not finding him. Who goes to the Rubens to get drunk? There's too much good food there."

We part ways at the corner of Mehringdamm, where he pauses to say: "Thanks for our little talk. I had all but one thing worked out. See you for end-play. I'll be at the airside tunnel after dark."

I head straight for the airport, skin tinged gray and blue, hair stiff behind my head like a flame in the wind. The sky is fast-moving, leaf debris escorts me tumbling up the street to the wagon, where I find a host of new faces.

Didier Le Basque is here, I catch him hurrying between trailers in a blur of whiskers and coats. He ushers me into a command post where, from the speed of his gaze and the jot of wine he pours, I sense the meeting will be short.

We raise our glasses: "To the exquisite and the strange," he toasts. "This is it, uh. Hope your costume fits well. And I should say thanks—without even knowing it you gave us a genius idea for the signature dish. The best we've ever had. I won't spoil the surprise—you'll see soon enough. As to your schedule, remember the closing alarum is at eleven fifty-five precisely. You must exit within four minutes of that. Lights-out will begin the countdown, uh? I've told the doorman to watch you, he'll activate the light switch. You appear, lights out, and then bon voyage."

I nod. "Very good."

"*Bon, allez*. The bookkeeper pays your fee at the exit. Then I suggest you leave the building quickly and don't return for at least a few weeks, although anyway the place will be closed. Thomas will leave before lights-out with two of the trailers, the kitchen stays until the end. Aircraft engines start at eleven-fifty. So—uh? Timing is everything." He dangles his hand to squeeze. "Good luck, my friend."

Outside I find Thomas near a closed kitchen trailer a few meters away, and we stop to share a cigarette on the street behind it. Anti-closure protesters are beginning to arrive, adding to the throng. In hushed tones, Thomas relays news from the kitchen hotline, a reliable telegraph the world over: that tonight's guests are inbound from Hotel Le Meurice in Paris and comprise extreme high-flyers from those quarters of banking and commerce responsible for the global recession, on a shindig before vanishing in advance of government investigations.

According to the kitchen only two are not billionaires.

As we smoke I overhear a chef on the phone inside: "What the fuck am I supposed to do with that?" he bellows, and my heart turns for Smuts, who should be here. While it remains a question whether the Basque will come through with his end of our bargain, I've anyway decided to fulfill my part, and have taken the matter of chastising the true culprits behind Smuts's detention into my own hands.

"Why have you messed with the menu?" yells the chef. "Well, the guest has no palate. Why invite someone without a palate?"

I tune out the call as half a dozen new faces file into the trailer, and in the opening and closing of its door I could swear I hear babies whining and gurgling inside. I turn to Thomas for clues, cocking an ear to the wagon; but his face remains blank, and after a last pull on his smoke he passes it over and walks off.

The weather clears toward evening, and this last Friday afternoon of a monument, a history, a dream, and a limbo comes to be graced by autumn sun. At first the glare hides behind buildings, throwing cool shadows, lighting the sky chalky blue. People come and go through these shadows, chrome glints from passing traffic, even Gottfried lurks in his work wear and gloves, sometimes posing beside the bistro, sometimes prowling. At a certain point a golden light bursts over him, and he looks to me without smiling—but I know it's a smile. The sky and its empty treetops grow clear and still. The road is quiet, but not too quiet. And there comes a moment when Thomas, dressed in black evening wear, returns to fold himself next to me on the curb, in the gap between command post and kitchen. The street before us suggests no gaiety or abandon, has no neon lures, no gushing enticements, no glare of trinkets or frippery. This Berlin street is dull and closed in a way that holds no promise of future openings. Its dwellers are upstairs. Businesses in ground floors don't scream or shout or even mention their trades.

And here, waiting for the greatest bacchanal since the fall of Rome, waiting for the feast of Trimalchio, Des Esseintes' last stand, Dorian Gray's big night out, waiting for the spirits of Salomé, Abbé Jules, Caragiale, Baudelaire, Hlaváček, Mirbeau, and Tonegaru, we smoke cigarettes at the curbside and bask in cool sun.

"So, my man." Thomas eventually squints into the sky. "This is it. Wonder how many souls we'll send to heaven." He punches my shoulder for luck.

I feel a shiver. The air is electric, all the more so for the scrape of cheap shoes on the street, the dull chime of truck engines. But the night is about to begin.

At sundown walkie-talkies start to crackle around the Columbiadamm side of the airport. I watch a rangy Frenchman swagger underground: the lookout with his starting pistol. Thomas introduces the bookkeeper, a small bearded man like a gnome. He shakes my hand and goes underground to take up his position, then another man passes whom Thomas seems more purposefully to introduce as the "courier."

Finally, in my flowing black cape, tricorn hat, and white half-mask, I get the call to move up the tunnel to the airfield. A stiff breeze strikes the tunnel mouth. The sky over Tempelhof is tiger-striped, gray over evening blue. A handful of stars already twinkle, and these are soon joined by flashing strobes and Gottfried's wheezing breath as he emerges from shadows alongside me. We watch a jet land and make a long taxi in profile, shrieking and sparkling, crouched like a predator. Gottfried's tongue stirs in his mouth. His eyes shine clear, almost white. Then he nudges me:

"Look at it gleaming. Some machine. Like a Porsche—eh?"

We pause to exchange a glance, then he melts away behind me. I shield my face as the jet bears down with its lights. Shadowy forms glow in the cockpit as it bounces to a stop, whistling and whining, its stairs already starting to unfold.

Seven guests descend in tailcoats and human masks. I pull my cape across my chest and spin about-face to lead them through the tunnels to Wonderland. But within seconds I find myself irritated by the men: they dawdle along, loudly talking shop, seeming not to care about the location, as if walking from their office to a sandwich bar. It makes me realize the Zentral Flughafen has become another secret Miguel, another friend, and I suffer the march listening to the men's echoes growing louder and more fractured as we penetrate the complex. Along the way I hear the following:

"Ask him," says one man. "I think it's third-generation theory."

"You mean like stochastic? A kind of Black-Scholes spin-off?"

"No, no," another says with a cough. "It's not about volatility, it's a consumer model. Trades on the fact that half of consumers are influenced by coupon offers, but only ten percent send the coupon back—it's that margin applied to manufacturing. For example, cut product quality by half, but a lower fraction will return the product. That margin is the market."

"Ah, working on the basis that cost of return is equal to repurchase, like with low-value goods? But then half the game must lie in making it impossible to return the merchandise, no? You're talking about the 'too hard' market."

"Kind of—but next-generation. We found a measurable acceptance factor over time. For example, who remembers a shoe that doesn't leak after ten weeks? A mobile phone that doesn't die? The market now accepts that they do, returns are down year-on-year. We calculate rate of acceptance based on units returned, then project it. Now a third-generation model applies to all markets—diminution of cost, rate of acceptance, increase in price. In seven years we could sell empty packaging."

"I guess it bit you, though, or you wouldn't be here."

"The model didn't bite, it was a corporate capital issue. But it won't break surface until at least the next quarter—I'll be on the nineteenth hole."

Something prickles me, listening to the men, something in their utter detachment from the world around, in the insulation of their jargon from human touch, and in the humdrum of their voices plotting such guaranteed dismay:

It's the shadowy forces themselves.

A thrill squirts through me as we round the last corner. The warbling strains of a close-harmony ensemble start to shimmer through the air as we near the salon, a chorus rising as if from history itself. The tune is sublime, quite modern, and somehow familiar—after a bar or two I recognize it as "Night and Day" sung in German, "Tag und Nacht," by the Comedian Harmonists, banned by the Reich in the thirties. Imagine the scene as it grows unreal, a pod of masked men in evening wear led by a sphinx in a cape through a tunnel of music. The salon door then opens onto a muslin-lined chamber awash with rare fabrics, where guests pay the bookkeeper a fee in diamonds. With the clank each one makes in a tray he passes a chunk of fruit to a splendid green bird hanging in a cage of gold and jewels.

"Feed the bird," he chants, "feed the decadent avian."

After they've paid the fee I follow guests through a curtain into the next chamber. There two attendants stand waiting in tails with a man-sized carousel of seven wedgelike cabinets between them. Seven naked persons bend head-down inside, trunks and limbs tucked away, sexes straining up through cushioned holes, a jamboree of vulvas and loins as diverse as faces, each with its nature and charm. The voluptuary's roundabout follows Didier's theory that hormones should simmer to a lusty boil during the course of a meal. Fleshy petals, curled lips, shy crevices, even two willowy cocks with their sacs invite delectation, while trays beside each juxtapose oysters, fruits, snails, cocaine, cheese, raw ham, and truffle, conjuring pubic musks of quivering rarity. From the carousel's crown, crystal glasses of infants' tears cleanse the guests between courses. I note that the men at this pudendum degustator can't disguise their individual natures, some skimming, others plunging and slurping, still others hovering in the hazes above.

After this the footmen lead them into Wonderland.

The concourse of arches overflows with rugs, cushions, plants, and entertainments, with a long table running under dazzling chandeliers. My gaze zooms through the arches to the painted sideshow creatures at the end, while through an arch to the right, nestled in a blast of foliage, sits a fountain of Marius. Light plays on its spout, glimmers in ripples across its black pool. At the table boys and girls wait with trays of abalone, cheese of human breast milk, pomegranates, and honeycomb, while maidens bear a beluga sturgeon on a bed of sea snails, scooping caviar from its gut with their hands.

With the guests seated, the time comes for me to withdraw,

though as I sweep out of Wonderland I meet the bookkeeper, who in a spirit of crew camaraderie invites me to peer through his curtain whenever I want.

"The bird isn't the best company," he says with a shrug.

Kitchen attendants pass me in the bahn tunnel with a course of steaming broth, attended by maidens whirling and naked beneath frocks. As they disperse I see a group of pretty figures in bathrobes beside the railway tracks, chattering and smoking in the shadows—surely sex organs on a break from the carousel.

Kiwi & Hummingbird Broth
with Porcini Agnolotti & Leeks

INGREDIENTS FOR BROTH

14 blue-capped hummingbirds	3 sprigs of thyme
(reserve cap feathers for decoration)	10 white peppercorns
4 brown kiwis	3 sprigs of parsley
50g mirepoix	2 bay leaves
2 sticks of celery	2 medium tomatoes, split
2 brown onions	2–3 juniper berries, crushed
1 head of garlic	2 bunches of leeks

INGREDIENTS FOR AGNOLOTTI

50g dried porcini	100g leg meat from the kiwis
1 clove garlic	500g egg pasta
1 dash of truffle oil	dry sherry
1 tbsp chopped parsley	egg white and flour

For the broth, first prepare a mirepoix (finely chopped onion, celery, and carrot in a ratio of 2:1:1) and sauté until aromatic. Trim the kiwis and hummingbirds of their breasts and winglets and add all other trimmings and remaining ingredients to the pan. Once colored and aromatic, add the mixture to a pot of cold water and bring to a boil, skimming as required until the stock has reduced by half. Remove and set aside any leg meat and return the bones to the pot, continuing to cook until the broth is full-flavored. Finally remove and strain.

For the agnolotti, steep the porcini in boiling water until soft, then strain and reserve the liquor. Finely chop the reserved kiwi leg meat, garlic, and porcini, then sauté the garlic in a pan, adding the porcini with parsley and a splash of dry sherry. Add the chopped leg meat and finish with porcini liquid, reducing until no liquid remains. Reserve in a bowl to cool.

To make the pasta, roll the dough through a pasta machine on its finest setting and lay the sheet out on a cool, floured bench. Cut 7cm rounds and place a heaped teaspoon of filling in the center of each, brushing around the edge. Put lids onto the disks and seal from the center outward, then reserve on a floured board. Bring fresh water to a boil for the agnolotti, and heat the broth. Boil agnolotti until they float to the surface, then place one in each serving bowl with breasts of kiwi and hummingbird stacked on top. As the broth comes to a boil add finely chopped parsley with truffle oil and spoon over the breasts and agnolotti. Serve with parmesan shavings.

SERVES 7. BON APPÉTIT!

I pause by the stairwell to light a cigarette. Thomas grabs it to take a drag: "An attendant recognized two guests. One from the news last week, the bank that went under. The other one's supposedly all over the papers too, she can't remember why. Same kind of deal. Bad vibe off the table, apparently."

"The kitchen's got ears." I take a turn with the smoke.

"It's always the way. The wire's hotter than usual here, the kitchen's got more contact with service and front-of-house. Big show tonight."

"I'm surprised the Basque manages to keep it secret."

"Everyone's tried and tested, that's what makes his jobs such golden gateways for the crew. He has to keep them sweet once they're in. Not that anyone really knows what goes on—behind the salon are other places where service can't go. That's where the real shit happens, I can't even talk to you about it. But this is a perfect location, nobody can just wander in. Amazing venue, you really pulled a miracle."

"How the police aren't all over us is the miracle," I say.

"Easy: there's a big film set in the terminal. Crew's just rotating up and down between here and there. Perfect cover, they're all in costume. Local cop's already been around, we gave him dinner. He thinks downstairs is wardrobe and makeup. Saw your other acquaintance up there too, with the mustache. Strange fellow, he was sitting on the steps in a sailor's hat. Probably wants a part in the movie."

It's Gerd. The image stabs me through the heart. Worlds have finally collided, one a voracious bottom-feeder devouring everything in its path, laughing over its shoulder, the other a world of simple pleasures, straight answers, and horses in hallways.

An urge takes me to find Gerd and run to the Piratenburg; but I couldn't face the pain. Instead I pull the night's deadline into focus, deciding to take care of the last few details before it gets too late. I turn to Thomas:

"Will you join me in a drop of *Symphony*?"

"It's in the fountain, we're not allowed in."

"There's some of my own left—wait here."

I hurry up the bahn tunnel and let myself into the kiosk store with the yellow key. Inside I unpack my kit bag, taking out the wine and my Bavarian suit. The Miesbacher hat makes me pause and remember my early days in Berlin, so recent but seeming like a lifetime ago, back when the mysterious Gerd Specht loomed so large. Innocent days, in retrospect. Limbo had a childhood, a middle age, and now falls away to its death. I feel it in a zeal for sleep, a new distaste for excess.

Perhaps also a pining for home, my teeming isles, for fish and chips, a pint of ale, and a game of darts. Ah, this limbo.

After repacking my bag with new contents, I leave the Marius with Thomas and hurry to the airside tunnel. Chugs from a generator meet me at the tunnel mouth, and a scent of kerosene haunts the air. I see the jet sitting open and glowing inside, frosty patterns grown on its wings. A second jet now sits behind it, and a man stands on the tarmac nearby. He seems familiar, and I tag him as one of Didier's crew. I linger by the tunnel mouth till Gottfried steps from the dark. The sentry sees him and nods, obviously taking me in my cape for a member of the event crew. I hand Gottfried the bag and he opens it to look inside, angling it to a nearby light.

"What time will they start engines?" he hisses.

"Eleven-fifty precisely. Is the timer accurate?"

"Of course! I built it myself. I'll set it for eleven-forty, I don't want any ground crew around." After fumbling for a few moments in the bag, he pauses to click his tongue: "I'll miss that early-morning cigar. And just wait and see Specht squeal like a little girl about his sixty-euro box. I bet you a brandy he does."

"All in a good cause. Sure you won't be at risk?"

"I'll be here at eleven-thirty to see that nobody enters the plane. I don't expect a problem, guests are flying themselves so they'll have a contract pilot to run checks and start up. I can give him a schedule change. Apart from that every risk is worth taking. Firstly, it's open ground, and the mess will mostly stay in the plane. Secondly, I'm unemployed after this weekend—everyone is, after many years, so we're not happy. My comrades won't shed tears over this. Thirdly, I'm not actually doing anything—you are." He hands me the bag and points to the open jet: "Inside to the left you'll find a storage hatch. Thank God it won't be airborne, then we'd really have a show."

He waves to the sentry, and I realize as I cross the apron that this will have looked like a routine security check by airport staff.

Now I understand Gottfried's choice of uniform, as sure enough the sentry waves me aboard.

When I step out I see Gottfried watching from across the apron, nodding to himself, wetness glistening around his mouth. I hurry back past him and hear him softly growl: "A little souvenir from Berlin. A memento from old Kreuzberg, and maybe tonight they have to catch the subway home with the rest of humanity."

Western Fanshell Mussel Soufflé
with Black Rhino Horn

INGREDIENTS

5 garlic cloves, finely minced

6 cups good Puligny-Montrachet

12 shallots

bunch chopped parsley

28 fresh western fanshell mussels

50ml olive oil

350ml double cream

50g black rhino horn, powdered, with
  occasional polished chips

SOUFFLÉ BASE

6 egg yolks

10 egg whites

350ml milk

8 tbsp unsalted butter

pinch of cornstarch

pinch of salt

Add 8 shallots, all of the garlic, and 2 cups of the wine to a sauté pan and reduce. Set the reduction aside and sauté the remaining shallots with the mussels and 4 cups of wine before straining both liquids and setting aside. Retrieve and clean the mussels, finely chop, and also set aside.

For the soufflé batter, bring the milk and butter to a boil, add the flour, and cook until stiff. Reduce heat and cook for another 5–7 minutes, until the batter is smooth and shiny. Mix slowly in a mixer until cool, then beat in each egg yolk individually while folding in the shallots and mussels.

For the sauce, reduce the reserved mussel liquids by half, then add cream and further reduce until thick.

To complete, heat an oven to 190°C, beat egg whites until

stiff, and fold into warmed soufflé batter. Bake in cups for 25 minutes. Serve fresh from the oven, adding the sauce and sprinkling the soufflé crowns with powdered rhino horn.

SERVES 7. BON APPÉTIT!

EIGHT O'CLOCK

Peering through the curtain, I see maidens lined up wearing dresses styled after wartime. Cheeky girls, rudely alive, bouncing, fidgeting. I briefly ponder what it is that bends a person toward such vitality. I suppose there was the child who snuck a finger beneath bedclothes to fetch a secret swipe; and others who held undergarments at a full arm's length, turning their faces in disgust.

The former line up here, then, behind the table.

An organ-grinder emerges with a monkey in a uniform of blue and gold, who jumps onto the table and removes his pillbox hat. Tiny envelopes tumble out, and as the soup course is cleared, the monkey pigeon-toes up and down the table handing one to each guest, frowning and twitching in that deranged, strangely familiar way of apes, who after all are cousins, little mirrors sent by nature to lampoon us. The envelopes contain cards printed each with the pattern of a maiden's dress. Quaffing wine, the guests search out their girl and hold up the card to call her over.

The bookkeeper and I step aside as dishes pass out—some barely touched, with tiny breasts and drumsticks inside—while waiters pass through with a bell-like oven full of perfect soufflés. A portly guest calls for a boy instead of a maiden, and after a moment a boy slips off a bathrobe behind us and passes through the curtain, shining white like silver birch. His eyes are pale and set wide apart, his nose small, lips long and full on a blank face. There's a seedy beauty about him, a gyroscopic elegance to his gait that shows him to be a creature whose boyhood has sailed over the apex of gender into something neither female nor male. On top of this, in the way he averts his gaze, in the sticky languor of his smile, he seems to advance a taste of himself, and this doesn't escape the guest, who mouths him hungrily when he arrives.

Sturdy dwarves follow bearing a miniature litter with a pagoda roof where live songbirds cling or perch around the gutters. On a velvet cushion lies the tiniest, most delicate and translucent Oriental woman the world can have ever seen. She lies on her side, naked, one leg drawn up beside the other, and all around her are instruments for the enjoyment of opium and fine cigars. Fingers reach out to touch her skin as she passes, or to slide between her perfect red lips, just deeply enough to be warmed and wet. By now the back of the room is obscured in a haze, and moving figures can no longer be seen in detail, though I can see certain boys or maidens go down on their hosts with tongues, while others drip honey into mouths from their fingers, or pass lilies and jasmine under noses, or have fingers dipped into themselves. Smoke plumes into a ceiling of cloud, making the space even more magical, distancing arches from each other, softening light and shade, muting color till the scene is a centuries-old bacchanal.

I observe the men's natures: after being hand-fed in various ways, some grope their maidens, whispering deals to possess them, others simply command them like whores. The eldest suffers a gasping orgasm at the table and hurriedly calls for cocaine. After the soufflé course, their moods upholstered by wine, they lean into alliances with each other, chuckling, trading maidens, inevitably falling into debauch.

The next course arrives with younger, darker-skinned maidens, and trays of rare fluids in glasses. With this the Basque makes his first appearance, encased in a shiny tailcoat, wearing the half-mask of a cat. A cheer rings out and he takes a deep bow.

With attention thus drawn from my curtain, I see another man enter without fanfare. Not decadently dressed but in a comfortable black suit and open collar. He moves to the fountain, takes up a goblet, skims it full of wine. After a taste he throws it back, filling again from the spout. Something sets him apart from the guests, he's not of their type—yet he enjoys the run of the salon. I study him for clues. Sandy-haired, lightly bearded, maybe nearing sixty; he's a man who observes, a neutral player here, but one whose neutrality safekeeps something, whose gaze challenges for credentials.

I'm spellbound at the curtain.

Here they are—the shadowy forces.

The shadowy forces, a stranger beside the fountain of Marius. And a sphinx lying in wait.

Olive Ridley Turtle Necks in Parmesan and Brioche Crumbs
with Celeriac Remoulade

INGREDIENTS FOR TURTLE NECKS

7 Olive Ridley turtle necks

½ loaf of brioche

(day-old, crust off, dry in slices)

160g grated Parmesan

INGREDIENTS FOR REMOULADE

2 whole eggs

½ tsp salt

¼ tsp pepper

50ml vinegar

¾ tsp Dijon mustard

340ml vegetable oil

INGREDIENTS FOR SEASONING GARNISH

1½ tsp chopped onion

15g chopped cornichons

5g anchovy, diced

1 hard-boiled egg, finely chopped

¼ head of celeriac, shredded

10g parsley

salt and pepper

Purée brioche and Parmesan until smooth, adjusting the Parmesan to taste before setting aside. In a robot coupe, mix eggs with vinegar, salt, pepper, and mustard. Add the oil a little at a time to fully incorporate until it's as thick as double cream. Add anchovies, cornichons, chopped onion, chopped hard-boiled egg, celeriac, and chopped parsley. Consistency should be very thick, the flavor full and robust. Adjust seasoning with salt and pepper.

Finally, crumb the necks in brioche and parmesan mix and deep-fry until golden brown. Serve with the sauce and garnish with fried Italian parsley.

SERVES 7. BON APPÉTIT!

NINE O'CLOCK

An extraordinary amusement makes the salon hush before the next course. Through the door I see the tail of an enormous snake appear, borne by a kitchen hand. More of the snake slides in with two more carriers, then another two, and another two, until finally a chef appears with the head of an anaconda. The porters move under the arches like pallbearers, pulling it over the table till it spans the whole length and droops to the floor at each end. A massive lump at the midsection, many times the girth of the head, suggests another creature might lie inside. Nature shows off an artwork on the skin, exquisite gold and chocolate ribs, rounded and serifed in a deco style with orbs seeming to peer from between them. To think, for all this display, which must have taken some time—nature forgot to give the creature empathy, or even legs.

It has made a rug that kills by strangulation.

One of the bearers stands at the head to announce: "For tonight's first amusement, a special adventure: this, the largest of all serpents, was flown today from its jungle lair. But we won't be eating it. Rather, what we have before us is the most precise tenderizer of meats the world has ever known. Our only question—what was its last meal? It's an adventure, and we hope you will commit, sight unseen, to savor whatever specialties emerge." He sweeps up an arm: *"Monsieur le chef!"*

Chef takes the snake's head and, on a count of three, bearers heave the animal onto its back, showing ivory articulations that gleam in the light. With a quick sawing motion Chef pulls the knife clean through its flesh.

"Ah," he says, "there's something here."

He rolls up his sleeves and thrusts his arms in up to his elbows, rummaging and scowling to one side. And finally he bends in, scooping deep with his hands.

And hoists out a perfect human baby.

I flinch, feeling the salon recoil as one being. But after a moment a hot breath finds my ear from below: "It's only pork and veal," hisses the bookkeeper, "with lobster eyes—we do it every time, bankers love it." After this he takes my shoulder and points me to the door, where apparently I have a caller.

"Slight concern." It's Thomas. "Some girl is down here, not attached to the event—small, with dark hair. Strange because it's after-hours. Would she have her own key?"

"She's terminal staff, they have a temporary store by the stairs."

He points me up the tunnel to find her and I set off, billowing in my cape. There's no sign of Anna around the stairwell, nor in the store. I poke around a bit more, and eventually see light softly glowing from a recess in the tunnel wall ahead. Approaching, I see that it's being used as a temporary storage area, stacked with cages and crates; at the sound of my steps, something moves.

"Pff—you frightened me," hisses Anna.

"What are you doing? Be careful," I say.

"God, you look like Dracula. Look down here, how cruel." She crouches to a box punched with holes. Inside stands a very fine little creature, perhaps some rare savanna deer or miniature gazelle, scratching around, squeaking.

"What is all this?" She squeezes my wrist. "It's horrible, and look over there—something's in that one, you can hear it moving. Who are these people, what's going on, it's like a zoo down here—they can't be making movies at night?"

"I'm sure it's all fine, they won't be here long—probably best if I walk you up, get some fresh air. Is the wagon still open? We could grab some coffee."

"Coffee? While these poor things are here like this? Look, he doesn't even have water, it's unbelievable. I'm going up to get water, and maybe they can give me some fruit or bread. My poor babies—keep watch until I come back."

No sooner has Anna gone than voices approach up the tunnel with a squeak of struggling trolley wheels and sundry clangs, knocks, and rattles.

"What the hell do they eat to get this heavy?" grunts a man.

"Just grass, I guess, or who knows." It's Thomas's voice. "Call for some help, though, we're running late—he needs to be on his feet by ten forty-five, and to the butcher truck by eleven-ten, it's our pièce de résistance—we can't mess it up."

"Big rush for something that lived a hundred years already."

I hurry down the tunnel to meet Thomas, heart racing when I see the massive crate. My stomach starts to heave.

"Look." Thomas beams. "I bet you never expected this—it was a great idea, we couldn't believe it. We're not a hundred percent sure it's the famous one, they all look the same—but as far as the guests are concerned it will be. The single rarest creature on earth, the last of its kind. A real coup."

I stand shaking my head. Between slats in the crate a wise but frightened old eye looks out, catching the light.

A giant tortoise's eye.

"Incredible, eh? And easier than expected—environmentalists have killed the native fishing industry by declaring everything off limits, you can barely swat a fly in the Galápagos. Which meant plenty of helping hands amongst the fishermen. Apparently these are very edible, you can use every part of them. We're tempura-battering some brain with a sea-urchin salad for the surprise course. But I'm gambling we could walk him into the salon first, guests should see him alive."

The odyssey unveils a new cone, a new point, a new end-play to deal with. My mind races, listening for Anna's footsteps to return. "Are you wheeling him up with the other animals? Because the girl will be back in a minute."

"Eh? Keep her out—call security if you have to."

Golden Lion Tamarin Monkey Brain &
Blue Cheese Ravioli
with Champagne Zabaglione &
White Alba Truffle

INGREDIENTS FOR RAVIOLI

1 Golden Lion Tamarin monkey brain

500g ravioli pastry

100g cave-aged *societé* Roquefort, cold

2 egg whites

INGREDIENTS FOR ZABAGLIONE

1 tbsp hollandaise

2 tbsp fish velouté

2 tbsp champagne

1 tbsp lightly whipped cream

White Alba truffle to shave

Remove the monkey brain fresh and slice into 7 equal rounds. Discard the carcass. Slice cheese into small enough slivers to cover half of each brain portion, then cut pasta into cup-sized rounds, brushing the edges with an egg-white wash. Nestle a brain portion with blue cheese into the middle of each circle and place a pasta lid on top, squeezing toward the edge with good pressure. Individually blanch the ravioli (very quickly) in rapid boiling water, then refresh in iced water with a few drops of olive oil.

For the sauce, add the champagne to a pot and reduce by half. Add velouté and bring to a boil before removing from heat, quickly adding cream and following with hollandaise. Buzz the mixture with a stem blender until a light, frothy zabaglione appears.

Garnish the ravioli with sauce and finish with truffle shavings.

SERVES 7. BON APPÉTIT!

TEN O'CLOCK

Tangles approach on a number of fronts. The guests are pigs, and now Thomas and Didier are set apart from me by their menu; set apart in the way a favorite dog is set apart by gobbling shit.

The situation is volatile. I run down the airside tunnel to see if Gottfried is there, maybe he can decoy Anna for a while. But there's no sign of him around the apron; and when I see the jet I find it has two uniformed pilots attached to it, one visible through the cockpit window. Running back up the tunnel, I turn my mind to the tortoise, who has barely an hour to live. But there's nothing I can do, the evening's machinery is ruthlessly engaged.

I burst around the corner into the bahn tunnel and bolt past the salon door toward the stairwell. Too late. Anna steps from the stairway with a paper bag and two bowls, on a collision course for Lonesome George. I watch her shadow glide close to the trolley and stiffen, halting on the wall like a stain.

Moments later, a damp cry.

Giant Panda Paw with Borlotti Beans
& Baby Root Vegetables
on Potato Skordalia

INGREDIENTS FOR PANDA

250–300g of panda wrist, trimmed
  and tipped with arm and claw
  joints removed

50g mirepoix (onion, celery,
  and carrot)

bouquet garni

420g borlotti beans, blanched and
  peeled

baby carrot, turnip, and parsnip

chopped Italian parsley

INGREDIENTS FOR SKORDALIA

1kg Pontiac potatoes

7 peeled garlic cloves

sea salt

125ml cream

25g butter

25ml olive oil

Boil all the solid skordalia ingredients until soft, then purée adding heated cream, butter, and olive oil. Season with salt to taste.

Season and rub panda wrist sections with oil, then sauté until brown and leave to rest. Add the mirepoix to a braising pan and color lightly, placing the wrists on top. Add bouquet garni and cover with cold water, sealing the pan and bringing to a boil. Move the pan into an oven and bake for 40 minutes at 180°C, checking progress, turning occasionally and cooking until tender. Cool and remove the meat, strain the liquid through a fine strainer, and reserve.

To serve, blanch the borlotti beans and baby vegetables in reserved liquor, reheat the wrist meat, and place with beans and vegetables onto the skordalia. Finish the remaining broth with olive oil and parsley, and spoon over meat.

SERVES 7. BON APPÉTIT!

TEN-THIRTY

The air outside has grown crisp, streetlamps show it to be grainy with haze. Activity has quietened around the building, even the bistro trailer pumps softer beats, while the protesters, still milling near the entrance, seem to be thinking of home. Moving past the trailers, I finally see Gottfried near the terminal.

"A little problem," he says. "Is there a turtle inside? Because Anna already reported it to a policeman. She's there, down past the vans, crying her heart out."

"Hm—I saw it arrive. Is the policeman responding?"

"He's not, your men are lucky, because there are protesters and other issues to deal with. Animal cruelty is an unexpected complaint today, he probably thinks she's crazy." Gottfried wheezes for a moment after his walk, looking around. When he faces me again his gaze is heavy. "I have to say—these are some swine you unleashed on our place. These people are devouring everything. Devouring me, Anna, you, your friends, and all the world around. We're on that table being eaten tonight, and they're not even chewing but gulping us down. Thank God I moved Gerd out to the Piratenburg."

I'm distracted by the whoosh and pop of a Roman candle in the monumental garden, followed by a pair of the Basque's foot soldiers charging through trees to stop the culprits. I find myself wondering why they would want to stop such innocent celebration, which must also serve them as a cover—and after running a few options through my mind an answer starts to dawn that makes me tingle, then shudder.

An end-play.

I ask Gottfried to meet me by the stairwell entrance at eleven, just before the tortoise is brought up to the kitchens.

With this, moving along the side of the building I search all the entrance porches for signs of life—and in one of them finally see a darker shape. Someone hunched almost double against the building, twenty meters away.

I take a step closer. The figure slowly stands.

A compact figure, arms loosely hung: Anna.

I'm suddenly aware of the cape floating around me, and step under a lamp to show myself. She waits there, gazing back.

And after a moment—just turns and walks away.

Confit of Koala Leg
with Lemon Saffron Chutney
Followed by a Digestive Elixir of Infants' Tears

INGREDIENTS FOR KOALA

7 whole koala legs

For glaze:

2 cloves of star anise

2 inches of ginger

1 cinnamon stick

70ml maltose

70ml light soy

70ml balsamic vinegar

a little orange peel

1 whole clove

For crust:

100g salt

100g Szechuan pepper

INGREDIENTS FOR LEMON SAFFRON CHUTNEY

3 large Meyer lemons

50ml white wine vinegar

½ peeled cooking apple

2 crushed cloves of garlic

1 onion, peeled and minced

1 pinch saffron threads

1 tsp horseradish

Boil all the glaze ingredients and reduce to a glaze. For the crust, heat a pan and roast the pepper until fragrant; add the salt, heat a little more, then cool. Rinse and dry the koalas, tying by the neck to allow air flow around the legs. Once dry, liberally sprinkle the legs with salt mixture and rest the marsupials for a minimum of 1 hour and a maximum of 4. Rinse off the salt under running water, and have a large pot ready with boiling water and a little ginger and spring onion. Blanch each koala leg for 30 seconds and remove. When dry, brush with the glaze and hang in a cool area for at least two days, repeating the glaze at least two or three more times. Finally, place the legs in a braising pan with a little mirepoix. Cook for two hours, covered, on 150 to 160°C, then remove cover and cook for 1 more hour.

For the chutney, zest lemons and reserve the zest before squeezing. Put the zest and juice into a large nonmetallic bowl with vinegar and 25ml water. Cover and leave overnight before emptying the contents into a stainless steel preserving pan. Add all remaining ingredients except sugar. Bring to the boil and simmer for 20 to 30 minutes or until fruits are tender, then add sugar and stir over heat until fully dissolved.

To serve, add a koala leg to the center of each plate and dot with satellites of chutney. Follow the dish with a 7ml shot of healthy infants' tears followed by 16ml of Ratzeputz liqueur.

SERVES 7. BON APPÉTIT!

TEN FORTY-FIVE

Thomas joins me at the curtain. We reflect that sea-horse tails and oyster mussels are too delicate a snack for the current mood in the salon. Watching a sea-horse tail disappear up the willowy boy's anus, Thomas makes a note to brief Didier for future events.

Didier has left, and so has the other man. Only the shadowy forces remain.

"Who was the man who came after the Basque?" I ask.

"Pike," he says. "You should've asked him the end of his story."

"Amazing. I don't suppose they'll be back?"

"No. The Basque always runs away in the end. And the company here isn't to their taste. It's many years since Pike was in Europe, I bet they got changed and went to Curry 36 on Mehringdamm. They'll be on the street with *pommes* and wurst. Didier loves to play the heavy Prussian on the street."

"I hate to ask if it's an irony, while sea-horse tails and tiger are being served up here."

"No irony. It's called class." Thomas pulls back from the curtain as a blob of shit flies through. "These fuckers wouldn't know."

The banquet has collapsed to the floor, Wonderland has become a writhing mass of cloth and flesh. All the room's cushions and rugs have been gathered, with guests squirming like maggots, grunting and rasping, skin glistening over Persian designs, sexual organs like weeping faces and veined worms forming unrepeatable artworks in the manner of Des Esseintes' jeweled turtle.

A gazelle carcass lies on its side in the fountain. The nearest of its long, arched horns makes a breakwater against which a variety of flotsam bobs and whirls. Before I can list all the different things floating there, a guest lurches up and urinates long and hard into the wine. His frothy jet sends debris eddying over the horn.

Another shadowy force crawls up and refills his goblet.

The portly man lies against an arch on a pile of cushions. The willowy boy is naked on all fours over his face. The man slurps at him, mouth flashing red, tongue darting and jabbing. A maiden sits astride the man, impaled and rocking, sometimes reaching down to squeeze his half-flaccid member. Then a wail takes my attention, and I see another boy bent over the table, head laid flat on its side, buttocks stretched open, with a guest's hairy arm making pistonlike thrusts behind him.

Our elegant place has become a level of hell.

A new girl passes into the salon before I can stop her. I feel sorry. She glows with good nature and whenever she smiles she gives a little shrug, a default to all the things a life might bring, which is just as well because it brings them all here. Her build is boyish, not quite plump, with proud neck and back, and candid brown eyes. As she purrs around I see an arm slowly emerge from under the table.

She disappears with a thud.

And a longing grows in me.

To just get away.

I'm about to turn when Thomas grips my arm:

"Even the Basque never saw anything like it," he hisses. "They're just a breed of animal. I'm getting out of here with one of the wagons, these pigs can go to hell. But before I forget, the Basque said as a matter of thanks you should choose something from the kitchen before you go. Check the shelves, the produce is superb: truffles, chocolate, smoked fish—many good things. Also a box you might recognize from a restaurant in Tokyo— still sealed, technically in quarantine, with samples of a biological nature, and signed papers from the restaurant, of course, guaranteeing authenticity. And in fact I have a friend who's a specimens courier—I think you even met him. So pick yourself something else from the shelf, let him return that one to Japan."

I feel a sweat of relief, my bones sag inside.

"It'll be there tomorrow night. Forensics are expecting it."

"And this was planned all along?"

"My friend, my friend." Thomas hugs me around the shoulder. "First of all, we hoped you would see that an excuse was needed to secure a specimen, one that didn't seem like the Basque was gathering evidence for the case. The banquet will be known in certain circles and was the first legitimate opportunity to serve a fish. How were we to know it would be stolen from the trailer? So as to your question, no, this wasn't planned—in fact it never happened. Remember?"

We stare at each other, running our adventures through our minds. And I know without wondering that this will be the last time I see the dashing Thomas Georg Philip Frederick Florian von Brandenburg Stendal Saxe fuck-knows-even-what-else, who needs a business card about a meter long.

As our gazes break apart—mine cloudy and sheepish, though perhaps with a new gleam, his like a bolt of lightning—we muse a moment on our limbos having touched this way.

Because they did touch, this once.

Then he steps back, clicks his heels, bows.

And is gone.

Caramelized Milk-Fed White Tiger Cub

Steamed Silken Tofu and Eggplant with Mushrooms,
Roast Garlic, Ginger, and Shallots
in Soy Dressing

Chiseled tiger-tooth toothpick

INGREDIENTS

1 milk-fed white tiger cub belly	2 shallots, julienned, white part only
1 medium eggplant	3cm piece ginger, julienned
500ml of grape seed oil	2 tbsp peanut oil
6 cloves garlic	7 oyster mushrooms
300g packet silken tofu	7 shiitake mushrooms
3 tbsp mushroom soya	fried shallots and coriander
2 tbsp *shao hsing* wine	sprigs to garnish

Reserve the tiger pelt with paws and tail for table decoration. Marinate the tiger belly for 24 hours with coriander seeds and shaved ginger, adding some palm sugar and ground white pepper to the marinade. Take care not to use too much sugar. Braise the tiger belly, covered with oil, for 6–8 hours. The slower it cooks, the better the result. Once cooked, it should be weighted to compress the belly flat. Cut the flattened belly into squares of between 180 and 220g. Make sure the belly is reheated skin-side down before serving, to allow the skin to crisp.

For the silken tofu and eggplant, cut the eggplant into large cubes and salt for 20 minutes before washing and patting dry.

Heat oil in a wok and add garlic, frying until golden. Remove the garlic and pat dry, then fry the eggplant until golden, also drying on a towel. Cut the tofu to the same size as the eggplant, taking care not to break when cutting. Place the eggplant and tofu in a heatproof container and drizzle with soy and *shao hsing* wine. Steam for 8 minutes until tofu is tender. Cook off the mushrooms separately and add to the dish at the end.

To serve, place the silken tofu and eggplant in the center of each plate and perch tiger belly squares on top. Swaddle with mushrooms, and garnish with julienned vegetables. Finally, drizzle with soy mix and sprinkle with crispy shallots.

SERVES 7. BON APPÉTIT!

ELEVEN O'CLOCK

The tortoise has withdrawn into his shell, leaving only his old man's face peering out with its look of sadness, eyes slowly curling this way and that. It takes four men to haul him onto a goods trolley, at which two set off pushing him to the salon.

"We're late," says one. "Just give them five minutes with him."

Making my way to the stairwell, I pass two messy nymphs beside the tracks, heads against the wall, smoking. The *alarum* lingers farther down, rocking to himself, studying the ground. I duck into the kiosk store, retrieve one of Gerd's firecrackers, and climb the stairs to find Gottfried outside.

"I saw the girl," he says. "She knows you're responsible for tonight in some way. She put the clues together herself, with only one deviation from fact—she doesn't think it's a situation spiraling out of your control. She thinks you let it happen. Perhaps you should find her and explain."

"Or perhaps," I say, "we should just kill the spiral."

Gottfried follows me underground to the stairwell door, where I point out the waiting Frenchman with his gun.

"Could you cover him? Keep him quiet?"

Gottfried raises his brow, at which I open my hand to reveal the fuse end of the cracker. We look at each other and over a few moments, with his mouth slightly open, I see him compute the move to its end.

"A big move," he whispers. "End-play."

The tortoise waits on its trolley in a darker patch of tunnel a few yards short of the salon door, while porters get clearance from inside. The door is shut behind them. After a pause to scout up and down, Gottfried gives my arm a quick squeeze and ambles off towards the *alarum*. I watch until he draws near, then hurry to the salon door, hissing an apology to the tortoise as I pass. When I see Gottfried reach the Frenchman, I crouch in the salon's doorframe and light the cracker.

An almighty bang shocks the air. After a moment the doorway explodes with porters, maidens, and boys flailing into the tunnel. I flatten myself against the wall, hearing forces stumble through Wonderland:

"Leave it, just run!" cries one. "Get out!"

The bookkeeper jostles past, trying to gather his tray and scales, till Portly Guest flies into him at the door, naked but for a trouser leg, and knocks the tray with all its diamonds to the floor. The gnome freezes, looking back—but with the guests all gone, footsteps echoing away, he quickly turns tail.

No cry of false alarm was ever called. Peering down the tunnel, I see Gottfried waddle into a recess with an extra pair of legs dangling between his. And with the salon as empty as the scene of a bombing, the floor sparkling with diamonds, ensuing moments eerie for their lack of noise, I step up the tunnel until a lonely shape appears, still huddled into itself. I watch its head crane out as my footsteps approach. And soon comes another set of steps, light ones flying down the stairs; then a small figure outlined at the stairwell, looking in.

She spots me crouched beside the trolley and stops dead.

I stroke the creature's shell till its head looks up. Then I lean close, put my face beside its face, and point it toward the girl.

I give her time to marvel.

And I say: "Whoosh."

ELEVEN FIFTEEN

Gottfried Pietsch and I step out of the Zentral Flughafen Tempelhof, Berlin, through a service entrance on the last night of the life she was designed for, never to return again. Chill night meets us at the door. The trailers have left Columbiadamm, protesters have dispersed. A piece of litter flaps along the sidewalk.

Behind us in the darkened terminal no sailors explain why Dieter is also called Gerd. No tubas play, no wurst is served. No horse stands in the hallway. Across three and a half million square meters of Berlin no American bombers roar, no children wait, no Berliners hope, no pilots wave, no communists watch from afar.

No Nazis flee, no Russians march, no flames rise.

A sphinx deceived into a life that didn't exist steps from a monument whose era never was, with a friend from a state that couldn't be, into a town that is once more.

Tonight all our limbos are over.

A breeze blows.

As we move up Columbiadamm toward the monumental garden, overlooked by the eagle on his plinth, lightly pummeled by the gravitational suck of a structure meant to outlast human history—a business jet screams into the sky over Tempelhof. It rockets up into the night, sparkling an urgent heartbeat in strobes of red and white. We pause, staring in silence till its pulse dissolves behind cloud, till its thunder wavers and echoes into whispers, and the whispers die bouncing off stars.

When we turn back to the street a familiar figure approaches. Gottfried waits still, ever so slightly nodding: "Piratenburg must have closed."

"*Haa.*" Gerd waves. "Nearly forgot our fireworks!"

Gottfried looks to me before glancing at his watch. I know he's thinking about the plane.

"Northeast," I answer instinctively. "Helsinki."

Gerd steps up, lanky from beer but falling quiet as he enters our airspace, seeming to sense our altered mood. At this, hauling us by the shoulders into a trio, Gottfried leads us slowly away, head hung as if to confess, till a few paces down the road, as a gust stirs our hair, he looks up into the night and softly says: "By my calculation, gentlemen—the fireworks tonight will be over the Baltic."

My senses withdraw before I hear Gerd's reply. Instead I rocket above the clouds, watching the last inch of a fuse burn away. This along with a hiss of speed through the air brings a perfect knowing—that what I watch is the last inch of innocence, the fizzle of a childhood burning away to its death. And there's no time left to ponder. I detonate, shattering like a pane of glass, and in the lucid trance that follows, from a hallway rug sticky with blood, I take stock and feel a new force: a breath nearby, and the weight of an arm—not a doctor's arm, nor a rich man's—just another human arm, a friend's solid arm over my shoulder, and another beyond it, and another and another, till I'm a thread in a mesh of fellows spanning all the world, spanning all of time before and after me, a shawl of unbreakable fibers. Of my fellows, in my world.

Finally, gingerly, I stand up from that hallway rug.

I stand pulling out shards, and throwing them down.

And after a moment, in a vivid dream, bloodied shapes begin to rise all around me on an infinite rug, that place where all childhood pain came to rest—small undaunted shapes in Pooh pajamas, kitten pajamas, whale pajamas, teddy-bear pajamas, wiping themselves off, smiling up into a sky that bursts with brilliant colors, popping and flashing and banging, spewing cinders through the clouds, dropping cogs of spent frustration, depression, and shock. And like a boy just landed from Mars I stand gazing in awe across this mass of junior comrades, eventually spying a ruffle among them, and soon a little figure carving a wake from afar. He runs barefoot, in cowboy-gun pajamas, with his tan fresh from Cape Town:

"*Cunts!*" he runs singing up at the clouds. "*You greedy cunts!*"

Grins break over our faces, but just then, as if I could soar any higher, as if my grin could stretch any more, a small hand slips into mine from another world, another time, squeezing to pull me forward like it was my first big day at school:

"Pff," she says. "I guess that's a normal Friday night for you?"

"Pretty much." I nod. "Though sometimes I go out for a drink."

LIGHTS ON

The Lada rattles along with its smells of old tobacco, plastic, and economy soap toward Berlin Tegel Airport. In my captive state between Gottfried and Berlin, a profound and quite pleasant fatigue settles in, akin to ten milligrams of Valium.

I flop back in the seat watching Gerd maneuver through a sparse rush hour, craning and jerking at the wheel. He wears an amalgam of clothes, a self-image carousel that never stopped at an outcome. Still, it's a casual carousel and his movements are freer, more loping and relaxed. In fact, a holiday ambience starts to lift the car, rising like the first notes of a dance, though only two of us will be traveling.

"You're sure we're back in time for *Tatort*?" grunts Gottfried.

"*Ja*, of course. We can see it at Dieter's, on the way home from the airport—if his television's working, you know what it's like."

"If we went to a bar we could watch it in color."

"Well, or a bar, *ja*. The problem is that people will talk over it."

Gerd catches my eye in the mirror. "Did you see *Tatort*? Great German crime series, national institution. On Sunday nights all Germany stops to watch."

He turns to Anna as rain starts to dot the windshield: "Are you fine doing the wipers? Sorry to separate you lovebirds, but Gottfried has arthritis, so he's excused." The wipers scrape to a stop every six or seven passes, and Anna reaches out to shake them. "The mighty Lada." Gerd slaps the wheel. "Built for Siberian conditions, just look—three hundred thousand kilometers and still going like a tank."

"Pff, tank is right." Anna tightens her coat around her.

As traffic thins, Gottfried reaches into an old Lufthansa bag at his feet and pulls out a beer, uncapping it on a door panel. He hands it over the front seat to Anna. Doing the same for me, then Gerd, he seems to observe a hierarchy of hospitality, making no sound apart from a wheeze as he reaches between seats.

"That's a known entry drug." I glance at Anna's beer.

"Must've gotten a bad one, I'm not even bleeding yet."

"*Gott*, at your age we used to drink vodka," says Gerd. "We would wake up green. Eh, Gottfried? We would wake up green!"

"You weren't doing it properly."

"Eh? There's no properly with vodka. You end up green."

"The eighty-twenty rule applies. Eighty percent of enjoyment comes from twenty percent of drinks. The art is to only drink that twenty percent."

"Oh, so you only want twenty percent of Gabriel's wine?"

Gottfried remains still, his mouth slightly open in a smile. "No—I'm having ninety-nine percent, as you'll certainly be on the floor after one glass."

"*Haa*"—Gerd thumps the wheel—"fighting words, Herr Pietsch, fighting words."

Skin creases around Gottfried's eyes, the seat crackles back with his weight.

"It's the reverse of your old system." Anna turns to me: "Eighty percent of drinks is one percent of enjoyment, and the remainder is throwing up blood."

"What?" I scowl. "That's unfair. You saw me on a bad day."

Gottfried's brow rises knowingly. "With the Englander it wasn't about drinks. He chased something else, a feeling." He looks at me: "Am I right?"

"Hm—I guess it's true."

"I know what it is," he says. "But actually it's here in front, the place you're looking for. In the moment just before."

"*Haa*, hear that, Frederick? Learn from the masters. Watch us next time, the next major party can be your debut."

"Ah, yes, yes." Gottfried rests back his head to muse. "We all have to grow up in the end. And actually enjoyment grows, once you master the secrets. I don't know when growing up became so unfashionable. When I was a boy we were expected to be little adults already. A better system, because you learned all the disciplines early, then at adulthood things suddenly got fun. You could have a drink, spend money—every door opened up."

"The markets would hate it," I say. "Half the economy is fed by children."

"Hnf, well. Maybe half your economy is fed by them. Half of my economy would be spent sending them early to bed."

"*Ja, ja*," says Gerd, "in Pietschland things would be different, eh, Gottfried?"

"Excuse me—things *will* be different. They'll be very different in my land."

"Ach, come on. Admit it, you're stuck with the world as it is."

"What?" Gottfried leans forward. "Nobody is stuck with anything as it is. We all must stand up and take control."

"Bah—it's easy to speak for a population of one."

"What do you mean, one? I have a foreign envoy." Gottfried nudges me. "Comrade Englander will take the mission overseas. He can't be depressed at the state of things, Britain is in a great position. They started this commercial experiment, so it's natural that they collapse first. It means they might be first to rise in the future. Naturally they have authoritarianism to come, but in the end it's always overthrown by the people. Now is the time to plant seeds for after that."

"Ach," says Gerd, "you're telling Berlin's story. The concept of the People was planted before the fascists came."

"You see? History has its rhythm."

"So, Frederick"—Gerd looks over his shoulder—"I warned you he would try and recruit you. You should warn your friend when he comes from Japan—watch out for Gottfried, you never know with him. He might look like a statue, but by the time you know him it's too late. When does your friend arrive?"

"Thursday night." I sip at my beer.

"Another recruit," he tuts. "Watch out, *mein Gott*. And then comes your mission for Pietschland, eh? What will you carry back with you for such a mission against the forces of decadence? Apart from a hangover?"

I ponder this while they laugh. "Well, decadence itself is now in a hangover—but I've taken a few notes, it's a small start."

"Pff." Anna turns. "You mean the little book? For monkeys and poets or whatever? The first paragraph said there wasn't a name for your situation because you were going to kill yourself."

"Eh?" says Gerd. "Not Frederick."

"Symbolic," says Gottfried. "He must be talking about the culture, the markets. Now all he has to do is put the same paragraph at the end, but saying that he's going to live. Then it's a perfect cycle—just like life."

"And what about Anna?" Gerd nudges her: "Are you joining Pietschland, am I facing a mass exodus of everyone I know?"

"Depends. If there's going to be a kiosk there, then no."

More japing carries us into the airport, until boarding passes are collected and we mill as people do around a departure gate, looking vacant, saying unimportant things, and even then leaving our sentences unfinished. When the flight is called for boarding and strangers start to crowd, I wonder if I detect a tear in Gerd's eye. We draw together, Gerd with the smile from his portraits, Gottfried with his stony glare, and we say the last-minute nothings that are the traveler's lot.

"See you Sunday," says Gerd.

"*Tschüss*," wheezes Gottfried.

Anna and I wave back—"Enjoy Stuttgart"—and a squeeze throbs between our hands, maybe the same lusty promise passed between parents when their kids leave them home alone. "Say hi to Gisela."

"Ah"—Gottfried turns to Gerd—"do you have the diamond?"

"*Ja*"—Gerd nods, "but keep quiet about the rest, she might come back too soon."

We laugh, and they bumble to the gate like a pair of maiden aunts, turning for a last wave from passport control. From the corner of my eye as I wave back, I spot a familiar shape entering the gate beside ours: with a jolt I realize it's Didier Le Basque's ominous form. I try to catch his attention but he vanishes without seeing me, leaving Gerd and Gottfried wondering who or what I've spotted. Then, before I can call an explanation, a second vaguely familiar figure appears.

I run a search of memory, and the answer lights up in a flash. "Pike!" I call out. "Hey, Pike—what's the ending to the story?" The man turns, frowning, trying to make me out.

"There you were," I say, "the sea was blue, the sky stretched tight, the air hot, you can smell the girl, the leather, and the sea. Ecstasy was guaranteed."

And as I watch, and now Gerd, Gottfried, and Anna watch and wonder, the man's face relaxes, his eyes narrow and sparkle such that I almost feel him touching the scene, scanning it emotionally, a hand in mine, real comrades nearby, adventures fresh behind us, and all the night and all of life ahead of us to come.

"*It doesn't get any better than this*,'" I prompt. "And then?"

He takes a moment, nodding gently to himself. And says: "I was right—it didn't."

Whoosh.

There isn't a name for my situation.
    Firstly because I decided to live.
    And then because of this idea:
    I don't have to do it all immediately.

The End

TERMS & CONDITIONS

We will all be destroyed
whether we like it or not.

I say let's like it.

May this small book of
certainties from a short life be
your compass in a decadence,
your mentor in times of ruin,
your friend when none is near;

And may its poking from your
pocket be a beacon to all who
share our spirit in these end times.

The odyssey raises a goblet to:

DAVID BODLAK,

who could have said more than this over a coffee.

"They come as God sends them."

———

Pony Hütchen and the bear of Berlin.
Chef de cuisine David Spanner.
Clare Conville.
Jill Bialosky & Norton crew.
The Aniversario De La Muerte.
Xavier, Hildegaard, and The List.
Baras, Strawberries, Carnales Baras.

———

Trinity College Literary Society.